INHUMAN TRAFFICKING

Also by Mike Papantonio

Law and Disorder
Law and Vengeance
Law and Addiction

Also by Alan Russell

No Sign of Murder
The Forest Prime Evil
The Hotel Detective
The Fat Innkeeper
Multiple Wounds
Shame
Exposure
Political Suicide
St. Nick
A Cold War
The Homecoming
Burning Man
Guardians of the Night
Lost Dog
Gideon's Rescue
L.A. Woman
The Last Good Dog

INHUMAN TRAFFICKING

A LEGAL THRILLER

MIKE PAPANTONIO
AND ALAN RUSSELL

Skyhorse Publishing

First Edition

This is a work of fiction. Names, places, characters, and incidents are either the products of the author's imagination or are used fictitiously.

Skyhorse Publishing books may be purchased in bulk at special discounts for sales promotion, corporate gifts, fund-raising, or educational purposes. Special editions can also be created to specifications. For details, contact the Special Sales Department, Skyhorse Publishing, 307 West 36th Street, 11th Floor, New York, NY 10018 or info@skyhorsepublishing.com.

Skyhorse® and Skyhorse Publishing® are registered trademarks of Skyhorse Publishing, Inc.®, a Delaware corporation.

Visit our website at www.skyhorsepublishing.com

10 9 8 7 6 5 4 3 2 1

Library of Congress Cataloging-in-Publication Data is available on file.
Library of Congress Control Number: 2021939202

Cover design by Erin Seaward-Hiatt
Cover photography: © Brian Caissie/Getty Images (boat); © Aaron Foster/ Getty Images (sky); © Mrs/Getty Images (hand); © Nico Blue/Getty Images (spatters)

Print ISBN: 978-1-5107-6887-1
Ebook ISBN: 978-1-5107-6892-5

Printed in the United States of America

INHUMAN TRAFFICKING

1

The unfamiliar red Mustang pulled up alongside Lily Reyes, matching her pace as she walked on the sidewalk. Lily didn't like the feeling of being stalked. She began walking faster, and looked around to see if anyone was outside. The Tallahassee heat and humidity had the neighborhood looking like a ghost town; everyone was at work or had retreated inside their air-conditioned homes. The Mustang continued to creep along and pace her. Its windows were tinted, only offering her a general outline of the male driver wearing a baseball cap.

Maybe I should run up to a house and ring the doorbell, Lily thought. But what if no one was home, and her stalker took that opportunity to come after her?

The car came to a hard stop right next to her. As the passenger window inched downward, Lily took a breath to scream.

"You getting in?"

"Oh, god," she said, blowing out pent-up air. "I thought you were like some disgusting creep. Where'd you get the car?"

"Borrowed it from a friend."

Lily opened the passenger door, tossed her backpack inside, and got comfortable in her seat. The cooling AC blew over her. "Nice ride. Must be a good friend to let you borrow it."

"It's a business thing."

Lily decided not to press him for answers. Carlos never liked it when she asked too many questions, and she didn't want him getting uptight. He seemed distracted about something. Why, he'd barely looked at her.

Lily was kind of hoping he would have noticed how she'd dressed up for him.

"I thought you were going to pick me up at Subway," Lily said.

"Decided to spare you the walk."

Lily's mom, Sylvia, didn't know about Carlos. No one knew about him, except for Lily's best friend, Madison, and even she wasn't supposed to know anything. Carlos was paranoid about being busted. When Lily had first started dating him, she'd lied about her age, telling him she was eighteen. It was only after they'd been going together for a month that Lily admitted she was only fifteen. Of course, she hadn't been the only one stretching the truth. When they'd first hooked up, Carlos had said he was nineteen, not the twenty-one he really was.

"Did you bring some change of clothes?" Carlos asked.

"In the backpack, even though you never explained why I needed them."

"Always nice to have options."

"Where we going?"

"It's a surprise."

Lily tried to play it cool and hid her smile. Madison seemed to think that Carlos was just using her, but she didn't know him like Lily did.

"Stopped and got you a wild cherry Slurpee," he said. "Better drink it before it melts."

He had remembered her favorite drink. She would certainly mention that to Madison. Lily reached for the Slurpee and took a long sip.

"Want some?" she asked.

"Not without adding some rum."

"I'm okay with that."

"Maybe later."

Carlos liked to party, and liked it even more when Lily joined in with him. She had to be careful, though. Her mom was always in her business.

As if reading her mind, Carlos said, "How long did your mom let you off the leash?"

"I told her I'd probably be eating dinner at Madison's."

"That gives us a little time."

"Sure does," she said.

Lily reached out her hand and ran it along his leg. Carlos needed to see she was grown-up and not some kid, but instead of positioning her hand on him like he usually did, Carlos acted preoccupied. Maybe he was just in one of his moods.

She withdrew her hand and began drinking her Slurpee. "Sure you don't want some?"

He shook his head, and she continued to sip. Halfway through the cup, Lily's skin began tingling.

"I feel weird," she said.

"We can get some fresh air at Cascades Park."

"Is that where we're going?"

Carlos nodded. He still wasn't looking at her, and seemed unusually attentive to his driving, continually checking the rearview and side mirrors.

"It feels like we're floating," she said.

Lily flapped the hand not holding her drink. "I'm flying. Whoa."

Something wasn't right. Why was she feeling out of it? Her gaze fell to the Slurpee. One look, and the pieces came together. Lily's accusation was shrill: "You put something in my drink!"

"Relax. I just made you a Molly and benzo cocktail to help loosen you up."

Lily tried to process her panic, along with Carlos's explanation. She wanted to feel reassured, but didn't. One by one, words emerged from her mouth. Each syllable felt as if it were weighted down on her tongue. "Why didn't you tell me?"

"I wanted you to be calm while I explained a few things."

"Oh, shit." This was bad. "You're breaking up with me."

"No, baby, never."

Lily struggled to find the words, and speak them. "We're. Still. Together?"

"Forever, baby. It's just that things didn't work out with my big plan. Remember we talked about that?"

"Big score."

"That's right. And it would have been, but my luck went bad, really bad."

Lily managed to say, "That's okay."

"No, it's not okay. Everything went to shit. It put me in the hole for almost five thousand bucks."

"I can help you . . ."

Lily had earned almost two hundred dollars babysitting. She'd give it to him. But Carlos interrupted before she could finish.

"Thank you, baby. I knew I could count on you. They were going to mess me up bad, maybe even kill me. You were my only hope."

Lily tried to follow what he was saying, but her brain couldn't find its balance. Everything was hazy.

"After you work off my marker, baby, we'll get back together. I promise."

"Don't understand."

"A guy I know fronted the money I owed, but he needed collateral."

"What?"

"I had to put up something of value. And nothing's more valuable to me than you. I love you."

Lily had been waiting for a long time to hear those words. But now they sounded wrong. Felt wrong. Love?

Carlos said, "You're a lifesaver. It will just be for a few months. And when you come back to me, things will be better than ever between us."

Too dizzy to support her chin, Lily's face dropped down to her chest. Talking was beyond her. She didn't know how long they drove, and was barely aware when they came to a stop. She heard two men talking, but it was like listening in to a dream.

"Is she good to go?"

Lily had never heard that voice before. She would have remembered it if she had. There was something scary about it, a rasp with a serrated edge.

"She agreed to work off what I owe."

"You explain what would happen to you if she didn't?"

"I told her."

"Okay, then. I'll find you if there's a problem. Count on it. Give me the keys."

Lily heard retreating footsteps. Carlos didn't say goodbye. There was a part of her that was still listening for his voice, that wanted him to declare his love for her once more.

She couldn't lift her head to acknowledge the new occupant of the driver's seat but heard the ugly voice.

"Hey, pretty lady," he said. "I'm your Tío Leo."

II

Seven days after Lily Reyes's disappearance

Though Sylvia Reyes tried to keep her emotions in check, Nick "Deke" Deketomis could feel the sobs racking her body as the two of them embraced. Deke was glad Sylvia couldn't see the guilt that he was sure was written all over his face. He'd been dreading this encounter since hearing the news, his years of having been negligent weighing on him.

"It's going to be all right," he said, knowing what he was saying was inadequate, but helpless to come up with anything better.

Sylvia nodded and disengaged from their hug. She ran a hand down her face, wiped away her tears, and gathered herself with a deep breath. Her dark circles and gaunt face spoke of her tiredness.

"I'm afraid I haven't slept in days," she said, but then tried to smile for him. "Please come inside. Can I get you something to drink?"

"I'm fine, thanks."

It had been fifteen years since Deke had last seen Sylvia. He was reminded of that as they entered her small house. Photos lined the hallway wall, and Deke spotted a picture of him holding a baby in a white baptismal gown.

His goddaughter, Lily. Deke hadn't seen her in all the years since.

They each took a chair and sat down in a tiny living room. Sylvia said, "I wouldn't have bothered you, Deke, but Bill Fuller suggested you might be able to help."

Bill was also in some of the pictures in the hallway. He had been the best man at the wedding of Sylvia and Art Reyes, and Deke had been a groomsman. Deke and Bill had both been prosecutors in the Broward County State Attorney's Office, and Art had been chief investigator there. The three men became close friends, their coworkers referring to them as the "three amigos." Bill was now the state attorney for Leon County.

"Bill and his office have been working with the police," Sylvia said. "What they've uncovered has left me feeling like a failed parent. I had no idea what was going on in Lily's life."

"Every parent of every teenager has said the same thing."

"That's what I want to believe, but it still doesn't excuse my not knowing that Lily has been seeing a twenty-one-year-old man for the last five months."

"I'm sure Lily did everything she could to keep you from finding out about him."

"She did, but I'm the parent, and should have been protecting her from a drug-dealing predator like Carlos Navarro."

"Has he been arrested?"

"Not yet. The police are still trying to make a case against him, but he's been questioned multiple times. His story keeps changing, or at least it did before he lawyered up. At first, he tried to claim that he and Lily were just casual friends, and that he wasn't with her on the night she went missing. After being confronted with evidence showing that was a lie, Navarro claimed it was his *pride* that made him say what he did, because he didn't want to admit that Lily had dumped him for another guy with money. He said he didn't even know the name of this other guy Lily drove off with."

Sylvia's lower lip began trembling, and she bit down on it in an effort to try and regain control. Deke could see how she was barely holding on.

"How about I get you a glass of water?"

Sylvia shook her head. "His lies make me want to scream. A confidential informant told the police that Navarro got burned on some drug deal, and was desperate to pay off his debt. According to this informant, Navarro made an arrangement with Leonel Rodríguez, who goes by the name of Tío Leo."

"Arrangement?"

Fighting back her emotions, Sylvia found the strength to finish her story. "Rodríguez is a sex trafficker."

The tears, held back with such effort, began pouring down Sylvia's face. Being witness to her raw pain was torture for Deke. Inaction wasn't his way. He much preferred confronting problems head-on. That's why he'd become a lawyer in the first place. It had given him a platform for taking on cases he believed were important. Needing to do something, Deke went to the kitchen and returned with a glass of water. Sylvia took a gulp and steadied herself with a few deep breaths.

"What can I do to help?" Deke asked.

"Bill Fuller said you and your firm were heading up a case going after human traffickers."

Deke met her desperate red-rimmed eyes and nodded. "We're bringing a case against Welcome Mat Hospitality, alleging that they've knowingly allowed their truck stops and motels to be used for the purpose of human trafficking."

"Welcome Mat's a big company, right?"

"More than five hundred truck stops, and three hundred motels with over twenty thousand rooms."

"Bill said the more eyes and resources we can put on Lily's situation, the better it would be, and he was pretty sure you'd be using investigators in your lawsuit."

"It's true we're looking into Welcome Mat's operations and putting eyes on select truck stops and motels, but we don't have the personnel or resources for extensive monitoring."

"But you could tell your people to watch for Lily, right? And Rodríguez? They might end up in one of those properties."

"We can do that and a lot more," Deke promised. He didn't want to raise her hopes, but he needed Sylvia to know he'd do everything in his power to help.

"I would be grateful." The relief could be heard in her voice and seen in her face. Even Sylvia's breathing looked less labored, as if a weight had been lifted from her chest.

Or maybe that weight had just been transferred over to Deke. He felt the need to make his own confession. "I need to say something before we continue. I want to apologize and say that I'm sorry."

"Sorry for what?"

She really didn't seem to know, Deke thought.

"For failing in my responsibilities as a godfather. And failing to do right by Art."

Sylvia began shaking her head, but Deke couldn't let her forgive him that easily. She opened her mouth to speak, but Deke got the words out first.

"I should have made it to Art's funeral. It was unforgivable of me to not attend. At the time I was in the middle of a huge trial, but that's no excuse."

"You explained that in your beautiful card," she said. "And I heard you made a generous contribution to the National Pancreatic Cancer Foundation in Art's name."

"I didn't honor the dead, and I failed the living by not being there for Lily."

"That's not how I remember it," Sylvia said. "After Art died, and we continued living in Fort Lauderdale, you never forgot Lily's birthday. Because of you, she learned about Benjamin Franklin."

Deke almost smiled. Despite the pain she was in, Sylvia was trying to do the comforting. "Four or five years ago, Lily's birthday card was returned to me. According to what the post office stamped on it, there was no forwarding address. I should have followed up. I meant to find out where the two of you were living. But good intentions aren't enough. I know that."

"That's as much on me as it is on you, Deke. A few years after Art's death, I decided Lily and I should start afresh. I was the one who didn't send out change-of-address notices or put out a mass email. I was going through a bad patch. I was mad at the whole world, and thought a new life would make things better."

"I appreciate your trying to share the blame. But I made vows saying I would look out for Lily, and promised God, and you, and Art. I broke those vows, but now I promise I will do whatever I can to make them right."

Sylvia blinked away some tears and nodded.

Deke said, "Out in the car is my friend and colleague, Carol Morris. Carol is head of Safety and Security and Investigative Services for our firm. If it's all right with you, she'd like to ask you some questions."

"You left her out in your car in this heat?"

"I didn't want to presume."

"Please bring her in before she melts."

* * *

Carol was a self-described "Southern steel magnolia." She had grown up in the South, the daughter of an army staff sergeant. That was the magnolia part of her; the steel part showed itself in her work. Before Deke had brought her into the firm more than a decade ago, she had had a long and successful career working in the mostly male world of law enforcement. She had never felt the need to posture, as had so many of her coworkers, but her effectiveness was never a matter of dispute. On the job, Carol was invariably polite, but no one questioned her firmness. When it came to ferreting out answers and tracking down people, no one was better than Carol. She had been a decision Deke never regretted.

It didn't take long for Carol to get Sylvia to open up, and Deke got to hear about a goddaughter he didn't know. According to Sylvia, Lily was too clever by half. She was smart but indifferent to schoolwork. As pretty as her daughter was, Lily was still insecure about her looks. She could be loving one moment and surly the next. The daughter that Sylvia had once been so close to had become increasingly distant and secretive. Deke was mostly an accessory in the conversation, letting Carol take the lead.

While the two women talked, Deke found himself flipping through some photos that Carol had asked for. Most were recent shots of Lily. She was petite like her mother, and slight. In almost all of the pictures, she had a small, self-conscious smile. But one thing about her features stood out more than anything else, something Carol took a moment to inquire about.

"Where did Lily get her beautiful green eyes?"

"They're from Art's side of the family," Sylvia said. "He had an aunt with almost exactly the same-colored eyes."

Deke stared at the picture, studying his goddaughter's eyes. They weren't eyes easily forgotten. Unblinking, Lily looked back at him with eyes that haunted.

III

Teri Deketomis stuck her head into Deke's study, expecting to find her husband sitting or standing while working at his height-adjusted desk. But Deke wasn't at his desk, nor was he working. He was sitting in an old leather armchair in the corner of the room, his chin resting on his hand. In the background he had one of his favorite albums playing, Johnny Cash's *At San Quentin*. Teri's arrival coincided with the song "A Boy Named Sue."

Deke straightened in his chair and smiled. "You caught me daydreaming."

"That's not a crime," Teri said.

"Then why do I feel guilty?"

Teri walked across the room, sat on the chair's armrest, and put a hand on her husband's shoulder. "Lily?" she asked.

He nodded. "I was thinking about the day of her christening. Art was so proud. He was crazy about his little girl."

"I remember."

"Usually, I don't look back in time."

She gave him a squeeze. "I know." More than anyone, Teri did know.

"I tell myself I don't have time for introspection. My excuse is I always have a case that needs my full attention. The truth is, I don't much like looking back to when I was Lily's age."

"Given what you went through, that's understandable."

"It wasn't an upbringing I'd wish on anyone."

Deke had been in the foster care system, going from one placement to another. He tried to bury the past and rarely talked about the parents who had abandoned him, but sometimes his childhood had a way of surfacing with a vengeance. Like today. Because of Lily. For a man like Deke, letting his goddaughter fall through the cracks was a personal failure.

In the background, Johnny Cash seemed to be commenting on that. On a monthly basis, the firm had a Bergman/Deketomis karaoke night. Every so often Deke joined in the festivities, and his standard was always "A Boy Named Sue." Deke wasn't much of a singer, but his rendition of that song always got wild applause. Most of his colleagues hadn't been aware of the song's existence until they heard him sing it, and now they had even learned the words and loved joining in. Deke believed his coworkers sensed it was personal to him, which it was. He'd felt the same abandonment as the boy named Sue but hadn't let his crappy upbringing and abandonment dictate the outcome of his life.

Teri gave her husband another squeeze, and Deke felt her love. It always helped to vanquish his shadows more than anything.

"I was an angry kid who made plenty of bad decisions, but was fortunate I didn't make one that sabotaged my future," Deke said.

"You beat the odds."

"That's for sure," he said. "Which is why I don't like to let my inner abandoned kid come out very often. He's a real downer."

"Maybe you shouldn't bottle him up as much as you do."

"It's a lot easier to think about my life after the age of twenty-eight."

Teri's gaze turned to a prominent photo hanging in Deke's study that showed him kissing his young bride. She found herself smiling, just as she'd been smiling in the picture.

"Sometimes I still can't believe the ways things turned out," he said. "I got the woman of my dreams, two great kids, and an unbelievable career."

"The woman of your dreams loves hearing that, but also thinks you shouldn't completely shut out that kid from foster care. He helped make you who you are."

"Lily made me think about him. She kept calling to that kid in my head."

"So, what are you going to do?"

"Carol says the best way I can help Lily is by putting all my efforts into the Welcome Mat case."

"That makes sense. It's your forum to take on human trafficking."

"It makes professional sense. But it feels wrong to not be doing more for Lily. I already made that mistake once."

"What else could you do?"

"I was thinking of putting up billboards," Deke said.

"Billboards?"

"You remember how they used to advertise missing kids on milk bottles? I could put billboards up with Lily's picture, along with the images of a few other children whom we know are being sexually trafficked, and advertise a reward for their safe return."

"That sounds like a great idea."

"It's something, at least. And there's a chance Lily might even see herself up on one of those billboards. If that happens, she'd know she isn't alone. She'd know someone cares."

Deke was aware that his own biography was coming out in his words. When he'd been Lily's age, no one had given a damn about him, but he'd been fortunate in that he'd never had to endure physical or sexual abuse.

"I'll help you set that up tomorrow," Teri promised. "But no more ruminating tonight. It's time you came to bed."

"How could I refuse the woman of my dreams?"

IV

Nine months after Lily Reyes's disappearance

Deke was working at the office when a call from Carol was put through. "We're pretty sure we found him," she said.

Deke allowed himself a single fist pump. Tracking down Tío Leo had been a long and difficult hunt, with many disappointments along the way. Carol had spent countless hours sifting through sexually oriented advertisements, and the dark web, to try and get leads on Rodríguez and Lily. They started closing in on their target when Rodríguez advertised her as a "green-eyed vixen," along with some leads from Deke's billboards.

A few months back they had almost landed their fish. If one particular sheriff hadn't been so intent on trying to turn the arrest into a photo op, Lily would now be free. That was something Deke couldn't forget. Even now it haunted him.

"How sure?"

"We have a tentative ID from one of our operatives who's watching a house we believe Rodríguez is staying in."

"Where is he?"

Instead of answering his question, Carol said, "Let me take care of this."

"Where?" he repeated.

"A suburb in Mobile."

Mobile, Alabama, was only an hour's drive from their offices in

Spanish Trace, and that was if you obeyed the speed limit. That wasn't something Deke was planning on doing.

"Is *she* there?" he asked.

"Our operative has identified several young women in the house, but we don't know if Lily is among them. I'm walking over to your office now so we can discuss the best way to handle this."

It was clear Carol was doing everything in her power to keep Deke from acting on his own, but that wasn't enough. Not this time.

"Save yourself the walk. My office will be empty. I need that address. Now."

Carol gave it to him.

* * *

Deke jumped into his ten-year-old Ford F-150 truck. His vehicle looked out of place in the firm's parking lot filled luxury sedans, and wasn't the kind of drive most people would have expected from a senior partner in one of the nation's largest plaintiff law firms, but the old truck suited his purposes just fine.

He threw the truck in reverse, hit the gas, but then slammed on the brakes. Jake Rutledge had suddenly appeared in his rearview mirror.

Deke lowered his window and barked, "Get the hell out of my way."

"I'm going with you."

In answer, Deke revved the engine, but the young man didn't budge.

"You want to keep working here?" Deke asked.

"Go ahead and fire me. I'm still coming with you."

"Then get in!"

Jake ran to the passenger door, opened it while the truck was moving, and jumped inside. Even before Jake had a chance to pull the door shut, Deke floored the accelerator. As the truck rocketed out of the underground garage, Jake managed to close the door and latch his seatbelt.

For ten minutes, the two men didn't speak. Deke finally broke the silence. "I thought you were supposed to be on vacation."

Jake worked investigations for the firm, and for much of the past month he'd been on special assignment working undercover as a trucker investigating Welcome Mat.

"It was a staycation. And I just happened to come into the office today when Carol recruited me to help."

"I don't need a babysitter, or a bodyguard."

"Then think of me as a traveling companion."

"Did Carol tell you what this is about?"

Jake shook his head. "She only said you were on your way to go confront some scumbag."

"He's far worse than a scumbag. Leonel Rodríguez, who goes by the nickname Tío Leo, sexually traffics girls."

"I'm familiar with him," Jake said. "Carol spotlighted him in her BOLO alerts to the team, along with one of the young women he's believed to be trafficking."

"My goddaughter Lily," Deke said.

"I wasn't aware of the connection," Jake said.

"Carol and I didn't see any need to advertise it."

"I had her picture taped to my dash, and kept an eye out for her at all my Welcome Mat stops," Jake said. "I kept hoping against hope that she'd turn up."

"You and me both."

Deke didn't volunteer anything more, and they drove without speaking for a few minutes. Jake finally asked, "Where are we going?"

"A suburb just outside Mobile called Saraland. Carol believes Rodríguez is holed up in a house there."

"Will we be meeting up with law enforcements?"

"We will not."

"Why not?"

"Reason one would be Sheriff Earl Jackson."

Jake's face showed his confusion. "I don't know him."

"You're lucky," Deke said. "Two months ago, we had Rodríguez dead to rights. Through Carol's investigative work, we knew where he was, and we passed on that information to the Cove County Florida Sheriff's Department. We counted on Sheriff Jackson to do his job, but instead of acting right away, he apparently decided it was a good time for a photo op. Not coincidentally, the sheriff's up for reelection in November. While Jackson was lining up the media, Tío Leo got away. I was the one who had to call Lily's mom, Sylvia, and tell her what happened."

"That couldn't have been easy."

"We shared some bitter tears. And afterward, I made a substantial political contribution to the candidate running against Sheriff Jackson."

"I can understand your disappointment, but just because one bad cop messed up doesn't mean we shouldn't be enlisting law enforcement in this."

"There are other reasons as well."

"Such as?"

"We can't chance having to wait before acting. Our coming in from out of state complicates matters, and could cause a delay in issuing a search warrant."

"So we call the local authorities now, and the paperwork might be in place even before we arrive."

"You're assuming that some judge won't have qualms about this or that. I don't want us jumping through judicial hoops while Rodríguez is pulling another disappearing act. He's slippery, and being constantly on the move is a way of life for him. It's not just the law he's trying to stay in front of. The word on the street is that MS-13 wants to settle a score with Rodríguez for having had a hand in the death of one of their own."

"That would keep me moving," Jake said.

"He avoids staying anywhere more than a few nights, and has a host of names he uses for short-term rentals in residential locations."

Deke turned onto Interstate 10 west, which would take them right to Mobile. "You've probably been along this route a lot lately."

Jake raised his left arm, displaying his "trucker's tan." "I traveled this way a few times, but mostly I worked along I-20."

"I guess there's a reason it's called the sex trafficking superhighway."

"From what I saw, there's lots of competition for that nickname."

Deke's scowl served in place of words.

"Were you close to Lily?" Jake asked.

"I wish I could say that I was, but I haven't seen her since the day of her christening fifteen years ago."

"That's not unusual. When I was growing up, I was told I had a godfather, but he was never part of my life. Hell, I don't even remember his name, and couldn't tell you anything about him. These days being a godparent is ceremonial."

"That's not what the vows say. I promised to be there for her, but wasn't. Until now."

* * *

The Mobile suburb of Saraland, with its stately trees and large homes on big lots, wasn't what typically came to mind when most people thought about sex trafficking. That was what made it, and places like it, perfect spots for Tío Leo's business. The short-term rental he was believed to be staying in was surrounded with fencing and greenery, shielding the house from prying eyes.

Carol's hired help was a PI who had set up shop on the residential street. Deke had passed by the nondescript delivery van while making his own slow surveillance of the street. Only one car was visible at the house: a Ford Transit van parked in front of the three-car garage.

After parking down the street, Deke called the operative on his cell phone and identified himself. "Any activity?"

"Nothing in the last two hours," the PI said.

"What about before then?"

"There was a TV on in the master bedroom upstairs where I believe the girls are."

"No visitors?"

"None I observed."

"So, it's just our suspect and the girls?"

"As far as I know."

"Thanks for your work. We've got it from here."

As Deke put away his phone, Jake said, "Why didn't you ask for his help?"

"Because what I'm about to do isn't exactly legal, so I'm thinking the fewer eyes on the situation, the better."

"You haven't told me the plan."

"The plan is to question Mr. Rodríguez, preferably without anyone around."

"If I recall correctly, Rodríguez is twentysomething? Besides being younger than you are, he's probably armed, and certainly dangerous."

"I'm hoping that means he won't be threatened when he sees me."

"What's your reason for knocking at his door?"

"I'm with the management company overseeing the rental, and the last tenants reported a gas leak."

"And you think he'll buy that?"

"I don't care if he does or not, as long as he lets me get within striking range. I'm wearing what's called a sap cap."

Jake's eyes went to the innocuous-looking baseball cap on Deke's head.

"There's steel bird shot sewn into a pouch and the back lining of the hat. It works just like a sap, and at my first opportunity, I'm going to try and drop Rodríguez."

"That's too risky."

"If I'm not back in ten minutes, call the cops. Give me that much leeway."

Jake began shaking his head. As he opened his mouth to object, Deke spoke before he could. "Give me a chance to make good on the promises I made to Art, and my goddaughter, and to God, all those years ago. I need you to do that for me."

"You and your damn closing arguments." Jake sighed in reluctant capitulation. "All right. Ten minutes. Not one second more."

* * *

"Hello! Rental management."

Deke knocked on the door for a second time. He had a sense of being watched and did his best to appear benign and nonthreatening. As the door opened a crack, Deke began speaking in a tone both friendly and apologetic.

"Good afternoon! My name is Nick Draper. Sorry to bother you, but I'm with the company that manages this rental, and I'm responding to a complaint made by the last tenant who reported that there was a strong gas smell in the unit. By law, we're required to follow up."

From behind the door a man's voice responded. "I haven't smelled no gas leak."

"Our company is all about accommodating our guests, but when it comes to safety, we have to follow company protocols. If you don't want me inside, that's fine, but I'll need to call the fire and police departments to come out here just to make sure we don't have a serious problem."

The door slowly opened, and Tío Leo showed himself. Deke kept a placid smile on his face and said, "Thank you so much." He made a move to tip his cap, but Rodríguez chose that moment to step back.

Deke followed him into the house, but Rodríguez remained wary and watchful. It was a hot day, but Rodríguez was wearing a sports coat. He had his right hand in his coat pocket, and Deke had no doubt but that a gun was leveled on him.

Pretending to be oblivious to the threat, Deke said, "You can't fool around with a gas leak. Better safe than sorry, right?"

"You said that you're with the management company?"

"That's correct."

"And what's your name?"

Deke recalled the name he'd used. "Nick Draper," he said, extending his hand, but Rodríguez kept his hand inside his coat pocket and maintained his distance.

"I was told the gas smell was coming from the kitchen area," Deke said.

"Is that so?"

There was a mocking note in Tío Leo's reply, but Deke pretended not to notice. He made his way farther into the house, Rodríguez following behind him, and found the kitchen. What he hadn't counted on was the electric stove and oven.

"Strange place for someone to have detected a gas smell," Rodríguez said, facing Deke down with a shooter's pose, the now visible gun centered on his chest.

Deke held up his hands. "Clearly, there's been some misunderstanding."

"Let's see your ID," Rodríguez said.

"My wallet's in the car."

"Really? Then why do I see an outline of it in your back pocket?"

Deke feigned surprise, patting his back pocket. "I guess you're right."

Tío Leo seemed to think that was funny. "I guess I am," he said. "No sudden movements. Toss your wallet my way nice and easy."

"Please lower your gun. Like I said, there's been some mistake."

"Your wallet. Now!"

Deke complied with the directive. With his gun raised and held at the ready, Rodríguez picked up the wallet, pocketed the cash, and then studied Deke's license.

"Nicholas Dekey-tomb-eyes," he said, struggling with Deke's surname.

"Deke-eh-tome-is."

"You work for the management company, but you live in Florida?"

"I recently resettled in Mobile."

"Don't bullshit me. Take off your clothes."

"What?"

"Now."

"Look, if you don't believe what I'm saying, why don't you call the cops? They should be able to confirm everything."

"Either you start stripping, or I start shooting."

Deke began removing his clothing, leaving on only his socks, underwear, and cap.

"Now, slide your clothes my way, and then sit on the ground, put your hands behind your back, and link your fingers together."

When Deke complied, Rodríguez went through his clothing with his free hand, pocketing Deke's cell phone and the keys to his truck.

"If you want to get out of this alive, I'll need to hear answers I believe. Who are you, Mr. Dinky Thomas?"

Deke gave up on his ruse. "I'm a lawyer representing Sylvia Reyes. She retained my services on behalf of her daughter, Lily."

Rodríguez started laughing. "You're a lawyer?"

"I am."

"And you came here to do what? Sue me?"

"That was one option."

"I got another option for you, old man. Putting a bullet in you."

"The police are going to be here any minute, Mr. Rodríguez. Or do you prefer to be called Tío Leo?"

Deke could see that got the other man's attention. "You've been in our sights for months. We know all about you."

"You don't know jack shit."

"By cooperating with me, you might get a reduced sentence. Let's start by having Lily and the others go outside."

"Who's this Lily you keep talking about? I don't know no Lily."

Deke called out, "Lily? Come downstairs now."

Rodríguez started laughing. "My three nieces from Mexico are upstairs, but there's no Lily."

"Where is she?"

"Don't know what you're talking about. But I do know I've heard enough."

Rodríguez pulled Deke's belt loose from his pants and then tossed it at his feet. "Loop the belt between and around your ankles, and then pull it tight and fasten it."

Deke slowly began wrapping the belt around his ankles. "Tighter," Rodríguez said. "And keep your head facing forward if you don't want it blown away."

He circled behind Deke, who tried to keep him talking to track his whereabouts.

"All I want to do is get Lily back safe and sound."

Rodríguez didn't answer. Deke was straining to hear. Was there a whisper of movement behind him? Reacting was dangerous; so was not reacting.

A kitchen window shattered, and Deke swept the cap off his head and blindly swung upward. The impact was enough to throw off Rodríguez's blow and lessen the impact of his gun's smashing into Deke's cheekbone.

From outside Jake's muffled voice yelled, "Police! Drop your gun now."

Rodríguez responded by firing two rounds in the direction of the voice. Deke swiveled his partially tied legs toward Rodríguez, trying to sweep him off his feet. The kick staggered but didn't drop him. As he steadied himself, Deke lunged for his arm, and the two men wrestled for the gun. From his knees, Deke lacked the leverage to turn Rodríguez, but he held tight to the other man's arm even while being kicked in his head.

Don't . . . let . . . go . . .

The gun went off, but Deke didn't loosen his grip. He took another vicious kick to his face, a blow that knocked him backward, but that also wrenched his opponent's arm and sent the gun flying.

Rodríguez froze, torn between going after the gun or fleeing. The sound of Jake kicking in the back door was enough to make Rodríguez race off. Deke staggered after him, but by the time he got to the front door, Rodríguez was driving away.

As Jake ran up to his side, Deke said, "Call the police! Tell them to put out an APB on a Ford Transit van."

As Jake made the call, Deke called up to the second floor, "Lily? Are you there?"

No one answered, but Deke heard several girls talking excitedly in Spanish.

"Lily?"

No reply.

Blood started pooling at Deke's feet from the gashes on his face, but he barely took notice. It wasn't his wounds that left him hurt and empty; it was his failure.

V

D eke tried not to wince as Teri applied makeup to his face, but apparently wasn't successful.

"You're in no condition to be working today," she said.

"I'd feel a lot worse sitting home," he said, but at that moment the movement of Teri's brush on his mangled face caused a sharp intake of breath.

"You sure about that?" Teri asked.

Deke didn't answer.

"Concealer's done," she said.

Deke moved to rise, but Teri said, "Not so fast. I still need to apply foundation, and then bronzer."

"My flight leaves in an hour."

"I'll be fast, even though I shouldn't be enabling you."

"If all goes well with today's deposition, I'll just be an observer," Deke said.

"For your sake, I hope so. With all your tossing and turning, did you even sleep last night?"

Deke wasn't sure if he had or not. His conversation with Sylvia kept replaying in his head. As bad as the failed rescue was, having to tell her what happened made it even worse. This time there wasn't some sheriff to blame. It was all on him. The beating he was still giving himself was far worse than what Rodríguez had administered.

"Hard to sleep with a guilty conscience," he said.

"But Lily wasn't in the house. You couldn't have rescued her anyway."

"If we'd captured Rodríguez, it's likely he could have told us where she was."

"You freed three young women. That's a good thing."

The girls Rodríguez had called his "nieces" were Mexican nationals. The oldest was sixteen and the youngest was thirteen.

"Freeing them makes what happened not quite a disaster. At least the girls confirmed that Lily was with them until the day before yesterday." He shook his head. "So close."

Teri finished applying the bronzer and studied her handiwork. "Not bad," she said. "You almost look human."

"High praise from you."

"Try to avoid touching your face and smudging my work," she said. "I would kiss you, but I don't want to mess up your makeup."

"Those are words I never expected to hear," Deke said.

* * *

Although Deke and Michael Carey were seatmates, neither man said much to the other during their flight to Indianapolis. Both prepared for the deposition. The philosophy at the law firm of Bergman/Deketomis was to allow their lawyers to gain experience by handing them the helm. In some ways it was the equivalent of having a child learn how to swim by throwing them into the deep end of the pool.

Usually, they started swimming.

Michael had been with the firm for about a year. Deke didn't know the associate very well, but had heard good things from others. Michael's background was a bit unusual. He'd been in the Air Force before being medically discharged and making a career change to pursuing law. When Michael had been hired, the firm believed they were getting a warrior.

Deke hoped so, but sometimes even promising young lawyers had trouble finding their footing. Today's deposition would be the opening salvo in what was expected to be a protracted struggle with Parakalo Pharmaceuticals, one of the biggest and most lucrative pharmaceutical companies in the world. Bergman/Deketomis had brought a mass tort suit against Parakalo and its diabetes drug, Aeos. Deke wasn't the lead lawyer in the action against Parakalo, but had agreed to help with the early depositions.

Over the loudspeaker, the flight attendant announced they were on final approach to Indianapolis International Airport. Corporate headquarters for Parakalo was only ten miles from the airport. The Parakalo Building was one of the biggest edifices in Indianapolis's skyline, a monument to Big Pharma and bigger money.

Ten minutes later, the flight attendant announced the local time and temperature and said, "From all of us, we hope you enjoy your stay in the Crossroads of America, Indianapolis."

To Deke's ear, it almost sounded as if she had said "crosshairs."

* * *

The two sides faced off across an oversized walnut conference table in a state-of-the-art meeting room. Judging by numbers, the Parakalo lawyers had the advantage. The Bergman/Deketomis legal team consisted of Michael, Deke, and a paralegal. Parakalo had double that number at the table, and a support system at the ready.

The court reporter had her hands poised, waiting on Michael to ask his next question. She wasn't the only one waiting. Deke fought the urge to shift in his seat. He didn't want his impatience to betray the doubts he was having about his associate's cross-examination of the witness. They were almost fifteen minutes into the deposition. By that time, Michael should have been engaged in what the firm called "combat training." You'd think that would be easy for a war vet. The associates were expected to conduct depositions in a prescribed manner only half-kiddingly referred to as "slash and burn." Michael knew the methodology, but he was blowing it. Deke considered slipping him a note saying, *Attack, attack, attack! And use the damn documents!*

By dint of Michael's softball questioning, Parakalo scientist Dr. Gerald Erskine was looking increasingly relaxed and comfortable. By now Erskine should have been feeling the heat over company emails and memos clearly showing criminal conduct by management. When a witness is in the hot seat, all the air-conditioning in the world shouldn't keep him cool.

Michael asked, "Is it your contention, Dr. Erskine, that Aeos is completely safe in managing type 2 diabetes?"

Deke bit down on his lip. Hard. It was a classic setup question that every experienced witness hopes for, and it allowed Dr. Erskine the opportunity to take control of the narrative. Erskine smiled, ready to recite the company talking points about how no drug is completely safe, and how even the most benign drug isn't without risks. He'd say how proud he was of his company and its important work, emphasize that the safety and efficaciousness of Parakalo's drugs were valued above all things, and claim that the pharmaceutical company set the gold standard for drug development that was just short of miraculous.

Erskine could have come out of Hollywood casting playing the avuncular voice of reason. He had gray hair, sympathetic eyes, and a calm voice. That's why it was essential that his mask be pulled back; Parakalo wanted Dr. Jekyll on display, but Bergman/Deketomis needed to reveal Mr. Hyde. Erskine and his team were putting out poison and calling it a miracle drug.

"As I am sure you are aware," said Erskine, "the safety protocols at Parakalo are second to none . . ."

Deke had heard enough bullshit, and knew Erskine was just beginning. He coughed hard, reached for his throat as if in distress, then began coughing all the harder. Deke's manufactured fit was enough to interrupt the direct examination. The way he looked, even with the damn makeup he was wearing, made believers of everyone there.

"Are you all right?" asked Michael.

The associate handed him a bottle of water; Deke managed to swallow a few gulps between bouts of violent coughing.

"Can we please have a short recess?" asked Michael, helping a still coughing Deke to his feet.

The two men exited the meeting room. When they were out of earshot of the others, Deke's voice magically returned.

"I'm going to have to drive this deposition," he said.

Michael couldn't hide his wince. "But I know this case inside out."

Deke tapped his head. "You know it here," he said. "But you either don't know it here"—he tapped his heart—"or you're not showing it."

"I can do better."

Deke was glad the kid didn't want to come out of the game. This was his first real experience coming to bat in the big leagues, and he clearly expected better from himself. As a young lawyer, Deke remembered a time when he'd had the reins taken away from him by a more experienced lawyer who hadn't liked the way he was handling a case. It had been a harsh but necessary lesson. In fact, there was something about Michael that reminded Deke of when he'd been a wet behind the ears lawyer.

"And you will do better, but not today," Deke said. "These opening depositions are critical to our ability to develop and control the themes we'll be showcasing in the trial, and we can't have you allowing this witness to develop their story line at the expense of ours. We need a blitzkrieg. We need rage. Every good trial lawyer has to channel controlled rage. If you're not angry, no jury is going to get angry. Where's your passion?"

Michael took a deep breath. "I was trained to be clear-headed."

Deke could tell there was more to that story, but there wasn't time for him to hear it. "And that's a problem," Deke said. "Righteous indignation needs to be a big part of your legal arsenal. How many people do you think Aeos has killed?"

The drug had been on the market for the better part of a decade. As Aeos sales had increased, so had the deaths associated with its usage.

"No one is sure what those numbers are."

Deke raised his voice. "You make that sound as if it's relevant. It's not. What if this drug had killed your wife? You think you could show a little rage then? We need to speak for the dead. It's our job to do that, whether we're talking about one individual or a thousand. We've got the documentation linking Aeos to a murderer's row of ailments suffered by its users, and you haven't brought in even one of those documents in the fifteen minutes you've been deposing this witness. We're talking about clinical data that shows bladder cancer, kidney disease, and liver failure, just to name a few. Parakalo's own internal company documents show us everything in black and white, but you've been wasting our time asking this corporate shill where he went to school and what courses he took. Really?"

Deke shook his head. He didn't like upbraiding an associate, but at the same time knew a wake-up call was absolutely essential to Michael's development as a lawyer.

"If all those documents we've accumulated showing Parakalo's cover-up of a dangerous drug don't make you angry," said Deke, "then I'll have to get angry for you."

* * *

Erskine and the two Parakalo lawyers were laughing about something when Deke and Michael returned to the conference room. When the proceeding was resumed, Deke said, "Dr. Erskine, isn't it true that you suspected Aeos was a dangerous drug the very first time you reviewed the clinical data?"

"I would object to your calling it dangerous," he said.

"I'm surprised at that, because I assume that before you came in here, you reviewed all the clinical data associated with Aeos going back over the last ten years."

"Naturally, I reviewed all data that I deemed important."

"In that case, you'll need to explain to me how seven years ago you wrote an internal memorandum describing some of the serious side effects surfacing in patients who had been prescribed Aeos."

"That sounds like wild speculation, Mr. Deketomis," said one of the Parakalo lawyers.

"Speculation? It's not speculation if that's what Dr. Erskine wrote, is it? In fact, Dr. Erskine, why don't you just read to us what you wrote seven years ago?"

Deke extended a document toward the scientist. Erskine collected it with a hand that suddenly had a slight tremor. Before beginning to read, he had to wipe away the slight sheen of sweat that had formed on his forehead.

Four hours later, it looked as if Erskine had taken a long steaming sauna in what had been an expensive business suit.

VI

Karina Boyko, like all the others, was curious about the new arrival. Everyone in their camp was an H2B worker from Ukraine, but this newcomer was an American. None of the other girls had yet been able to talk to her. She was being kept in her own private quarters separate from the others.

"They're bringing in American girls to take our jobs," Oksana said.

Around a dozen women were clustered together in one of the "tin cans," their name for the shelters in which they were housed. Karina had been told the units were converted military surplus called Quonset huts. When the women were recruited in Ukraine for work in America, they had been told their housing and food would be provided for. What hadn't been mentioned was that they would be sleeping in some old metal barracks, in what was essentially a prison. For almost a year that had been Karina's home.

Nor had they been told the real nature of the work expected of them. Their "hospitality" job was quite different than what they'd been promised. Despite that, Oksana's rumor was spreading and causing alarm among the others.

Karina decided to speak up. "Who would want our jobs?"

Most of those inside the tin can started nodding. All of them worked at the Pussy Cat Palace, an adult entertainment club. Stripping wasn't the only thing they did. The downstairs of the club was for so-called private dances. Viktoria Yevtushenko Driscoll—the woman who had arranged for them to get H2B visas to work in America—had made it all but impossible for them to make money without doing the "extras" expected of them. What made their situation even worse, if that was possible, was Vicky pocketing almost all the money earned from the selling of their bodies.

Oksana said, "Better half a loaf than none."

Oksana was vain and stupid, but that didn't stop her from having followers and influencing others. Karina had grown up with her grandmother living in their apartment, and Babulya always had a saying for every occasion, such as, "The obliging fool is worse than the enemy." But that wasn't something Karina voiced in the moment. She didn't want Oksana to pout for the rest of the day. Instead, Karina responded with another one of her grandmother's sayings.

"The devil always takes back his gifts."

Her words resonated with those in the room. They all knew Vicky gave nothing to them without getting much more in return.

Oksana changed the subject rather than trying to argue. Logic was never her friend. She was much better at sowing discord.

"The American is getting special treatment. Did you smell the chicken soup they brought to her yesterday? Its aroma was better than perfume even."

One of the girls said, "I hear she's sick."

"I heard from Timofy that she's getting off drugs," whispered another girl.

Timofy was one of their guards, or as Vicky referred to them, "escorts." The guards controlled their movements both inside and outside the camp. It wasn't exactly a prison, but close enough. When not working, they were sequestered from the outside world. Inside the compound were half a dozen of the Quonset huts and little else. There were no neighbors, or at least none that could be seen, and the gated, private road kept any potential visitors at bay.

"You see?" Oksana said. "They are bringing in sick, drug-addicted Americans to take our jobs. And they are spoiling them. She has her own special room, and gets to eat whatever she wants."

"Do you think this American would be here if she had a choice?"

Karina was speaking as much to their own situation as to the American's. None of them had bargained for their own circumstances.

Oksana made a dismissive sound and muttered disdainfully, "*Rusalka.*" A few of the girls laughed at hearing the mocking nickname. A rusalka was a malevolent water sprite with long red hair. Karina's hair was also long and red. She pretended to ignore Oksana's jibe, but once again wished her best friend, Nataliya, was there at her side. It had been easier when the two of them presented a united front to the others. But three months ago, Nataliya had disappeared while working at the Pussy Cat Palace. Vicky wanted the others to believe that Nataliya had run off and married a rich American, but Karina knew better than to believe her bullshit story and kept pressing her for answers. The others wanted to believe Vicky's fantasy, because it played into their own dreams. Or what had been their dreams when most had come to America. Now they knew better, even if they didn't want to believe it. No American Prince Charming is coming for me, Karina thought. And she was sure none had come for Nataliya, despite Vicky's lies.

The door to their hut was thrown open. Timofy stood at the entrance, posing in a self-important stance with his hands on his hips. "What are you hens doing? It's time to start getting ready for work."

All the women, except for Oksana, ignored him. As she made her way out of the tin can, Oksana paused to run her hand on his chest and said, "Time to make ourselves beautiful, right, Timofy?"

Karina suspected that she probably wanted some of that chicken soup she'd smelled the day before.

The others took their leave of the Quonset hut. Since Nataliya's disappearance, there were only three girls in the unit where Karina was housed. The space felt empty without friend. With a heavy heart, Karina picked out an outfit and began dressing.

From outside their quarters, Karina heard Timofy talking, or at least trying to. He was speaking in broken English. Curious, Karina ventured outside.

Timofy stood in front of the Quonset hut where the American was housed. "Out," he said. "Sun needs."

In Ukrainian, Karina asked him what he was trying to say. "Vicky said the American has to get out in the sun so she doesn't look so white and sick," he said.

"Do you want me to talk to her?"

Timofy looked around, afraid that others might hear or see what was going on. "Vicky doesn't want you girls getting near her."

He turned his attention back to the American. "Here. Out."

The hidden woman didn't respond to Timofy's command. He considered what to do, made a frustrated face, then said, "Talk to her."

Karina's heart was pounding as she walked over to the door of the Quonset hut. The quarters were dark, but in the shadows, she could just make out the figure of a woman lying on a cot.

"Come outside in sun," Karina said in English. "There is chair to sit."

The woman didn't respond, but Karina was sure she had heard.

"Breeze nice," Karina said. For a moment she struggled to remember the name of an English word that eluded her, but then recalled it. "No stuffy."

The American finally stirred. She groaned and then slowly raised herself. With slow, unsteady steps, the woman made her way forward, easing her way out of the shadows into the light.

When Karina caught a glimpse of her face, her breath caught. Nataliya!

But as the girl moved into the sunlight, Karina saw she was mistaken. It wasn't Nataliya, although she could have passed as her sister. The American was small and slight, just like Nataliya, but that wasn't the real resemblance. This girl had Nataliya's beautiful green eyes. Karina couldn't look away from them.

"Sit," Karina said, gesturing to the chair.

It was a hot day, but despite the warmth, the American was trembling. As she took a few uncertain steps forward, Karina reached out to steady her arm and help her into the chair.

The girl acknowledged her help by turning to her and nodding, and Karina found herself staring at the girl's eyes.

"Go, go!" Timofy shooed Karina away.

She backed up. The green eyes—Nataliya's eyes—continued watching her as she retreated back into her hut.

VII

Michael tried to hide his surprise when Deke appeared at the door of his small office. In the Bergman/Deketomis pecking order, Michael knew he remained an unproven associate. He stood up; his impulse was to salute, but he managed to keep his right arm at his side. Still, his body language suggested someone had called out, "Attention!"

Deke said, "Rather than both of us standing, is it all right if I sit down?"

"Please."

Michael waited for Deke to sit before he followed suit. Even then, his posture was rigid. The tiny space was just big enough to accommodate the two of them. "Relax," Deke said. "We haven't really had a chance to talk since the Parakalo thing, so I stopped by for a little chat."

"I'm ready to submit my letter of resignation if that's what you want."

"Whoa!" Deke's open palms were in the air, motioning for Michael to take it down a notch. "Clearly, we need to get a few things straight. I didn't come over asking for a letter of resignation, nor would I accept it if offered. So, just take a deep breath, loosen your collar, and unstarch your shirt."

Michael's rigid posture eased a little.

"Truth to tell, I actually came here to apologize," Deke said.

That wasn't what Michael had been expecting to hear, and it showed on his face. "For what?"

"For being too impatient. You had a slow start in the deposition, but that's not surprising, seeing as it was your first time out of the gate.

I should have waited for the break, where we could have discussed a better plan of attack. And if I'd been thinking a little clearer, I would have realized I wasn't lashing out as much at you for your shortcomings as I was for mine."

Michael still felt taken aback. As much as he appreciated Deke's apology, he didn't think it was earned. "But you were right. I wasn't pressing Erskine like I should have. In retrospect, there are a hundred things I'd do differently."

"Welcome to the club." Deke shook his head and sighed. "Like I said, it wasn't you whom I was really pissed off at. The day before we flew up to the depo, I did some major-league stupid things, and paid the consequences for being an idiot. Worse, the person I was trying to help bore the consequences of my stupidity. By the way, thanks for not asking me why my face looked the way it did."

"It wasn't my business."

That didn't mean Michael hadn't been curious. The condition of Deke's face had been a favored topic of the Bergman/Deketomis team for days. No one seemed to know the story of what had happened to him, or if they did, no one was talking about it.

"Maybe it is your business," Deke said, "or could be."

Michael waited for Deke to continue speaking—or not. After a few seconds of deliberation, he finally did. "When I was riding your ass at the deposition, there is one thing I wouldn't take back. I told you that every good lawyer worth a damn has to be passionate, and they have to channel that anger and put their righteous indignation on display."

"I remember," Michael said. Deke's words were forever burned in his memory.

"Why did you join the military?" Deke asked.

There were a hundred reasons, but Michael spoke from his heart. "I wanted to help people who might not otherwise have been able to help themselves."

Deke nodded. If Michael was reading him correctly, his answer seemed to be just what the other man was waiting to hear.

"I don't want to take you completely off the Aeos/Parakalo case.

We'll still need you on that team. But I'm working another case that I think might be more up your alley, and I could use your help."

"What is it?"

"You might have heard about the lawsuit we've brought against Welcome Mat Hospitality, and our contention that their truck stops and motels are being used for sex trafficking. You want an opportunity to help those who can't advocate for themselves? This is it."

Michael's answer was immediate and unequivocal: "I'm in."

VIII

The compound was mostly empty of occupants, and Karina had a rare afternoon off. The others were off working housekeeping shifts at the Emerald Hideaway, a luxury hotel that Vicky owned in Destin. Karina's respite from work would be brief, though. Tonight, she would be "entertaining" at the strip club.

"You are all entertainers," Vicky liked to tell them.

Bitch.

Karina half sat, half lounged on the steps leading into her quarters. She took a languid puff on her cigarette and blew smoke in the air. Before coming to America, she had never smoked, but now that seemed the least of her sins.

A door opened in the hut across from her, and the American emerged. She blinked at the sun. Draped over her hunched shoulders was a coat. It was a hot day, but the American looked cold. Karina was only wearing a T-shirt and shorts and was still sweating. The girl moved her head and took notice of Karina. Karina felt as if it were Nataliya looking at her.

Andrei, their escort for the afternoon, had fallen asleep while sitting in a chair near the American's hut. The girl silently bypassed the big man and made her way over to Karina. With a slight tilt of her head, Karina directed the girl to sit down on one of the steps.

Keeping her voice lowered, the American asked, "May I have a drag?"

Karina handed over the cigarette and said, "Finish."

The girl nodded, accepted the cigarette with trembling fingers, and took a puff. "I needed that," she said. Her trembling became less pronounced.

Karina spanked her pack of smokes, loosened a cigarette, and extended it toward the American. She shook her head and said, "If they find it on me, they'll just confiscate it, like they did the rest of my stash."

In a hopeful whisper she added, "Got any drugs?"

"No drugs."

"Shit," the girl muttered under her breath. "They're giving me some kind of pain reliever with codeine, but it's not doing the job."

She took another deep drag of the cigarette, blew out some smoke, and said, "I don't know what their game is, but they're forcing me to get clean."

Although Karina only understood about half of what the girl was saying, she offered a nod. That was enough encouragement for the American to keep talking.

"What is this place?" She gestured to the fenced-in enclosure with its concertina wire. "Is it like a prison?"

"*Tak*," Karina answered, and then remembered to say it in English: "Yes."

"So, where is everybody?"

"We work hotel. And strip club at night."

"You're a stripper?"

Karina didn't want to fully answer, or even answer at all, but she could not deny the American with Nataliya's eyes. "Stripper, hooker," she said.

"Sucks, don't it?" The American tried to take another drag on the cigarette, but her hands began trembling anew, making it difficult. "I keep asking myself what the hell happened to my life, but the only thing I can figure out is that hell happened."

The American turned her green eyes Karina's way, almost as if she expected her to offer up some answers. Karina looked away. She didn't have any answers. And she didn't want to be hypnotized by the other's eyes.

"I've been a zombie, you know, like the living dead. It was easier when I could just check out with drugs. It was like I was there, but not there. That was the only way I could deal with all those pervs. I kept thinking about killing myself, but it just seemed like too much effort. You sure you don't have a stash? I just need something to tide me over."

"No drugs."

"I can find some way to pay."

Karina shook her head. "No have."

"Shit. What do they want with me? Why am I here?"

Karina offered a shrug.

"You ever do really, really stupid things for a guy? My boyfriend, Carlos, played the love card on me, and I was crazy enough to believe him. That's how that asshole Lie-o controlled me at first. I thought I was saving Carlos's life, and that the two of us would get back together. Lie-o would pass on a message to me that he said was from Carlos. And I was stupid enough to believe him. Then, after two or three months of that bullshit, I realized it was all a big lie."

"Big lie," Karina agreed. It was the story of all their lives.

"That's when I fell into this hole. It was like I died. Lie-o gave me zombie drugs. It was like I wasn't really alive. And then a few days ago, that scumbag Lie-o sold me for a big bag of money. What kind of world is this that you can sell someone? Bastard."

The hate showed itself in the girl's features. Her anger must have warmed her. She stopped trembling and looked more focused.

"In this life we go from slave to grave," Karina said.

The American didn't seem to hear her, which was just as well. "What month is it?"

Karina didn't know the name for it, but counted out on her fingers. "Nine," she said.

The American thought about that and said, "September. I'd be a junior. A year ago, I thought school was so lame. I was too stupid to know how good I had it."

The girl was even younger than Karina had imagined. "How old?" she asked.

The question seemed to catch the American off guard, but then something approaching a small smile came over her face. "What's today's date?"

It took Karina a few moments to remember. "I think twenty-two."

"The twenty-second," the girl mused. "If you're right, in two days, I'll be sixteen." And then she whispered, "Feels like seventy."

"Tak."

"What's your story?"

"Story?"

"Why are you here?"

"Came from Ukraine on H2B visa. Supposed to be one year. Vicky now try to extend for all of us. She say might be three year."

"Do you want to stay?"

Karina shook her head. "Want home."

"Me too." Her sad voice sounded like a little girl's. "Do you have a phone?"

"No phone."

"Can you borrow one from somebody at the strip club?"

"They watch." Karina pointed to a nearby security camera to make sure the girl understood what she was saying. "At club, eyes always watch."

"I need to call my mom. I need help."

Karina shrugged. For the likes of them, there was no help, and little hope, but she didn't have the English to say that.

"Where are we?"

"Florida."

"Where in Florida?"

The question wasn't an easy one for Karina to answer. She couldn't really say where the compound was. It wasn't near any city she could name, but was off by itself on a private road.

"Here I no know. But hotel I work in Destin. Strip club Panama City. Hour drive from here to each."

The American seemed excited by that news. "My mom's house is outside Tallahassee. That's like a three-hour drive from Panama City. She'll help. She's probably going crazy. I need to get ahold of her."

The girl looked expectantly—and beseechingly—at Karina. It was almost like Nataliya was looking at her.

"Your eyes like Nataliya, best friend of me. She gone. Taken, I think. Don't know where is now."

The girl was still looking at her, hoping she would agree to help. That made it hard for Karina to say no.

The words came reluctantly out of her mouth. "I try help you."

Karina would have said more, but a loud voice yelled, "You!"

Andrei had awakened from his nap and was angrily gesturing to the American. "Here! Now!"

As big as Andrei was, the girl didn't look intimidated by him. In her short time sitting with Karina, she seemed to have gotten some of the fight back into her. The American inhaled the last of the cigarette and then tossed the butt to the ground.

Blowing out a plume of smoke, she said, "About time you woke up. Spare me your roid rage and give me my codeine."

"Not time yet," Andrei said.

"Is that so? Tell me that while you're cleaning up my puke, because that's what's going to happen if I don't get my dose."

The prospect of doing that kind of cleanup clearly didn't appeal to Andrei. "Come here for pills."

As the girl got to her feet, Karina was treated to the green flash of her eyes. "Later, gator," she said, and began walking away before stopping to turn around.

"What's your name?"

"Karina. What yours?"

One last glance, a glimpse of green, and a single word: "Lily."

IX

Gina Romano came running into Deke's office, waving her phone and interrupting a meeting he was having with Carol. "Sorry for the interruption, but this is something Deke needs to see. Social media is blowing up."

Holding her phone in front of Deke, Gina began playing a video. An African American woman wearing a platinum-blond wig and sunglasses was addressing a roomful of cameras and reporters.

"I've always tried to be real with my fans," the woman said. "But there was one period of my life I never talked about. I was just too ashamed. But the more I tried to put what happened behind me, the more it kept hurting. I couldn't bottle it up no more. It had to come out. *Chains* is raw, and ugly, and real."

Reporters started yelling questions, and Gina paused the video. "Could we have asked for better timing?"

Gina was one of the most talented lawyers at Bergman/Deketomis, but she was as mercurial as she was brilliant. For her, upsetting the apple cart sometimes wasn't enough; blowing it up was more her style.

Deke tried to understand Gina's excitement. "What am I missing here?"

"You know who's doing the talking, right?"

Deke shook his head.

"It's Storm!"

Gina turned to Carol, who was also shaking her head in disbelief. Even though Carol was a few years older than Deke, she gave him her "you've got to be kidding" look.

"All right, tell me who this Storm is, and tell me why you're so excited."

Almost as if she were explaining to a child, Gina said, "Storm is the hottest hip hop singer on the planet, and at her press conference today, she came out and said she was sexually trafficked as a teenager. She was, and I quote, 'Used, abused, bruised, and utterly confused,' and peddled from one man to another at truck stops and motels. Storm said that what she endured wasn't human trafficking, but inhuman trafficking."

"She said that?"

"More than said it. She sang it on her single 'Inhuman Trafficking.' They even teased a couple of lyrics at the press conference. Her album *Chains* comes out next week. I'm all for beating the drums and making it our anthem for the trial."

"Tomorrow's hearing suddenly got more interesting," Deke said.

"My thoughts exactly," Gina said.

The two lawyers were going to appear in federal court in Atlanta. When they had filed their human trafficking suit against Welcome Mat Hospitality earlier in the year, the media had been remarkably disinterested in reporting on what Deke called the "invisible epidemic." With Storm's new revelation, that would probably no longer be the case.

Deke said, "Try to reach out to Storm's people to see if she might be willing to talk to us. Short of that, try and determine if she has gone on record as saying she was trafficked at any of the Welcome Mat properties."

"Will do," Gina said, and with a wave to the others hurried out of the office.

Deke turned his attention back to Carol. "Let's get back to Tío Leo."

"I wish we had better news, but he's fallen off our radar. We know he doesn't have any shortage of false identities, so he's probably using a new name."

"I want to turn the heat up on him. Give me your best guess as to where he's likely to be, and I'll saturate the area with billboards that have his name and picture, and most of all, the promise of a reward for his capture."

"I'd target the corridor between Tallahassee and Jacksonville. That's where he grew up, but there's no guarantee that's where he is. In the past six months, we know he's done his trafficking from Mobile to Miami."

"Were the girls we freed able to tell us anything about Lily?"

"The sixteen-year-old, a girl named Guadalupe, saw two big white guys carrying Lily out to a large van. She said Rodríguez was expecting them, and thinks he gave Lily enough drugs to be out of it. Guadalupe said the two men spoke English to Rodríguez, so she couldn't understand what was being said, but judging by their accents, she said they weren't Americans."

"She wasn't more specific than that?"

"Afraid not. Before coming to America, she'd never been out of her village."

"How long were the girls with Rodríguez?"

"He's been trafficking them for almost two months. They came into the country on a classic bait and switch, believing they'd be working as housekeepers. Rodríguez manipulated them through all kinds of threats and coercion. They feared not only for their lives but the lives of their families. In fact, he had the girls convinced that he was a *brujo*—a male witch. Rodríguez cut a lock of hair from each of them and said that were they to cross him, he would use their hair to cast a spell on them, and they would waste away. I guess Lily wondered why the girls were so scared of Rodríguez. She only spoke a little Spanish, though, so it took her a while to figure out what was going on. Lily assured the girls that Tío Leo was full of bullshit—*está lleno de mierda*—which I guess was one of the few phrases she knew in Spanish. Guadalupe said Lily was protective of them."

"What's the current status of the three girls?" Deke asked.

"They want to go home, and the sooner the better."

"I would too," Deke said.

X

"Stinking rednecks on table nine," Oksana said. She spoke in English. Vicky didn't like it when the girls spoke Ukrainian. "They think they should get hand jobs with their drinks."

Even though dawn was less than four hours away, the Pussy Cat Palace was still half full.

Redneck. Before coming to Florida, Karina hadn't known that word, and after hearing it for the first time, she asked her countrywomen what it meant. They told her that *redneck* pretty much meant the same thing as asshole, unless it was used in a joking way, in which case it meant "good old boy." Karina hadn't known what that was either, but had come to learn that good old boys weren't typically good, or old, but neither were they complete assholes.

"*Mudak*," Oksana said, breaking Vicky's rule about speaking Ukrainian.

There was no question about the meaning of that. *Mudak* meant asshole in Ukrainian.

Karina suspected Oksana was much more upset about getting a small tip than she was with the table's suggestion that she be their very own sex toy. Since Vicky appropriated almost all their tip money anyway, Karina wondered why Oksana even cared. She ignored the other woman's complaints. Karina knew if she agreed with Oksana, word would get back to Vicky of what she had said. Oksana was all about money, complaining, causing trouble, and tattling to Vicky. Behind her back, the other women called her "the vulture," because she was always waiting for something bad to happen to someone else.

The bartender finished making Karina's drinks. After she put them on a tray and gathered cocktail napkins and straws, Karina went to deliver the cocktails to two men sitting at the tip rail at the club stage, or what the girls referred to as "pervert's row."

Sofia was finishing up her set to a Cardi B song, moving up and down suggestively on the dance pole. The two men were staring at her, and ignored Karina as she delivered their drinks. It was just as well, she thought. The men were running a tab, which allowed her an easy escape. For once, she wasn't required to smile and laugh and pretend what they said was clever.

The Pussy Cat Palace was located on the outskirts of Panama City, which was halfway between Pensacola and Tallahassee. Karina had heard people refer to Panama City as the capital of the Redneck Riviera.

Sofia finished with her gyrating, and her efforts were greeted with some applause. Karina was glad that she wouldn't be dancing any more that night on the stage. Faking happiness, and feigning sexiness, wasn't something she was good at. She had heard the men describe her performances as "McDance." Karina didn't know what they meant, but knew it wasn't a compliment.

"Last call," announced the bar manager.

The announcement was more for the dancers than it was for the patrons, a signal to hustle the customers not only for drinks, but for a last private dance. It was 3:30 a.m., and the city's ordinance allowed alcohol to be sold until 4:00 a.m.

Whenever last call was announced, the Pussy Cat Palace played the Donna Summer song "Last Dance." There was no disco ball at the so-called gentlemen's club, but the lighting system allowed for reflective lights to shimmer along the surface of the stage and the surrounding walls beyond. Now was the time for Karina and the other dancers to begin suggestively singing the song's lyrics in the ears of their marks.

As usual, Karina didn't rush to participate in the frantic manhunt. If she was lucky, maybe the man she targeted would be content ending his night doing what Americans called a "dry hump" in one of the private rooms downstairs.

By that time of night, most of the dancers were as tipsy as the patrons. Vicky allowed all the girls to run a bar tab. That was one of her traps. Much of the money the dancers made went to booze. It was just one of many ways in which Vicky controlled them. She was the company store for the girls to buy their "four Cs" of clothing, cosmetics, chocolate, and cigarettes. At the end of every month, Vicky sent money back to their families in Ukraine, but it never seemed to amount to much.

The drinks were expensive, but they also seemed like a necessity. "*Cope* rhyme with *hope*." That was what Nataliya would always say when she got buzzed. And after she made that declaration, a sad smile always came to her face, and she would add, "But it really don't."

Karina could feel her own lips transforming into that same sad smile.

By this time of night, Nataliya would always be shit-faced. That was a favorite expression of hers. "I need to get shit-faced," she would say.

Shit-faced, thought Karina. That was another strange American word. There were plenty of words for getting drunk in Ukrainian, but there was no equivalent to *shit-faced*. Still, Karina could understand Nataliya's need to drink herself senseless.

Karina wished her friend were here. None of the others even mentioned Nataliya's name anymore. It was almost as if they were afraid to acknowledge her existence. They even seemed annoyed that Karina persisted in asking about Nataliya, and made it clear they thought she should leave things be. But that wasn't something Karina could do. Only three months ago she had disappeared on a night just like this. Karina heard that Vicky had called her into the office to talk. And then she was never seen again. Without Nataliya around, Karina felt lonelier than ever.

Over the speakers, Donna Summer sang her last dance anthem.

Most of the dancers had already disappeared downstairs. By now they were settling into a small room with their john for a so-called private dance. Karina continued to put off finding a mark. She didn't want to abandon the memory of Nataliya; this was her chance to spend time with her once more.

Seeing the American earlier in the day had brought back all sorts of memories. It wasn't only that they had the same eyes. At her core, Karina sensed that the American was feisty like Nataliya. Now that she was coming off the drugs, Karina suspected the girl's spirit would begin to show itself more and more.

Lily had said some man had sold her. If that was true, it must have been Vicky who had bought her. But why? Vicky's only motivation was money. How could she profit from Lily? They were bringing good food to the American and weaning her off drugs. Vicky wanted her out in the sun, to look fit and healthy. There had to be a reason for that, even if Karina didn't yet know why.

The American wanted her help, but Karina knew that sticking out her neck could be dangerous. Still, maybe she could do something for her. But Karina didn't have a cell phone. Vicky had taken all their cell phones away when they'd arrived in America. She said it was for their safekeeping, but everyone knew better. Once a month, Vicky allowed them to make calls back home. There was a script they had to follow, and Vicky listened in on what was being said. Deviating from what was allowed meant suspension of future phone privileges, so they willingly spoke in lies, that they might hear the voices of their loved ones.

Before Nataliya had disappeared, she had discovered a secret way in which they might make a call. The two of them had even discussed calling the police, but they were too afraid because Vicky frequently dropped hints that she had friends in law enforcement who looked out for her. They were scared of the authorities and knew of no one else who might help them.

The lights continued to flash, and the disco beat went on. Disco had come and gone before she was born, thought Karina. It was supposed to be long dead, but its ghost continued to haunt all these years later. In the absence of Nataliya, and in the presence of all these *mudaky*, she couldn't help but feel lost.

As Donna Summer sang, Karina wondered if the singer was still alive. She seemed to recall that the Queen of Disco was now dead, but her song still played in this room of despair. It hadn't seemed so bad when Nataliya was there, though. Sometimes the two of them danced to this song. Usually Nataliya would be drunk and would yell out, "Last dance, Karina!"

They didn't dance for the men, offering them some parody of sex in the hopes of payment. They danced for fun. When the song ended, they would usually go in search of a man to go downstairs, but not always. Sometimes Nataliya would insist that the two of them just keep dancing. Each of them wanted to think that the choice of who they shared their bodies with was their own. But was that ever really the case?

"Last dance, Nataliya," she whispered.

XI

Those who worked late at the Pussy Cat Palace were allowed to sleep until midmorning. The workers were shuttled to the hotel in two shifts, morning and afternoon. From there, workers were normally either taken back to the compound or to the Pussy Cat Palace.

A bell rang, calling to those sleeping. The women were slow to appear, and the bell was rung more vigorously until everyone assembled in the open area. Yawning and grumbling, they waited on the day's announcements.

"Change of plans for some of you today," Timofy announced. "There's a strip trip going out an hour before sunset."

Shit, Karina thought. She had never learned to swim and was uncomfortable being on a boat. She didn't like the conditions, or the lack of security. At least there was a bouncer and manager at the Pussy Cat Palace. On Vicky's party boat there was only a crew of two, the captain and his first mate. Both men stayed in the wheelhouse and put no limitations on the partying. Karina had heard stories that in addition to doing Vicky's booze cruises, the crew was also involved in human trafficking. If that was true, she wouldn't be surprised.

Timofy began reading the names of those Vicky had assigned to the booze cruise. Not me, thought Karina, not me, but it was wishful thinking. She was one of the five women assigned to work the ship.

"Those going out on the *Seacreto*"—that was the name of Vicky's boat—"will be transported to the marina from their afternoon shift at the hotel."

Karina knew some of the girls preferred working the strip trip over working at the club. There was usually good food, and the clients paid for all the drinks.

"Who wants to switch club for cruise?" she asked.

Timofy shook his head. "Vicky said no switches."

"*Layno*," Karina said, cursing in Ukrainian.

Only one person seemed to take notice of how upset she was, and that was the American. She emerged out of the tin can she had all to herself, looking concerned at the sound of Karina's angry outburst. Everyone's gaze turned to her, which started Timofy on one of his lectures.

Speaking in Ukrainian, he said, "Ignore the American. I don't want to see any of you talking with her."

"Why?" asked Karina.

"Because Vicky said so."

The girls began grumbling to one another. "And what are we supposed to do if she walks anywhere near us?" Petra asked. "Should we run away?"

Oksana voiced concern. For herself, of course. "Is the American contagious with some kind of disease?"

Even though they were supposed to be ignoring her, everyone stared at Lily. The American knew she was the topic of conversation, but had no idea what was being said.

Timofy said, "She isn't sick, but has been detoxing here. You can see what rest and good food have done for her."

It was true that she had lost her pallor, and looked much better than when she had arrived.

Timofy wasn't done warning them, though. "But to be safe, everyone needs to stay away from her. Besides, she won't be around for more than a day or two."

"Where is she going?" Karina asked.

Timofy didn't hide his annoyance. "Why do you care?"

"She is probably going somewhere nice," Oksana said.

Lily was looking at Karina. Clearly, she wanted an explanation of what was going on, but Karina could only shake her head slightly, signaling this was not a good time for any interaction between them.

Timofy put an end to the conversation. "The van will be leaving soon. Go get ready."

Karina went off with the others. She knew Lily's eyes followed her, but she didn't acknowledge them.

* * *

The Emerald Hideaway was a small waterfront luxury hotel. Karina much preferred working there than at the Pussy Cat Palace. She was not daunted by the physical labor of toiling in the laundry room or cleaning hotel rooms. Making beds and cleaning toilets suited her much more than being one of Vicky's entertainers at the strip club. The hotel work felt honest, and she got a certain satisfaction from taking something dirty and making it clean. At the club, it felt like just the opposite.

Working as a housekeeper gave Karina an invisibility she liked. She wore a uniform, not the provocative clothing required at the club. The anonymity suited her. At the hotel they were forbidden from engaging with the guests other than exchanging the briefest of pleasantries. Vicky's guards monitored them, and their movements were strictly controlled. The laundry room was located in the subterranean garage, an area closed to guests. Laundry was taken in carts by means of a service elevator that could only be utilized by staff. The three-story block of suites was accessed by outdoor walkways. There was one maid to each floor. Today, Karina was assigned the top floor.

The room she was cleaning had been vacated. Karina picked up the dirty towels in the bathroom and took them out to her cart. Her movements didn't seem to draw any interest from Danylo, one of her keepers at the hotel. As usual, he was parked out in the courtyard, pretending to be a guest. His vantage point allowed him a good viewing spot to monitor the maids, or anyone bringing up laundry. Karina carried some clean linen back to the room. Even though she wasn't supposed to turn on the television while cleaning the guest rooms, she always did. At their compound, no television, radio, or internet was allowed.

Using the remote, Karina turned on the television and began

flipping through the channels until she found CNN. On occasion, she was able to catch up on news reports about Ukraine. Today, though, she saw an angry man standing in front of a group of reporters on the landing of what the words on the screen told her was the Richard B. Russell Federal Building in Atlanta, Georgia.

Karina tried to make sense of the writing at the bottom of the television screen, where a scrolling message said, *Hip hop star Storm claims to have been a sex slave on the trucking circuit.*

A female reporter shouted, "Mr. Deketomis, your case is drawing international interest after Storm went public with her assertion that when she was a teenager, she was sexually trafficked at truck stops and motels throughout the southeast. Your comment, please?"

The man being asked the question, Karina could see, looked troubled. "I know Storm's disclosure is why most, if not all of you are here. I only wish the media's newfound interest in human trafficking had occurred previous to today, because as of this morning a gag order was put into effect by Judge Irwin, which precludes my discussing any particulars from the Welcome Mat case. As for Storm, I can only say that I'm glad she is coming forward to speak of her own terrible experiences, and I hope her voice will speak for the voiceless and help to spotlight the more than a half million individuals in this country who at this moment are being trafficked."

At the bottom of the screen, a new chyron read, *Storm says her latest album* Chains *will detail her life as a sex slave.*

A male reporter shouted, "Your case alleges the collusion of Welcome Mat's truck stop and motel management with human traffickers. What can you tell us about that?"

"Believe me, I'd like to do nothing more than share that information with you, but Judge Irwin's gag order applies to all material uncovered during our interrogatories and depositions, which leaves me muzzled and extremely upset."

"Is it safe to say, Mr. Deketomis, that you don't agree with Judge Irwin's ruling?"

At the bottom of the screen, the speaker was identified as Nick "Deke" Deketomis, attorney for the law firm of Bergman/Deketomis of

Spanish Trace. That city, Karina knew, wasn't far from the hotel where she was working.

The lawyer's red face bespoke his anger. "I'm extremely troubled by it, especially because this kind of ruling is becoming all too common-place among judges who are disconnected with the realities surrounding a case like this. When you hide what is unfolding in the courtroom on a day-to-day basis, you end up keeping the public in the dark about dangers of which they need to be aware. Many of those being trafficked are minors, so doesn't it make sense to warn mothers and fathers that there might be a clear and present danger to their children? Why is the public's right to know put aside in favor of shielding the criminal offenses of corporations and offenders?"

"Can you answer your own question, Mr. Deketomis?" shouted another reporter.

"I wish I could," Deke said. "The First Amendment to our Constitution ensures the freedom of speech, and yet too many judges seem to forget that."

"Are you referring to Judge Irwin?" asked a reporter.

"I'm referring to the all-too-common court practice of denying the public the right to know. What makes that situation even worse is that nobody, including the media, gives a damn, or at least they don't give a damn unless some recording star's commentary drives the latest news cycle."

The lawyer's condemnation seemed to momentarily silence all the reporters.

"Look, there's a reason that I brought this lawsuit. In America today, we have slavery in plain sight, and the government and the corporate media are turning a blind eye to it. Where's the DOJ? Where's the Department of Homeland Security? Where is the Department of Labor?

"Most Americans seem to be of the belief that this is some third world problem, but the truth is that there is more human trafficking going on in the United States than any other country. What that means is that we as a society are condoning slavery. That makes this an American tragedy. The problem is massive and systemic. I'm talking about individuals being placed in a position where they have no recourse but to submit to whatever their human traffickers tell them to do, with failure to comply resulting in beatings, sexual abuse, and even death."

Tears welled up in Karina's eyes. It was rare for her to cry, but this man was speaking to her life, and to her misery. And he was speaking to Nataliya's disappearance and perhaps death. She stopped breathing so as to hear his every word.

"Do you think you will win your case, Mr. Deketomis?"

"If our Constitution is still viable, we will win. In 1865, the Thirteenth Amendment abolished slavery in this country. 'Neither slavery nor involuntary servitude, except as a punishment for crime where the party shall have been duly convicted, shall exist within the United States, or any place subject to their jurisdiction.'"

Deke took a breath. "Thirty-two words. That's all that was needed to establish that vital law of this land."

"But why are you going after Welcome Mat Hospitality?" asked a female reporter.

"Because it's no secret that Welcome Mat's truck stops and motels have been used for the purposes of prostitution. But putting it in those terms makes it almost sound respectable. It isn't. They have conspired to provide venues for illicit sexual trafficking."

Nick Deketomis took another deep breath. Karina could tell he wanted to say more, but couldn't. She knew his dilemma; it was her own.

"Thank you," he said and walked away from the microphones.

Karina used the remote to turn off the television. First, she felt numb, but then her anger began building, stirring up her insides. The lawyer had awakened so many things that she had bottled up. It was almost as if he had been speaking to her, and to her personal misery. She didn't understand why this judge had constrained him from talking, but she did understand that this man was on her side. Now, she wasn't feeling quite so alone.

Pacing the room, Karina thought about what to do. She stepped out onto the balcony and looked out to the Gulf of Mexico. The hotel guests paid a lot of money for just such a view, but Karina rarely had the luxury of being able to see as they did. She stole a few moments to take in the sight. The colors of the water changed with the conditions and were now a postcard-perfect emerald.

Like Nataliya's eyes. And the American's.

Thinking about her missing friend was enough to make Karina turn away from the view. She walked back into the hotel room. The suite still needed to be cleaned. It was her last room of the day, but that only made Karina feel more uneasy. The booze cruise awaited.

Instead of starting in on her cleaning, she went and opened the bedside table. Inside the drawer were a Bible and a local telephone directory of businesses. From Karina's experience, it was rare for either one of those books to be opened. When guests wanted to look up any local attractions, they used their cell phones.

Trying to make sense of the listings in the business directory was much like working on a puzzle. Her excitement grew when she saw that some of the businesses listed on the pages had addresses in Spanish Trace. That's where the lawyer's firm was located. There were many listings and advertisements for AC techs, accountants, account services, actuaries, and administrative resources, but when she looked for the listings under the Ls, she couldn't find any category for lawyers. Why had they been excluded?

Karina went back to the L listings and saw the entry she had overlooked.

Lawyers—see Attorneys at Law.

Her heart was beating hard as she began her search anew. This time she found several pages of listings, but making sense of what she saw was still challenging. There were headings, and subheadings, but she didn't see the name Nick Deketomis. Then something caught her eye under the letter B. There was a telephone number for the law firm of Bergman/Deketomis. Karina reached out and reverently touched the entry. It was real. It was there. And so was the number.

She held her breath, thinking of what to do. You couldn't make calls from the phones in the guest rooms; the guest could only call the operator or front desk. It was Nataliya who told her it hadn't always been that way—before cell phones, guests made calls from the phones in their hotel rooms. How Nataliya knew this, Karina didn't know. There were a lot of things her friend had known that no one else did.

It shouldn't have come as a surprise to her, then, when one day Nataliya announced that there was a way to make a phone call. She directed Karina to secretly meet up with her in the service elevator. At the time, it had felt like a spy mission behind enemy lines. Karina feared the consequences of being discovered, but did as Nataliya asked.

Nataliya was waiting for her inside the elevator. They spoke in whispers, afraid of being overheard. According to Nataliya, when the elevator phone had originally been installed, it would have come with its own dedicated line. She opened up its panel, and showed Karina the faded directive inside of it. *In Event of Emergency Dial O.*

But Nataliya hadn't dialed O. Somehow her friend had imagined there was a way to bypass the hotel operator in order to get an outside line. And she showed her.

She announced her discovery in an excited whisper, "All you have to do is hit nine! And then when you hear the dial tone, enter the number you want!"

Her green eyes danced when she told Karina the news. But then Nataliya admitted there was one problem with her magical solution. The elevator phone line could only call what her friend said were "local" numbers.

Was this Bergman/Deketomis number one of those?

Karina and Nataliya had discussed the possibilities of who they should call from the elevator phone, but before they had a chance to do that, Nataliya had been taken away. The thought of what had happened to her friend strengthened Karina's resolve. Like someone possessed, Karina hurried through her cleaning. There was a call to make.

XII

Diana Fernandez, Deke's longtime office administrator, picked up yet another call. For almost twenty years, she'd been Deke's "gatekeeper." Organizing Deke, as she often told him, was a full-time job in itself.

The phone had been ringing nonstop for the last hour. Many people had caught clips of Deke's interview on CNN, and wanted to talk to him about it.

"Office of Nick Deketomis," she said. "This is Diana."

There was breathing on the line, but no one said anything. Anyone else probably would have hung up, but Diana had experience with reluctant callers.

Diana spoke into the silence. "May I help you?" she said.

"Mr. Deke, please," said a heavily accented and very nervous voice.

"Who is calling?" asked Diana.

"I see him on the TV," the woman said. "I need bad help."

The voice was muffled, like the woman was speaking from within an enclosed space. She could hear the woman's desperation in her strained voice. The caller sounded young, probably close to the age of her own teenage daughter. Diana tried to put her at ease.

"I'm glad you called. We'll certainly help you if we can. Unfortunately, Mr. Deketomis won't be in today, but you can sure talk to me. My name is Diana."

Shallow breathing could be heard from the other end of the line. Diana sensed the frightened caller was ready to hang up.

"Let me help you, dear. And I will be glad to pass on any message you might have for Mr. Deketomis."

"No, no," the woman said, clearly frustrated, clearly afraid.

"What's your name, sweetie?"

After a moment's hesitation: "Karina."

Was her accent Russian? "That's a beautiful name."

Karina said something in her native tongue. Diana reached for a legal pad and wrote down, *Jock—o—u?* She assumed Karina was thanking her. The fact that the woman was still on the line, despite her fears, demonstrated her pressing need for someone to hear what she had to say.

"And what's your last name, Karina?"

The woman spoke quickly. Diana wrote down *Boyko?* She decided to not ask her to repeat it. The young woman was already too nervous. Instead, Diana said, "Over fifty years ago, my family came from Cuba. I wasn't even born yet. My grandparents arrived in this country with nothing. I know how difficult it was for them. It's not easy to try and make your way in a country you don't know."

The intake of Karina's breath told Diana that she had spoken to her own experience. The immediacy of her response also suggested the girl was able to comprehend English much better than she could speak it.

"Yes," she agreed. "Bad hard."

Karina's sigh said more than her words could. "Mister Deke talk about slaves on the TV."

The CNN segment, Diana thought. She had caught a replay of Deke's comments, and knew Judge Irwin would not be happy with what he'd said. But despite the potential legal tempest of Deke's violating the gag order, Diana was proud of her boss. If he hadn't spoken his conscience to the world, this frightened young woman would never have called.

"Mr. Deketomis is very passionate in his beliefs, and he says exactly what he means."

"I am slave," Karina said.

Diana's intake of breath was involuntary. The mom in her wanted to hug this scared girl, and try and make everything better.

"I'm so sorry. What can I do to help you?"

Karina spoke in a whisper, almost as if she herself was afraid to hear her own fears and confession. "Not me only. My friend Nataliya *Na-hurny* go missing."

Diana added the name to the legal pad.

"I think something bad, something bad," said Karina, her voice still hushed.

"Something bad happened to Nataliya?" asked Diana.

Karina made a sound much like a pirate's—"Yarrr"—and then added, "Nataliya like me."

Diana tried to understand what Karina was telling her. Was she saying that Nataliya liked her? No, that wasn't it. Then Diana figured it out, or thought she did. Karina was telling her that Nataliya was in her same situation.

"Nataliya is also a *slave*?" asked Diana.

Just saying that word felt wrong. It made her feel unclean.

"Dalk!"

Karina's response was immediate and emphatic, and Diana made another entry on the pad. Unsure of the spelling, she wrote down what she had heard.

"Nataliya work at club I work. Vicky call her to office. She never come back."

"When did this happen, Karina?"

"Three month, maybe?"

"Do you want us to look into this? Are you asking to see if Mr. Deketomis might be able to help you? And help Nataliya as well?"

"I want him to lawyer for me. And for Nataliya."

Diana tried to soothe the frightened woman. "Can you meet with Mr. Deketomis for a consultation, dear?"

Panicked breathing was all Diana could hear. She quickly added, "If you can't meet in person, Nataliya, I could schedule a phone interview."

"Phone hard, but I try again. Must go on strip trip."

"Strip trip?" Diana asked.

"Booze cruise. We soon to go on boat."

"Do you have a number where Mr. Deketomis could call you tomorrow?"

"Knee. No number. I call."

"That's fine. I hope we can talk again soon."

Karina spoke hurriedly, clearly pressed for time. *"Amerikanski* also need help."

"I don't understand," Diana said.

"Amerikanski who look like Nataliya prisoner where we live."

Diana didn't get a chance to ask any more questions.

"Can't talk," Karina said. "Must go."

There was a click, and the line went dead. Diana found herself shaking the phone in frustration before reluctantly returning it to its cradle. Then she looked down at her pad. There was one other thing she needed to write down.

Emerald Hideaway.

That was the name displayed on Diana's phone. Curious, she typed the name into a search engine. The first entry that came up showed a beautiful resort hotel located on the Emerald Coast on the outskirts of Destin, about an hour's drive away.

Karina must have been calling from the hotel, thought Diana. But if the woman was a slave, as she said, what was she doing there? The property looked posh, but maybe that was just a veneer.

Diana consulted the pad where she'd made all of her entries. Then she used a search engine to try variations of the foreign words she'd written down. Making sense of most of her phonetic translations didn't take long. Karina hadn't said *jock-o-u* and *dalk* and *knee.* What she had said were *dyakuyu* and *tak* and *ni. Thank you* and *yes* and *no.* Although she couldn't translate everything Karina had said, Diana was sure of one thing.

Karina was Ukrainian.

XIII

"Hurry it up!" Danylo was standing outside the van, scowling at her. "We've all been waiting for you."

Karina hustled up to the white van and took an open seat. Her heart was still racing, and she dared not talk for fear of her excitement giving her away. Luckily for her, the others were talking among themselves and seemed to take little notice of her presence. Most of them looked happy to be going on an outing that was different from their usual routine. It wasn't as if they had any choice but to go along with whatever Vicky told them to do. By this time most of them had been in America for almost a year. Disillusionment had come early in their stay.

"It's a perfect night for going out on the water," Valentyna said. "Hot, but not too hot."

"Good thing we sail tonight and not tomorrow," Yana said. "A customer at the club said a big storm was coming our way."

"Storm?" Oksana made a dismissive sound. "There was barely a breath of wind all day."

Yana said, "Haven't you heard about the calm before the storm?"

As the others kept talking, Karina closed her eyes and pretended to rest, but what she was really doing was thinking about her conversation with Diana. She tried to remember every word the two of them had exchanged. In retrospect, there was so much more she should have said but didn't. When her call actually went through, it had felt like her heart was jumping out of her chest. If only Nataliya had been there with her. Without her friend showing her the way, she never could have made the call.

Next time she would be more organized, Karina vowed. She would plan better, and try to make things as safe as possible. During her talk with Diana, she had only been able to listen to her with one ear, so fearful was she of being discovered.

The girls were still chattering. "Tonight, we get to eat party food," Valentyna said. "It will be nice to have something other than borscht. I hope they have salmon."

"I hope they have blow," Oksana said.

Everyone except for Karina laughed. Naturally, Oksana noticed. "What is the matter, rusalka?"

As Oksana reached to touch her red locks, Karina pulled her head back and said, "I'm afraid of where those hands have been."

"Always so high and mighty, rusalka. You and Nataliya. But where is she now?"

"I don't know where she is. Do you?"

Oksana's answer was a smug smile.

The van pulled into the marina's parking lot, and Danylo hustled them over to the *Seacreto*. "Move it! Move it!"

"Why?" Karina asked. "I don't see the passengers."

"Why do you always ask questions?"

Instead of hurrying with the others, Karina slowed her pace. Everything felt wrong. Danylo came back to her. "Come along!" When that didn't get her moving, Danylo said in a voice the others couldn't hear, "The clients will be meeting up with the ship later."

"Where?"

"I don't know."

"That makes no sense."

"You think Vicky tells me her business? Now, come along. Don't make me have to drag you to the boat."

The other girls were already boarding the *Seacreto*. With great reluctance, Karina went to join them.

From the yacht, Karina watched the retreating shore. They had never before gone out without their clients already aboard the boat. As usual, the crew of two did not communicate with them. The other girls were acting carefree, most of them leaning against the railing. Karina kept to the interior of the yacht. The open water scared her.

This whole situation scared her, even if she wasn't sure why that was.

They were well away from shore, and away from any seacraft, when she saw a speeding Zodiac approaching them. The captain of the *Seacreto* idled the yacht, and a line was thrown to the other craft. One by one, five men climbed the ladder.

Hard, dangerous men. Karina knew this the moment she saw them.

"We're here to do some deep-sea drilling!" one of the men yelled.

They thought that was funny.

* * *

The party was in full force when the anchor was finally thrown. Never before had Karina and the others ventured this far from shore for a booze cruise. The sun had just set; the lights on shore were beginning to show themselves.

Everyone else was drinking and doing drugs. Karina stayed on the periphery of where the others were gathered. In her hand was a beer. She was actually grateful that Oksana was the center of attention. When the cocaine had come out, Oksana had stripped off her clothes and offered her naked body for lines. The men and women lined up to do their snorting. All the noses were white; Oksana's was whitest of all.

Even though the *Seacreto* was a large yacht, Karina knew there was no place to hide on it. That was the story of her life. She had always looked for a good hiding spot, but had never found one.

I ran from the wolf, thought Karina, but ran into a bear. The old Ukrainian saying almost made her smile, but this was not a time for even grim humor.

"Hey, Red," shouted the man who was clearly in charge. "Come join the party."

Karina pretended not to hear. She leaned over and retched. By feigning seasickness, she hoped the man might turn his attention to one of the other girls.

"I'm talking to you, Red."

His voice was louder now, and more insistent. Karina could see his look of impatience and hear the hunger in his voice. Karina knew there were those who envied her good looks, but for her it had always been more of a curse than not. Men like this one had sought her out since she was a girl. After her father had abandoned her mother and family, their advances had only gotten worse.

"Sick," Karina said.

A few of the girls offered up scornful laughs.

"Rusalka," shouted Oksana.

"What the hell does that mean?" the man asked.

Oksana was glad to explain: "Rusalka, red-haired kind of fairy-girls that live in water. They use long red hair to pull men under and drown them."

"Is that so?" The man looked amused. "Always had a thing for red-heads, rusalka or not. Get your ass over here, Red. We paid your boss top dollar, and she promised us VIP treatment."

Karina covered her mouth with her hand, and made more retching sounds, but the man was unmoved. It was clear to Karina that whether she was sick or not made no difference to him.

"I'm not asking again," he said.

Karina started forward, trying to buy time by pretending her legs were wobbly. There were no other ships around, not even any fishing boats.

One of the men began playing rock and roll music on his phone. An already naked Oksana began bumping and grinding with Sofia, eliciting whistles and cheers.

"Girl on girl," hooted one of the men.

Unfortunately for Karina, the man who had called her over wasn't distracted. His gaze remained fixed on her while she made her approach. Finally, she stood in front of him.

"You took your damn time," he said.

"Big sick," Karina said, making a waving motion with her hand. "The sea."

"Champagne will settle your stomach."

He extended a glass of champagne to Karina, but when she reached for it, he grabbed her arm and pulled her close. Everyone seemed to think that was funny.

"You better drink up now," he said. "Because in another minute, your lips are going to be occupied."

The man's pack of followers made appreciative noises. Karina tried to pull away, but that just made the spectators that much rowdier.

Unbidden, the word came out of Karina's mouth: "No."

The man's smile was even more threatening than his scowl. "Maybe I didn't hear you right, Red."

His arm shot out, and he grabbed Karina's long red locks and yanked. She screamed from the pain and cried out even louder as the man began swinging her from side to side. Wherever he pulled, her body followed, until the man wrenched her down to her knees.

"Now let's get busy," he said.

Karina no longer had to pretend she was sick; her stomach roiled. She clawed at the man's arm, raking his flesh, but he didn't release his grip on her hair. His smile broadened, and with his free hand he slapped her.

As her head snapped back, she caught a glimpse of the captain and first officer seated comfortably in their helm seats. Both of them were leaning forward and enjoying the show. There would be no help from either of them, she knew, just as there would be no help from those watching.

"No," Karina said again.

She wanted to sound defiant, but failed. She was tired. So tired. All her life she'd fought. This was not a battle she could win, but neither could she bring herself to surrender.

Her refusal was met with another slap and demand. "Mister Johnson doesn't like to be kept waiting, Red."

"Get screwed, asshole!" Karina screamed.

Karina expected a beating. But the man surprised her by yanking her up. His fingers locked in under her armpits, and Karina's feet left the deck. She had always been thin. There wasn't much weight on her.

That made it easy for him to toss her over the railing.

There wasn't even time to scream, not at first. She plunged into the water and then came to the surface, thrashing and flailing. Even then, her scream was muted. She grabbed one desperate breath, cried out, and then splashed frantically. But all her flailing was not enough to keep her head above the water.

No, no! She swallowed salt water and began gagging and choking. Her panicked floundering succeeded in getting her head above the water a second time, but then she went under again. In a desperate attempt to get air, she swallowed more water. As sick as Karina was, she still fought. When she broke the surface for a third time, a light from above shined down upon her.

Somehow a moment of clarity superseded her panic. Karina could see the shadows on the railing looking down at her. The music was still playing, but that wasn't all that Karina heard. The others were laughing at her.

Laughing.

Her wet clothing began pulling her down, and Karina's panicked attempts to breathe only filled her lungs with seawater that much faster. Her throat burned and her stomach convulsed. A lack of oxygen made her light-headed.

Karina heard Diana's concerned voice in her head. When they'd talked, the woman had sounded as if she truly cared. Karina would not be able to call her back as she'd promised. A part of her knew that death had come for her. It felt as if invisible hands were pulling her into the depths.

Not hands, she thought, but hair. The rusalki were claiming her. But it wasn't only the water nymphs. Nataliya was there as well. As her struggles lessened, Karina's panic receded. The water no longer felt like her enemy; it embraced her in its warmth.

I am now a rusalka, she thought. It was the fate of women spurned by life and love. But she wasn't alone. Nataliya and the others were with her. If the stories Karina had heard were true, their cruel deaths would make their spirits haunt these waters. They would only be able to rest in peace if someone avenged their deaths.

She swam with the rusalki.

XIV

Michael ran up the stairs to get to their apartment. It was the last leg, so to speak, of his workout. The PJ regimen alternated push-ups with a combination of sprints, and only took him half an hour to get a good sweat. For good measure, he always added another five minutes of core workout to help strengthen the broken back that had ended his military service.

It was easier talking about that than it was the traumatic brain injury sustained during the same crash. He didn't want to come across as some kind of head case. The doctors hadn't been able to give him a long-term prognosis for his brain injury, but they had pulled the plug on his service. When you have blurry vision, and dizziness, and difficulty concentrating, you can't do the duties required of a PJ. The decision to leave the military hadn't been his, but Michael had come to look at the discharge as a blessing. It had allowed him to marry Mona and start a new life. Each of them had helped the other with their injuries. Mona's wounds had been even more serious than his.

He announced his presence at the door by rapping out "shave and a haircut—two bits," and then unlocked the dead bolt. Mona met him at the door, where they kissed.

"It is good to have you home, husband," she said.

Michael found himself smiling, as he usually did, at Mona's form of address to him. He still wasn't sure if it was a cultural thing, or Mona's way of speaking. Mona's father had been educated in England, but had refused to be part of the Assyrian diaspora, and had returned to his homeland in Iraq. It was her father who had taught Mona her flawless English.

"It is good to be home, wife," he said, offering quaint for quaint. "But I know why you're so glad to see me."

He handed her the two takeout bags he was holding. "Cuban picadillo and black beans and rice."

The Cuban picadillo was similar to one of her favorite Assyrian entrees. On Michael's nights to "cook," it was one of his go-to dishes.

"You read my mind."

"As I'm reading it right now. That's why I'll shower before we eat."

"That is not something to which I will object."

They kissed again, and Michael went and showered. In the military he'd grown used to showering in under two minutes. Even now, his showers held to that time frame. Within five minutes he was clean, dressed, and back out in the living room. By then Mona had doctored the dishes with a few of her favorite condiments, adding a spritz of lime to the rice and some coriander seasoning to the picadillo. As she served up the dishes, each smiled at the other.

"Good day?" Michael asked.

"Busy day, mostly spent in front of the computer."

"Sounds like we had a similar day then."

"I doubt you were learning about scabies."

"I don't even know what scabies are."

"It is a condition caused by an infestation of microscopic mites that have burrowed under the skin, and shows itself through bumps or redness."

"If I wasn't a hypochondriac before you started nursing school, I'll surely be one by the time you become an RN."

"Please wait until next semester before manifesting any symptoms, because that's when I will be taking a class on health anxiety."

Michael stuck his tongue out at her. Instead of responding in kind, Mona peered intently at his tongue and said, "Did you know the color of your tongue can say many things about your health? Its shape, texture, and color all tell stories."

"And what does my tongue say?"

"It says you are incorrigible."

Both of them tried to hide their smiles; both failed.

Fate had brought the couple together not once, but twice. Two days after Michael's combat search and rescue team had flown a seriously injured Mona to the Air Force hospital in Belad, Michael had been brought there for his own injuries. Their unusual courtship had been conducted while both of them were convalescing. Adjusting to life after the military hadn't been easy for Michael, but he knew his adjustment was a cakewalk compared to Mona's. She had given up her world to join Michael in his. In many ways they were opposites in looks and temperament, but neither could now imagine life without the other.

"Did you happen to watch CNN today?"

Mona shook her head. "The wider world was ignored in favor of the study of microorganisms, germs, and bacteria."

"You missed Deke on national news. He was talking about the Welcome Mat Hospitality case that I'm now working on. Or maybe I should say he was *not* talking about it, or trying to not talk about."

"You are being cryptic, husband."

"The judge on the case issued a gag order, and Deke wasn't supposed to discuss of any its particulars. But when the media started asking him questions, he didn't exactly comply with the order."

"Is that bad?"

"There's going to be some fallout. How much, I don't know."

"You approve of what he did?"

"I respect what he did." Michael thought about it a little more, nodded, and said, "He's the kind of guy you'd want to go into battle with."

Those were not words that he offered up lightly.

"I am proud that you have taken on this case," she said. "It is too easy, and too commonplace, for innocent people to get caught up in terrible circumstances and be placed in abhorrent situations."

It was her own biography, Michael knew. She had been caught up in a war that had killed her family, and almost killed her. "It's a good mission."

It didn't matter that Michael was no longer a PJ. To him, everything was still a mission.

XV

The man the others referred to as "Rock" stood on the deck of the *Seacreto* and debated his options. By then, the laughter had stopped, and the party had come to an abrupt end.

"Turn off that music, dammit," he said.

His order was immediately complied with.

He stared down the whores. They were afraid to meet his eyes. There was good reason for their fear. He was deciding whether to kill them or not. Morality wasn't a factor in his decision-making process. He had no qualms about murdering them. What it came down to was whether it would be better for him if they lived, or if they died.

Doing away with the remaining four whores, and the crew of two, was an order away. His men were ready. Thumbs up, or thumbs down? He made his answer based on the numbers game. The death of one individual could be covered up, but there was no way killing so many people would go unnoticed.

It was a good thing that he and his men had kept a low profile. In their line of work, that was SOP. You didn't advertise to the world that you were going out to party hearty with whores. He'd known mixing drugs, booze, and whores made for a volatile mix. In retrospect, it wasn't surprising the shit had hit the fan. But it was annoying. It was that damn redheaded whore's fault. She had pushed him over the edge. Later, after everything was under control, he would enjoy thinking about what had happened and revel in the memory of her struggles and screams. Her terror had been a turn-on. But now he had to deal with the pain-in-the-ass ramifications that came from her final act of defiance.

"What happened tonight was a bad accident," he announced.

The faces of all the whores were filled with relief. They started breathing again. He was offering them a stay of execution.

"Accident," one of them said, getting nods from the others.

"I'll discuss this matter with your boss. We'll come to an understanding. And even though we all know that what happened was an accident, it's not something we can talk about. It's important you keep your mouths shut if you don't want to end up in prison for a long time. You got that?"

Heads nodded.

"I'm going to make sure your boss rewards you for your troubles. You follow what I'm saying?"

One of them said, "We get money."

"That's right. You get money."

"Vicky cheap," she said.

"I'll talk to Vicky."

His words were almost a growl, and caused the women to shift uneasily, all except the naked whore whose body they'd been doing lines of coke on. The prospect of money had her smiling. It looked as if she'd already forgotten about the redhead who had drowned.

He moved closer to the women, invading their space, until he was just inches away from them. He made them see who he was, what he was, and what he was capable of doing.

"Any questions?"

There were no questions. Most of the whores were shaking by that time. Yes, he'd made himself clear. They understood who they were dealing with.

He turned to his aide-de-camp. "The whores aren't supposed to have phones, but search them to be sure. And toss the captain and first mate's phones in the drink. After that, go around and make sure there are no cameras or surveillance devices anywhere on this ship."

"Yes, sir," the man said.

The rest of his team were awaiting their orders. "Quite a night, huh?" he said.

His men laughed.

"The way that redhead disappeared makes me think she must have had a hot date with Davy Jones, but let's keep our eyes open to see if she resurfaces."

He looked out to the water, as did the others. There was nothing to be seen.

"In the meantime, let's party."

The music began anew.

XVI

While driving in to work, Diana Fernandez kept looking to the dark skies. The rain hadn't yet hit, but it was definitely on its way. Dark thunderclouds were approaching from the south. It was a dramatic turnaround from the perfect weather they'd had just the day before. Soon, it would be raining the devil and pitchforks, as Floridians liked to say.

More than the weather, though, Diana was thinking about yesterday's call that she'd received from Karina Boyko. The previous night she had kept recalling how troubled the young woman had sounded. Even now, Diana couldn't stop ruminating. It's not every day that someone tells you they're a slave. The girl had brought out Diana's maternal instincts. She wanted to try and help.

A quarter hour later, Diana walked into the office. Even though she was among the first to arrive at work, Diana wasn't surprised to find Deke already at his desk.

He looked up from the paperwork he was reading, smiled, and offered a cheery "good morning."

Anyone else would have thought all was fine. Diana could see the strain he was trying to hide.

"That bad?" she asked.

His sigh was answer enough. "I'm hoping it will just blow over, but yesterday Judge Irwin read me the riot act for my remarks to the media, saying they violated the State Bar of Georgia's Rules of Professional Conduct. Irwin couldn't argue the substance of what I had said, but that doesn't matter. He warned me that I was facing disciplinary action, up to and including removing me from the case."

"Is he serious?"

"I'm hoping he'll reconsider and just give me a slap on the wrist, but I'm sure Nathan Bines is egging on his hard-line position, wanting nothing better than getting me removed."

Bines, a renowned lawyer frequently seen on television commenting on legal matters, was heading up the Welcome Mat defense.

Deke said, "I'm hoping that by making a public apology to Judge Irwin, he'll put this behind him. That's what I'm working on now. Problem is, I hate capitulating, especially when I think the real judicial misconduct is Irwin's gag order."

"The sooner you get your request for forgiveness out of the way, the easier it will be."

"I suppose. I'm just trying to come up with the best nonapology apology."

"I've heard that's now referred to as a *fauxpology*."

"I like that," Deke said.

"What do you have so far?"

"I'm not sure if I should start with, 'To anyone who might have been offended,' or go with the classic, 'If my remarks were interpreted as being disrespectful.'"

"Each has its merits."

"I'm looking more for demerits."

Diana nodded in commiseration and said, "You can't go wrong with, 'I'm sorry if you feel that way.'"

"I'm considering, 'I hope no one came away with the impression that I believed Judge Irwin's gag order to be idiotic.'"

"Are you that intent on digging your own grave?"

"I'll work on my fauxpology some more," he promised.

"And run it by me first."

"Yes, Mother."

Diana stood there a moment longer than usual. She didn't want to bother Deke, but felt the need to tell him about Karina's call.

Deke responded to her hesitation. "Something else?"

It wouldn't do to delay telling him about the call, Diana decided. "Yesterday a woman who identified herself as Karina called this office and asked to speak to you."

* * *

The Welcome Mat team of lawyers and investigators were gathered in one of the upper floor conference rooms. The meeting space commanded one of the best views in Spanish Trace. Below them, the fury of the storm was on display. The driving winds were stirring up the waters in the Gulf of Mexico, turning the normally emerald expanse a brownish blue.

Deke spoke over the noise of the rain slapping the windows. "I know everyone here is busy, so let's make this short. But before we get to the most recent developments in the Welcome Mat case, I wanted Diana to tell you about a call that came in yesterday."

He acknowledged Diana with a nod, and she briefly recapped Karina's call, including her detective work pointing to the fact that she was Ukrainian.

"My impression of Karina is that she's young, probably no more than twenty-five. And it was clear from the tone of her voice that she was frightened and didn't know what to do or where to turn. I just wish we'd had longer to talk, but she was pressed for time."

Michael looked up from his note-taking. "She used the words *strip trip*?"

Nodding, Diana said, "As well as *booze cruise*."

Carol asked, "When Karina told you that she was a slave, how convincing was she?"

"Not a moment of doubt crossed my mind."

Diana's involuntary shudder convinced the room. "This morning I've had a chance to review my notes. Unfortunately, between Karina's switching from Ukrainian to English and back, some of what she said was lost in translation. What I can say with a certainty is that Karina asked that Deke and the firm represent her. In a broader context, she also wanted us to help her friend Nataliya, who she said went missing several months ago. Karina told me Nataliya was in her same straits."

Deke spoke up: "She told Diana they were both slaves. I've gotten some pushback for using that word yesterday when I talked to the media, and I'm sure some of you don't think it's appropriate, but that's how Karina described her situation. I'll have more to say about that in a minute, but please continue, Diana."

"Karina also said there was an American slave. That came up at the end of our conversation, and I didn't have a chance to clarify what she was telling me because I was taking notes as fast as I could. I'm still trying to decipher what she said and what I wrote down."

"Sometimes two heads are better than one," Carol said. "Would you like my help?"

Diana enthusiastically nodded. "Maybe between the two of us we can code-break my hieroglyphics."

Deke turned to Michael. "As everyone here knows, Michael is now on board with the Welcome Mat case. But based on what we just heard, are you ready to take on another case as well?"

The offer caught Michael off guard. "Do you mean Karina's asking us for representation?"

"I mean Karina, Nataliya, and the unnamed American. Karina essentially requested we represent all those parties. That means in all likelihood you'd be heading up a civil suit."

Michael's big smile came with the words, "That sounds great."

His enthusiasm didn't go unnoticed by Deke. "Only an associate would be grateful for having his workload doubled. Any more questions or comments for Diana?"

Gina said, "It's a good thing you took the call, Diana. You're the only person in this room with any patience."

There was laughter, but also a consensus of agreement seen in the nods.

"I haven't been able to get her voice out of my head," Diana said. "She was terrified. But she wasn't going to be deterred from asking us for help."

Jake said, "So, let's help."

Though Jake was supposed to be getting some much-earned R&R from his undercover work, he had insisted upon coming back to work early.

Deke said, "If we're to help Karina, we'll need to learn whatever we can about her circumstances. Karina was calling from the Emerald Hideaway, a resort hotel located in Destin. We need to do a reconnaissance of that property and make some discreet inquiries."

Michael said, "Since I've been given her case, I'd like to volunteer for that assignment."

Carol began shaking her head. "You were asked to represent her as a lawyer, not as an investigator."

"I understand that, but before becoming a lawyer, I served in the military for the better part of ten years. While I certainly don't have the expertise in law enforcement that you and your team have, I've been trained to read and react to my environments."

Deke could tell from Carol's expression that she was skeptical. She'd told him on numerous occasions that lawyers tended to think they were infallible, and that they invariably overestimated their abilities in arenas outside the law. That overconfidence, Deke feared, was part of his own character.

She asked, "What branch of service were you in, Michael, and what did you do?"

"Air Force, and PJ."

That got a double take from Carol. "You were a pararescue specialist?"

Michael nodded.

Deke didn't know what a PJ was, and doubted whether anyone else but Carol did. It was clear, though, that hearing about Michael's background reassured her. "In that case, per Deke's approval, I'm more than fine with your scouting the hotel."

The two of them turned to Deke, who said, "Okay by me, but sooner is better than later."

"I'll be on the road at the conclusion of this meeting."

A jagged flash of lightning filled the sky, illuminating those gathered in a lightboard effect, much like X-rays on display. A roar of thunder rattled the floor-to-ceiling windows.

"You might be looking at some washed-out roads," Deke said.

"I drive a Jeep."

Deke was glad to see the associate's quiet confidence. He seemed to have put the Parakalo deposition behind him.

"As you know, Karina's call was prompted by comments I made in Atlanta yesterday," Deke said. "One of the takeaways from her conversation with Diana is that human trafficking is going on all over this country, including our own backyard. I know some of you in this firm expressed reservations about our taking on the Welcome Mat Hospitality case because you didn't like the idea of having the firm's name associated with sex trafficking. I can understand that. Few things are more sordid. But I think it's important for us to be on the right side of this one."

"Damn straight," Gina said. "And if some partners in this firm can't see beyond the end of their noses, screw 'em."

"I applaud your passion, Gina, but I hope you never consider seeking employment in the diplomatic services."

Laughter swept through the conference room.

"Still, I know our plaintiffs are greatly appreciative of Gina's passion, which became apparent starting with Jane Doe number one."

"I met with her two days after her escape," Gina said.

She opened a folder and tossed its contents onto the middle of the conference table. The photos that spilled out showed a young Caucasian woman with bruises and cuts on her face, and especially her nose. Her low-cut top was remarkable not for its décolletage, but for all the bloodstains that had soaked into it. Gauging her age from the photos was difficult, mostly because of her beleaguered brown eyes, which looked so weary as to appear ancient. In them was the thousand-yard stare usually only seen in the gaze of soldiers who had witnessed too much death and destruction.

"Our Jane Doe was seventeen years old when these pictures were taken," Gina said. "After she was beaten by a client, her handlers were distracted long enough for her to wander away from a truck stop south of Atlanta off of Interstate 75. She avoided being recaptured, and found her way to a church where she hid in the bushes. The next morning a parishioner discovered her and took the pictures you see in front of you. Jane Doe's savior just happened to know a volunteer who worked at PEACE—an acronym for Prostitutes Escaping Adversity and Captive Environments. Through PEACE, Jane found a way out of sex trafficking, and out of slavery.

"Every Jane Doe has a different story. Our Jane was a runaway, and first trafficked as a fourteen-year-old. If that sounds young to you, it's actually on the older side for a first-time victim of sex trafficking. And if you're wondering how big the problem is, it's estimated that every year at least a quarter of a million Americans under the age of eighteen are lured into the commercial sex trade. Our Jane grew up in poverty and came from an abusive household. Her uncle started molesting her when she was eight. All those factors made her easy pickings for the sex trafficker who recruited her when she was just off the bus. He pretended he cared for her, a lie she was desperate to believe.

"For almost three years she was forced to work night and day at truck stops and motels. Lots of people and businesses profited from her enforced slavery. Drugs you can only sell once. Our Jane had to submit to a dozen men a day, and more. I promised her that I would do my best to nail those who exploited her, and by god I'm going to."

Gina reached for one of the pictures and held it up. "I know these pictures are difficult to look at, but to Jane they're a record of the best day of her life. It's the day she was finally free."

The room was silent. Jane Doe number one now had a face, and a story. She was no longer just a name symbolizing anonymity.

Deke said, "That's the story of our first plaintiff, but as you might imagine, we're now representing dozens of Jane Does. The way I look at it, this could be our Spartacus moment."

Deke took a read of the mostly blank faces. "Anyone familiar with that name?"

When no one answered, Jake said, "Didn't he lead a slave uprising against Rome?"

"That's right. A Rome which at the time had the most powerful government and army on the planet. Hollywood made a movie of Spartacus, with Kirk Douglas playing him. One of the great scenes of all time is when a defeated Spartacus tries to turn himself over to the enemy in the hope that the other slaves would be allowed to live. But his comrades refuse to let Spartacus die alone. One by one, they stand up and tell the Romans, 'I am Spartacus.'"

Deke let those words sink in before adding, "That needs to be our message, and the message of our Jane Does. We have to stake out our position against this modern slave trade."

"Damn right," said Gina.

"I know enforcing the law shouldn't fall to trial lawyers," Deke said, "but I'm convinced that is where we now find ourselves, especially since it seems the government and law enforcement are asleep at the wheel."

Deke's gaze turned to Jake, and then to Carol. Her smile and nod encouraged him to keep talking. Time for my confession, he thought.

"There've been whispers here recently about the condition of my face, and how it looks even worse than usual. There's a reason for that. I recently tangled with a human trafficker. My hope was to liberate a young woman named Lily Reyes. My connection with Lily is that I am her godfather, or at least that's what I was supposed to be. Truth is, I failed miserably in that responsibility. While Carol's team continues to track down Lily, I'm trying to find what atonement I can by doing whatever it takes in the Welcome Mat case to assist other women who have been trafficked."

Deke shook his head and sighed. His goddaughter was still out there. He stopped talking and sat there, lost in thought. People stirred, unsure if the meeting was over. Deke knew he should say something, but the words wouldn't come.

There was movement in the room, and someone cleared his throat. Deke looked up to see Michael standing up from his seat.

"I am Spartacus," Michael said.

The unexpected words reverberated through the room. At another firm, with a different group of associates, Michael's announcement might have been met with laughter, or even derision. But for those at the table, the rallying cry brought everyone to their feet.

One by one, each announced, "I am Spartacus."

Deke swallowed hard, multiple times. "Thank you," he said. "I don't feel like I deserved that, but . . . thank you."

He found his smile again, and said, "I suppose I should mention that Spartacus and his slave rebellion were utterly crushed, and the Romans were anything but merciful. Crucified slaves lined the Appian Way for miles and miles. I can only hope the slave insurgence that we're a part of has a much better outcome."

XVII

Michael took to the road right after the meeting. There were fewer drivers than usual; the pounding rain was discouraging traffic. For Michael, taking a drive in these conditions was a playtime of sorts, giving him an opportunity to enjoy the challenge of the elements. His Jeep Grand Cherokee Trailhawk had been specially modified for adverse weather. It was equipped with a lift kit that had premium coil springs and bigger wheels, as well as a snorkel attached to the air intake to keep it from being clogged by mud or water.

The Jeep's modifications weren't designed to stand out. Even its color was understated: a flat gray. Most Jeep owners went with black, or flame red. They wanted their vehicles as much for show as for go. Michael saw that as a liability. Cops targeted showboats. Michael didn't see any reason to make himself a bull's-eye to the police or anyone else.

During the drive, Michael's thoughts kept returning to the meeting he'd just attended. Deke's spilling his guts, and not making any excuses, had reaffirmed his good opinion of the man. That was what had brought Michael to his feet. By nature, he was reserved, but doing that had felt right. In the car, he found himself once more saying the words, "I am Spartacus."

Maybe his decision to become a lawyer hadn't been so crazy after all. Not all battles, he was learning, needed to be waged with camos and M16 rifles. Sometimes the better weapons were suits and briefcases.

Michael used the GPS to direct him to the Emerald Hideaway, but pulled over a mile short of the destination in the deserted parking lot at James Lee Beach. The storm was keeping people home.

Using voice commands, he opened his phone's search engine and began preparing for the mission. The Emerald Hideaway described itself as a "boutique hotel." From what he could determine, being a boutique hotel meant that it had only fifty guest rooms, with room rates starting at five hundred dollars a night. All the suites had full water views.

Michael was interested in more than the brochure description. He tweaked his search engine commands and studied the property's layout, including areas of ingress and egress. Unlike most of Florida's lodgings, which featured open layouts and catered to walk-in business, the Emerald Hideaway was enclosed on all sides. At the front entrance was a bellman's stand that controlled foot traffic entering the property. The subterranean garage offered the only other access to the hotel, with parking attendants and security gates controlling all comings and goings. That was enough for Michael to decide to park away from the property. He didn't want to surrender his keys to a valet, or allow the hotel's security system to record his Jeep's license plate number.

According to the GPS, he was only five minutes away from his target. Michael exited the beach parking lot and as he drove familiarized himself with the area, pulling over on a side street two blocks away from the Emerald Hideaway. Before setting out, he pulled an umbrella from the back of the Jeep. After adjusting his tie and putting a comb through his hair, Michael started toward the hotel. In under two minutes he arrived at the property.

The two attendants eyed him as he began his ascent up the hotel stairs leading to the entrance. Both men wore shirts that announced them as staff. One of the men, in particular, stretched the fabric almost to the breaking point.

"Good afternoon, sir," said the smaller of the two. His name tag identified him as Frank. "Are you checking in?"

It was a good way for Frank to learn his business and control his movements without seeming obtrusive, Michael thought. Though it wasn't yet noon, Frank already had a heavy five o'clock shadow. Under his right eye was a patch of skin that stood out for its whiteness, a spot where Michael suspected there had once been a teardrop tattoo. A laser had removed it, but had left a telltale mark.

"Actually, I'm here to scout out the property." That much, at least, was true. "My brother is getting married next June, and he wants me to pick out the perfect location in the Destin, Fort Walton Beach area. I need to talk to someone in sales."

"You have appointment?" asked the muscle-bound guard, speaking with an accent that sounded Eastern European. His name tag identified him as Andrei. Michael immediately nicknamed him Andrei the Giant. The man stared at him with shark eyes, a dark pupil surrounded by blue. His features looked Slavic, with prominent cheekbones, a broad face, and ears low on his head, one of which appeared to have cauliflower scarring. His nose was flattened, likely as a result of having been broken.

"Appointment?" Michael's tone made it clear he wasn't used to being questioned in such a manner. "Why? I'm here to have a conversation with someone who can tell me about having a wedding at this establishment. This isn't some kind of private club, is it? I was under the impression that it's a hotel."

Frank took over from his companion. "Because we get lots of celebrities here, we look out for the privacy of our guests."

"If you want me to be a future guest, can we finish with this TSA routine so that I can just talk to someone in sales?"

"I'll take you to see our director of sales," Frank said.

Michael was led through the courtyard. The sales office was located off the garden patio, where a blond fortyish woman sat at her desk. As the men entered the office, she raised her index finger to signal that she would need a minute.

Dismissing his escort with a twenty-dollar bill, Michael took a seat in one of the chairs. Frank didn't linger. Michael tracked his movements until he passed from sight, then it was his turn to raise his index finger, signaling to the sales director that he'd be back in a minute. Before she even had a chance to respond, he was out of her office.

The three-story property was spread out over almost two acres, but Michael was only interested in the guest suites. In one hand he held the umbrella, in the other he palmed his phone, ready to surreptitiously snap pictures. He played the role of a well-heeled guest, covering ground quickly while trying to appear unhurried.

The pool area was absent save for a fortysomething male sipping coffee while sitting under a table with an umbrella. At first glance the man, in a blazer and tan linen pants, looked like a typical guest. But Michael thought it strange that someone would be sitting outside on a rainy day. He also didn't think it was a coincidence that the spot where he was sitting offered a good vantage point for the hotel rooms.

But what was he surveilling? There was no obvious activity to be seen, or was there? He followed the gaze of the sentry and saw him studying a maid on the second floor gathering some towels from a linen cart parked on the walkway outside the room where she was working. When she disappeared back inside, the man turned his attention toward Michael. Avoiding any eye contact, Michael raised his wrist as if checking the time on his watch, all the while walking toward an elevator. That's when he discovered you needed a guest key card to access the elevator. Michael stopped to remove an imaginary rock from his shoe, time enough to think about what to do next.

Pretending to feel the vibration of his phone, Michael studied the display, then put it up to his ear and said, "Bret! How's it going, buddy?"

As he talked, Michael reversed course, returning in the direction from which he'd come. "Yeah, I'm in Destin," he said, was silent for a moment as if listening to a response, then offered a short laugh. "Destin's in Florida, of course. I'm doing a favor for my bro. He's getting married, and I've got best man duty."

The one-way conversation continued past the pool and most of the way back to the sales office. The sales director was standing outside and looking around with a concerned air. Unescorted tours, thought Michael, did not seem to be encouraged.

"There you are," she said.

"Call of nature, or it was supposed to be, but I couldn't find the bathroom."

"There's one in the lobby."

"I'm okay for now, and I got to see some of this beautiful property." He extended his hand. "Grant Conway." The name came easily to him.

He and Grant had gone through PJ special operations training—known as the pipeline—together.

"Mia Jacobson," she said, and the two of them shook.

"I won't take up much of your time, Ms. Jacobson. My brother is getting married and I'm the best man. He's looking for the perfect property, and I'm his eyes. Derek is a doctor, and his wife-to-be is an oral surgeon. Talk about bucks, right? So, they've got plenty of money, and are looking to do this top drawer. If you can give me the grand tour, I can report back to them."

The woman was ready to be apologetic. "I am afraid, Mr. Conway, we'll need to schedule a time for your tour of the property . . ."

"That's why I'm here."

"I am sorry, but I'm the only one in the office and have other obligations . . ."

Michael cut her off again. "I'm a lawyer. My time is limited. You can give me a five-minute tour, can't you?"

"I wish I could, but . . ."

Once more, Michael didn't let her finish. "If you can't take me around, then I guess I'll have to do a self-tour."

She was already shaking her head. "The ownership requires that you be accompanied around the premises by an employee."

"Then how do we make that happen right now?"

Michael could see that she was wavering, and did his best to seal the deal. "Tell you what, you give me the fifty-cent tour, and I'll be glad to provide any free legal advice you might need."

The offer captured Mia's interest. "I suppose I shouldn't be saying this, especially with your brother's impending marriage, but I'm considering filing for divorce."

"I'm all ears," said Michael.

* * *

Of all the areas of law, none interested Michael less than divorce law, but that didn't stop him from doing his best to advise Mia Jacobson. He was familiar enough with family law to be able to answer most of her inquiries, although he did stress that his area of expertise was real estate law. In truth, he was about as interested in real estate law as he was in family law. However, the more helpful Michael was in answering Mia's questions, the longer the tour extended. Both held umbrellas over their heads and tried to ignore the relentless pelting of the rain.

"The weather, as you know, is usually picture perfect," she said.

As they approached the first-floor guest room wing, Michael observed a housekeeper getting linen from one of the maid's carts. While pretending interest in a towering bird of paradise, Michael studied the housekeeper, a young woman who appeared to be in her late teens or early twenties. Her name tag identified her as Yana.

"Here we are," Mia said, coming to a stop in front of a hotel room. "All of our accommodations are suites, and while we don't have a honeymoon suite per se, as you'll see all of our rooms are quite spectacular."

Michael followed her into the room and gave an appreciative whistle. "Almost makes me want to get married."

It was a good thing he'd remembered to put his wedding ring in his front right pocket.

The room, with its long, panoramic balcony, offered a view of the water that should have adorned a postcard. Even on a stormy day it looked beautiful. Mia pulled back the sheer drapes, then cracked open the sliding glass doors. Between the room and the sand stood a high wrought iron fence capped with spikes. It was a visible deterrent to anyone thinking of entering—or exiting—the property.

"Look, a rainbow."

As Michael followed the direction of her hand, his attention was diverted by the nearby sound of a sliding glass door opening. A maid wearing a shower cap came out to the balcony with a brush and began scrubbing the railing, cleaning away the calling cards of seagulls that hadn't been washed away by the rain.

"Isn't it beautiful?" said Mia, transfixed by the rainbow Michael had yet to look at.

The sound of her voice caused the maid to turn. She looked uncertain as to whether to keep cleaning or to retreat back into the room. After deliberating for only a moment, she withdrew, but her momentary indecision allowed Michael to see her name tag. For a moment, he thought that luck was with him, but on closer inspection saw the name tag said Katrya. It was another Eastern European name, but not the one he wanted to see.

Michael returned inside the room, and feigned interest in its accommodations. He paused to look at a guest phone. It wasn't like a typical hotel phone that offered extensions within the hotel, or information about getting an outside line.

"How would I make a local call?" he asked.

"Most guests just use their cell phones, but I suppose you could ask the hotel operator for an outside line."

"And what if my brother wants extra towels, or room service?"

"The hotel operator or front desk facilitate all guest requests. We've found it easier to have them deal with any issues our guests might have."

It was also a great way of limiting contact with service staff, he thought.

* * *

When Michael returned to work, he stopped by Diana's desk and offered a regretful shake of his head. "No luck spotting her, I'm afraid."

Diana didn't look surprised by the news, but Michael could still read her disappointment. "I keep staring at my phone waiting for her call."

"Maybe the next one will be her."

Diana motioned with her head to Deke's office. "Better catch him while he's free. Carol and Jake are due to see him in five minutes."

Michael thanked her and stepped over to Deke's office. He stuck his head inside, and Deke waved him in.

"I was eavesdropping," Deke said. "No luck finding your client?"

"I saw a few other maids. Judging by their names, I suspect they're Ukrainian nationals as well."

"If that's true, they're probably H2B visa workers. That's the status of one of the Jane Does we're representing in the Welcome Mat case."

"Excuse my ignorance, but what's an H2B worker?"

"It's a designation for a visa given to a nonimmigrant. Basically, it allows foreign workers to temporarily reside and be employed in the US. We'll need to determine if that's the status of Karina and the others."

"Will that have a bearing on my case?"

"If Karina represented her working conditions accurately, and she and the others are in enforced servitude, her nonimmigrant status won't matter. Slavery is against the law."

"I would hope so."

"Your case could have important legal consequences, and potentially establish case law defining the government's responsibilities when it comes to overseeing H2B workers."

"I'm glad you entrusted me with the mission."

Hearing the case described in military terms seemed to amuse Deke. "So, what was it you said that you did in the Air Force? PJ, was it?"

"Yes," Michael said, managing to bite off the "sir."

"Doesn't have anything to do with pajamas, does it?"

"No, it's an old abbreviation for parajumper. PJs are the special service arm of the Air Force."

"Funny, I've heard of Navy Seals, Army Rangers, Green Berets, and Marine Raiders, but I've never heard of PJs."

"I think most of us prefer it that way."

"So, your duties involved parachuting?"

"That's one important component of our duties, especially when you're being sent out the chute at forty thousand feet in the air."

"I imagine so. I've never done any parachuting, but I have been a private pilot for more than a quarter of a century, and love to go wheels up. I guess I've always been more comfortable with the thought of landing on wheels, rather than landing on my feet. Are you a pilot?"

"I've got my license for single-engine, but that barely qualifies as piloting, at least not compared to the kind of birds my former employer used to like to put me in."

The appearance of Carol and Jake at the door prompted Michael to stand up, but Deke motioned for him to sit back down.

"I'd call this good timing," Deke said. "Michael was just telling me about what he saw at the hotel."

With a nod from Deke, Michael began.

"The Emerald Hideaway is a beautiful property, but it's also kind of spooky. In fact, it reminded me of some American embassies I've visited where the compounds are secured by having one entry point so as to limit traffic."

Everyone listened to his detailed account. It took him about ten minutes to recount what he'd seen, with his listeners holding off their questions until he finished.

"Do you think prostitution is currently taking place at the property?" asked Deke.

"I don't believe so. Or maybe I should say that nothing I saw suggested that, but my time there was limited."

"We'll need to do a closer look to make sure. When you study our complaint against Welcome Mat Hospitality, you'll read how we detailed telltale signs of human trafficking going on in their establishments."

"Such as?"

Deke raised his hand, and used his fingers to count off some of those signs. "Paying in cash, insisting upon interconnecting rooms, entertaining visitors at all hours of the day and night, refusing maid service, and not bringing any luggage."

He ran out of fingers, but also added, "The women are forbidden to engage with staff, and they're confined to their rooms."

Jake said, "We've even documented instances where staff was advised to ignore any noise complaints coming from rooms with women clearly being trafficked."

Carol said, "If you're right about no sex trafficking going on at the Emerald Hideaway, why do you think security is so pervasive?"

It was Deke who offered a potential answer. "It might go to controlling the H2B workers. We already know the employees are used for purposes other than hotel work. Karina told Diana she couldn't talk because she needed to go work a booze cruise."

"Not just a booze cruise. A strip trip," Michael said.

"As good as the hospitality business is for laundering money, massage parlors and strip clubs are even better," Carol said.

"We need to look at the ownership of the Emerald Hideaway," Deke said.

"We're on it," Carol said.

"And I'll be seeing if I can pick up some leads on Karina," Michael added.

Deke said, "You might mention that to Diana on your way out. I don't think she's been away from her desk all day for fear of missing Karina's call. I can certainly empathize. And speaking of which, anything new on Tío Leo?"

Jake said, "We've been dovetailing with your reward message on the billboards by chumming the water and offering bounty money to Rodríguez's known associates. If they tip us off to his presence, we're promising a nice payday."

"Good," Deke said. "And this time I promise I'll let the cops do the takedown on him."

XVIII

The violent storm that descended on Florida's Panhandle and eastern coast, what the media called the "fall squall," blew itself out over a period of twenty-four hours. In the wake of the storm was the usual litany of downed trees and upended boats. The saving grace was the fall squall's coming and going as quickly as it had.

For the second day in a row, Diana remained at her desk during her lunch break. Each passing hour of not hearing from Karina made her worry that much more. She had been the sharer of Karina's distress, and its impact still haunted her.

Because it was her break, Diana decided on the distraction of the radio. She tuned into WUWF-FM, the local public radio station at the University of West Florida in Pensacola. It was almost time for Terry Gross and *Fresh Air*.

National news signed off, giving way to local news. Diana was only half listening, but then heard something that caused her hand to shoot out and turn up the volume.

". . . where the Coast Guard reported that the woman's body was found. The victim was not wearing a life vest. Although it appears that she drowned, law enforcement is actively looking into her death. At this time, according to the Coast Guard and Florida Fish and Wildlife Conservation, there are no reports of any recent boating accidents in the area. Although the victim has not yet been identified, local authorities are reviewing all current missing persons reports. Anyone who might have information as to the victim's identity is asked to contact Detective Jeff Tanner at the Bay County's Sheriff's Office . . ."

Without thinking about what she was doing, Diana wrote the name and number down, making the notations in the same pad where she had taken notes from Karina's call.

It's nothing, Diana thought.

Booze cruise, Karina had said.

What were the odds? Those had to be common occurrences along Florida's coast, right?

We soon to go on boat, she had said.

Was it her imagination now, or had Karina sounded as if she was dreading going on that cruise?

Diana sent out a group text to Deke, Carol, Jake, and Michael. They needed to find out about the drowned woman.

* * *

The five o'clock meeting in Deke's office made for a somber gathering. Jake directed his comments to everyone at the room, but mostly to Diana.

"We're by no means certain that the woman who drowned was Karina Boyko, but there are indications that she might be a Ukrainian national."

Diana's sigh filled the space.

"Let's not jump to conclusions," Deke said, his gentle voice meant to comfort Diana. To Jake he said, "What makes you think the victim is Ukrainian?"

"After talking to law enforcement and asking about any identifying features on the drowned woman, I was told she had two unusual tattoos. Initially, the sheriff's department wasn't happy that I was at their office asking questions, but they warmed up to me when I said it was possible the victim was one of our clients. Because Carol and the Bay County captain have friends in common who vouched for us, he okayed the medical examiner's releasing of the pictures of the victim to me, including shots of her tattoos."

In a slightly apologetic tone, Jake added, "I neglected to mention that we'd never actually laid eyes on Karina, but I did say our client was a Ukrainian national. That's how we were able to identify the victim's unique tattoos, one on her inner thigh, and the other on her upper right arm. I have those pictures on my phone."

He brought up the photos and extended the phone to Deke, who then handed it to Michael. When it was Diana's turn, she shook her head, not wanting to see what was there. Carol reached for the phone, handed it back to Jake, and then rubbed Diana's shoulder.

"Tell us about her tattoos," Deke said to Jake.

"Ukraine was the key. That three-pointed tattoo on her thigh that sort of looks like a spear turned out to be one of the country's most prominent symbols. It's actually a depiction of an ancient trident, and a symbol that comes from the Ukrainian national coat of arms. That particular trident, what Ukrainians call a *tryzub*, has been around for more than a thousand years.

"The other tattoo wasn't as easy to identify. I thought it looked like the kind of pattern you'd find embroidered on a shirt or dress, and I wasn't completely wrong. The tattoo is a representation of a *vyshyvanka*, which is the traditional embroidery used in Ukrainian clothing. On special occasions in Ukraine, you'll see women wearing outfits with that embroidery. Those who wear the vyshyvanka believe it affords them good luck and protection from evil."

"If only warding off evil was that easy," Deke said.

"It didn't bring good luck to the dead woman, but the tattoo might be what allows her to speak from the grave. Every region in Ukraine has its own special vyshyvanka, with colors and patterns unique to the area. Although our victim's tattoo doesn't definitively identify her, it does offer us a map of what part of Ukraine she came from."

Carol took over the talking. "After Jake sent me the shots, I spent an hour looking at vyshyvankas. Although I can't yet be certain, I'm pretty sure the tattoo pattern came from the Poltava Oblast region of Central Ukraine."

"Great detective work," Michael said, "but where do we go from here in establishing the victim's identity?"

Carol directed her words at Diana. "We asked the Bay County Sheriff's Department to float the name Karina Boyko through USCIS—US Citizenship and Immigration Services. They're the governmental agency who maintains fingerprint and photographic records of H2B workers."

"What's the ETA when USCIS will get us answers?" Deke asked.

"Whenever you're dealing with a bureaucracy, things take longer than you'd want."

"What about going through management or ownership at the Emerald Hideaway?" Michael asked.

Carol said, "I already tried doing that. The front desk said there was no one in-house who could help me with personnel records, and directed me to the management company overseeing the hotel. When I contacted them, they kicked the can and stonewalled about giving out any information. Since they're refusing to cooperate, tomorrow I'll start my cyber-sleuthing with the State of Florida's database of registered businesses. From there, I'll be searching Bay County's list of business licenses, and if necessary, Florida's Division of Hotels and Restaurants. Within twenty-four hours I should be able to tell you the ownership of the Emerald Hideaway.

"We will get answers," she promised.

The usually upbeat Diana had the last word, whispering, "Whether we like them or not."

XIX

This place, thought Lily, was getting creepier and creepier. It was especially bad tonight. No one was in the compound except for her and Muscles. What was worse, he wasn't letting her out of his sight.

If only she could talk to somebody. The silent treatment she'd been experiencing was freaking her out. These days, no one even made eye contact with her except for the damn guards. And the one person she'd felt a connection to was no longer around. On the day after Karina had told her she would try and help, she had up and disappeared.

When was that? It was at least three or four days ago, and maybe even longer. Time played strange tricks on you in this place.

Something was definitely wrong. She wasn't the only one who had the heebie-jeebies. On the night Karina didn't come back, she had been waiting outside in the hopes of getting a private moment to talk to her. When the other women returned without Karina, Lily could sense their vibe was all wrong. They looked and moved like they were in a state of shock and just disappeared into their tin cabins.

Since then, none of the girls had said a word to her. Not a single word. They hadn't been talking much with one another either. Everyone was keeping to herself. The only one who seemed to have any inclination to speak was the girl who was always shooting her dirty looks, the one they called Oksana.

Ox, thought Lily. Big, dumb ox. That's what she thought of Oksana.

Lily suspected the tension in the air had to do with Karina. She had tried talking to the girl they called Yana, catching her when she was standing off by herself. With no one in earshot, she'd said to her, "What happened to Karina?" The girl had recoiled, acting like Lily was coming at her with a weapon, and then she'd actually run away. What had scared her off like that?

It was easy to be paranoid, Lily knew, especially with no one talking to her. But it also seemed to her like there was a lot to be paranoid about.

Despite everything, she was feeling better physically than she had in a long time. Tío Leo had given her all the drugs she wanted, but it wasn't like some act of kindness on his part. He'd supplied her with drugs because it made it easier for him to control her. Lily had known they were slow-acting poison, but at least they'd allowed some escape from her situation.

Getting regular meals, sun, and exercise had lifted her fog, but it hadn't made her any less anxious. Her guards were acting under the orders of this Vicky bitch, and Lily was sure of one thing: this Vicky was no social worker. She had seen how Karina had made a face when she spat out Vicky's name.

Her personal guard for the night, the big guy with the muscles, was watching her much more closely than usual. What was up with that? Normally he wasn't so attentive.

"What's your name?" she asked.

In a heavily accented voice he said, "Andrei."

"How about the two of us party, Andrei?"

"No party."

Lily pretended to pout. Getting Muscles to like her might allow her the opportunity to use his phone.

"Don't be boring. The two of us could have a little fun together."

Instead of responding, Andrei checked the time on his watch. Then his gaze drifted toward the gate before returning back to her.

Trying to seduce the guard was a nonstarter. Maybe he was afraid of the cameras in the compound. Or maybe it was her. It was like she was bad news that everyone knew to avoid.

Screw that.

Lily got to her feet and started walking. The only route available was to circle the compound. The space was enclosed by electric fencing and topped by razor wire. She walked the perimeter; Andrei trailed behind her. To play with his mind, Lily picked up the pace. He did as well. Where did he think she was going anyway?

She came to a stop in the middle of a clearing. A light illuminated the area, showcasing Lily's elongated shadow. Lily extended a tentative hand, formed her fingers into a shape, and a bunny's head showed itself. She wiggled her fingers; the bunny's ears began to move. When she was younger, one of her favorite games had been to make shadow figures. All you needed was a light like this one. She remembered a sleepover with her friends Brooke and Candy—how old had they been then? Maybe ten. The three of them had gathered around a book that showed them how to position their hands and fingers to make different shadows. For an hour or two, they had put on shows for one another. The other girls had particularly admired Lily's bat; everyone agreed it was the best shadow figure. It had looked so real that Candy said she thought it was going to fly away.

Lily brought her hands together, trying to remember how she had gone about making her bat.

Her show was interrupted by bouncing lights, and Lily suddenly became aware of the sounds of an approaching vehicle. A large SUV with a camper shell, its headlight beams on high, was pulling up to the gate.

Lily had been held long enough to know there was little traffic in or out of the compound. The gated private road made sure of that. Vans took the girls to their workplaces and then returned them. This wasn't one of those vans. It was a vehicle she had never seen before

This wasn't usual.

Lily reacted, but too late. Andrei had crept up behind her. She struggled in his grasp, but there was no escaping his iron grip. He pressed something foul-smelling over her nose and mouth, forcing her to breathe in. She grew light-headed, but before passing out, her struggles seemed to produce a new set of shadow images in the clearing.

A spider was wrapping its prey as the insect wriggled. Then the struggle stopped. The spider secured its prey, and the shadow image faded to black.

XX

In the ten minutes he had been waiting inside the rental on a deserted cul-de-sac on the outskirts of Fort Walton Beach, no cars had passed by. The nearest streetlamp was far enough away that his vehicle was in darkness and out of sight of the closest residence. He had picked the spot for its privacy.

A car pulled up and a blond, mid-forties, well-dressed woman exited her vehicle and crossed over to the passenger side of his car. She knocked on the window before opening the door, then stood there with a fake smile. Was the bitch waiting for some kind of engraved invitation?

Viktoria Yevtushenko Driscoll might have fooled Florida's business community into believing she was a successful entrepreneur, but he knew exactly what she was. His intelligence team had compiled a thick dossier on Driscoll. Not having to worry about burdensome governmental regulations had made it easier for his people to turn over lots of rocks. And there had been plenty of dirt beneath them.

"You screwed up big-time," he said as she slid into the seat.

"I did what?"

"You heard me. You were paid a substantial amount of money to provide beautiful, compliant whores. That's not what we got. So now, you're going to be making it right."

"What happened was not my fault."

"Your whore drank too much champagne. She got drunk, slipped, and fell over the railing. Aren't you responsible for your employees?"

Vicky opened her bee-stung lips to voice her objections, but then under his hard gaze seemed to think better of it. "It was an unfortunate accident."

He knew Vicky didn't want to openly challenge him. Things hadn't turned out well for the last bitch who had done that. Taking it down a notch, he pretended to offer a carrot.

"An accident, but one you're going to have to make right. Your whore's clumsiness makes potential problems for all of us, but especially for you."

His words set her off like an alarm. "Me?"

"You want the cops looking through your affairs? It didn't take my team long to find out how dirty you and your businesses are."

"I don't understand," she said.

Her innocent act, her suddenly pretending not to understand English, wasn't cutting it with him.

"You understand very well. I hope you're not starting to believe that Cinderella story you like to tell about a Ukrainian girl who came to the US and found her fortune and true love. Before your crooked husband died, he salted away millions in illegal funds, money you parlayed into the ownership of a resort hotel. That's your legitimate front, and it's a good one. Where I was brought up, we'd say you got more money than you could say grace over. I imagine that property is a great place to launder the money from your strip club/whorehouse."

Vicky was the definition of a Judas goat, he thought. She brought in young and pretty workers on H2B visas and led them to the slaughterhouse.

"I am not without friends," Vicky said.

"You mean those politicians you bought off? There's a big difference between those leeches and vampires you deal with and what I represent."

He turned on a light, so that she could get a good look at him and what he was. That made her very nervous, and for good reason.

"Your friends are minnows, Vicky. They're not sharks."

He looked at her and smiled. She saw his teeth and shrank back from them.

"On the night of the accident, I talked to your people. They understood when I told them how it's in everyone's best interests to forget what happened. Loose lips sink ships, right? So, we can't have that. If word gets out, we'd all be held liable. Including you. Especially you. Those who were there understand we're all looking at some serious jail time. That's why we have to put all of this behind us. And the way we do that is by having you incentivize their silence with some money."

The extra precautions might not be necessary, but he wasn't going to take chances. If matters went as hoped, the drowned girl's death wouldn't be carefully scrutinized. Cops typically weren't very vigilant if they believed the victim was a prostitute. In law enforcement jargon, a hooker's death was sometimes referred to as an "NHI" death—no human involved.

As expected, though, the whore didn't like the idea of paying out of pocket. "Karina's death is already costly to me. And it poses problems."

"If you don't spread some money around, that could pose a lot more problems. You're not stupid. What you're doing is buying an insurance policy. By taking the blood money you're offering, it further implicates them and ensures their silence. That's why you're going to arrange for everyone who was working the party boat to get ten thousand dollars apiece."

"That's too much!"

"This isn't a negotiation. It's the market price for guaranteeing collective amnesia."

"Shouldn't you pay half?"

His hand shot out, grabbing her chin. "I'll pretend I didn't hear that." Over the scent of her too-strong perfume, he suddenly caught the smell of her fear. He ground her chin between his thumb and index finger before removing his hand.

Vicky offered him an appeasing smile. She had probably done some oppo research of her own, and knew that not complying with his demands could be very dangerous to her health.

"I will do as you say."

"I'm glad we understand one another. And I don't have to tell you that I'll be keeping tabs on you to make sure you comply with everything we discussed."

She responded to his threat with a nod.

"Shame your girl fell overboard, but she shouldn't have been drinking, especially since she didn't know how to swim. Then again, she paid for her carelessness. None of us can be careless, right?"

Vicky was sitting very still. His insinuation wasn't lost on her. Still, he was surprised at how compliant she had been. He had expected more of a fight. Was he missing something? He tried to get a read of her eyes, but she was avoiding eye contact. She was afraid of him. That must be it.

Her fear turned him on. For being forty-six years old—Vicky claimed to others she was forty-one—she still looked youthful. Although he preferred redheads, she would do.

"If we're done with business, let's move on to the next subject."

He turned off the car light. To his thinking, he was still owed for what the dead whore hadn't provided. Pulling down his zipper, he looked at her expectantly.

XXI

It was getting late in the day by the time Michael arrived at Panama City Beach. So far, he'd stopped at eight marinas, making inquiries at each to find out more about Karina's strip trip. Unfortunately, he was still looking for answers.

At five o'clock, there were still plenty of people milling about Captain Randy's Marina. Sunset cruises were setting out, and tourists were settling into the perfect dining spot to look out upon St. Andrew's Bay. At the dock, a fish market was tending to the day's catch, where many sunburned fishermen were getting their redfish and grouper filleted.

Michael went to the marina's office, hoping to talk to someone about boat charters or tours, but found the office had just closed for the day. A sign on the window listed the private charter boats, dive boats, and tour vessels operating out of the marina. No one was advertising booze cruises, or the availability of strippers for hire, but he did see a handful of listings for party fishing boats.

The party boats were identified with a captain and a contact number. Michael called the first number and clicked off when a message came on. The same thing happened with the second number. The third time proved to be a charm. Captain Ernesto "Moss" Macias, who operated the Easy Way Out, answered.

Michael tried to be folksy. "Glad to hear a human voice. My name's Michael, and I'm standing at the marina charter office, but it's closed up tight. I came by hoping to get some information on a party boat rental."

"I might be able to help you if you can hang tight for five minutes," he said.

"Much appreciated," Michael said.

* * *

The Captain was good with his time frame. "Michael?"

The man coming toward him was tall and heavyset with a short white beard. On his T-shirt was a picture of a fisherman casting a line and the words, I CAN'T WORK TODAY BECAUSE MY HAND IS IN A CAST! Work jeans and mesh-lined fishing shoes completed his outfit.

"Moss," said the man, and they shook.

His hand was callused from years of angling and working the sea. Michael said, "Thanks for stopping by. You have a good day out on the water?"

"Pretty fair. Nobody got skunked. And right about now they're telling anyone who will listen how they had a whale on the end of their line, but it got away."

"I once caught a fish this big." Michael stretched his arms out wide, before bringing his hands almost together.

"I have a T-shirt with those words written on it. My kids say I'm impossible to shop for, so they always get me one fishing shirt or another. Some of them my wife doesn't let me wear."

Michael didn't reference his own wife. As he had done during his visit to the Emerald Hideaway, he'd put away his wedding ring in order to better work his story.

"The reason I stopped by was to get some information about hosting a party on your boat."

"A fishing party?"

"The fishing wouldn't be as much the priority, as would the partying. You see, my brother is getting married, and I've been put in charge of his bachelor party. There will be about twenty-five of us. We'll want a booze cruise with some extras."

"Extras?"

"The guys want me to get some strippers."

Moss began shaking his head. "I won't be able to help you there, son. I know this area has the reputation for being a crazy spring break hot spot, but that's not the kind of business me and my crew cater to."

"Is that just your boat, or is it all the party boats in this marina?"

"I'm pretty sure you're not going to find that kind of a charter here."

"Any suggestions on where I could find it?"

The captain's formerly accommodating attitude turned dismissive. "I'd try one of the other marinas in town."

As Moss walked by him, Michael said, "I'm sorry to have bothered you, sir, and I certainly didn't mean to insult you. If I had a choice in the matter, I'd be all for pole fishing instead of pole dancing, but a couple of the guys are insisting on strippers."

The apology was enough to make Moss pause. "No offense taken. And it's not as if that kind of business doesn't go on around here. In fact, I just had a fishing charter where I overheard some of the guys talking about a sunset party cruise that was in the works with girls from a local strip club."

"You happen to remember which strip club it was? I know Panama City doesn't have a shortage of nudie bars."

"Sorry."

Michael tried to keep him talking. "Was this a recent charter?"

"Four, five days ago."

"Out-of-towners, I bet?"

The captain nodded. "They were in this area doing some kind of military recruiting."

"Different kind of fishing," Michael said.

"A much more lucrative kind. I got paid in cash. Rock said they were celebrating a very successful recruiting trip."

"Rock?"

"That's what the others called him. That, and General."

Michael did his best not to react. The name was likely just a coincidence, he thought. Still, hearing the name "Rock" had him curious, as did the man's being addressed with a military title.

"Not to be pushy, but I'm wondering if you could provide me with the contact information from that charter. I'd be curious about their experience with that party boat."

"No can do," said Moss, his answer abrupt and suspicious.

Michael held up his hands in a posture of surrender. "Completely understood. I'm just trying to navigate this whole bachelor party thing."

"Like I said, I can't help you with that. But I will give you my opinion on the matter, son. I'd be thinking more about your brother's future wife than his friends. You don't want to do anything that might cause trouble between your brother and his bride-to-be. I'm speaking from the experience of having been married for almost forty years."

"That sounds like good advice."

"Don't mean to sermonize, but my wife is always telling me I shouldn't only be a fisherman, but a fisher of men, like it says in the Good Book."

"You won't get an argument from me," Michael said.

"Not that I'm what you'd call a regular churchgoer. I always tell my wife that it's better to sit in a boat thinking about God, than sit in a church thinking about fishing."

"I like that."

"It's on one of my T-shirts," the man confessed.

Then he made one more confession. "If you're still inclined to find entertainment, you might ask around the Suncoast Marina. Seems to me a friend once mentioned a special kind of trawling takes place on a yacht that he called the 'melon boat.'"

"Much obliged," Michael said.

XXII

Even though the cruise control was on and set to seventy-six miles per hour, which was one mile over the speed limit along Interstate 40, JJ still eyed the speedometer. Yes, he confirmed, they were traveling at 76 mph. If anything, that was slowpoke speed along this stretch of the highway, but you could never be too careful, especially when you were carrying contraband.

The two men had driven nonstop except to fill up. The sooner they delivered their cargo, the better it would be.

With that thought came some muffled sounds from deep inside the Chevy Suburban's camper. Not good, he thought.

JJ turned to his right. Keebler was asleep in the passenger seat, as he had been since they'd last stopped for gas. Damn Keebler could sleep anywhere. JJ's associate had the face of one of the Keebler elves: big cheeks, big ears, and a doughy expression. His resemblance to the elves ended there. Keebler was a big guy. His talent wasn't in making cookies; he was good at hurting people.

"Hey, Keebler. Wake up."

The man blinked a few times, then gave him a non-elf-like scowl. Keebler didn't like having his sleep interrupted, but what he liked even less was waking up to someone calling him by his nickname.

JJ said, "I need you to keep your eyes open for a quiet place to pull over. It's time for you to play doctor with our cargo."

"Shit. Let's just pull over and get it done."

They were about fifty miles east of Flagstaff. Around them was Arizona high desert country mostly devoid of any towns or structures.

"I'm not just pulling over on the shoulder. That would be an invitation for any curious cop to stop and talk."

Keebler pointed to a sign and said, "Meteor Crater, next exit."

"You think it's a good idea for you to play doc in the middle of some tourist attraction?"

"I go in the back, I shoot her up," Keebler said. "No fuss, no muss. And maybe we take a look at that meteor."

"It's no meteor. It's a big hole in the ground where a meteor struck."

"That's all that's there? A hole in the ground?"

"It's like a mile wide. It's what they call an impact crater."

"Lucky me, that I get to travel with Dr. Science," Keebler said.

A third voice entered the conversation, a moan finding its way out of the confines of the cargo hold. JJ didn't want to admit it, but there was something spooky about hearing the woman's disembodied voice.

"Get the dose ready. We're no more than five hours from Vegas. Let's play it safe and make sure she's out of it for the next eight hours."

Sighing, Keebler reached into the glove compartment and took out a medical traveling pouch. He unzipped it, revealing syringes and vials. Keebler started going through the vials, studying the different dosages.

"Not too much, but not too little. I'm sure MM is going to want to meet his new friend tonight, and he won't want her all drugged up."

"If you're so concerned with it being just right, Goldilocks," Keebler said, "maybe you should be playing doctor instead of me."

"Take it easy. I'm just trying to spare you from getting on MM's bad side. But if you don't care about that, do whatever you want."

MM was their employer, Max Miller—or at least that was their explanation for the acronym if others were around. But the truth of the matter was that MM was an abbreviation for something else. Moon Man. There was some history that came with that nickname.

Mentioning MM made Keebler look around uneasily. "We're not looking at the next full moon for another couple weeks, right?"

"We're good. We're entering the waning gibbous cycle."

JJ liked saying things like *waning gibbous* and *waxing crescent*. Then again, knowing the phases of the lunar cycle allowed them to be forewarned.

"Thought so," said a relieved Keebler.

MM did not stand for Max Miller as much as it did for Moon Man. Both of the men had worked for their employer long enough to be convinced his psyche—and his madness—could be tied to the lunar cycle. Their boss's behavior became more and more erratic with the approach of the full moon.

One could go so far as to say their Moon Man was a true lunatic.

"Twenty-three more days until the next full moon," JJ said.

Both men exhaled some pent-up air. Each of them was exceedingly well paid for their work, but for a few days every month it meant walking around on eggshells and trying to keep their boss from being totally bonkers.

"Sign says there's a rest stop at Meteor Crater," Keebler said.

JJ blew out a little more air. "We'll pull over and see what it looks like. But it's a no-go if there's anyone nearby."

He raised his nose, did some sniffing, and thought he detected an acrid odor. "You're also going to need to change her Depends."

"Shit," Keebler said.

XXIII

Nathan Bines made the rounds of the Brookhaven Ballroom in Atlanta's exclusive and private Capital City Country Club. His firm was sponsoring a weekend getaway for a select group of invited guests, and Bines was working the room, his silky and polished behavior embodying noblesse oblige. The smile on his face suggested he was having a great time. His smile lied. The only reason for Bines's being there was to serve the interests of his publicity-shy client. Over the course of the last decade, that same client had come to expect more and more of Bines. There was a time when he would have eschewed this kind of behavior and manipulation, but now it just seemed easier to capitulate to his client's demands. He kept drawing imaginary lines in the sand that he believed he wouldn't cross, and then did so.

It would stop. That's what he told himself. But not today. He exerted his will upon his face, growing his smile. At least he was the only one who could hear his teeth grinding.

Even though Bines lived most of the year in Manhattan, he was spending most of his time these days renting in Atlanta while working on the Welcome Mat Hospitality case. His firm had twelve offices nationally and another half dozen internationally. Bines had earned a spot as one of the names on his law firm's letterhead. The weekend function was ostensibly being paid for by the firm, but a certain benefactor was subsidizing most of the costs, just as he was the legal fees associated with the Welcome Mat case.

Bines circled like a shark, making an incremental approach to his fish. That was the primary reason for his being there. The client who could not be named—sort of like Voldemort—had insisted upon this backchannel meeting. Judge Allen Irwin was Bines's target. Their crossing paths had to look as if it was aboveboard. That would be good for all concerned. As expected, the judge had declined the weekend activities of golfing and meetings, wanting to avoid any notion of conflicts of interest with Bines or his firm. If he was ever questioned, the judge's attending the reception could be explained away as being nothing more than a common courtesy extended to one of Atlanta's preeminent law firms.

Of course, the judge knew full well that at this particular reception the finest wines and champagnes were being served, as well as a selection of hors d'oeuvres fit for royalty, including premium charcuterie, cutting boards of exotic cheeses, and crystal containers filled with beluga caviar. Servers circulated the floor offering up appetizers of carpaccio, oysters, and wagyu beef and asparagus. It was the rare offering that the judge refused. He seemed as driven to eat as a bear fattening up for winter's hibernation.

Bines watched Judge Irwin flag down a waiter offering grilled lobster tail skewers. He made his approach a few moments after he was served, arriving as the judge bit off half the tail in a single chomp, leaving a trail of butter on the side of his mouth.

"Judge Irwin, what an unexpected pleasure to see you."

The judge pretended to be as surprised by their encounter as Bines. He finished chewing down his huge bite of lobster and extended his hand. The lawyer managed to keep the smile on his face even as he pressed flesh with the judge's greasy hand.

"Mr. Bines, I would have thought you'd be spending this weekend in New York with those two apples of your eye, your beautiful and accomplished wife and daughter."

The two men drew closer so that their words would not extend beyond them.

Bines said, "The reason I stayed in town was to help host this gathering. Our firm wanted to get the best and brightest legal minds together, in the hopes of convincing a select few to join our ranks."

"Best wishes on your headhunting," Judge Irwin said.

"I am hoping for more than your best wishes. There's one name at the top of our firm's wish list: yours."

Judge Irwin acted surprised. "I had no idea."

"I need to know if we even have a chance."

Irwin shook his head and looked regretful. "I am very happy on the bench. It is a most satisfying position."

"I am sure. And yet you are overworked and underpaid."

With a laugh, Irwin said, "I wish I could argue with that."

"It doesn't have to be that way. If you were to join our firm, you would be looking at a substantial increase in pay."

"Substantial?" Irwin asked.

"Unofficially, three or four times your current salary."

As a federal judge, Irwin was making close to quarter of a million dollars a year. Bines could see Irwin doing the mental calculations.

"That is certainly something to think about," the judge said, all but salivating while he considered the merits of the bribe—that is, job offer.

"Good, good. Officially, of course, such an offer couldn't come from me."

"Of course not. We mustn't muddy the waters of the current proceedings."

"Absolutely, but I am hoping you can do me a favor that has nothing to do with the current case."

"And what might that be?"

Bines baited the hook a little more. "As you are probably aware, I help with the club's Downtown Speakers' Series. I am sure you know we have a long tradition of having notable individuals give talks to our membership. Winston Churchill honored the club and the city of Atlanta with a talk in 1932, and we've had club functions where a number of US presidents have given addresses."

Irwin was nodding. "Didn't I read somewhere that you have Geofredo Salazar as this month's speaker?"

Geo Salazar, as most called him, was a Spaniard who had made his fortune in the founding and managing of his international hedge fund, but was now better known for his philanthropic endeavors.

Smiling, Bines said, "Since Mr. Salazar was already planning to be in town to award academic scholarships to several deserving African American youths to attend the University of Barcelona and the University of Madrid, he agreed to speak at the club. We are always on the lookout for securing preeminent thought leaders as lecturers. And that's why I am hoping to get you onboard for a talk. The honorarium would be generous, of course."

"I would be pleased to speak, but I am afraid my position precludes me from accepting any honoraria."

Bines looked surprised. "But aren't you allowed to receive teaching income? I have no doubt that your audience will be learning a great deal from your insights."

Irwin clearly liked that argument, but did not overtly commit to it. "For now, let's just say I will agree to speak."

"Of course, of course, but if we can come to some acceptable financial arrangement, let's get it done."

With the hook now in the judge's mouth, Bines knew he could land his fish at his leisure. Looking at his Patek Philippe Grand wristwatch, Bines expressed surprise. "I'll have to take my leave of you shortly to take part in a conference call with the other partners."

He leaned in close to the judge, and spoke in a lowered tone that suggested he was confessing something. "I don't want this to be an ex parte discussion per se, but this Deketomis thing has got the partners upset. They're not pleased by his vicious insinuations and aspersions, not to mention his egregious violation of your gag order."

Irwin made a face and shook his head. "Everyone knows Deketomis is a hothead."

"But, Your Honor, his theatrics made you a laughingstock. And that's not acceptable when it comes to one of the most respected jurists in the land."

"His comments were out of line," Irwin said.

"Out of line? What Deketomis said showed absolute contempt for the court and your position in it. I'm afraid Deketomis now thinks he can get away with his carny barking without any repercussions whatsoever."

"That is not the case. As I've already informed Mr. Deketomis, there will be consequences."

"I would hope so."

"I've even been pondering whether Mr. Deketomis's outburst is reason enough for his removal from this case."

Bines made a small grimace. "That might play into his hands, and give him a soapbox he would not otherwise have. And his second chair, that Romano woman, isn't any less obnoxious than he is."

But then he added in a low, secretive voice, "To her credit, though, she does have a very nice ass."

The judge covered up his laughter behind his hand.

Bines wasn't finished with his influencing. "No, you wouldn't want his removal being part of the court record, seeing as this case will clearly never advance to a trial."

Irwin offered an almost imperceptible nod. The court record was a public document that could be reviewed—and second-guessed. Because of that record, most judges did their best to try and appear unbiased and evenhanded.

"It's a shame Deketomis even had a forum for his rant," the judge said. "If it hadn't been for that singer talking about being a truck stop prostitute, the media wouldn't have taken any notice of the proceedings."

"Deketomis played up to the cameras, and in the process put you in a bad light. He knew that things weren't going well for him. I can't imagine any forward-thinking jurist would allow an ambulance chaser like Deketomis to waste the court's time with fantastical speculation."

Irwin looked a little uneasy. Bines wondered if that was a result of a twinge of ethics, or the judge's having finished the rest of the lobster tail.

"Clearly, sanctions are in order," Bines said. "Last month Judge Aberdol in Alabama fined a loudmouthed trial lawyer fifty thousand dollars for saying far less than Deketomis did."

The judge's head was bobbing up and down. "That's pretty much in line with what I was thinking."

The lawyer patted the judge reassuringly on the shoulder. "Business calls, I'm afraid, but I don't want to leave before making sure you sample some of the foie gras. It's not to be missed."

Bines flagged down a passing server and made sure the judge got his foie gras. As he walked away, he thought about how foie gras was made. Feeding tubes were forced down the throats of male ducks and geese; the force-feeding distended the livers of the birds. It was a cruel practice, with the birds forcefully stuffed with corn and meal until they could barely breathe.

He reached up to his own collar, loosening it. I'm not a Strasbourg goose, he thought. Still, he wondered at the consequences of being forced to swallow his pride, almost until he could no longer breathe.

With an effort, he kept the smile on his face until he exited the meeting room.

XXIV

While driving around and researching private charters, Michael had put his cell phone on silent mode. Now that he was on his way back home, he was catching up on missed calls. Jake's message from an hour earlier had been brief.

"Call me when you get a chance," he'd said.

Jake picked up on the second ring. "You in your office?" Jake asked.

"About two hours from it. I'm just leaving Panama City."

"What are you doing there?"

"It was my last stop of the day. I traveled the Florida Panhandle coastline finding out who does booze cruises. And more to the point, strip trips."

"Find anything?"

"Several charter companies do sunset specials and booze cruises. But it seems there's only one 'gentlemen's charter' in the area that comes complete with party girls. The outing isn't advertised as a strip trip, probably to avoid liability, but I confirmed there's a Panama City strip club that arranges for a party boat with what they call their 'first mates.'"

"Let me guess: the name of that strip club is the Pussy Cat Palace."

"Bingo. How'd you know?"

"That's what I was calling you about. Carol and I navigated a maze of shell companies through databases and determined the ownership of the Emerald Hideaway. The proprietorship is one PDL Properties, an abbreviation for Ponce de Leon. The owner of PDL Properties is Viktoria Yevtushenko Driscoll, a naturalized citizen originally from Ukraine."

"It seems like that's where all our roads are leading."

Michael considered telling Jake about Captain Moss's charter, and how there might be a potential tie-in with the strip club party boat, but decided saying anything would be premature.

Instead, he said, "When Karina called Diana, she mentioned a friend of hers by the name of Nataliya who went missing months earlier. If I can establish that both the drowning victim and Nataliya worked at the Pussy Cat Palace, that should help me demonstrate to a judge that it's a dangerous workplace."

"Which might get you access that much sooner to depose Viktoria Driscoll."

"That's the hope. Any word on when an autopsy will be performed on the victim?"

"I'm told best-case scenario is by the end of the week, but we're pushing for it ASAP."

For Michael, even ASAP didn't feel like it was soon enough. His gut told him time was not on their side.

* * *

It was half past seven when Michael arrived home, but he decided dinner could wait for a few more minutes. Hearing Captain Moss saying that he'd taken out military recruiters on his fishing charter had piqued Michael's curiosity. It wasn't just a casual interest on his part. Michael had a distinct bias against private military contractors, and one in particular. Peter Stone was the founder and CEO of Darkpool Security International, the biggest private military contractor in the world. There were a lot of things Michael detested about Stone and his organization. To his thinking, they were vultures feeding on the carrion of war.

Because of his surname, Stone was known by the nickname of "Rock." And in Stone's army, not the US army, he held the rank of general. It was probably nothing, but it was a coincidence Michael felt compelled to pursue. The drowned woman deserved at least that much.

Michael began doing searches on his phone, calling up multiple profiles of Peter Stone. In one posed picture, Stone was wearing a white

Uncle Sam top hat complete with a blue band and white stars. The caption featured a quote from Stone: "I want you for my army." The corporate offices for Darkpool were located in Virginia, in near proximity to Washington, DC. Given that there were so many military bases in Florida's Panhandle, it would have been more surprising if Darkpool wasn't recruiting throughout the area than if they were. But Michael couldn't find anything linking Stone or Darkpool to having traveled to the area in the past week.

All the articles Michael scanned were in agreement on one thing: the business of war had been good for Stone and his company, and had made him rich.

"Some people refer to my fortune as blood money," Stone was quoted as saying. "I'm okay with that."

"I'm not," Michael said, putting away his phone.

He had already kept Mona waiting too long and jogged to the stairs, taking them two at a time. Michael signaled his arrival by knocking, then unlocked the dead bolt and stepped inside. He was greeted by the aroma of the onions and peppers that had gone into the making of the riza shirwah, and the cinnamon, allspice, and mint in the rice dolma. Mona emerged from the kitchen. Her large dark eyes had beguiled him from the first. Mona's arched eyebrows seemed to have their own vocabulary, telling stories with the way they rose, and lowered, and furrowed. The two of them kissed.

"You are hungry, I hope," she asked.

"I am."

"Then let us both eat."

"I hope you weren't waiting for me."

"I sampled the food while preparing it, as any good cook must."

"Did you leave any for me?"

"Only a very little. Enough for a mouse, and no more."

They kissed again. "Need help serving the food?" he asked.

"I do not. Why don't you select your beverage of choice?"

"I will get my beverage of choice," said Michael, trying to hide his smile.

Mona had a unique way of saying, "Get yourself a beer," the same way she had a unique way of saying most things. He grabbed a bottle and took a seat at the table. A plate of dolma wrapped in grape leaves was waiting for him, as was a basket of lavash and baba ghanoush. Mona came with their stew and joined him.

"You work late, husband."

"And I'm afraid I will have to leave quite early."

"You will forget what I look like."

"Not in a million years."

Judging by her smile, his remark pleased her. Mona had barely been holding on to life when the two of them had first met in the carnage of war. She had been the only one in her family to survive an ISIS attack, and at the time she was being evacuated by helicopter, Michael had wondered if the wounded young woman would ever smile again in her lifetime. Now, she smiled for him.

It felt like a miracle.

XXV

In fits and starts, Lily began to awaken, the passage to her regaining consciousness marked by the increasing volume of her moans. As her eyes gradually opened, she had trouble understanding what she was seeing. The room's windows seemed to fade in, then fade out. Colors shimmered, appearing and disappearing like will-o'-the-wisps. She reached out a tentative hand, grasping for one of the mysterious reflections, wondering if the light was something that could be touched.

Was she in heaven?

No, she decided. In heaven her head would not hurt this much, and the veins around her temples would not be pounding. She gingerly touched the sides of her head and tried to make sense of things. Then, Lily realized she wasn't alone and screamed.

A man in a white linen suit was seated in a chair staring at her. He had a dark, carefully trimmed beard. In his hand he held a plastic champagne flute, which he was lightly tapping with a long thumbnail that tapered out like a knife.

"Would you like some champagne?" he asked.

"Champagne?" Her reply sounded more like a croak than a word. Lily's head felt as if it were exploding.

"Yes. Champagne."

She made the mistake of looking at him and was confronted by his unblinking eyes. For her, it felt like she was looking at something reptilian, or alien.

"No. Water."

Her throat was so dry it was hard getting the words out. Lily tried to lick her parched lips, but her mouth was too dry for her to moisten them. Her body told her she'd been on a bender. How long had she been out of it? She remembered being forced to inhale something, and seemed to recall a hypodermic needle being inserted into her arm, but everything was hazy.

And crazy.

"I'm afraid we only have tap water available at this time. I'll get you some."

What was she doing in this strange place? Lily sat up on the sofa and tried to focus. A number of questions came to mind, but she resisted asking them. It wasn't only that her head and throat hurt, making speaking difficult. Instinctively, Lily knew not to trust the man in the white suit. His politeness didn't fool her. During the past year, she had gotten a terrible education in reading men. The guy was twisted, of that she was sure. His playing nice didn't fool her. It just put her more on edge.

He returned with a paper cup filled with water. Lily gulped it down. "More?"

She nodded, and he went to get her a refill. The water made her feel a little less like a corpse, but not much. The man came back, handed the refilled cup to her, and said, "I would drink it more slowly."

Lily didn't like the man hovering over her and leaned away from him. The only thing good about Tío Leo was that he'd watched over his sex workers. Not that he gave a shit about them; he was protective of what he thought was his merchandise. But Lily had learned to be careful as well, ready to run, ready to scream, ready to defend herself. She was glad when the man returned to his chair. Once more she noticed lights casting colors and making strange patterns in the room, prompting her question.

"What is this place, and where am I?"

"You are in a penthouse suite in Las Vegas."

Las Vegas? Why? How?

"What am I doing here?"

"You are my guest."

This whole thing made no sense. It was almost like she was that girl who dropped down into a rabbit hole. Alice. But Lily wanted nothing to do with this place.

"I want to leave."

"But you just arrived."

"You said I was a guest."

"And you are. If there's anything you want to eat or drink, a special dumbwaiter will bring it to you. The menu selections are virtually unlimited. And if there's any particular music you want to hear, I will arrange for it to be played."

"When can I leave?"

"We'll talk about that after you've settled in for a few days."

Lily trusted her vibe a hell of a lot more than his less-than-reassuring words. "I'll scream."

"I'd like that," he said.

It was his expectant smile that dissuaded her from screaming. But he did not allow the silence to last and suddenly offered his own scream. Lily started, covering her own mouth as if hoping to muffle his shriek. His demonstration clearly pleased him.

"What exceptional acoustics," he said. "This suite was designed to my specifications. It's been soundproofed so that the noise doesn't carry far. The penthouse is subdivided, so I'm your only neighbor. And beneath us is my special staff. There is no one to hear your cries. It's sort of like the Zen koan of a tree falling in a forest. If no one is around to hear it, does it make a sound?"

He looked at her. "Do you make a sound if no one can hear you?"

Lily found herself trembling.

"Or are you visible if no one can see you?" He swept his hand, gesturing to the room's expanse. "All the windows in this suite have been treated so that you can see out, but no one can see in. Like those special windows in interrogation rooms where the police can observe the suspects being questioned without being seen."

He went back to sipping his champagne.

"I don't understand why I'm here," Lily said.

"That is the beginning of the road to understanding, Nataliya."

Lily wondered if she'd misheard. Had he mistakenly called her Nataliya? It was a name she had heard recently. But where?

"Your situation can potentially provide you a path to enlightenment. There was once a man being pursued by a tiger. His only hope for escape was to leap into a precipice, and as he fell the man was able to grab at a vine. Above, the tiger stared down at him. The man looked below and saw another tiger waiting below. As he hung on to the vine, a mouse began chewing at his only support. And that was when the man saw a plump wild strawberry growing next to the vine. Holding on to the vine with one hand, he was able to pluck the strawberry and eat it. How delicious it tasted."

He pantomimed the eating of the strawberry. "The man was able to live in the moment. Do you understand?"

Lily wanted to tell him to shove his strawberry up his ass, but she held her tongue, not wanting to provoke him. She got to her feet and took a few steps toward the window before abruptly coming to a stop. The room was high up. Real high. Heights scared her; the sudden onset of vertigo made her feel unsteady and she retreated.

"No need to be afraid. The windows here are more than secure."

He put down his flute of champagne and smiled. Then he made sure Lily was watching him, and ran as fast as he could at the glass.

Lily couldn't help herself. "No!" she screamed.

The man hit the glass with his shoulder, ramming into it. The impact could be heard throughout the room, but even louder was the man's laughter. He bounced from the window, much like a basketball off a backboard, landing on his feet near to the point from where he had taken off.

"That never gets old. Never." He looked at her. "Again?"

Lily shook her head.

"Do you want to try?"

This time she shook her head even more vigorously.

"Wait until the full moon arrives. There is no better time to window dance. That's when I turn the music up high. That's when I howl to my heart's content. That is when all is revealed."

The man was now leaning his back against the window. Directly behind him was only space, and the abyss.

As much as Lily didn't want to know, she had to ask the question. "How high up are we?"

"Such a good question, but the answer is not so easy."

He turned around, bringing his face up next to the window and looking down. "Two floors below us is the Peak of Heaven Restaurant and Lounge. If you were to ride an elevator up to it, you would push the button for the fifty-eighth floor. But that doesn't tell the full story. You see, even though everyone likes to say the restaurant is on the fifty-eighth floor, and in TV spots and magazines it's always described as such, that's not true. It is one of the secrets of the Yin-Yang. That's where we are, by the way. You've heard of it?"

She shook her head.

"It's also known as the Y, or the Double Y, although its official name is the Yin-Yang Casino and Convention Center. At the Y, things are not always as they seem. For example, if you were to try and take an elevator to the fourth floor, you would discover there is no button with the number four, just as there is no fourteen, or twenty-four, or thirty-four. In fact, the number four does not exist in this building. If you look at the bank of floors listed on the elevator panel, you will see the next number after thirty-nine is fifty. Why do you think that is?"

"I don't know."

"Tetraphobia."

It wasn't a word Lily had ever heard of, but the perv seemed to think it was important. He kept staring at her eyes. It was almost like he was trying to see beneath their surface.

"Repeat it for me."

Shit, she thought. She couldn't remember the word. "What was it again?"

"Tetraphobia."

"Tetraphobia," she said.

"Perfect. It means the fear of the number four."

"People are afraid of the number four?"

"Terrified. That sounds silly, doesn't it? And yet many Asian people are tetraphobic. The number four is bad luck for them. It's like our superstition over the number thirteen, but much worse. For the Chinese and Koreans and Japanese, the number four is associated with death. To assuage those fears, this building was structured without the number four on any of the floors."

It sounded batshit crazy to Lily, but no crazier than what she was experiencing.

"In this place we have tried to create a balance between the seen world and the unseen. Are you familiar with the notion of yin and yang?"

Lily shook her head.

"Think of dualism. Some people try to explain it in extremes, like negative and positive, but I see it as something that is more complementary than oppositional. We need light, and we need dark. The north needs a south, the east needs a west. What is fire without water, or winter without summer? For me, the cycle of the moon is an expression of the yin and the yang. From darkness, we proceed into the light, and what is invisible becomes visible.

"We need disorder as much as order, although it is in our nature to try and deny this. The yin and the yang do not define what is good and what is bad. It is a philosophy of understanding the balance between them and the swaying dance that is the universe."

Lily couldn't follow the man's babbling, but something in his words made her remember an image. "Black-and-white fish," she said.

"That's right. Yin and yang are often portrayed in black-and-white tai chi fish. We have incorporated that very symbol into the marketing of this property. Every night the fish illuminate the hotel's walls. You can even see them swim."

He stared into Lily's eyes. This predator made her afraid, and she sought to divert him.

"Tetraphobia," she said, remembering the word central to his lecturing.

"Yes! Fear of the number four."

His eyes focused, and he seemed to remember himself. "Let me offer a belated introduction. I am Max Miller. Feel free to call me Max, although most call me MM, the owner of the YY. They find that ironic. The initials of my name tell a story in themselves. Each is the thirteenth letter in the alphabet. They fall directly in the middle of twenty-six letters. I have brought you here as my honored guest, Lily."

He did know her name. Lily would have preferred he didn't. "Honored?" she asked.

"In a yin-yang kind of way," he said, pointing one of his thumbnails at her. "You must remember what I said about duality, and the balancing act therein."

His smile faded. "And given those parameters, I would say welcome to heaven, welcome to hell."

XXVI

To Deke, it almost felt like the Sword of Damocles was hanging over him, with only a single thread sparing him from being impaled. Even though he and Gina and the Welcome Mat team had continued with their lawsuit preparations, everyone was waiting for the other shoe to drop. There was little question that Judge Irwin was going to come down hard on Deke, but no one could predict the severity of his response, or when it would happen.

Tired of the wait, and knowing he needed a pressure release, Deke was more than looking forward to his favorite stress-buster. Once a month he and his good friend Robin Clark went out spearfishing.

"All set?"

Robin finished stowing the gear and saluted Deke in the wheel-house. "Aye, aye, captain."

The irony was that in real life Robin was a commercial airline pilot whom others called captain. Out on the sea, though, Deke took the helm. For almost twenty years, the two men had been diving together.

Dawn was still a few minutes off as Deke piloted their dive boat out from the gray harbor. From experience, Deke knew it was best to get to their dive spot early. Their destination was fifteen miles offshore, a spot where a Navy transport boat had been sunk in ninety feet of water more than a quarter of a century earlier. Wreck diving was popular in Florida, with the artificial reefs attracting clusters of fish.

Once clear of the harbor, Deke put the twin Yamaha 250 horsepower outboard engines to good use. In the calm waters, the thirty-two-foot dive boat sailed along at a fast clip.

Over the loud motors, Robin shouted, "Wonder if we'll see your colleague today."

Deke knew where Robin was going and didn't bite. That didn't stop his friend from saying, "At least you don't have to worry about him biting you, what with professional courtesy and all."

It was the punch line to one of the oldest lawyer jokes in the world; what surprised Deke was that it had taken Robin this long to use it. The "colleague" his friend was referencing was a twelve-foot bull shark the two men had encountered during several of their dives. The much more common apex predators were the barracuda. There were always plenty of them hanging around in the vicinity of the old sunken boat. The presence of the bull shark was always good to get their adrenaline going.

"Nowadays it's debatable whether it's lawyers or sharks who have a worse PR problem," Deke yelled.

Healthy oceans needed sharks as an essential part of the ecosystem, Deke knew, just as healthy societies needed lawyers defending the rule of law. He was always dumbfounded at how most people never understood that connection until they, or a loved one, desperately needed to retain a lawyer for one dire circumstance or another.

"Maybe lawyers should do the TV equivalent of Shark Week. That programming has changed a lot of negative opinions toward sharks."

"Couldn't hurt, and maybe it could dispel some of the legal stereotypes that plague the profession. But I bet even that wouldn't stop people from calling us and asking to be represented by the biggest and meanest shark in our firm. That, or pit bull."

Deke knew Robin was just kidding with his shark reference, but the lawyer stereotypes still grew old. The powerful forces that lawyers opposed had done a good job painting the legal profession as rapacious and predatory. Having worked in the trenches for as long as he had, Deke knew just how influential and deep-rooted the opposition was. There were plenty of forces allied against the rule of law. If lawyers were to fail, autocracy and corporatocracy would win the day.

There were some days when Deke thought that already seemed to have happened.

Over the noise of the motors, Robin shouted, "I suppose it's better to be feared than loved."

Deke offered a noncommittal nod. For this morning at least, he didn't want to think about being a lawyer. His resolve lasted about ten seconds, until he started dwelling on the drowned woman. Carol Morris was moving mountains trying to get a positive ID on the woman they believed was Karina Boyko.

As the sun began to rise, the waters seemed to transform in color, going from a dark navy blue to a bluish green. With the calm seas around them, Deke knew that by the time they arrived at their dive spot, the visibility would be upward of sixty feet. As the shoreline grew farther and farther behind them, Deke experienced the kind of calm he was never able to obtain on land. It was his form of detox, Deke liked to tell others, with the worries and pressures lifting from him.

The tranquil waters allowed them to make good time. As they approached the wreck site, they observed that they were the sole boat for as far as the eye could see. The anchor was dropped, and final preparations for the dive were made. Deke and Robin knew they shouldn't be diving without a third person staying in the boat, a role usually filled by Deke's son Andy when he was available. Such a precaution made sense in the event anything went wrong during the dive, but today they were violating that fundamental rule. Their concession to safety would be to strictly limit their dive times.

Both men were wearing a spring suit, or what Robin referred to as a "shorty." The neoprene wet suits didn't completely cover their arms or legs, allowing for easier movement. The spring suits were perfect for the Gulf's warm waters. It was only after they descended below sixty feet that the waters started getting nippy. For today's dive they had decided they wouldn't be swimming in the interior of the old navy boat, but instead would be circling around its exterior, much in the manner of the prey they were hunting. Their routine was to do two dives, each twenty minutes in duration. Depending on the conditions, they sometimes traveled a short distance away to another favored spot for their second dive. That dive was for sightseeing; the first dive was for bragging rights.

"I'll remind you that in our fish-off contest I'm ahead four to three," Robin said.

Although in his mid-fifties, Robin's competitive juices still ran deep. His idea of recreation was doing triathlons. Every time the men went out to dive, each of them vied to land the biggest fish. This was their eighth excursion of the year.

"We'll be tied after today. And speaking of reminding, let's not forget that last year you looked stunning in orange and blue."

Robin was a graduate of Florida State; Deke of the University of Florida. On the big game day in November, the loser in their annual fish tallies had to wear the victor's school colors.

"I can't wait for your walk of shame this year. You can help cheer the Seminoles on to victory."

Deke waved a dismissive hand, then both men turned to checking their equipment. As many times as Deke had been diving, he always felt that same thrill of excitement just prior to entering the water. On the surface the diving gear felt cumbersome, but once underwater Deke was in his element. They clipped their lines to the two fish buoys and tossed them into the water. Each man offered the other a thumbs-up. Robin went into the water first, and Deke followed.

Before starting his descent, Deke took his bearings. He made a point of taking measured breaths, letting his body adjust to his surroundings. For Deke, it always felt like a *Wizard of Oz* moment, going from black-and-white Kansas to the striking colors and unusual sights of Oz. Still, you had to be mindful of any potential witches.

Deke checked his watch, then started down.

Their prey was amberjack. The state of Florida had a bag limit of one; for Deke and Robin, that meant making the best of their opportunity. State law mandated that the fish be at least thirty-four inches long, but to win bragging rights for the day would likely require taking a fish that weighed at least fifteen pounds. The guessing game was to take your shot early, or wait for just the right fish to come along.

Now that they were drawing near to the sunken boat, they could see there was no shortage of potential prey. Both divers stayed within sight of one another, but not so close as to impede the other's hunt. Deke's attention was drawn by a familiar flash of silver blue and the telltale brown band over the eye of the approaching fish. The amberjack drew closer, coming into range. Deke liked to take the shot from no more than five feet away. He sighted with the tip of his spear shaft, but then lowered his speargun. The amberjack was certainly legal in size, but he knew it wouldn't tip the scales at much more than ten pounds.

Deke was a gambler; he was willing to wait to try and get the bigger fish. Sometimes his strategy paid off; sometimes, by not taking the early opportunity, he ended up being skunked. Robin always thought it was better to take the sure shot, and five minutes into the dive he landed his fish. From a distance, Deke could see it was good-sized, a minimum fifteen pounds. He watched Robin quickly gather in the amberjack and put it into the fish bag that was attached to the float line. It was important to get your fish squared away as soon as possible; leaving a floundering or bleeding fish in the water was sure to attract predators. Nearby, watching with interest, Deke sighted half a dozen barracuda, some as big as four feet. They weren't a threat to their person, even if their big, bad teeth suggested otherwise, but they would happily snag any unsecured fish.

The clock, Deke knew, was running. Instead of trying to hunt down the fish, Deke settled on the bottom, positioning himself near the wreck. There wasn't a game trail per se, but the fish were creatures of habit that liked to move along familiar routes.

Deke didn't move; air bubbles were his only giveaway. Amberjack came his way. Some gave him a wide berth, others came close enough for Deke to get a clean shot, but they were clearly undersized compared to Robin's catch.

From the corner of his eye, Deke was able to catch the time on his watch. He was almost at the fifteenth minute of the dive. Taking measured breaths from his Nitrox mixture of air, Deke knew he still had at least a quarter of a tank. The more immediate concern was he only had five minutes to land his fish.

He continued to remain as motionless as possible. The passage of time was trying his patience, but he didn't alter his hunting plan.

Three minutes remaining.

Patience didn't come easy to Deke, either in his job or in his fishing, but he had learned that sometimes it was a strategic necessity to let events unravel.

An amberjack slowly came his way. Deke's breath caught. This could be it. But as the fish neared, Deke could see that it wasn't large enough to win the day. Still, it would mean plenty of fish for weekend kabobs. Some fishermen mistakenly believed amberjack didn't make for good eating; those same fishermen had clearly never dined on Deke's marinated amberjack kabobs.

The shot was there. Deke's trigger finger tightened, but he decided not to take it. There was still time, and Deke wasn't yet ready to make his concession speech.

He saw the shadow before he could make out the body, a moving patch of darkness that appeared more spectral than substance. As the figure materialized, the silver-blue fish showed itself more clearly. It was a big amberjack, at least twenty pounds. Deke willed it to come closer. Adrenaline surged through his body, but he remained still, barely blinking. The big fish didn't seem to notice him. Maybe he didn't register as a threat. Maybe the fish thought it was well out of harm's way.

Twenty feet, ten. Just a little closer for a clean gill shot, Deke thought.

The fish met its end at eighteen minutes and forty-eight seconds into their dive.

* * *

As Deke made his victory official by weighing the fish, Robin kept talking about Deke's "lucky win."

"Fluke win you might say," Deke said. "By the way, we're looking at twenty pounds, four ounces. Your fish is just under sixteen pounds."

"You made that shot at the last possible second."

"There was plenty of time still on the clock. And speaking of a ticking clock, I wouldn't wait on making your purchase for the big game.

There's a sale going on right now at the University of Florida gift shop. What do you think about modeling a Gator dress at this year's party?"

Robin made it clear he didn't think much of that idea, which only made the grin on Deke's face larger as he iced and stowed the fish. Both men recovered from their dive by hydrating with water. They usually rested for at least an hour before their second dive. In the last few years, they'd started to devote a part of each trip to spearing as many lionfish as possible. The invasive species was wreaking havoc on Florida's reefs and fisheries.

Deke tried to keep diving sacrosanct and not let business intrude, but he still found himself reaching for his phone to scan the morning's texts and emails. One of the texts was from Diana. She knew he was out diving that morning and wouldn't have encroached on his private time without good reason. He read her note, ground his teeth together, and said, "Dammit."

"What is it?"

"We're not the only ones out spearfishing. A federal judge is trying to impale me with a motion to show cause. But if he thinks I'm going to be easy to land, he's about to learn differently."

"You want to go in?"

"It wouldn't be fair to cut our trip short," Deke said.

"Your last-second win already ruined my day. There's no need to prolong my misery."

XXVII

Gina Romano looked up from Judge Irwin's motion to show cause order and said, "It's not like any of this came as a surprise."

Deke rolled his eyes. For the past half hour, he and Gina had been hunkered down in his office studying the email file sent out that morning by the judge. The motion to show cause asked for Deke to appear in open court on the following Tuesday morning to defend his actions. By filing the motion, the judge asserted Deke had done something sanctionable by the court. The fallout from such a motion typically resulted in a fine or judicial rebuke, or both. When taken to an extreme, it could also result in Deke's removal from the case.

"The best-case scenario is that Irwin will use this motion as an opportunity to browbeat me, and while I don't relish the idea of being his whipping boy, what bothers me most is that you can be sure he'll use this opportunity to reiterate the terms of his gag order. That's the real issue here, and one I'd like to find a way to push back on. When gag orders start being used in this manner, they might as well be called gag and shackle orders."

"We can ask for more time to prepare. It would be very hard for him to refuse that. Three days to prepare for this motion is a ridiculous turnaround time."

Deke shook his head. "Let's not. I expect that's what Irwin wants us to do, and by granting us more time it would allow him to look reasonable in the court record. My assertion is that he's not acting reasonably, and I intend to show that."

"Wrong. I'm the one who's going to show that. You're not going to say a single word during the proceeding. Your only job will be to sit there and look like a choirboy."

"I don't do choirboy very well," Deke said.

"Then you had better start practicing your singing."

"But . . ."

Gina didn't even allow him to start his argument. "Don't even think about it. You know I'm right, and that it makes no sense for you to represent yourself. If you and Irwin get into a pissing match, you'll lose the high ground. That's not a position we want to give up. In fact, I intend to build on it. So, while I sing your praises in court, you need to appear to be the wronged victim."

"I am the wronged victim."

"The *contrite* and *humble* and *silent* wronged victim," she said.

Deke sighed.

"Judge Irwin is clearly going to make this about your violating his gag order. He thinks he's going to make an example of you. When he's not looking, we'll make it about him. I intend to show him the error of his ways."

She smiled. Deke was glad he was on the right side of this particular smile, knowing it was a portent of things to come. Even though Gina was an attractive woman, she wasn't showing her teeth to look pretty as much as she was baring them.

"What's your plan?"

"My plan is to leave this office, enlist two of the firm's best associates, and have them help me research case law all weekend. We'll comb through appellate court ruling and find as many instances as possible where it was determined that the lawyer's First Amendment right to comment about political or social issues was not superseded by the judicial overreach of a protective order, especially as it pertains to serious public health and safety issues."

"I like the sound of that. I'm going to be tied up for the next few hours, but after that I'll have some time to brainstorm with you and your associates."

Gina shook her head. "I've got this. All you'd be doing is getting in the way."

Deke opened his mouth. Gina's look made him shut it. She nodded with satisfaction, and stood up.

"I'm going to go find my legal eagles. They'll be doing a sleepover at my place this weekend."

"I'll be available if you want to discuss strategy," Deke said.

Gina covered her ears, pretending she hadn't heard a word he'd said, and walked out of his office.

"It's been great listening to you," Deke called out to her back.

* * *

Ten minutes later, Deke's office was occupied again, this time by Jake, Carol, and Michael. Deke didn't even wait for them to be seated before starting in with his questions.

"What's the latest?"

Carol handed Deke a pile of paperwork. "That's what we have on Vicky Driscoll. The short version is that Mrs. Driscoll is a naturalized American citizen by way of Ukraine. She uses her ownership of the Emerald Hideaway to get H2B workers into the country, but they do more than work at her hotel. Driscoll owns a strip club called the Pussy Cat Palace in Panama City, and operates at least one massage parlor in Bay County. She also owns a yacht called the *Seacreto* that is used for suspect boat charters."

"Suspect in what way?"

"It's a vehicle for prostitution. While we were doing our investigation, Michael was making his own inquiries into the matter. He found a witness who said dancers from the club regularly entertained at sea."

"So, we're pretty sure the woman who drowned was on that boat for the purposes of prostitution?"

Carol nodded. "That's our working theory."

"But we still don't know her identity?"

"We're hoping to get word from USCIS today. So far all they have confirmed is that Karina Boyko is in this country on an H2B visa as a hospitality worker in the employ of Mrs. Driscoll."

Deke asked, "Do we know if Driscoll reported Karina's being

missing to either the local authorities or to the governmental agencies overseeing the temporary workers?"

Shaking her head, Carol said, "From what we know, there wasn't any missing person's report submitted to the sheriff's office. Ditto the Coast Guard. No nautical accidents were reported either. As for USCIS, they refuse to comment on that subject, so we don't know if she contacted them."

Deke couldn't help but notice that Michael was leaning forward in his seat, anxiously waiting for his chance to jump into the conversation.

Making eye contact with him, Deke said, "Better speak, before you burst."

Michael took the invitation to discuss his investigation of private charter boats in the area and his conversation with Captain Moss.

"You've been busy," Deke said.

"Much to my surprise," Carol said.

"Oh?" Deke turned to Michael for an explanation.

"I should have talked to Carol before investigating the marinas. Next time I will."

"Seems to me I've made that same promise to her a few times myself," Deke said.

"Seems to me that whenever you've failed to do so, bad things have happened," Carol said. "Like almost having your head caved in."

Deke gingerly touched the side of his head. "Point well taken. And speaking of which, any news of our fugitive?"

Jake's head bobbed up and down. "We actually just got off the phone with a contact in the Jacksonville area who knows Rodríguez. According to him, Tío Leo was in the area. We told the informant if he wants his payday, we'll need to get a specific address of where Leo's holed up."

"Let's hope the informant is on the up and up," Deke said. "Anything else?"

"The drowned woman . . ." Michael said, letting the words hang for a moment before continuing. "I'm pursuing a potential lead. It might be nothing, and my thinking could potentially be compromised because of my own personal biases, but my gut tells me something's there."

"Let's hear it," Deke said.

Michael took a moment to get his thoughts together. "There's one thing in particular I haven't been able to get out of my head since my visit to Panama City. The charter boat captain told me that he'd taken out a group of military contractors, and that he overheard them talking about their plans for going out on a party boat with some dancers from a strip club.

"The timing of their planned outing seems to align with the drowned woman's death. They would have gone out the day before the fall squall. And as far as I have been able to determine, only one strip club in Panama City sends its dancers out on a party boat."

"So, what's your hesitation in following up?" Deke said.

"I want to make sure that this isn't wishful thinking, that I'm not seeing some kind of synchronicity in all of this because it suits my own purposes."

Deke said, "If you want my two cents' worth, I'm a big believer in synchronicity."

"I can't even offer one cent, because I don't know what that means," Carol said.

"I'll offer my definition without *The Twilight Zone* sound effects," Michael said. "Synchronicity is when seemingly random things happen at the same time, but it's almost as if those events were meant to be connected."

Half skeptical, half curious, Jake said, "Is that like the universe is talking to you?"

Michael said, "I'm not going there. What I do know is what the charter boat captain told me. He said the military contractors were celebrating a successful recruiting campaign, and they were arranging for an outing with strippers. Without any prompting, he even offered me the name of their group leader: Rock. That happens to be the nickname of Peter Stone, the founder and president of Darkpool Security International."

"Darkpool," Deke said, recognizing the name.

"My buddies in the service called it Dark Ghoul. They're the biggest PMC—private military contractor—in the world. That's a fancy way of saying they're an army of mercenaries. Peter Stone is a modern-day war-lord who dispatches his private army to the highest bidder. His biggest client is our own government. Most American citizens are completely unaware of how dependent we've become on these mercenaries. These days it's not uncommon for private military contractors to outnumber US armed forces. In Iraq and Afghanistan, half of the soldiers were contracted. The reason these mercenaries have been so popular with our government is that they don't count as boots on the ground. That means in a numbers game it appears we are not as heavily committed in a military action as we really are."

"You don't sound like a proponent of using them," Deke said.

"I detest the idea of using PMCs in a war zone."

Deke liked the fire he was seeing in his associate and stoked it a little. "Why?"

"Because I don't think multinational corporations should be in the business of war. It's too easy for bad things to happen in a war zone, especially if you're not accountable like you are in the military. PMCs don't need to abide by the Uniform Code of Military Justice. Perhaps as a consequence of that, they've been involved in all sorts of bad shit."

"Such as?"

"There have been stories of bribery, torture, rape, kidnapping, murder, and even sex slavery rings. When there's a profit motive for war, it's a lot more difficult to establish a peace. Most of these mercenaries aren't even Americans, which means they don't serve our government; they serve the contractor. And if you have rot at the top, what do you expect to happen down the line? Peter Stone was tossed from the Navy Seals with an OTH—other than honorable—discharge. For Stone, getting bad paper was no big deal. In fact, it allowed him to fully embrace the business of war by starting up Darkpool. And he got to walk away from war crimes because the navy didn't want the embarrassment of trying to prosecute him."

"What kind of things did he allegedly do?"

"He tortured prisoners. Witnesses say he even murdered one of them. And he beheaded an enemy corpse for a photo op."

"So, he's bad news and bad things happen around him. And it

wouldn't surprise you if one of those bad things was a woman who drowned?"

"It fits right in with his CV."

Deke prodded Michael a little. "Is that why you sound so pissed?"

"It's part of it. And just the thought of Stone potentially being involved in this young woman's death stirred up some things from the past. Bad mojo all around made it feel personal."

"Synchronicity?" Carol asked.

Michael shrugged. "Maybe. A good friend of mine in the service, a PJ named Cal, died because of Darkpool's lax security and failure to follow protocols on a military base. We were almost overrun by the enemy. Cal was shot and killed during a firefight."

An incredulous Jake said, "Private military contractors were handling the security for a US base?"

"Crazy, right? Look, I'm not saying all the freelance soldiers are bad. Most of the securing and staffing transport lines fell to them, and they did a mostly good job under bad circumstances. But these contractors were never invested in the overall mission. They were there for a fat paycheck; we were there for our band of brothers. And those who were bad apples really muddied the waters for the rest of us. It was hard for the citizenry to distinguish between the mercenaries and us. Before she became a US citizen, my wife, Mona, said the people in her own village distrusted our military because the mercenaries had extorted them."

Carol asked, "Your wife is an Iraqi?"

"Yeah, of Assyrian descent. Most of her fellow Christian Assyrians had already fled the country in a series of diasporas. Mona's family stayed too long."

Deke got the question in first: "What happened?"

"It's a long story."

"I think we can spare a few minutes," Deke said.

Michael took a deep breath. He shifted in his seat, clearly uncomfortable at being put on the spot. "I'll give you the abbreviated version," he said, then offered a bare-bones account of his team's rescue of Mona.

When he finished, Carol said, "I'm so sorry."

"Don't be. That's how I met the woman I love. And getting back to an earlier subject, maybe it explains why I don't discount the notion of synchronicity. After delivering Mona to the Air Force hospital in Belad, I couldn't get her out of my thoughts. Just two days after her arrival at the hospital, I was brought there myself with a broken back."

Deke did a double-take. "You broke your back?"

"I fractured my spine as a result of a helicopter landing gone wrong." Michael took a breath and then added, "There was also a traumatic brain injury, which healed over time, thank god. I look at all of that as a small price to pay, though. Mona and I convalesced together in the same hospital. For as long as possible, I put off being transferred for treatment to the Landstuhl Regional Medical Center in Germany because I didn't want Mona to be alone. By the time I finally relented, Mona and I were engaged."

"Did the military make it hard for you to marry an Iraqi woman?" asked Deke.

"They didn't make it easy. But when I was cashiered with a medical discharge, it smoothed the way. Mona had seen enough of war to never want to be touched by it again, and was delighted when I told her I would be leaving the military."

"Were you planning on being a lifer?"

Michael nodded. "But I'm not complaining."

Deke feigned umbrage. "I would hope not. We're the ones who should be complaining. How are the rest of us mortals ever supposed to compete with that story of how you met the love of your life? Talk about making all of us look bad."

Much-needed laughter swept through the office. Deke said, "I think you've answered your own question about synchronicity. This time, though, don't feel as if you have to fracture your spine before following your gut, or your heart, or both."

"But do keep us informed of your movements along the way," Carol said.

"Yes, ma'am."

Carol turned to Deke. "If it's all right with you, I'd like to engage the services of Miami Maritime Investigations to look into the party boat. They have connections with all the marinas in Florida and beyond, and should be able to get us answers and footage of when the party boat went out, and who was in it, and who was on it when it came back."

After Deke voiced his agreement, Carol added, "I'd also like to send an undercover team into Viktoria Driscoll's strip club in Panama City ASAP. If we're lucky, we'll find Karina Boyko still alive and working there."

"If tonight's ASAP enough for you, I'd like to volunteer," Michael said. "I know I'm not one of your investigators, but I am Karina's lawyer."

"Yes, you are her *lawyer*."

Michael responded to Carol's reproach: "Eglin Air Force Base and Tyndall Air Force Base are both in the area. Strip clubs always target the military as customers, and I still look the part."

"You're not going into that strip club by yourself," Carol said, drawing a line.

"I'll go with him," Jake said.

Carol turned to Deke, who offered an almost imperceptible nod. "All right," she said. "Jake will be in charge tonight. You are both to keep a low profile, and not put yourself in harm's way. Understood?"

Jake nodded and Michael said, "Yes, ma'am."

Deke sat back and took the measure of everyone in the office. "Are we good?" Heads nodded. "In that case, carpe diem, all."

Instead of following Carol and Jake out of the office, Michael stayed seated. "Got time for a quick consult on my civil case?"

"I'm all ears."

They were ten minutes into their discussion when Deke's private line buzzed. He looked at the display, saw Carol was calling, and picked up. Her news wasn't good.

"Dammit," Deke said, hanging up the phone. "The dead woman has been identified as Karina Boyko."

Michael cursed under his breath. "I guess this puts the brakes on my civil case."

"Why would you think that?"

"Karina was my client."

"Her death doesn't change that relationship. It alters matters, of course, but there won't be any abandoning of the case. And we're not going to wait on getting Karina's personal information from UCSIS. That could take forever. I'm going to direct Carol to try and contact her family in Ukraine. If we're lucky, that tattoo of Karina's, the thing-amajig . . ."

Michael offered up the Ukrainian word: "Vyshyvanka."

"Right. If its geography proves accurate, that should narrow the search. We'll use an operative in Ukraine if at all possible. After locating her family, you'll ask questions of them, such as if Driscoll perpetrated a bait and switch and brought these young women into our country without telling them the illegal nature of the work they would be forced to perform. And though it's illegal to solicit family members to represent the deceased, don't be surprised if they bring up that topic. If that happens, your case would morph into not only a civil suit, but a wrongful death suit."

"That's all the more reason for me to depose Driscoll as soon as possible."

"Agreed."

"So, how do I make that happen?"

"You petition the court for expedited discovery, and make your motion for exigent circumstances. Karina's death was on Driscoll's watch. Hammer that point. You'll need to stress the dangerous work-place angle, and how it was Driscoll's duty to maintain a safe work environment. Frame your cause of action by asserting that the H2B workers were clearly invited business guests of Driscoll."

"What's the best-case scenario for getting expedited discovery?"

Deke's head wobbled from side to side, as if doing his own scale of justice weighing. "Even with a sympathetic judge, it's rare to get a fast-track discovery."

"If I did, what's the time frame?"

"Ordinarily, you'd be lucky, very lucky, in getting a three-month window."

"That's too long."

"By judicial standards, that's light speed."

Michael's hands were clenched in fists. Deke spoke to his anger. "I know that seems like an unnecessary eternity, but you're going to need time to prepare for your case. There are a lot of nuances in Florida's liability laws pertaining to licensees and invitees, and that's just the start of it. You need to keep your eyes on the prize. The world has turned a blind eye to these victims for too long."

"I'll do what I can to change that," Michael said, standing up to leave.

Deke got to his feet as well. His long sigh didn't go unnoticed by Michael. "Problem?" he asked.

In a voice that didn't carry beyond the office, Deke said, "I need to go tell Diana the bad news. They only talked the one time, but Karina has been in her thoughts ever since. I've seen Diana studying the notes of their conversation, trying to make sense of everything. This is going to hit her hard."

XXVIII

Michael waited for his ride in the white zone fronting the Bergman/Deketomis building. As Jake pulled up with his SUV, Michael could see that he was eyeing him uncertainly. Michael lowered his aviator glasses and nodded. He had changed out of the suit that Jake was used to seeing him in and was wearing faded blue jeans, cowboy boots, and a tight United States Air Force T-shirt with an American flag and the words FLY, FIGHT, WIN.

He climbed into the passenger seat and tossed his workout bag behind him.

"I almost didn't recognize you," Jake said.

"Given a choice, this is what I'd be wearing to work."

"That's one thing I like about my job. Most days I don't have to wear suits."

"I understand you used to be a lawyer," Michael said.

"Guilty as charged."

Instead of pressing him on the subject, Michael left it up to Jake to decide whether or not to elaborate. He didn't have to wait long.

"I was practicing law in West Virginia where I managed to get Deke and the firm involved in what ultimately turned out to be that big opioid multidistrict litigation case in Ohio. Long story short, I released privileged information to the public, which got me disbarred. And I should also mention how I managed to get addicted to opioids while everything was playing out. Anyway, after all was said and done, and since a career change was necessary, Deke offered me a job in legal investigations. I've been here for two years."

"Ever consider a return to practicing law?"

Jake nodded. "My plan had been to petition to have my law license reinstated after a year's hiatus, but the longer I worked in legal investigations, the clearer it became that I was better suited to doing that."

"I've had my own career doubts of late," Michael said. "I'm not sure if I have the patience to be a lawyer. Somehow I never envisioned that the best way to take on the enemy was to write a brief. I was envious hearing about your working undercover."

"You mean my truck stop assignment?"

When Michael nodded, Jake said, "There's nothing glamorous or exciting about that work. In fact, that assignment was as hard as anything I've ever done. By day I drove a big rig, and at night I worked surveillance at the truck stops. I hope I never have to do anything like that again. Human trafficking is worse than a sewage spill, and if what I witnessed is any indication, it's becoming ever more prevalent throughout this country."

"How common is it?"

"I'm not saying that the trafficking is going on at all the truck stops, or even most of them, but it's not hard to find if you're looking for it. Many truck stops discourage what truckers call 'lot lizards,' but in some places I found management and ownership in cahoots with the traffickers. And I'm not talking about the old arrangement of prostitutes and their pimps, but worse."

"Worse in what way?"

Jake shook his head and sighed. "The old system had women going from truck to truck looking for johns, and while that's still practiced, as hard as it is to believe, the sex trade is now even more impersonal. These days you can find traveling bordellos, including trucks with cargo areas that have been set up as sex shacks. The trucks drive in with trafficked women who work the stop, then they drive out. Those women are there to serve one purpose: their entire existence is relegated to that cargo area of the truck, or in some cases to the motels associated with the truck stops."

"And that goes on out in the open?"

"I think it would be impossible for management to be unaware of what is going on. In fact, that kind of activity seems to be built into many truck stop operations. It is actually part of their business plan for increasing revenues."

"So, everyone is profiting except the sex worker?"

"*Sex worker* implies that these women have a choice as to whether to be engaging in sex or not, but the truth of the matter is they don't have any choice, or any say. They have been coerced, manipulated, and brainwashed. Some don't speak the language. Some have actually been sold by their families. Some think they'll be killed, or their loved ones will be if they don't do as they're told."

"I'll take back what I said about envying your undercover work. How in the hell is this going on here?"

"That's a good question. But an even better one is: How is it going on out in the open? Deke hopes to go after Welcome Mat's truck stops and motels by having a forensic accounting done, but so far, the judge doesn't look inclined to allow that to happen. We suspect there are multiple sets of books, with profits being funneled to the owners in the shadows."

"As in the mob?"

"Let's just say if that turns out to be the case, Deke won't be surprised. And neither will I."

Even the conversation was depressing, Michael thought. Being forced to confront that misery still weighed on Jake. You could hear it in his voice and sighs.

"Did you have the opportunity to talk to any of the women being trafficked?"

"I had some limited contact, mostly brief conversations with women knocking on my cab after midnight, asking if I wanted to party."

Michael tried playing devil's advocate. "Don't they say prostitution is the oldest profession in the world?"

"Prostitution isn't the same thing as human trafficking. These women aren't selling their bodies; their bodies are being sold for them."

"Mind if I steal that line for my civil case?"

"Please do."

By unsaid mutual agreement, the two men decided to take a break from their weighty conversation. They rode in companionable silence until Michael said, "Your trucking assignment must have been tough on your wife."

"It was, but Anna was the one who insisted that I do it. She said if my work helped trafficked women, then it would be worth it."

"What did she think about tonight's assignment?"

"She wasn't thrilled, and I don't blame her. What about your wife?"

Michael took a moment before answering. "I wasn't exactly forthcoming. I told Mona that you and I were seeking out background material on my client."

"That's all true, sort of."

"I wanted to come clean, but I was afraid of the fallout," Michael said.

"You want to do right, but not right now."

"That pretty much covers it."

"Lots of women wouldn't be happy with the idea of their husbands going to a strip club," Jake said.

"I think Mona would have been okay with that part of it."

"Really?"

"Don't get me wrong. I'm not saying she would be happy with my doing that, but I'm pretty sure the bigger stumbling block for her would be the idea of me putting myself in a potentially dangerous position. Mona is a worrier. After what she experienced, and what happened to her family, she wants me to stay clear of battle."

"But going to a strip club isn't like going into battle."

"That remains to be seen," Michael said.

Jake laughed at what he thought was a joke.

XXIX

At Michael's urging, Jake parked a block away from the strip club. The Pussy Cat Palace was several miles north of Panama City's coastline, situated in an area that was more industrial than commercial. Michael studied the street view of the club and aerial shots of the area. Based on his online recon, he knew that on one side of the Pussy Cat Palace was a parking lot and on the other a dead-end street. At the back of the building there was a service entrance for deliveries. As far as Michael could determine, all human traffic entered and exited through the front doors of the club.

Michael was used to military operations where knowing the lay of the land was essential, but even with the best intelligence you had to expect the unexpected.

Like his suddenly seeing the unmistakable hulking figure of Andrei, one-half of the greeting committee he'd encountered at the Emerald Hideaway, sitting on a stool at the entrance to the strip club.

Abort the mission, thought Michael, or continue? Andrei was already eyeballing the two of them. Michael's interaction with him at the hotel had been brief, only long enough to hear Andrei offer up a few words. As far as Michael could see, there was no glimmer of recognition in the bouncer's bored eyes. His main interest seemed to be in appraising the men for concealed weapons; he was far less interested in their faces. Michael was glad he'd worn a suit when he visited the hotel; today's outfit looked far different.

Brazen it out, he decided, and be the opposite of the haughty lawyer he'd been pretending to be at the hotel. "Hope this guy doesn't recognize me," Michael whispered, then slapped Jake on his shoulder. In a loud voice he said, "Cold beer, hot women. Sounds like heaven, don't it?"

Jake amplified on Michael's Panhandle patois, offering up his own West Virginia twang: "As close to heaven as the two of us are ever likely to get."

The bouncer raised one of his meaty hands and motioned them to a stop. "ID," he said.

"No problem, bro." Michael kept his face turned to the side while reaching for his wallet.

From inside the club they could hear the chorus of Jessie J, Ariana Grande, and Nicki Minaj singing their song "Bang Bang." Andrei didn't offer any small talk and showed no interest in engaging with them other than to look at their licenses. Michael wished they had brought fake IDs.

As he handed back their licenses, Andrei said, "Pay for entrance to club inside." Then, sounding almost funereal with his thick accent, he insincerely added, "You have good evening."

"You too, Bela Lugosi," Jake said, making his speech sound slurred. Michael's wingman had his back, getting Andrei's scowl and all of his attention.

The interior of the club was hidden by curtains. Michael suspected that barrier might be in compliance with state or county law so as to keep passersby from seeing any vestige of the "Full Nudity" advertised on the signage. The two men parted the curtains and stepped inside. The space was air-conditioned, but that didn't mask the smell of sweat and desperation, scents Michael had encountered too many times in too many places. They passed through a metal detector and were observed by a second man with dark, slicked-back hair who was positioned near the cashier's booth. Slick looked to be in his early thirties. The blue blazer he was wearing suggested he was the club manager; the bulge in his sport jacket told Michael something else. Slick was carrying.

"Goot even-ning, gen-tull-min."

The accented woman's voice was broadcast from the inside of an enclosed cashier's booth. Jake and Michael turned toward the speaker. The acrylic windows did nothing to hide the fact that the cashier was naked.

Michael swiveled his head all around, apparently looking for someone else in the area. "Gentlemen?" he said to Jake. "She can't be talking to us."

Laughing, Jake said, "That's for damn sure."

As Michael and Jake approached her window, the cashier pretended to be amused. Her smile was posed and fake. The woman was wearing lots of eye shadow, eyeliner, and mascara, but all of that couldn't camouflage her hard eyes.

"You are members here, yes?" she asked.

"We are members here, no," Michael said.

"It goot deal. All member get five dollar off each visit. Membership good for year."

Jake looked the woman up and down. "Never seen—I mean heard—such a good sales pitch."

Michael said, "Fifty bucks for membership? That's a rip-off."

The cashier pretended to pout. "You no like women?"

Jake laughed and slapped his buddy on the shoulder.

"She was talking to you," Michael told him, then pushed three twenties through the slot, the price of admission for the two of them.

"No tips for tits?" the cashier asked, giving a shake of her chest.

"Now you got my attention, darling," Jake said.

Abraham Lincoln was pushed through the slot, then vanished.

Jake looked impressed. "Now that's magic. Woman's not wearing a stitch, and yet she makes my money disappear from sight without so much as saying 'abracadabra.'"

* * *

The men found two open seats next to one another at the stage. Their location allowed for a good vantage point for the bar and the room, as well as the stairway that led to what the signage identified as the Underground Club.

The lights were kept low, with most of the lighting directed to the dancer. At the moment, she was moving suggestively up and down on a pole positioned in the middle of the stage. Half a dozen women were working the tables and bar area. Within fifteen seconds of their being seated, a server approached them. Her outfit concealed very little, but did allow for a name tag that identified her as Oksana. She ran her hands up and down each of their arms.

"Strong, sexy men. Buy Oksana a stiff, stiff drink?"

"Hello, gorgeous," Michael said. "As pretty as you are, I'm afraid we've got to disappoint you. The last time we were in here we promised Karina that we'd let her take care of us. So be a darling, and go tell her that Mickey D and the Dude are here."

For a moment, Oksana's false smile vanished, and perhaps a touch of uneasiness showed itself. Then again, with the amount of makeup she was wearing, Michael didn't have the easiest time reading her expression. Most clowns weren't as generous in their application of ruby-red lipstick as was Oksana.

"Karina no working," she said.

"Well, that's not what I wanted to hear."

"What about her friend?" Jake said. "What was her name?"

"Natasha?"

"No, that don't sound quite right."

Michael snapped his fingers. "Nataliya!"

"You got it."

Michael turned his attention back to Oksana. "Do me a favor, pretty lady, and tell Nataliya the boys are back in town."

Clown makeup or not, this time there was no doubt about it. They'd hit a nerve, and Oksana's face showed it.

"She not here."

"Strike two. I told you we should have gone to Booty Y'all," Jake said, referencing a nearby strip club.

Oksana said, "Pussy Cat Palace much better. What you want drink?"

Jake cupped his hand over his eyebrows and looked around. "You sure Karina and the love of my life, Nataliya, aren't here? Every time we've been here, both of them were working."

Without even a pretense of a smile, Oksana said, "No here."

"You got their telephone numbers?" Michael asked. "I'd like to invite them to join our party."

"No number. What you want drink?"

Michael sighed, and lifted his hands to Jake as if to say, "What can you do?" Aloud he said, "Vodka on the rocks."

"Make that two," Jake said.

"And speaking of getting our rocks off, the Dude and I are going to need two big glasses of ice water."

"What vodka you want?"

"None of that Commie stuff. What's in your well?"

"Smirnoff," Oksana said, clearly disdainful.

"Works for us, and don't forget our ice water in big glasses."

"You run tab?" she asked.

"We pay cash as we go," Michael said.

Grumbling under her breath, Oksana left them, and Michael and Jake turned their attention to the dancer, or at least gave the impression of doing so. Michael leaned forward, holding his face up with his palm while resting his elbow on the bar. That shielded half his face and allowed him to surreptitiously observe the room. After Oksana punched in their drink orders at the point-of-sales station, he saw her make a beeline for Slick. As she gestured toward them and began talking, Michael pretended to be caught up by the dancer's performance.

* * *

Michael and Jake stayed seated at the stage for an hour. During that time, they ordered four drinks apiece, and their speech became louder, their behavior more obnoxious. When the ice water was delivered, they downed the liquid, leaving only ice. While appearing to drink the vodka, they never actually swallowed it, but transferred the contents from one glass to the other through their periodic sipping. With every second drink they insisted upon getting some "fresh ice." Their charade allowed both men to be stone-cold sober.

The propositions had started within five minutes of their being seated. The men were repeatedly encouraged to join the women downstairs for a "private dance" in the Underground Club.

Oksana was the first to offer a lap dance, to which Michael said, "No offense, darling, but you're no Karina. Now that's one sexy girl. Any luck finding her?"

"Nataliya was the one who did it for me," Jake said.

As the two men argued about the attributes of each woman, a fuming Oksana once more sought out Slick, furiously whispering to him.

After that, different women visited the men, trying to entice them downstairs. One woman told Jake, "I do best lap dance in world. Follow me to private place. Maybe free for you."

"My daddy always told me there's nothing more expensive than free," he said. "You happen to be friends with Nataliya, darling? The two of us had an understanding that we'd be meeting up the next time I came into town."

The woman's name definitely had a chilling effect on the woman. She all but ran away.

The last dancer visiting them didn't have better luck than the others. Michael told her, "You kind of look like Karina. You know her, right? Where is she?"

The woman couldn't get away fast enough.

At the hour mark of their visit, Jake said in a voice that only Michael could hear, "Looks like we've done a good job of upsetting the hive."

The two of them, Michael thought, had certainly managed to get noticed. He said, "I'm going to the head. Don't be surprised if I'm not back for five or ten minutes."

Jake gave Michael a skeptical side glance. "You need to do better than that. What's up?"

"I'm hoping to ask the help a few questions without being observed. That's why I need you to stay here and chill so that everything looks like it's on the up-and-up."

Jake still wasn't buying it. "Don't bullshit me. We're a team, or we're supposed to be."

"Sorry," Michael said. "You're right. What I'm hoping is that my bathroom break will give me the opportunity to have a private chat with the manager."

The explanation seemed to work for Jake. "I'm just a shout away," he said.

Michael patted Jake's shoulder, rose from his barstool, and pretended to catch himself from falling. Then he started out unsteadily in the direction of the restrooms. On stage a dancer was gyrating to Nicki Minaj's "Megatron."

Pretending to be the embodiment of the drinking lyrics that were part of the song, Michael sang his way toward the restroom. He didn't turn around to take notice of Slick trailing after him; he didn't have to.

Once he entered the unoccupied restroom, Michael considered his options, then chose to go into the stall farthest from the entrance. He heard a soft whoosh of air and knew the door to the restroom had been quietly opened. From inside his stall, Michael continued humming the music from "Megatron." He wanted Slick to know exactly where he was.

The man was there to ask questions, Michael knew, and to threaten him. In order to get Michael's immediate compliance, he'd probably have his gun leveled and waiting as he exited the stall. Still humming, Michael gauged where Slick was standing.

The stall opened inward. Slick knew that. What he didn't know was that Michael hadn't latched the door shut but was propping it closed with his hand. Slick also didn't know that Michael had pocketed a shot glass while walking away from the stage. He lofted the shot glass, tossing it in the direction of the main door to the restrooms. As it shattered, Michael charged out of the stall.

The noise had drawn all of Slick's attention. As Michael had expected, the man's gun was drawn. Three things happened almost instantaneously: in half a second, Michael grabbed Slick's wrist, pointed the gun away from him, and kicked him in his balls. In the next half second, Michael disarmed Slick, swept his legs out from under him, and left him stunned and sprawled on the floor.

Speaking in a conversational voice, Michael asked, "Let's talk about Karina and Nataliya, shall we?"

Slick began cursing. Without offering any warning, Michael's left foot slammed into the side of Slick's face, snapping it back and opening up a cut on his cheek. While Slick's glazed eyes were having trouble focusing, Michael grabbed him by the ankles and threw him against the door, effectively blocking it.

"Let's go over the ground rules here," Michael said, his voice calm, his breath even. "The first rule is no cursing, and along with that I'd like you to keep your voice down."

Slick pretended to think about that, then lunged for Michael's legs. This time Michael used his right foot to catch Slick on his jaw and drive him backward against the door.

"There's a second rule you'll need to follow, and that's no lying. I ask you a question, and you answer honestly."

The downed man told Michael to do something that was physically impossible.

"You forgot rule one." Michael's kick connected with Slick's mouth, driving his head against the door again and sending a tooth flying.

"Let me reiterate: there are only two rules. Do I need to repeat them for you?"

Although he was holding Slick's gun, Michael wasn't brandishing it or leveling it at the man. There was no need to. He was the threat, not the gun. Slick shook his head.

"I want to talk about Karina Boyko. You knew her, right?"

Slick offered up a reluctant "Yeah."

"What about Nataliya?"

"She hasn't been around the last coupla months."

"What's Nataliya's last name?"

"Who remembers all those crazy Uke names? They got about a million vowels."

Something in Michael's stare helped Slick to remember. "Nahorny," he said. "Only reason I remember it is I always thought it was a funny last name."

Michael didn't look amused. "Where is Nataliya now?"

"I hear she went back home to Ukraine."

Michael shook his head, made a few tsk-tsk sounds, and said, "I'm afraid you're not complying with rule two."

Slick wiped some blood from his mouth and looked warily at Michael's boots. "I really don't know where she is. Maybe Andrei could tell you. He's the big guy out front. The two of them would sometimes speak Uke to one another."

"Have you ever had your nose broken before? It's not pleasant."

"Fu—" said the man, before remembering rule number one. Then he revisited rule two. "Andrei told me she wasn't coming back. I don't know nothing other than that. Vicky called her into her office to talk one night, and that's the last time I seen her."

"Tell me about Karina Boyko."

"Sh—" The man bit off the rest of the word. He flinched a little, fearing Michael's sweeping kick, but it never landed. "Just today I was told she's dead. That's all I know."

He gave a side glance at Michael's boots. "Really."

"You don't know how she died?"

"I know enough to not ask any questions."

"I want to know about your party yacht that goes out with the dancers for booze cruises."

"The *Seacreto* is Vicky's thing. I got nothing to do with it. But I did hear when Vicky got the boat, she thought she was being clever with its name."

"In what way?" Michael asked.

"*Secreto* is Spanish for 'secret,'" Slick said.

* * *

Michael stumbled as he exited the club, caught himself, and started uncertainly down the walkway. He came to a sudden stop, seemed to reconsider where he was going, and turned around as if returning to the club. As he neared the entrance, he exited the pathway, staggering toward the side of the building and moving into the shadows away from the lights. He stumbled over to a concrete planter box with a shade tree, spread his legs, and reached for his zipper.

"No piss there," Andrei shouted. "No piss there."

Michael was swaying on his feet and showed no indication of having heard the bouncer's yelling.

"You stop!" Andrei roared, rushing at him.

Michael was a shade over five eleven, and tipped the scales at 175 pounds. Andrei was six four and weighed at least 250 pounds. It wasn't a fair contest.

Like a bullfighter, Michael used Andrei's momentum, sidestepping and letting him slam into the concrete planter. In quick succession, Michael used a palm strike on Andrei's nose, a cup slap to his ear, and a low kick that dropped the big man to one knee. With the staggered giant reeling and down, Michael methodically stepped behind his prey and applied a choke hold. While the vise tightened around his neck, Andrei bucked, then reached back and used his hands to try and break Michael's hold. When that didn't work, the bouncer raised himself from the ground and with a backward push drove Michael against the planter. Michael merely tightened his grip. Denied oxygen, the big man panicked. He whirled around, desperately trying to reach back to dislodge Michael; that only depleted his oxygen faster. Goliath crashed and burned, dropping to the ground. He slapped his big hand down once, then a second time, desperately tapping out. Michael loosened his hold just enough for Andrei to fight for a few breaths, all the while keeping the giant's neck locked in the crook of his arm.

Speaking over Andrei's sucking in of air, Michael said, "If you don't want to be choked out, you need to answer my questions without lying. Understand?"

Between heaving breaths, the giant said, "Yes."

"What happened to Nataliya?"

The lie was automatic. "I don't . . ."

Michael's vise grip tightened, cutting off Andrei's air. Instead of submitting, the big man pushed backward, driving Michael against the wall. The bouncer writhed and twisted but, denied air, he fell to his knees. As he began blacking out, Michael allowed him enough air for a few labored breaths.

"Just so we understand one another, if you try my patience again, things will not go well for you. Consider this your last warning. Is that clear?"

The giant rasped, "Yes." Judging by his slumped shoulders and beaten expression, there was no fight left in him.

"Good. I've already talked to your manager, and he told me the two of you were here on the night Nataliya disappeared. What happened?"

"Two men," gasped Andrei, "take her."

"What two men?"

"I don't . . ."

Michael began tightening his grip, stopping the big man's lie midsentence. Andrei desperately tapped out, and Michael reopened his air supply.

"It happen few months back."

"Tell me about the two men."

"Same men who just take *Amerykans' kyy.*"

Michael tried to understand what the man was telling him. "You're saying the same two men who took Nataliya also took an American?"

"Same men. Vicky arrange."

"And you were there when these men took each of those girls?"

His grunt affirmed that.

"Describe these men."

"Both Amerykans'kyy."

"I need more than that."

"One big, the other not so big. Both white. The small man call big man Keebler."

"Keebler?"

"Like favorite cookies of me."

The Keebler elf, thought Michael.

"What else?"

"No else."

Michael ratcheted up the pressure to help Andrei remember more. "You were there when the girls were taken, right? What did you see?"

Andrei signaled his compliance, and Michael eased his hold. "Nataliya taken from here. Vicky call her outside in delivery lot. Men put her in SUV with camper shell and shaded windows."

"What about the American?"

"They take her from place she stay with others. Compound on private road on outskirts of DeFuniak Springs."

The sound of footsteps on the pathway alerted Michael to company. "Almost didn't see you in the shadows," Jake said.

"Just finishing up."

After Michael had tied the manager up in a restroom stall, he'd told Jake to hold off for five minutes before joining him outside.

"Do you know where Nataliya and the American were being taken?"

The bouncer hesitated just long enough for Michael to tighten his grip. That brought on a fit of coughing. When Michael eased the pressure, Andrei said, "Each time they drive big SUV with license plate from Nevada."

In the distance the sounds of boisterous young males could be heard making their way toward the Pussy Cat Palace. Though the three men were in the shadows, Michael thought it was time to finish his interrogation.

"I wouldn't mention this encounter to Vicky, or to anyone. Your manager, who is tied up in the men's bathroom, agreed that it was in his best interests to keep quiet on the matter. We're going to tie you up now, but we'll do it in such a way that it won't take you very long to free yourself. Don't even think about following us. We've got your manager's gun and prefer not to shoot you. Understood?"

Andrei nodded, or at least tried to nod over the obstruction of Michael's crooked elbow.

"Nylon cuffs in my back pocket," Michael told Jake.

XXX

Lily wiped the perspiration from her forehead. The crazy asshole was playing with the heat again. It was a favorite tactic of Mad Max. A few years ago, Lily had gone to a sleepover where she and her friends had binge-watched all the Mad Max movies. She couldn't remember all that had happened but did recall some nightmarish figures. Her Mad Max would have fit in nicely in all that madness. The nickname seemed perfect for her captor.

Max loved being in charge of everything. There was no thermostat that she was able to access, just as she had no control over the air-conditioning. It was a power thing for him. He was like this creepy spider, and she was an insect in his web. The asshole didn't even try to hide his monitoring of her through his spy cameras. In fact, it seemed a point of pride to him. During his visits, he liked to drop comments on what he'd seen her doing. Not that there was a hell of a lot she could do. The bastard could even control what she watched on TV, changing the channel whenever he wanted. And playing with the volume to annoy her. She was his TV show. There was no privacy from him.

She raised her hand and flipped off the camera nearest to her. His response was to turn on the air-conditioning to high. Bastard.

Lily wasn't sure who was worse, Tío Leo or Max. At least with Lie-o it had been all about the money. It wasn't as easy to figure out Max's game, but that didn't make him any less scary.

Although it was late, Lily resisted trying to sleep. Max usually waited until she was in a deep slumber before revealing himself. She'd awaken with the sense that something was wrong, and something was. The perv would be standing at the foot of her bed, staring at her. Staring. She never knew how long he stood there watching her, whether it was minutes or hours. The jolt was in opening her eyes, and finding him there. She had screamed the first two times, and he'd laughed, almost like he was getting his rocks off.

Maybe he was. Mad Max had an agenda, even if she didn't know what it was. That scared her.

Last night he hadn't awakened her, but Lily wasn't sure if that was better or worse. Max had left calling cards behind, images he had positioned around the room. They were all different, but similar. The girls in the drawings resembled Lily. They had her dark hair, fair skin, and large green eyes. Most wore sheer gowns. The young women were human, but there was an otherworldly quality to them.

In some of the images, the women were bathing in the outdoors, their bodies embraced in the reflected light of the moon shimmering off of the water's surface. In some others, girls her age were happily swinging from the moon, or serenely perched in the middle of a crescent moon. Not all of the drawings were modern. She suspected some of the images came from old paintings.

Lily gathered all the images of her look-alikes, and put them away in a drawer. She wanted no part of these moon maidens. She wanted no part of Max, but there was no getting away from him. Awaking to the images only confirmed her worst fears. Chance hadn't brought her to this prison; her captor had been looking for someone like her. He had been seeking his moon woman.

Max had said she was his guest. Max had lied.

Lily wondered if there had ever been a prison like hers. The bars might not be visible, but she was completely confined, hidden behind the darkened windows. There was only one door in her suite, a heavy steel security door. Max had told her that he was on the other side of it. There was a slot in the door that opened from his side for the purpose of sliding food through, just like how prisoners in movies got their food delivered. That was much more preferable to Max delivering it in person.

Her living space had been stripped down to its essentials, with everything bolted down, from the lamps to the television. There were no utensils and no tools. The prison had been designed so that there was no potential for weapons or projectiles. There was nothing sharp or heavy. It wasn't enough to put her in a birdcage. They'd also clipped her wings.

The room was getting colder, but Lily resisted covering herself in a blanket. She didn't want to give Max the satisfaction of thinking he could control her every movement.

There was no clock to tell Lily what time it was, but she suspected it was after midnight. The Las Vegas lights drew her close to the window, although her fear of heights kept her a few feet away from the glass. Lily avoided looking down, but instead took in the distant lights. They twinkled like stars. And they were just as unreachable, she feared.

She thought of the film *Tangled*. This was her high tower. In the movie Rapunzel had seen distant lights in the sky that she had thought were stars, but after discovering they were floating lanterns, she yearned to follow them. As much of an asshole as Tío Leo was, most mornings he let the girls watch Disney movies. Lily knew he hadn't done that to be nice; it was how he kept them occupied and controlled them, but it was the only good part of their day. The three other girls he'd been trafficking hadn't spoken English, and Lily didn't know much Spanish, but they'd still found a way to talk with one another. The girls liked singing the songs from the movies, even though they didn't know what the words meant.

Lily hummed softly under her breath. She didn't want Max to hear. But looking at the lights, she thought of Rapunzel singing "I See the Light." It had been one of their favorite songs. In a whisper, she sang, like Rapunzel had, of how blind she'd been.

Too bad she didn't have long golden hair like Rapunzel's. But even if she had, Lily knew there was no one out there waiting to climb her hair. She was by herself. That made everything worse.

Lily went to bed, but not so much for sleep as to hide under the covers. She wasn't going to let Max see her tears. It was only under the covers that she could express her feelings without the need of putting on a front. Where she could admit to herself that she missed her old life.

She missed her mommy.

After a time, Lily cried herself to sleep.

* * *

It was not a prince who came to her.

The loud bang caused Lily to awake with a start. She threw up her arms to ward off the perceived threat.

Max was wearing workout clothes, a black-and-white yin-yang sweatshirt and sweatpants. But the yin-yang fish had been transformed into the faces of black-and-white snarling wolves.

"It's a beautiful night to dance, is it not?"

Lily was too scared to answer, but that didn't seem to make a difference to Max.

Laughing, he backed up half a dozen steps, then ran at the window, throwing himself at it again. The impact knocked him back, but he landed on his feet. His toothy grin, pale face, and dark beard confronted her.

"Would you like to dance with me?" he asked, clicking his long thumbnails together, like a crab brandishing its claws.

Fighting her trembling, Lily shook her head.

"Such a shame. But at least we can have a late-night snack together. I took the liberty of ordering some of your favorites."

"I'm not hungry," she said.

There had been a few times when Lily had eaten with him, only to fall into a deep sleep afterward. She didn't think that was a coincidence and suspected Max of drugging her.

"Suit yourself, Nataliya, but I still expect you to join me in the next room while I dine."

Lily felt the hairs on her arms rise. Nataliya. He had called her by that name again. And now Lily remembered where she'd heard that name before. It was Karina who had said that Lily looked like her friend Nataliya. That couldn't be a coincidence, could it? What else had she said? Lily struggled to remember. And then it came to her. Karina had said Lily's eyes were just like Nataliya's.

Shit. That explained why Max was always studying her face. It was like he was trying to look into her skull. But now she knew it was her eyes.

Lily took a seat in the living room, trying to keep as much distance between herself and Max as she could. The creep's eyes were on her now. She refused to meet them. What had happened to Nataliya? She wanted to ask the question, but was afraid to.

Max gestured to the food in front of him. "You really should avail yourself of the cuisine we have. Our kitchen employs some of the best Chinese chefs in the world. Their *baozi* is unsurpassed, not to mention the *shou mian*."

He pointed to some noodles that were laid out on a plastic sheet and said, "We have patrons who travel many thousands of miles to partake of this dish."

She watched Max eating with his plastic fork. All the food was delivered precut without silverware or even plates. Her choice was to eat with her hands or with a plastic fork.

He was looking at her, expecting her to say something. "No thanks," she said.

"That is your choice, of course, but I think it to be an ill-advised one. The English translation of *shou mian* is 'noodles of longevity.' If I were you, I would make a point of eating them."

Despite being afraid, Lily looked into the black holes of his eyes. He smiled and said, "After all, it wouldn't do to tempt the fates."

XXXI

Nathan Bines felt the vibration coming from his wallet. In a slot designed for a credit card, his special cell phone—the size and thickness of a credit card—was vibrating. Bines found himself grinding his teeth. He didn't like being at the beck and call of another. The vibrating stopped, but that only meant the clock was ticking. Bines had two minutes to drop everything and find a spot to take the call in private.

Geofredo Salazar didn't like to be kept waiting.

Bines wished he could ignore the summons. He felt the clench in his gut. For the better part of a decade, Salazar had been represented by Bines, an arrangement kept secret by both parties. Several other law firms worked for the billionaire hedge fund manager and were his on-the-record lawyers. All clients have baggage, but Salazar had more than most. Now, looking back to the beginning of their relationship, Bines wished he had known just how much baggage that was.

He finished another conversation and closed the door to his office. Salazar didn't keep him waiting.

"I hope I didn't interrupt your golf game," Salazar said.

"As I've told you before, I rarely have time to play golf."

"What lawyers say, and what really is, I have often found to be contradictory."

Salazar sounded as if he were joking. His mellifluous Spanish accent—Bines thought it reminiscent of the late actor Ricardo Montalbán—certainly sounded affable. But Bines knew Salazar was neither genial nor good-tempered. Despite his image to the contrary, he was as cold and calculating an individual as Bines had ever met. At the same time, Bines and the firm had grown dependent on the billable hours charged to their anonymous client and his shell companies. That tended to happen when you were billing up to fifty million dollars a year in legal fees.

"Tell me about our case," Salazar said.

"Everything is proceeding as hoped. Tomorrow morning, Judge Irwin is going to publicly smack down Deketomis. After he gets through with him, Deketomis will be hamstrung. I expect he'll be so judicially constrained that his case will wither up and blow away."

Instead of being pleased, Salazar said, "That's not enough."

"Excuse me?"

"Deketomis needs to be humiliated."

Nathan Bines did not like Nick Deketomis, but he liked even less what he was hearing. It was one thing to work the legal system to your advantage, but quite another to endorse the equivalent of beating a dead horse.

"I can assure you that his ultimately losing this case will be punishment enough for him. Deketomis would sooner eat excrement than he would a serving of humble pie."

"*Excrement?*" By his tone, Salazar was clearly mocking Bines for his euphemism. "He needs to be dragged through a pile of *excrement*, so that when he comes out on the other side he will be fouled, and bowed, and beaten. Deketomis must be an example so as to discourage any other foolhardy lawyers from ever considering taking up a similar case."

"I cannot endorse anything inappropriate or illegal."

Salazar began laughing. Bines wasn't sure if he had ever heard him laugh before. "Inappropriate? We have been in bed together for far too long for you to start making protestations of your virtue."

"I am an officer of the court," Bines said.

"You say that with pride, but the only difference between you and those who work on their backs is that your hourly wage is so much more expensive than theirs. And so much less gratifying."

Bines could feel his throat tighten. Salazar had a reputation as a great philanthropist. The stated purpose of his international foundation, the Global Union Manifest (GUM), was to advance justice throughout the world. Those in many progressive camps liked to proclaim themselves as "gummies" or "gummy bears." But by no stretch of the imagination was Geo Salazar a gummy bear, or the good guy he pretended to be.

"I assume you called me for a reason other than offering insults."

Salazar said, "No insult was intended. I merely offered what seemed to me was a needed reality check. As for the purpose of my call, I wanted to discuss the amicus brief you filed last week."

"Amicus brief?" Bines said, puzzled. An amicus brief was filed by nonlitigants in cases where interested parties wished to make their opinions known. The Latin translation of *amicus curiae* meant "friend of the court." An outsider writing the kind of brief Salazar described was essentially endorsing the action.

"I filed no such brief."

"The record speaks to the contrary."

"There must be some mistake."

"No mistake. We took one of those law firm letterheads where your name is so prominently featured and attached it as a cover letter to the legal document that you filed in an ongoing appellate court case."

"What!" yelled an outraged Bines.

"It's only a three-page opinion."

"You're telling me *my name* was put on an amicus curiae brief. *My name.*"

"That's right. We had a need to use *your* name. Aren't you the voice of reason for the media? Don't they always call upon you to comment on the legal story of the day? And didn't you tell me you had thousands of Twitter followers?"

"You make my point," Bines said. "All those are reasons I need to be protective of my name and what it stands for."

"I doubt whether your amicus brief will get much attention, but should anyone take notice, I am certain you will be able to justify your arguments."

"You submitted a forged document to an appellate court, and I'm supposed to go along with that?"

"You are paid more than an ample sum to go along with it."

"What case?" Bines said.

"It was one that you didn't want to dirty your hands with. You might remember its particulars. I wanted you to challenge the government's age restrictions requiring all H2B workers to be eighteen and older. Our position is that the legal age should be lowered to fifteen so as to allow the kind of internship programs that exist in many countries around the world. When you begged off representing my interests, I retained another firm to take up the action."

"I told you in good conscience I couldn't take that case," Bines said. "I was against the idea of minors entering the workplace."

"And I accepted your decision."

"Yet you submitted an amicus brief in my name that supports positions you knew I was not comfortable endorsing?"

"Everything in the brief was in keeping with your usual First Amendment arguments and your well-documented distrust of the government overstepping its bounds and impinging upon individual freedoms."

The knot in Bines's stomach loosened a little. Maybe the amicus brief wasn't as bad as he'd feared.

Bines said, "Were those arguments solely applied to adults they might very well fly, but that is not the case. We're talking about children here."

"That's where your brilliant legal mind took on ageism," Salazar said, not sparing his sarcasm. "In the brief you referenced American cultural exceptionalism and detailed how it was out of step with much of the world."

For a moment, Bines couldn't speak. This was worse, far worse, than he ever could have imagined. "That's—that's—"

He struggled to find a word adequate to his outrage, but couldn't.

Salazar blithely continued, "I'm not saying we'll win this case, but it will give us traction for the next case, and the one after that. If we can erode the laws bit by bit, we will ultimately prevail."

"Do you realize that by signing my name to that brief, you have put my legal reputation in jeopardy, and potentially undermined my effectiveness in working the Welcome Mat case?"

"*A mal tiempo, buena cara*," Salazar said.

"What the hell does that mean?"

"It's a Spanish saying that translates to, 'In bad weather, a good face.'"

"Having a good face won't help me represent your interests in court, especially if I have the reputation of being morally bankrupt."

"Oh, that's right. I forgot that you are a man of the people, and fight for the rights of individuals."

"I need to withdraw that amicus brief," Bines said. "I'll say someone in my office mistakenly sent it. I won't go on record publicly defending the notion that a fifteen-year-old child from another country should be allowed to enter the workplace and treated like an adult. My daughter is fifteen. I am of the belief that she and all other teenagers need to be afforded the protections that come with being a minor."

Salazar made tsk-tsk sounds. "I am afraid you painted a very different picture in your amicus brief. You pointed out that culturally, and historically, the notion of adulthood has been an extremely fluid concept. Even the age of consent, as you so sagely noted, isn't something necessarily written in stone. Was not Romeo's beloved Juliet only thirteen years of age when she succumbed to his charms? That work of fiction, as you were quick to note, was certainly within the norms of its time."

"This is insane! I am your advocate. What possible advantage is there in setting me up as your fall guy?"

"Don't be a drama queen. At most, you have dirtied your hands, even though they have never been nearly as clean as you've imagined them to be. We needed a spokesperson to go along with the positions we are advocating. You were the logical choice."

"Who is 'we'?"

"Friends of mine. The same friends who have significant, if not visible, positions in Welcome Mat Hospitality."

There were long-standing rumors of Salazar being involved with criminal enterprises. When Bines had first begun representing Salazar, he had thought he could keep clear of those potential entanglements and not have to be concerned about the Spaniard's silent business partners.

But sometimes there was no avoiding stepping on gum, despite your best efforts to avoid it. And when that happened, the gum somehow found its way into clothing and hair.

"I am asking that my name be removed from the amicus brief," Bines said.

"*Hacer la vista gorda.*"

"You know I don't speak Spanish."

"Then I will translate. The literal translation is 'do the fat view,' but what the saying really means is that you should pretend not to notice what is being thrown your way."

"You've seen to the forging of my name, and the counterfeiting of my words, and that's all you have to say?"

"Consider it good advice. If your brief generates any attention, ignore whatever is said."

"You would have me go about pretending I agree with positions totally antithetical to what I believe?"

"You are paid to believe what I want you to believe."

"That's not how it works."

"So, you dictate to me now? When your partners learn of this noble stand of yours, will they admire your taking the moral high ground, especially after I take my business to another firm?"

Bines didn't answer.

"I thought as much. And do acquaint yourself with your amicus brief. As its author, you need to know its particulars."

Salazar clicked off, and Bines found himself staring at his phone. Among his peers, Bines had the reputation of being calm and collected. Nothing was supposed to be able to shake him, but at the moment his hands were trembling uncontrollably.

Bines was reminded of a story he'd once heard that was supposedly attributed to George Bernard Shaw. During the course of Shaw's conversation with a beautiful actress, the playwright asked if she would consider going to bed with him for a million pounds.

The actress said, "For a million pounds? Why, yes."

Then Shaw asked, "Would you go to bed with me for a sixpence?"

The actress indignantly replied, "What do you take me for?"

Shaw said to her, "We've already established that. Now we're just quibbling over price."

That's what he and Salazar had been establishing, thought Bines. His price. Along with the price of his soul.

XXXII

Deke and Gina bypassed a markedly smaller media contingent compared to the last time they'd been at the Richard B. Russell Federal Building. Storm's revelation about being sexually trafficked on the truck circuit was now yesterday's news. Most of the media was following something newer and shinier.

Only eight individuals were being allowed into the closed courtroom of Judge Allen Irwin. Deke and Gina entered ten minutes early. Bines and his team, which consisted of another lawyer as well as a paralegal, were already seated. Deke was used to the defendant's legal team making a show of force in their numbers, but today the wolf pack—what the plaintiff's lawyers called the opposition—had decided that three representatives were more than sufficient for a proceeding that they likely believed wouldn't even require their participation.

Judge Irwin was ten minutes late. Deke suspected his tardiness was all about making an entrance. Irwin wanted a show of power, because he believed such empowered him.

Gina was busy studying her notes, and Deke knew better than to interrupt her. Normally he felt at home in the courtroom, but today he was a passenger, not the driver. Gina's directive to him was to let her do all the talking. Deke knew it made sense, but relinquishing control still didn't come easy for him.

Deke looked at his watch. Again. This was the only case on Irwin's docket for the day. Without anything else to do, Deke studied the rest of the captive audience. Nathan Bines was supporting his chin with his hand and looked preoccupied. Usually Bines went around with a self-satisfied little smile; today he was frowning. Something was bothering him, Deke thought. That brightened his outlook a little.

The bailiff and court reporter were positioned at the ready. Both appeared to be daydreaming. In their jobs there was a lot of hurry up and wait.

Deke turned his eyes to the trappings of the court, including the flags and displays. It was ironic, thought Deke, that the Northern District Court of Georgia was located in the Richard B. Russell Federal Building. Atlanta was home to arguably the most vibrant African American community in the country, which was at odds with the name on the building. During his long tenure as a United States senator, Russell had done all he could to block civil rights. As a strong supporter of racial segregation, Russell had defended white supremacy. Having his name on the building was almost akin to its flying the Dixie flag. It was a shame, Deke thought, that Russell hadn't lived long enough to see Atlanta's renaissance of African Americans.

"Quit fidgeting," Gina whispered.

Deke realized he was shaking his foot. "Sorry," he said.

Thankfully, the judge chose that moment to grace them with his presence. The bailiff called for all to rise, waited for Judge Irwin to sit, then told everyone to be seated.

After the court came to order, Judge Irwin said, "I don't expect this proceeding to take very long. Last week Mr. Deketomis offered his thoughts to the media in regards to a case that was proceeding under a gag order.

"Transcripts of what Mr. Deketomis said have been provided to all plaintiffs and defendants in this action. There is no refuting that Mr. Deketomis's comments violated this court's order. Some might try and excuse his behavior as the theatrics of a lawyer merely venting. Were that the case, we would not be here."

Judge Irwin stared at Deke, shook his head and offered up a regretful sigh, then continued.

"You suggested, Mr. Deketomis, that my restrictive order when it came to making public any comments on the case was somehow unfair, despite its having been equally applied to both parties in this action. One of your major points of contention was that everyone should have the right to a fair trial. In that, I couldn't agree with you more.

"How can the defendant have a fair trial with you making your case to the media? What you did, and the comments you made, was akin to jury tampering. Your failure to follow the rules could yet result in all sorts of negative repercussions. When we try and seat a jury, how many potential jurors will be disqualified because they were witness to your televised rant?"

Deke could taste the blood in his mouth from biting down on the inside of his cheek. What the court record wouldn't show, but that was clearly in evidence, was Irwin's visible pleasure at twisting the knife in him.

The judge continued his sermon. "There are consequences to such actions, Mr. Deketomis. As an officer of the court, you cannot engage in such egregious disregard of the rules of law and make a mockery of the system. I am not rebuking you for any personal slights you made that were directed at me, but I am sanctioning you for challenging the standing of this court. It seems you think you are above the law, Mr. Deketomis. That is not the case. You are supposed to be acting in accordance with the law, and abiding by the jurisdiction of this court, but instead you have done the opposite by challenging this court's rulings, and violating its pronouncements."

Deke could feel the veins on his forehead pulsating. Gina must have sensed his rage. Although no one could see, she reached out and lightly patted his clenched hand. Her human touch allowed Deke to begin breathing again.

"As you know, Mr. Deketomis, I am within my rights to have you removed from this case. I have no doubt that many judges would do just that, but I am hoping by allowing you some forbearance in this matter that you will not ultimately force me into having to take that step. This court chooses to give you the benefit of the doubt, whether merited or not. I will allow you the opportunity to learn from your mistakes, Mr. Deketomis. I don't know if that will be possible for you to achieve, but let us hope for both of our sakes that it does. Let me reiterate that a gag order is in place, and that you are prohibited from commenting in regards to the Welcome Mat Hospitality case. Should you violate that order again, the consequences will be most severe. Is that understood?"

Grinding his teeth, Deke managed to say, "Yes, Your Honor."

Although Deke tried not to show it, the process was about as painless as chewing down on sharp shards of glass.

"The court has already received your written apology, Mr. Deketomis, and it has been entered into the record. While I appreciate your admission of being at fault, the seriousness of your offense cannot be mitigated by a mere apology."

Deke made a point of not reacting. He wasn't surprised that Irwin was opting to be punitive, but didn't want to give the judge any additional satisfaction from displaying his anger. Deke's poker face was at odds with Irwin's self-satisfied, even smug expression.

Irwin said, "At this point of time, should you like to address the court, I would like to hear from either you or your counsel before passing judgment."

Gina stood up. "If it pleases the court, Your Honor, I am Gina Romano representing Mr. Deketomis in this motion to show cause."

"Proceed, Ms. Romano," the judge said.

"Yes, Your Honor."

Gina turned to Deke, nodded, then looked back at Irwin. "Your Honor, I would like to introduce you to Mr. Nick Deketomis."

Irwin's eyebrows wrinkled, his puzzlement evident. "I am well acquainted with Mr. Deketomis, counselor."

"My mistake, Your Honor," Gina said, pretending contriteness. "I assumed you didn't know Mr. Deketomis based on some of your statements today. I would like to speak to the character of Mr. Deketomis, since it was somehow suggested that he does not fully understand his obligation to this court, or to society."

Gina was counting on Irwin giving her latitude, especially after already having had his say. Both Deke and Gina knew the judge had carefully chosen his words throughout the proceeding so as to appear evenhanded in the court record and not offer any obvious grounds for an appeal. Because he was constrained by trying to appear above reproach, it required him to let Gina speak.

"Go on," he said, the words begrudgingly offered.

"Thank you, Your Honor. For the record, I believe no one has more respect for the law than Mr. Deketomis. As a lawyer, he has few rivals. In fact, he was one of the youngest lawyers ever inducted into the Trial Lawyer Hall of Fame. As for his understanding of the law, Mr. Deketomis has prevailed in some of the biggest court cases in history, winning billions of dollars for the plaintiffs he has represented.

"More than the money, though, Mr. Deketomis can take justifiable pride in the causes he has championed, and the lives he has saved. By my conservative estimate, Mr. Deketomis has saved upward of fifty thousand lives. That might sound unlikely, if not impossible, but through his efforts Mr. Deketomis has had dangerous drugs pulled from the market and toxic chemicals banned from these shores, and has won landmark decisions against hazardous products that maimed and killed. The work that Mr. Deketomis has done has been remarkably beneficial to our entire American culture and to our way of thinking. When I state that Mr. Deketomis directly and indirectly saved fifty thousand lives, I haven't even taken into account the tobacco or opioids wars where my partner, of whom I am incredibly proud, served on the front lines on behalf of injured victims. If we were to include those figures, I don't doubt that Mr. Deketomis has saved well over one hundred thousand lives. Is that not a tangible benefit to our entire society? In going up against the corporations who caused the tobacco and opioid disasters, Mr. Deketomis was there for the mothers, fathers, sisters, and brothers whose lives were turned upside down by nothing less than corporate manslaughter."

The longer Gina spoke, the more florid was Judge Irwin's face. He didn't like what he was hearing and finally interrupted.

"I think you've made your point, Ms. Romano," he said, trying to cut her off.

"That was background information, Your Honor. If you let me continue, I will get to my point."

"Let's hope so," he said, gesturing with his hand for her to speak.

"This court has chosen to punish Mr. Deketomis for violating a gag order. I wish to go on record now and state that we are more than ready to challenge the propriety of that gag order in appellate court."

The court became preternaturally silent. What Gina had just done was throw down the judicial gauntlet and proclaim her willingness to challenge the court on appeal.

Gina continued speaking. "Mr. Deketomis had no choice but to speak out on the patently unfair order limiting his effectiveness to represent the plaintiffs. Your order clearly favored corporate interests at the expense of the public's interest. The public needs to know the risks associated with criminally forced prostitution. In our action we represent girls who were as young as thirteen when they were first lured into their terrible bondage."

Deke was suddenly enjoying his time in court. The redder Irwin's face, the better he felt. As a spectator, Deke was able to take the measure of the court. What surprised him most was the reaction of Nathan Bines. Gina's words seemed to be hitting him like body blows.

"When there is a clear and present danger as profound as human slavery, Your Honor, we believe it our moral responsibility as officers of the court to make that danger known to the public. It is our contention that public safety should never be put at risk by judicial overreach. And frankly, we believe it is time that appellate courts begin to better analyze that issue."

Irwin had heard enough. "You are getting dangerously close to being cited for contempt of court, counselor."

"I apologize, Your Honor, if any of my remarks were construed as being disrespectful to this court, but I thought it necessary to explain why my client had acted as he did. I know your specialty was corporate law, Your Honor, and not trial law."

Deke allowed himself a small smile. Gina's "apology" was actually a way of pointing out Judge Irwin's complete lack of experience as a trial lawyer. If only, Deke wished, that wasn't now so commonplace in America's courtrooms.

Gina kept talking, not even pausing to take a breath for fear of giving Irwin an opportunity to shut her down.

"You said your gag order was equally applied to both sides, Your Honor, but how is that possible? That statement is, at best, a false equivalency. Your ruling did not impact Mr. Bines and his team in the least. In fact, I am sure Mr. Bines was completely delighted when a gag order was applied to this case, especially after the singer Storm's comments about being sexually trafficked in truck stops resulted in media attention. Silence is Mr. Bines's complicit ally; silence serves the corporate interests he represents. If your corporation was killing American consumers with defective drugs or toxic chemicals, would you not be thrilled by the prospect that those murderous misdeeds couldn't be disclosed to the public?"

Deke was surprised Bines didn't object. Judging by Irwin's expression, he also found it strange. The judge glanced over to Bines, as if willing him to say something, but the lawyer remained mute.

Forging ahead, Gina said, "As stated earlier, we contend that our duty to warn the public of imminent danger takes precedence over any gag order. Mr. Deketomis was particularly concerned that parents needed to be aware of the threats that face their minor children. While Mr. Bines contends that this case is about protecting individual freedoms and reining in governmental overreach as applied to restricting business, he was uncharacteristically silent in discussing the merits of his case even before you applied your restrictive order. In fact, your gag order actually spared him from having to provide fashion statements as to the emperor's new clothes, and what is there and, more importantly, not there."

Judge Irwin turned his attention from Gina to Bines, but his obvious hint was still not acted upon. Without any stop sign placed in her way, Gina floored it.

"While preparing for this motion to show cause, I came upon an amicus brief that Mr. Bines submitted only last week. In this brief Mr. Bines contended that H2B workers should be allowed to work in this country starting at the age of fifteen. In fact, Mr. Bines went so far as to imply that when it comes to the age of consent, American exceptionalism shouldn't preclude our taking into account the mores of much of the world. In other words, when it comes to consent, he believes fifteen is the new eighteen."

Deke actually saw Bines wince.

The runaway train that was Gina kept speaking: "As you know, our undercover investigation into trucking and hospitality revealed an epidemic of minors being forced into sex slavery. If fifteen-year-old H2B workers are allowed into this country, there is no doubt in my mind that sex traffickers would try and target them. So why is it that Mr. Bines is advocating for that to happen? What shadowy interests is he representing?"

Deke saw Irwin look over to the defendant's table. "Mr. Bines," he said, his whisper a plea.

The prompt finally got through to the lawyer. "I object," Bines said.

Deke didn't think he'd ever heard a judge respond faster: "Sustained."

Gina said, "Your Honor, I—"

"I have allowed you more than ample time to make your record," Irwin said. "You will have the opportunity to add whatever you determine is relevant to the pleadings in your appeal."

"But Your Honor—"

"Not another word, Miss Romano, unless you want to spend the night in jail."

Deke knew the "damn the torpedoes, full speed ahead" look in Gina's eyes. As she opened her mouth to reply, Deke surreptitiously banged the side of her chair. Gina turned his way, took a read of his eyes, and swallowed her commentary.

Irwin's heavy, angry breathing could be heard throughout the courtroom. He turned his eyes to Deke, as if daring him to say or do anything to provoke him.

"Mr. Deketomis, you are sanctioned by this court, and are being fined fifty thousand dollars."

Deke refrained from saying that it was money well spent, though the expression on his face might have suggested that.

"The court is adjourned," Irwin said.

Mustering what dignity he could, the judge gathered his robes, then nodded to the bailiff.

"All rise," the bailiff said.

The judge was much faster in taking his leave of the courtroom than he had been to take his seat on the bench.

Hiding his smile, Deke whispered, "That's what you call a cool head?"

"Said the man who just got fined fifty thousand dollars," Gina said.

XXXIII

After their hour-long flight from Atlanta, Deke and Gina took leave of each other in the parking lot of Pensacola International Airport.

"Thanks for having my back," Deke told Gina.

"Irwin has certainly given us plenty to work with for a solid appeal," said Gina.

Deke's expression made it clear he wasn't thrilled with that prospect. "I'd rather win the case outright, even if this whole gag order abuse by the judiciary is something we need to keep attacking."

"Agreed, but as your lawyer, I have two final words of advice for you based on Irwin's directive. When approached by the media, your answer to everything is 'No comment.'"

Deke said, "If you promise to do the same, then I will as well."

The two hugged one another, then Gina got into her car and drove off.

* * *

Deke debated going into the office, or finishing off the day working at home. Despite the fact that he'd only been an observer in the courtroom, he couldn't ignore his tiredness. His drive home to Spanish Trace took him through Brownsville, an unincorporated area northwest of Pensacola. As he approached an intersection, Deke became aware of a woman standing next to a car with its hood up who was flagging him down. Without thinking, Deke immediately pulled over to the side of the road.

The woman said, "Thank god you stopped."

"Car trouble?" Deke asked.

"Life trouble," she said. "My phone isn't working, and my car broke down. What a great start to my vacation."

Despite her troubles, the woman gave him a big smile, which brightened her attractive features. She appeared to be in her early forties.

"Can I call you a tow truck?" Deke asked.

She hesitated a moment before saying, "That's very kind of you, but I think I'd prefer going the mobile mechanic route after I research my options from my motel."

"How can I help then?" he asked.

"If it's not too much trouble, can I impose upon you for a ride to where I'm staying? Even though I'm all turned around, I know the motel can't be much more than a mile or two from here."

"Glad to help," Deke said.

"Do you mind if I bring my golf clubs? I don't want to leave them in the car."

"No problem. I'll even be your caddy."

"I'm ever so grateful," she said, offering him her hand. "By the way, I'm Mindy."

He took her hand and said, "Deke."

After stowing her clubs in his trunk, Deke asked, "Where to?"

"To 'the Pensacola area's foremost lodging bargain,' or at least that's what the ad said. I think I better lodge a complaint with them to the BBB, or somebody. The place is a dump."

"Sounds like they target out-of-towners," Deke said.

"No doubt about it. As soon as I arrived, I tried to cancel my reservation, but they said because I hadn't given them a forty-eight-hour cancellation notice, they'd have to charge my credit card for one night's stay."

"So, do you have an address for the Pensacola area's foremost lodging bargain?"

She laughed. "Unfortunately, I do," she said, supplying him with an address on Cervantes Street. Deke entered the information into his GPS, which showed the motel was just under two miles away.

As they set out, he asked, "First time in this area?"

"How did you guess?"

Her reply made Deke laugh. "Where are you from?"

"I hail from a spot four hundred miles due north from here."

Deke thought about that and offered his guess: "Nashville?"

She nodded and said, "The Athens of the South."

"One of my favorite cities in the world."

"It's a lot more than just Music City," she agreed.

"What do you do there?" Deke said.

"I work in public relations."

"You're not a singer?"

"I think I'm the only person in Nashville who isn't," Mindy said.

Deke turned onto Cervantes Street. It looked long removed from pleasant dreams, or even the impossible dreams of Don Quixote.

"I'm beginning to think you should cancel your reservation and eat the cost. If you're short on funds, I'd be glad to cover a night's stay."

"That's a very generous offer, but I refuse to let you reward my stupidity."

"Better safe than sorry," he said.

"I'm supposed to be meeting a friend tonight for dinner. I'll be okay."

Deke pulled into the parking lot of her motel. What he saw didn't make him feel any better. "Offer still stands," he said.

"The room's interior is actually better than its exterior," she said, then added, "Thank heavens."

"How about I carry your clubs to the room?" he asked.

"You're a lifesaver, Deke."

Hoisting her bag, Deke followed her up a set of stairs to the second floor of the two-story motel. Mindy's room was halfway down the exterior walkway. She opened the door and Deke carried the clubs inside. A queen bed took up most of the room. As Deke put the bag down next to a small vanity, he heard the door close. Turning around, he saw Mindy walking toward him.

"I don't know how to thank you," Mindy said, but as she draped her arms around Deke's neck, it seemed she had an idea as to how to try.

Mindy tried pulling Deke close. He managed to avert his head while her lips sought his.

"Whoa!" said Deke, putting his hands on her arms while trying to disentangle himself.

"No?" she asked.

"No," he said.

"I'm sorry. I was sure you were giving off signals."

"It was a simple misunderstanding. Don't worry about it."

"I want you to know that I'm not in the habit of making passes," she said.

"Then I will take what happened as the great compliment it was," Deke said.

XXXIV

Deke was buzzed on his private line, interrupting the meeting taking place in his office.

"I'll try and make this quick," he announced to the four seated individuals.

When he picked up the line, Diana said, "I hate to intrude, but you have a call from Jack Stadler of the *American Enquirer*. Mr. Stadler says he needs your reaction to a story he's working on. I tried to take a message, but he insisted on talking to you, and said this might be your sole opportunity to respond to allegations he claims are being made against you."

"Sounds like classic ambush journalism," Deke said.

"Do you want me to tell him you're unavailable?"

"No, I'll take the call, but tell you what, have him stew for a minute before putting it through."

Deke thanked Diana, clicked off, and acknowledged the curious gazes of the others.

"A reporter from the *American Enquirer* wants to talk to me," he said.

Gina started shaking her head. "Remember our conversation yesterday? I stand by what I said, and I advise you to say nothing beyond, 'No comment.'"

Carol was quick to chime in. "That sounds like good advice."

"I'm not disagreeing, but I'm curious as to what story he's working on."

Carol wasn't done. "*American Enquirer*? I won't even line my bird-cage with that rag."

The weekly tabloid was known for being long on sensationalism and short on facts.

"I don't like the timing of his call, especially on the heels of what happened in court yesterday," Gina said.

Deke's phone began ringing. Motioning for silence, he picked up. "Nick Deketomis."

The caller said, "Mr. Deketomis, my name is Jack Stadler, and I'm a reporter with the *American Enquirer*. The reason for my call is I want to get your reaction to a story I'm working on."

Deke said, "Before we continue speaking, Mr. Stadler, I would like to not only tape this call but put you on speakerphone. Is that all right with you?"

"I have no problem with your doing that, Mr. Deketomis, but before you proceed, you should know that my story involves some very unsavory allegations being directed your way."

"Should I be surprised? That's the stock-in-trade of your paper, isn't it?"

"We stand by our stories." The reporter's voice could now be heard on speaker.

"You better not be standing downwind of those stories," Gina said.

Deke gave Gina a look, and she mouthed the word *sorry*.

"As you've surmised, you are on speaker, and this call is being recorded."

Stadler said, "That's fine by me. The piece I'm working on revolves around your apparent conflict of interest regarding the plaintiffs you are representing in the Welcome Mat Hospitality case."

"And what conflict of interest might that be?"

"My sources allege you have a long-standing history of consorting with prostitutes."

"*Consorting*?" Deke was barely able to control the outrage in his voice.

"How often do you hire prostitutes, Mr. Deketomis?"

The ugly question hung in the air. Gina began waving her hands, warning Deke to not respond. The faces of everyone in the room registered shock—Deke's most of all.

He allowed himself a moment of disgust before responding. "Since I want to be unequivocally clear about this, I'll speak slowly for you. I have never been with a prostitute in my entire life."

"You are stating for the record, then, that you don't frequent prostitutes, or avail yourself of escort services?"

Despite Gina signaling for him to hang up, Deke said, "That's exactly what I'm stating."

"Your claim is at odds with photographic evidence that has come into our possession," the reporter said. "We have pictures showing you spending time with an individual we determined is a very high-priced escort."

Deke again ignored Gina's gesture for him to cut off the call. "I can't explain any pictures you are referring to, other than to speculate they might have been photoshopped, which is something I don't doubt your paper has a history of doing. Aren't you known for running pictures of flying saucers and aliens?"

"The pictures we obtained were taken yesterday, Mr. Deketomis," he said.

"You're kidding." Deke knew his words were meant more for him than for the reporter.

"I'm not kidding. The photos show you in the company of a call girl."

"Unbelievable," Deke said.

"How long have you known this woman, and what is your relationship with her?" asked the reporter.

"I don't know this woman, and there is no relationship."

"Our sources assert that the only reason you are representing sex workers in their action is because you frequent them."

Deke was shaking his head in disbelief. "Yesterday I gave a ride to a woman who waved me down and told me her vehicle was disabled. Before stopping to help her, I had never seen her before. After taking this woman to her motel, I carried her golf clubs up to her room. I don't imagine I was in her room for more than a minute. If you are truly doing an investigative story, and not just a hit piece, you should be able to confirm everything I said."

"The pictures speak volumes, Mr. Deketomis."

"The only thing those pictures will show is that I was set up. I have told you exactly what happened. Now, you can roll the dice and run those pictures, but should you choose to do that I will do my best to bankrupt you, as well as your employer, in a jury trial."

"Don't you find it a strange coincidence that your personal life seems to be intersecting with your professional life?"

"The coincidence I find strange is how these pictures just happened to land on your desk, but I suppose I'll find that out when I take your deposition."

"My copy deadline is the day after tomorrow," the reporter said. "If you can provide any information that backs up your assertions, I will be glad to include it in my piece. I'll email you my contact information."

"I stand by what I already told you, Mr. Stadler."

Deke ended the call. No one in the room said anything, but waited on Deke to break the silence. Finally, he said, "I'm sorry, Gina. I'm sure I would have been better served had I just followed your advice from the onset. But right now, I'm pretty damn angry. And I'm kicking myself for being stupid enough to get blindsided."

Gina said, "You were set up. We'll show that."

"You think anything is going to stop the *American Enquirer* from running those pictures? They'll muddy the waters, give themselves an out with a disclaimer, and bury a retraction a few weeks from now."

"Not if I can help it," Carol said. "That story hasn't been filed. If we can provide incontrovertible evidence that it's false, we might get the powers that be at the *Enquirer* to kill it. We'll establish your time line from the airport, to the motel, to your home, through footage from security cameras. And we'll run a parallel investigation into identifying the woman that the reporter identified as an escort."

"Someone went to a lot of effort to make me look dirty," Deke said. "What do you want to bet that this woman is already out of the country and incommunicado?"

Carol said, "You're probably right, but that affords us an opportunity to investigate this fraud and discover its perpetrator."

"Bines?" Gina suggested.

Deke shook his head. "I can't see him engineering anything like this. Yesterday I got a chance to be an observer in the courtroom while you were doing all the work. The most surprising thing I witnessed was how Bines reacted during the proceeding. He acted preoccupied, except when you said things that I suspect struck close to home. In two or three instances, I even noticed him flinching. Those looked like tells."

Closing his eyes for a moment, Deke tried to visualize what he had seen and heard in the courtroom. What he remembered made him start nodding.

"Bines became agitated when you started focusing on his amicus brief where he advocated for the H2B inclusion of fifteen-year-olds. He almost looked guilty when you pointed out how teenage guest workers would be targeted by sex traffickers. Bines knew that what you were saying was true; the shame showed on his face."

"If it wasn't Bines who went after you, then it had to be someone associated with Welcome Mat," Gina said.

Deke wasn't sure about that. "Those are the obvious suspects, but what about the suspect, or suspects, we don't see?"

"I'm not following," Gina said.

"I could never understand why Nathan Bines took the Welcome Mat case. It wasn't in his usual wheelhouse. But what if he had been pressured into taking it? It looked to me as if he wanted to be anywhere but in that courtroom. His body language said the last thing he wanted to do was argue the merits of his own brief. I think you hit a nerve when you talked about him having to defend the emperor's new clothes. But who is the emperor?"

"You think someone gave him marching orders?"

"That's how it looked to me," Deke said. "And clearly Bines wasn't happy playing the role of foot soldier."

"Maybe Bines himself was blackmailed," Jake said.

"At the very least, I suspect someone has leverage over him."

"That kind of influence peddling doesn't come cheap," Carol said. "We can try and follow the money."

Deke cautiously nodded. "We could do that, but it would take time. I'm thinking a better way to go would be to follow the amicus brief."

Gina's eyes opened wide. "I like that. We might be able to figure out who Bines is fronting by studying his brief."

"We could conduct a legal search on similar briefs or cases," Michael added.

"Why stop there?" Gina said. "We'll look into those groups or organizations advocating similar positions to those put out in the brief. That might put some light on who went to so much effort to put Deke in a compromising position."

"As much as I appreciate everyone's concern, let's not forget why we're here," Deke said. "What happened to me is infuriating, but it's not life or death, whereas a lot of the matters you're working on are. If the story runs and temporarily blackens my eye, I can live with that. What I can't live with is you all dropping the ball on more important matters to try and help me. We're not going to let ourselves be distracted. Got it?"

Deke looked around the office, meeting the eyes of everyone there. Reluctantly, they all offered up nods.

"Good. Let's get back to what Michael was telling us. You said witnesses told you Vicky Driscoll was the one who arranged for her dancers to go out on her yacht *Seacreto*."

"Correct," Michael said.

"And you also said Nataliya was taken away by two men driving some large SUV with a camper shell and Nevada plates?"

"Yes, sir."

Deke looked at his notes. "And the bouncer, Andrei, told you that the bigger of the two men went by the nickname of Keebler. Is that right?"

Michael nodded.

"You must be an amazing conversationalist, Michael, to have both the club manager and its bouncer opening up to you like they did. You care to tell us how you got them to be so forthcoming?"

Speaking carefully, Michael said, "The manager followed me into the men's room at the club, where he drew a gun on me. I defended myself and removed the threat. Self-defense dictated my responses. It was *only* after he attacked me that I asked him questions."

Jake wasn't going to leave Michael sitting alone in the hot seat. "I want to make it clear that I backed Michael's decisions based on the circumstances we found ourselves in."

"You thought it wise for Michael to take on an armed thug?"

"I don't think it's wise for *anyone* to take on an armed thug."

Deke couldn't help but smile at the barb thrown his way. "After finishing your *talk* with the manager, Michael, you went and *talked* to the bouncer. How did that conversation come about?"

"He attacked me as well. Only after he charged at me, and tried to take me down, did I respond with force."

"Force?" Deke asked.

Michael said, "There is audio confirming everything I've just told you. The tape recording documents the attacks on my person, and the threats directed my way."

"And you don't think that having such a recording shows premeditation?" Deke asked.

"In Florida, you have a right to defend yourself."

Deke didn't hide his skepticism. "You're arguing this was a 'stand your ground' situation?"

"I believe that could be successfully argued, but I also believe it will never be necessary to make that argument."

"And what makes you think that?"

"I'm pretty sure that neither man will want to discuss the outcomes of our interactions, as the stories did not end well for either one of them. And their speaking about what occurred would not enhance their prospects for continued employment."

Carol's glower put an end to Michael's account. Deke unsuccessfully tried to hide his smile.

"Don't encourage them," Carol said. "I already read Frick and Frack the riot act."

"I would never encourage that kind of behavior," Deke said, winking.

"You're all children," Carol said in mock reprimand.

"What else?" Deke asked.

Michael continued, "The bouncer told me that a few months ago, Driscoll lured Nataliya out of the back of the strip club to the delivery lot, where the two men from Nevada were waiting for her. That wasn't the only time Andrei saw those guys. Last week they showed up again at the compound where I was told the workers are being housed, a remote area not far from DeFuniak Springs, and this time they took away an American girl."

"Where? Who? Why?"

Michael shook his head. "I wished I'd had time to press him further. Perhaps I can interview him again."

"Not a chance," Carol said.

"As much as I'd like the idea of you getting a redo with him, I'm afraid Carol is right," Gina said. "In court we could explain away one encounter, but not a second."

"Any update on Nataliya?" Deke asked.

Carol said, "We passed on her last name to UCSIS and are waiting to hear back from them."

"Let's hope they're more responsive this time," Deke said.

"In their defense, citizenship and immigration is overwhelmed," Carol said. "Every year there are more visa overstays than there are illegal immigrants. I was told there are at least six hundred thousand people with visa overstays currently living in this country. It's no wonder the disappearance of Nataliya Nahorny didn't raise any red flags, especially if her employer explained it by saying she ran off."

"Let's make sure we get a complete background on her, and what, if anything, Mrs. Driscoll told UCSIS. I know Michael's chomping at the bit to depose Vicky, but before that happens we need to make sure he's got all the ammunition he needs. Speaking of which, what's the latest on Karina Boyko and the party boat?"

Carol said, "Miami Maritime Investigations has run into a little complication with the tracking of the *Seacreto*. The yacht left its marina the day after the fall squall and hasn't been seen since. They're on that. In the meantime, they were able to view footage from the marina's

CCTV. It's grainy, but they confirmed five women went out, but only four women came back. They're trying to make positive ID on the missing woman being Karina."

"What about the *Seacreto*'s other passengers?" Deke asked.

"The footage doesn't show any other passengers either coming or going."

Deke's brows furrowed. "Explain that."

"I can't, and neither can Miami Maritime. The logical assumption is there was a meetup offshore. They are gathering footage from all nearby marinas and yacht clubs to see who went out during the time in question."

"That sounds like Dark Ghoul's MO," Michael said. "They're experts at keeping to the shadows, especially if they're engaged in something illegal."

"Karina still seems determined to speak to us from the beyond," Carol said. "I'm taking that as a sign she wants to be heard. By using her vyshyvanka tattoo, the Ukrainian investigator we hired has already located her mother."

"Great news," Deke said.

Carol's body language suggested something else. "Unfortunately, we were the bearers of bad news. Mrs. Boyko was unaware that her daughter had died."

Deke shook his head. "Poor woman."

"She was understandably distraught," Carol said. "But as upset as Mrs. Boyko was, she didn't blame the messenger. She told the operative she wants justice for Karina, and wants to go after those who were responsible for her death."

"I've arranged for a Ukrainian translator and will be talking to Mrs. Boyko tomorrow," Michael said.

"Let's give Karina the justice she deserves, and more," Deke said.

Everyone nodded. There were no smiles; just grim resolve.

XXXV

What Deke hated most about the allegation that he was a serial john was the likely impact it would have on his wife. Only three years ago, Deke had been wrongfully accused of murder. The knives had come out when his back was exposed, and Teri had been forced to bear the brunt of the attacks. He feared that was how it would play out again.

Despite Deke telling the others to not involve themselves in the campaign being waged against him, his defenders had ignored his stated wishes and on their own time had tried to establish a time line using photographic evidence that should have killed the story.

Should have.

Judging by the conversation taking place at that moment between Gina and the managing editor of the *American Enquirer*, it didn't appear that would be the case.

". . . and the horse you rode in on," Gina said.

Gina waited to hear a response, but there wasn't one. She looked at her phone, shook her head, and said to Deke, "He hung up."

"And you're surprised?"

"That bastard knows everything was a setup," she said.

"At least you got his promise that they'll detail our denials, along with our time line."

"They're still going to run one or more of the pictures, and you know what they say about a picture being worth a thousand words."

"More like a thousand lies," Deke said.

"Especially if they run the picture with some clever headline like,

Hooker Lawyer Caught in Cozy Embrace." She shook her head. "I'm sorry, Deke."

Deke pretended to be unfazed by what he knew was going to be ugly. "I've been in worse spots."

"After the story comes out, we need to go after your accuser, as well as the publisher of the *American Enquirer.*"

They had discovered that "Mindy's" real name was Madeline Parsons, an escort who worked out of Atlanta and provided companionship to "older, successful gentlemen." According to her still-active website, an evening of her "discreet" company came with a price tag of two thousand dollars.

Deke said, "She'll say it was a case of mistaken identity, at which time the *Enquirer* will print their retraction right under some advertisement for adult diapers."

Gina nodded, but her attention was still directed at her phone. Sounding surprised, she said, "Hannah Barber, the legal correspondent for the *New York Times*, left me a message. She wants to interview me for a story she's working on."

Deke's groan was visceral. "You don't think the *Times* is dignifying the *Enquirer's* gutter journalism, do you?"

"I doubt it. Usually their focus is on important legal issues, or court battles."

"Call her," Deke said.

Using her cell phone, Gina called the reporter's number. Barber picked up on the first ring.

"Thank you for calling me back, Ms. Romano," she said. "I understand you represented Mr. Deketomis in a motion to show cause hearing earlier this week in Atlanta. I'm interested in what took place."

"I'm sorry, Ms. Barber. Judge Irwin has put a gag order on the Welcome Mat Hospitality case, so I really can't comment."

The reporter said, "I don't need you to directly comment, but I would like you to confirm what I have heard from others."

Gina had turned up the volume of her phone, and was holding it out so Deke could hear as well.

"Why don't you ask your questions, Ms. Barber, and I'll decide if it's appropriate to comment."

"Thank you. Is it all right with you if I tape this conversation?"

"Go right ahead," Gina said.

"Ms. Romano, it was reported that Mr. Deketomis was sanctioned by the court, and your firm was fined fifty thousand dollars."

After a short eye consultation with Deke, Gina replied, "That's correct."

"And I understand that during the proceeding you vigorously defended Mr. Deketomis after he was upbraided by the judge."

"I can't comment on that specifically, but I will say that I vigorously defend all of my clients."

"Understood. But for the sake of clarity, I'm told that in the courtroom you challenged the impartiality and validity of Judge Irwin's gag order and further amplified upon Mr. Deketomis's publicized remarks."

Gina mouthed the letters *WTF* to Deke before responding, "I'm afraid I can't talk about that, Ms. Barber."

"I have it on good authority that you told the judge that because you and Mr. Deketomis were officers of the court, that it was your moral responsibility to alert the public to the known dangers of sex trafficking, and that public safety should always trump judicial overreach. Is that accurate?"

Deke began writing on a legal pad, and held it up for Gina to see. A single word was written: *Source?*

"Where did you hear this, Ms. Barber?" Gina asked.

"I can't reveal that, but as I explained at the onset of our conversation, the purpose of this call is to merely confirm what has been stated to me on the record."

Deke wrote something else on his pad and held it up: *Comment generally, not specifically.*

"I can't discuss what occurred in the courtroom, but our firm has a long history of advocating for public health and safety. And I do think that young women, in particular, need to be cautioned about the predatory practices of human traffickers."

"Do you deny that you told Judge Irwin that his gag order serves corporate interests?"

Deke and Gina exchanged glances. Finally, Deke wrote: *Non-denial denial?*

"Ms. Romano?" asked the reporter.

"I can't comment specifically, but I will say that I'm not a fan of gag orders being weaponized."

"I'm told Judge Irwin threatened to hold you in contempt of court."

"I think that's something you had better ask Judge Irwin," Gina said.

"I already have a call in to him."

Deke covered his mouth to mute his laugh.

"Well, good luck with that," Gina said.

"One more question, Ms. Romano, and I don't think it violates the gag order muzzling you."

"Ask it."

"Did you say to Mr. Bines that it fell to him to have to defend the emperor's new clothes?"

Deke offered a thumbs-up to Gina.

"I might have said something like that," Gina said.

The legal correspondent laughed. "That might be part of our headline."

Gina's smile bespoke her approval. But the idea of something else appealed to her even more. "It would make an even better illustration."

"Illustration?" The reporter sounded confused.

"I make that suggestion off the record, of course, but just imagine the visual of Judge Irwin wearing only a white horsehair wig."

"We don't do those kinds of illustrations in our daily paper," the reporter said.

"Pity."

"But sometimes illustrations are used in our Sunday magazine."

"God, I love the First Amendment," Gina said.

"Thank you for your time, Ms. Romano."

"It was truly a pleasure, Ms. Barber."

XXXVI

The demographics of Bay County Florida skewed very Republican, very white, and very conservative. Near the entrance to the Bay County Courthouse, however, was a historical marker that offered up a short history lesson to passersby, a reminder that even in the unlikeliest spots, landmark civil rights cases can take root.

In 1961, Clarence Earl Gideon was charged with breaking and entering into a pool hall in Panama City. Because Gideon couldn't afford a lawyer, he requested that an attorney be appointed to represent him, but was told that Florida only provided attorneys to indigent defendants whose crimes could result in the death penalty if they were found guilty. After Gideon was convicted, he petitioned the Florida Supreme Court for release because of his not having had a defense attorney present at his hearing. In 1963, the United States Supreme Court overturned his conviction in their landmark case of *Gideon v. Wainwright*. Their unanimous conclusion was that all defendants had a right to counsel. In the more than fifty years since that ruling, the rights of the indigent to receive legal representation had become an accepted part of American jurisprudence. In fact, those arrested were informed of this during the reading of their Miranda rights.

Just as few could have imagined a landmark civil rights case emerging out of Bay County, neither did it seem likely that a state court judge like Kenneth Mobley would be practicing at its courthouse. The iconoclastic African American judge was not afraid to question the usual conventions of the day. Mobley could not be categorized as either liberal or conservative, but more as a free thinker who didn't adhere to any singular ideology. He based his rulings on the tenets of the law, along with the litmus test of his soul.

From the privacy of his chambers, Mobley sorted through the morning's paperwork that had been prepared by his staff. Mobley's chambers were on the small side when compared to those of his peers around the country. The yellow-brick Bay County Courthouse had been built in 1915, and although its neoclassical architecture was pleasing to the eye, the structure had never been designed to serve the 185,000 residents that now lived within the county's borders.

Still, the best read of a judge often wasn't seen in the courtroom as much as it was in their chambers. Mobley's chambers were warm and personal. It contained the requisite legal library, of course, but the volumes didn't look like a photo-opportunity backdrop as they did in so many other chambers. Framed pictures dominated the space, the biggest of which showed Martin Luther King Jr. walking arm in arm with others during the Selma to Montgomery march in 1965. The judge rarely advertised the fact that one of the individuals walking in the vicinity of King was his father. The picture was significant to the judge because a year after it had been taken, his father had disappeared. Although his body never turned up, federal law enforcement was convinced that the senior Mobley had been murdered. At the time of his disappearance, Kenneth Mobley had only been five years old.

Even with the void of his father not being in his life, the apple ultimately did not fall far from the tree. Just like his father before him, Judge Mobley was passionate about civil rights.

As he drank his morning coffee, the judge began reviewing a motion that had been filed for not only an expedited hearing, but an expedited deposition. The requests in themselves were unusual; expedited relief was not something normally granted. The more Judge Mobley read, though, the more the motion intrigued him. Among its allegations were wrongful death, false imprisonment, and violations of RICO statutes.

At its heart, Kenneth Mobley recognized that the motion was asserting the ongoing violations of the civil rights of H2B workers. These individuals, the motion stated, were in potential if not actual danger.

Mobley loved his country, but he hated its notoriously short attention span. It wasn't until 1965 that most of the country's Jim Crow laws—which enforced racial segregation—were ruled unconstitutional. Before his death, his father along with many others had worked tirelessly to advocate that those laws be struck down. For too many years, those efforts had been for naught; judges who knew better, but shirked their duty to their office and to the Constitution; judges who refused to do the right thing and found excuses to turn a blind eye and deaf ear to the civil rights arguments made in their courtrooms. It wasn't until after the Civil Rights Act of 1964 was passed that courts across the country were forced to do what was right. If the courts hadn't erred on the side of caution for so long, Judge Mobley wondered if his father's life might have been spared.

He read through the motion again. The judge was well aware that the lawyer for the plaintiffs was asking for a Trojan horse. His hope—his Hail Mary pass, some might say—was that if granted an expedited discovery, he would have the chance to gather evidence that might otherwise be denied him. It was a fishing expedition, of course. But was it a fishing expedition that was merited?

Mobley thought of his father and the protests he'd led against Jim Crow laws. The vestiges of slavery had died hard—or maybe, if the allegations in this motion were accurate, they hadn't died at all.

The lawyer wanted immediate deposition access so as to allow him to ask his questions, and ask them without delay. Although Judge Mobley was familiar with the firm of Bergman/Deketomis, the lawyer who had filed the motion was unknown to him.

That was about to change, the judge decided. He would give Mr. Michael Carey a chance to make his arguments for expedited discovery, as well as an expedited hearing, in person.

Mobley opened his court calendar. There had been a cancellation; three weeks from now there was an opening. Judge Mobley wrote a note to his court clerk to immediately contact the parties and schedule the expedited hearing on his docket.

XXXVII

P eter Stone had warned Vicky Driscoll to not contact him unless it was an emergency and stressed that all communication needed to go through his encrypted email. An hour earlier she had sent up an email flare saying they needed to talk, and Stone had responded by telling her when to expect his call. In addition to having an encrypted phone line, Stone took the extra precaution of making the return call using a voice changer.

"You said we needed to talk."

"Your voice?" she said, put off by his strange-sounding speech.

"Don't worry about it," Stone said. The app he was using gave him the voice of Darth Vader.

"Papers arrived today from a lawyer," she said, her voice shrill. "Legal papers. Lots and lots of pages. They look like trouble, bad trouble."

"You're being sued?"

She whispered her answer. "Yes. In the papers there is the name Karina Boyko everywhere. They know she was one of my H2B workers, and they say I'm responsible for wrongful death. When her body turned up in the ocean, I was afraid bad things would happen. Her spirit won't rest."

"It's her lawyer you need to worry about, not some spirit. Who is suing you?"

"Michael Carey is the name of the lawyer."

"Does he represent the US government, or the state of Florida?"

"Papers say he works for Bergman/Deketomis."

"Are they a local firm?"

"Main office is in Spanish Trace, Florida."

"That's good. He sounds like some local-yokel scum-sucking lawyer who thought he could make easy money by shaking you down for your whore's death."

"Karina Boyko isn't the only name in the papers. How does this lawyer know about Nataliya Nahorny?"

"You're not making sense."

"Nataliya was a close friend of Karina's."

"Was?"

"She went away a few months ago."

"Where?"

Vicky paused before saying, "I don't know."

Stone got the sense that Vicky didn't want to know, at least not officially. The whore was definitely worried.

"You need to relax. In the next hour or two, I'll make sure you get contacted by a lawyer I know. He will make all your problems disappear. Understood?"

"Yes," she said.

Stone clicked off. And then he spat out an expletive. His curse sounded a lot harsher and uglier in his own voice than in Darth Vader's.

The whore was scared. She was worried about someone discovering all the skeletons in her closet. He didn't care about that. But he had to make sure her problems didn't become *his* problems.

That's where the Big Bad Wolf would come in.

BB Wolf—Barry Benjamin Wolf—was an attorney renowned for his scorched-earth tactics. If anyone could shut down the lawsuit, BB could. Ostensibly, he'd be serving the interests of Mrs. Driscoll, all the while reporting to his true client.

He hoped Mrs. Driscoll wasn't going to prove too much of a problem. Stone didn't like problems.

XXXVIII

Lily was afraid to speak, but it was just as scary as saying nothing. She had awakened to find Max standing at her bedroom window, the light of the moon illuminating him in the darkness. For the longest time she watched him, scared to do anything else. He appeared to be listening to something, occasionally nodding at what only he could hear.

That was bad enough, but what frightened her even more was when he spoke back to the void. Between her shaking and his indistinct speech, it was difficult to hear what he was saying. Maybe that was for the better, for what she *could* hear made her that much more afraid. Like what he was saying now.

"I will see to the proper timing of the sacrifice," he whispered.

As much as Lily wanted to believe otherwise, she was sure that Mad Max was talking about her. She stifled her urge to run out of the room, knowing there was no place to hide. Worse, her movements would awaken him to her presence.

If only she had some kind of weapon. For weeks now she had desperately searched for anything in her cage that was sharp or heavy. There was nothing. Lily had tried to make a knife from toilet paper, wetting and wrapping the paper into tight layers, but her efforts hadn't gone unnoticed. The cameras, she knew, had caught her. When her half-formed knife disappeared, Lily found a single playing card left in its place. A joker. It seemed as if the malevolent thing was sneering. His mocking look reminded her of Max.

Lily had been no more successful when she'd tried to create a flood by plugging up the bathtub. The floor wasn't even wet before Max was on the scene. There was no escaping the cameras, even though she did her best to keep her back to them.

With each day, Max seemed to become crazier. She watched and listened as her jailer continued to talk to something that was not there. Dare she sneak up on him? He was too strong for her to fight, but what if she surprised him from behind and tried to strangle him? She could twist her gown around his neck and use it like a garrote. Could she do it? Could she squeeze until he breathed his last?

Yes, she could. Lily visualized sneaking up on him. If she was to have a chance, she needed to be unnoticed, unseen. At least she wouldn't have to worry about him seeing her reflection as she approached. The treated windows didn't cast a reflection.

Max was absorbed in what was beyond the window; now was her chance. She needed to remove her gown, twist it silently, then creep up behind him. Lily considered every necessary step, then braced herself, as if getting ready to jump into icy water. Shifting under the covers, she began removing her gown. There was no rustling, no noise, but something alerted him. Lily froze as he turned his head slightly. The monster had awakened.

Could he divine her intentions? Was he smelling her desperation? Did he sense murder on her mind? That wasn't possible, of course, but Lily still felt the desperate need to do something to distract him. Say something, she thought, do something, anything.

"What are you looking at?" she asked.

"I stare at the abyss, and it stares back at me."

How in the hell was she supposed to respond to that?

"I turned around when I felt your green eyes upon me. I'm sensitive to the rays that they cast."

Max wasn't even hiding his eye obsession anymore. With each passing day of captivity, she was witness to his mask slipping off. Lily was afraid of what would happen when his creep show turned into a freak show.

"The Cheshire Cat smiles even when you cannot see it," he said. "Sometimes you see its complete form, and sometimes not. But always it laughs at you."

He pointed in the direction of the moonlight, as if that should explain his words. She didn't say anything, but Max was hearing something else. He tilted his head toward the window, as if trying to hear better.

"Yes, I agree, music is needed."

He turned back to Lily. "I would not insult you by playing Debussy's 'Clair de Lune.' The entire song is a fraud. He changed the title. It was supposed to be about a stroll. This is not a night for lies.

"Genie," Max called.

A female voice answered him from the ether. "What is your wish?"

"Play 'Let Slip the Madness,'" he commanded.

Hidden speakers revealed themselves; music began to play. At first Lily thought the song was a church requiem, but its contemplative notes did not last for long. Drums began pounding, and Max's head with them. He looked like some kind of freaky metalhead.

A low, gravelly voice began to roar, and Max joined in the singing: "Embrace now the dance of the dead, scream with the damned as your sanity is bled."

The speakers could not contain the beating of the drums. The room began shaking. Max joined in with the beat. He rattled the window, pounding it with his fists, then with his head, violently ramming himself into it. A trickle of blood began running from his forehead.

Lily tried covering her ears, tried to keep the madness from entering her head, but there was no relief. Max turned from the window to look at her. His eyes were large, black holes that were drawing Lily in.

Over the music he screamed, "Dance with me," and extended a hand her way.

Lily shook her head.

Droplets of blood were falling on his body. Max ran his fingers along the blood and painted his face. There was no looking away from him, as much as Lily wanted to.

His voice became more demanding. "Come, dance with me."

Lily dared not move, dared not say anything, but that didn't spare her. In one bound he was on the bed, grabbing her arm.

Touching her. Pulling at her. He had spared her any physical contact until now. This was the first time he'd violated her, or the first time he'd done so while Lily was conscious. She screamed as he dragged her toward the window. The music pounded as if the gates of hell had opened and all its demons were screaming.

He pulled her toward the edge, her stomach doing flip-flops. Death drew closer. They were so high up. Lily thrashed, trying to pull away from him, but his grip tightened. The bones in her hand threatened to break. Her screams seemed to be part of the dissonant music.

Max released his hold, not as a mercy, but as a prelude. It took Lily a moment to realize her captor was mimicking the position assumed by a man at the onset of a slow dance. His right arm was at her waist, his left arm extended to her back.

"Shall we dance?" he said.

Her answer was to try and desperately push him away, but he took that as an invitation to wrap her in a bear hug. She tried kicking, but he only squeezed harder. Lily couldn't catch a breath. Then he ran with her, running toward the window. She closed her eyes, afraid of the impact, afraid of falling from so high up. They slammed into the glass. For a moment Lily was sure they had broken through it and that she was plummeting to the ground, but the window rebuffed their assault and they fell backward. Max landed on his feet, Lily in his arms.

Over the raucous graveyard music, its beat trying to pound her into submission, she heard him say, "You dance divinely."

XXXIX

The day after the *New York Times* Sunday edition published its article on the ongoing theatrics in the Welcome Mat Hospitality proceedings, Judge Irwin requested that all lawyers involved in the case meet in his chambers on Wednesday morning.

The judge's "request" was in name only. There was nothing optional about the parties showing up. And though the judge didn't offer a reason for the meeting, all concerned knew it had to have been prompted by the story in the *Times*. Much to Gina's delight, the article had been accompanied by the illustration of two tailors pretending to be outfitting an obese and very naked Judge Irwin. The illustrator had even seen to the detail of Irwin wearing the white horsehair wig associated with British barristers.

Although Deke and Gina arrived fifteen minutes before the meeting was due to start, they were immediately shown into Judge Irwin's chambers. Nathan Bines and his associate Linda Sabin were already seated.

Irwin remained sitting behind his desk. He did not stand up to greet Deke and Gina, and his "take a seat" was noticeably brusque.

With everyone gathered, the grim-faced judge held up a copy of the article for all to see. Deke knew better than to turn Gina's way. If their eyes were to meet, he feared the two of them might start laughing. The illustration of Judge Irwin was not flattering. The drawing made him look porcine, his folds of flesh accentuated by his nakedness.

With undisguised wrath, Irwin said, "Explain this," and began shaking the paper in the faces of Deke and Gina.

His attempt at intimidation only succeeded in provoking Deke's own ire.

"To be abundantly clear, I can't explain that any more than I can explain this."

Having anticipated Irwin's use of the *Times* article, Deke raised up a copy of the *American Enquirer*. The headline of the article—*Bottom Line Explored. Lawyer's Happy Ending?*—had managed two double entendres in just six words. The accompanying picture showed Deke in the arms of a woman the tabloid identified as a high-priced call girl.

"I am certain you know this court had nothing to do with that, Mr. Deketomis," Irwin said.

"And we had nothing to do with the article in the *Times*."

Irwin's face soured. "How is it that Ms. Romano was quoted in the piece?"

"Mr. Bines was also quoted, as were you."

Irwin continued to glower. "The only individuals who stood to benefit from that article were you and Ms. Romano."

"If that's so, it would suggest that the terms of your gag order were detrimental to our side, and prejudicial to our case."

"I warn you not to poke the bear, Mr. Deketomis," Judge Irwin said. "I am in no mood for your word games."

Deke allowed himself a slight smile. "Word games? How can I be playing word games when you've forbidden me from saying anything other than 'No comment'? When this completely fabricated hit piece came out in the *Enquirer*, I couldn't even respond to it because your gag order prohibited me from commenting on anything having to do with the Welcome Mat case, which I believe was the motivating factor for my having been set up. Clearly, I believe certain vested interests wanted to undermine my credibility in that case, but under the terms of your order I was not allowed to make that assertion. I had to bite my tongue while my character was being assassinated."

The two men, vying newspapers still held aloft, stared each other down; it was Irwin who finally looked away and lowered his newspaper. Deke followed suit.

Irwin said, "For the record, you are stating that you are not the source behind the story in the *Times*?"

"That's correct."

"Same question to you, Ms. Romano," the judge said.

Gina's unblinking gaze was just shy of a glower. "I did not initiate the story, and I was not its source. The reporter for the *Times* called me up and told me the purpose of her call was to verify what her source had already told her. It was clear from her questioning that she knew every word that had been spoken during that hearing."

"There were only eight individuals in the courtroom that day," Irwin said.

"And five of those eight people are seated right here." Deke looked pointedly over to Bines and Linda Sabin.

Bines spoke for the two of them. "As we already told Judge Irwin, the article did our side no favors. Indeed, we were clearly cast as its villains, which has forced us to have to deal with the ongoing fallout. Ms. Romano's erroneous assertion that I have been trying to move the goalpost when it comes to the age of consent has painted me in a very poor light."

"It was your *own* amicus curiae brief that told us that, counselor," Gina said. "I sure didn't write it."

"It was a brief unrelated to this case, but from which you managed to derive an apples-to-oranges comparison. I'll have you know that I have a fifteen-year-old daughter."

She said, "That being the case, I find it strange that you attached your name to a brief so reprehensible."

"It speaks to governmental overstepping," Bines said.

"That's enough," Irwin said. "It's clear everyone in these chambers believes they are the aggrieved party. What isn't clear is how a seemingly verbatim transcript of what transpired in a sealed court proceeding was obtained by the *Times*."

"Or who was behind the *American Enquirer* story," Deke said.

Everyone in chambers looked as suspicious as they looked unhappy.

XL

"Like your wheels," Deke said as he opened the passenger door to Michael's Jeep.

"I guess it's not the usual lawyer ride."

"Don't ask me. My commute vehicle is an old truck."

"It's official. You're my role model."

As the two men got into the Jeep, Michael said, "Got us both coffees for the ride."

"Breakfast of champions." Deke lifted the coffee with his name on it from the cup holder, took a satisfied sip, and said, "Many thanks."

The two men had arrived early at the office for the drive to Bay County. For the last two weeks, Michael had been spending long hours preparing for this hearing. In that, he wasn't alone; the work had been nonstop for everyone.

Deke thought his role today was more for moral support than anything else. It was going to be Michael's game to win or lose, and it would likely be the latter. It was rare for any judge to grant an expedited hearing. Deke had warned the associate that the odds were against him, but that had only made Michael work all the harder.

Normally, Deke preferred driving to being the passenger, but Michael was so sure at the wheel it wasn't hard to relax. He drove with an assuredness most drivers lacked, easily dancing with the flow of the traffic. Deke was content to just sip his coffee.

"I heard the *Enquirer* printed a retraction," Michael said.

"Too little, too late," Deke said. "It's not going to stop me from going after them, but I'm glad for Teri's sake that they did that. My skin's thick enough to slough off their lies. It hasn't been as easy for her."

"What happened?"

"Some little things that felt like big things. Teri volunteers as a court-appointed special advocate for foster children. It's something that's near and dear to both our hearts. But last week she overheard a woman asking whether Teri should be allowed to continue working with children at risk because of 'her husband's whoremongering.'"

"That's ugly."

"I'm not sure what's uglier, what the woman said, or her need to say it."

"Schadenfreude."

"That's a fancy way of saying 'asshole.'"

Both men laughed.

"Anything on Tío Leo?" Michael asked.

"We thought we were close in Jacksonville, but he went ghost on us. Carol tells me I just need to be patient."

"She tells me the same thing when I press her on why the authorities haven't been pushing harder in their Karina Boyko investigation."

"Cops like to get their ducks in a row," Deke said.

"I hope those ducks don't fly away."

They didn't talk for a few minutes. Michael broke their silence when he said, "We're ten miles out. Got any last-minute advice for me? I don't want a Parakalo replay."

"Then put what happened in Indianapolis out of your mind. I've found that what the best lawyers and athletes have in common is they play in the moment and don't think about the past. Even if they're coming off a lousy game, that doesn't enter into their thinking."

Deke noticed Michael's smile. "Something funny?"

"I was just thinking that in my former career, I didn't have the luxury of having a bad game. Lives were saved or lost, including my own, based on succeeding in the mission."

"I'm glad the legal profession doesn't have those same standards. If it did, I'm afraid I would be dead many times over."

"One of my vivid memories of the Parakalo deposition was you telling me that I needed to get angry. You said every good trial lawyer has to be passionate about what they are arguing. Hearing that was almost the opposite of my military training, where we acted upon calculations and intel. Under hot fire, you need a cool head, not anger."

"In the legal arena, you need cool passion."

"That's an oxymoron," Michael said.

"It's also truth."

"Any advice other than cool passion?"

Deke thought for a few moments before answering. "The judge will ask his questions. Don't say what you think he wants to hear, but say what you think he needs to hear. When he plays the devil's advocate, answer his questions thoroughly, but don't belabor points you've made before. And answer the questions that aren't asked."

* * *

Before being shown into Judge Mobley's waiting room, Deke and Michael could hear the loud voice of a man saying, "Tell him to go screw himself."

The speaker's voice was just shy of a shout. His accent was from out of town, what Deke guessed to be Chicago. As he and Michael entered the antechamber, they found it occupied by two other men. The man with the loud voice continued talking into his phone.

"Of course I'm working on the RICO charges. Thing is, it's not like I can make them disappear by waving a magic wand."

The speaker stood up and began pacing around the small space, encroaching on where Deke and Michael had just taken their seats. The man's swagger, thought Deke, seemed to have been modeled on that of an NHL enforcer, even though his mouthful of complete and overly white teeth weren't exactly in keeping with that image.

"I got a numbers guy already on that," the man said.

Definitely Chicago, thought Deke. *That* sounded like *dat.*

Deke casually glanced over to Michael to see if his associate looked unnerved by the other man's posturing. He didn't appear nervous. If anything, Michael reminded Deke of a watchful predator just biding its time.

Judge Mobley appeared at the entrance to his chambers. The more informal nature of the proceedings was on display at its onset. Instead of wearing black robes, Mobley had opted for a sports coat. He wore a necktie, but even that came with a little wink: its prominent design elements were small scales of justice.

The two opposing lawyers elbowed their way forward so as to be the first to enter. "BB Wolf," said the man who had been talking on the phone. "It's a pleasure."

As the second man shook the judge's hand, he said, "Dan Perry. Pleased to meet you."

Deke did not need to introduce himself. He'd appeared before Judge Mobley on two previous occasions; they greeted each other warmly.

"Mr. Deketomis, a pleasure to see you again."

"The pleasure is mine, Your Honor," Deke said, then motioned for Michael to step forward. "I'd like to introduce you to one of our firm's rising stars, Michael Carey."

The two men shook hands, and Judge Mobley asked, "Have you been practicing the law for long, Mr. Carey?"

Michael shook his head. "I have not, Your Honor. As Mr. Deketomis would be quick to tell you, I am what he would charitably describe as a work in progress."

The judge smiled and ushered them inside. He introduced everyone to the court reporter, a serious-looking woman who'd set up her work station in the corner, before taking a seat behind his desk. "Thank you for being here," he said. "As you know, I have described today's hearing as a fact-finding session. All of us have read the motion that was submitted to the court. At its heart is its request for expedited discovery. Let's begin there, shall we?"

BB Wolf started talking the instant Judge Mobley finished his question.

"Thank you, Your Honor," he said. "I must say that in its motion to this court, the only thing opposing counsel didn't ask for is the moon, and it wouldn't surprise me if that appears in an amended motion. Asking for expedited discovery, and trying to use exigent cause as a launching pad, is a nonstarter, Judge. The motion tries to establish cause and effect, but to do that you need to start with cause, which isn't there. There's a reason that expedited discovery is rarely granted. Doing so violates the basic due process rights of the defendant."

The judge lifted a hand to the lawyer so as to allow the other side a chance to speak. "Let's take this in small steps. It's your turn, Mr. Carey."

"Thank you, Your Honor. Mr. Wolf is right when he says that expedited discovery is not commonplace, but where he is wrong is in stating that we don't have cause for its being applied. In our motion we referenced the wrongful death of Karina Boyko. We believe that delaying our inquiries into what occurred, and forestalling our examination of dangerous working conditions, could very well jeopardize other lives."

Wolf said, "That's mere speculation. You're not only asking to conduct a fishing expedition; you're asking for the bait to be provided."

"The death of Karina Boyko was a tragedy, not a fishing expedition. And we wonder at the fate of others, such as Nataliya Nahorny."

"That's nothing more than speculation on your part," Wolf said. "Just because you got a few names of employees who worked for the defendant doesn't give you the right to try and dig up random dirt while you turn the basic rules of discovery on their head. As pertains to the defendant, I am not even sure if you have established a case for discovery, let alone expedited discovery."

Judge Mobley again raised a cautionary hand. "One at a time. Mr. Carey?"

"Karina Boyko contacted our firm and asked us to represent her, Your Honor. She said the conditions of her employment constituted human trafficking. Ms. Boyko went so far as to say she was a slave. Before her death, Ms. Boyko referenced Ms. Nahorny and said she disappeared a few months earlier. Ms. Boyko's death and Ms. Nahorny's disappearance greatly concern us, Your Honor. Based on those individuals, we have good reason to fear for the safety of all of Viktoria Driscoll's H2B workers."

The judge turned to Wolf, who was shaking his head. "And that's how a minnow becomes a whale. Yes, there was an unfortunate death, but that doesn't mean there is an imminent emergency for everyone working in the same place of employment as the young lady who died. Mr. Carey certainly hasn't made his case in trying to establish that connection. The law is not designed to respond to supposition and exaggeration, nor does it countenance a violation of the rights of my client. Simply put, what Mr. Carey wants is neither warranted, nor is it reasonable."

"Your Honor, Mr. Wolf speaks about doing what is proper, while advocating that we turn a blind eye to the mysterious death of a young woman that might, just might, be an indicator of pervasive violations of the law. As one great man observed, the time is always right to do the right thing. In this instance, that would be to allow us to ask appropriate questions . . ."

A nodding judge made Deke think Michael's words were striking a chord. Wolf probably sensed the same thing, which was why he interrupted Michael in a vocal show of force.

"What Mr. Carey is trying to do is make his argument sound all noble and caring, but sentiment does not make the law. In the unlikely event that you were to grant Mr. Carey what he is requesting, we all know your ruling would be slapped down by an appeals court. He hasn't made his case; what he has constructed is a house of cards."

Wolf tried to continue talking, but this time it was Michael who interrupted, speaking over him. "Your Honor, it is my hope that Mr. Wolf can stop throwing around poorly disguised threats to this court so as to allow me to build a foundation for my so-called house of cards."

Judge Mobley said, "Mr. Carey's point is well taken, Mr. Wolf, and from this point forward I will be the only individual doing any interrupting. Is that understood by both of you?"

In unison, the two lawyers said, "Yes, Your Honor."

Judge Mobley turned to Michael. "I would hear more about what constitutes your foundation, Mr. Carey."

"Thank you, Your Honor. When I expressed concern for the welfare of Nataliya Nahorny, it was not idle conjecture or alarm mongering on my part. Where is Ms. Nahorny? We need access to the defendant's records to determine if there are other H2B workers who might have gone missing."

The judge swiveled his head. "Mr. Wolf?"

"It seems to me that opposing counsel is doing a fine job making a criminal case, while at the same time completely failing to make a civil case. It's an all-too-common occurrence for visitors to this country to overstay their visas, but that certainly doesn't constitute an emergency. If Mr. Carey truly believes the lives of workers are in danger, then he should bring the matter forward to the authorities. Our law is based on due process. Opposing counsel wants to bypass that, which is reason enough to disqualify his petition to this court for expedited discovery."

The judge turned to Michael, who immediately started his rebuttal. "Mr. Wolf keeps talking about the letter of the law, but not the rest of the alphabet. He wants the court to be confined by a narrow legal norm, even in this most extraordinary situation. Isn't the true purpose of the law to seek the truth?"

In the more than a quarter century that Deke had been practicing law, he had grown inured to most of the legal maneuvering and wiles that came with being a trial lawyer. It was like being a master magician and knowing how the tricks were performed. When you knew every variation of those tricks, it was hard to be surprised. This morning, though, was a surprise. It wasn't that Michael had grown as a lawyer; it was almost like he'd had a metamorphosis. Normally, Deke found himself playing armchair quarterback while observing other lawyers, second-guessing their presentation and arguments. With Michael today, it was hard to find fault. The same lawyer who had seemed so timid and overwhelmed during the Parakalo deposition, the attorney who had stumbled to find his voice, was now a force to be reckoned with.

Hammers and tongs, the two lawyers went at it, battling unabated for an hour. There was no flag of truce offered, only the briefest of pauses in battle when Judge Mobley asked his questions. Deke suspected he wasn't the only one there who was surprised. BB Wolf looked as if he was used to steamrolling other lawyers, but now was on the defensive.

Judge Mobley's face remained impassive throughout the session. Usually, Deke liked to think he could read a judge; not today.

No bell for the final round sounded, even though it felt as if a bout had taken place. "I've heard enough, gentlemen," the judge finally said, "but I would like to offer both of you the opportunity to finish up today with brief closing remarks."

BB Wolf took the opportunity to speak first. "In the end, Your Honor, we are at the same place we were when we started. The phrase *rush to judgment* has negative connotations for very good reasons. When you try and hurry along a proven course for rendering justice, the invariable result is injustice. Our courts have legal and ethical obligations to proceed in a prescribed manner. As you so correctly noted, Your Honor, at the heart of today's session was the request by opposing counsel for you to grant expedited discovery, along with a fast-track trial. That is not the norm, and there is a reason that is not the norm. The court has to be deliberate. The court has to be above reproach. We cannot put track shoes on Lady Justice and expect justice to be served."

Judge Mobley said, "Thank you, Mr. Wolf. And now we'll hear from Mr. Carey."

"Thank you, Your Honor, and thank you for the many thoughtful questions you have asked today," Michael said. "But now I'd like to close by answering a question you didn't ask."

Deke was probably the only one in chambers who caught the young lawyer's side-glance and smile. Son of a gun, he thought. The kid was referencing the advice he'd given him. No, that wasn't quite right. The kid was acting on that advice.

"Mr. Wolf used the phrase *rush to judgment*. That is not what I have advocated. My request to this court is for it to allow me an opportunity to act not in a rush, but in a time frame that speaks to the urgent matters addressed in our motion. I would submit that for this court to not allow expedited discovery is akin to justice delayed being justice denied. There is no need for me to quote the Sixth Amendment to anyone in these chambers. We are all aware that criminal defendants are supposed to have a right to a speedy trial. But it is my contention that the same right should apply to claimants in civil cases. Shouldn't they have a right to a speedy trial, especially if delaying that trial could potentially result in terrible or even fatal consequences?"

Michael took a deep breath, allowing himself a moment of reflection before continuing.

"I know from experience what can happen when you're a minute too late. In my former career, I served as a pararescueman for the United States Air Force, and even did some of my training at Tyndall Air Force Base. The Air Force pararescuemen motto is 'These things we do, that others may live.' Our missions are both military and humanitarian. Of all the missions I was involved with, one stands out over all the others.

"With limited intel, my CO had to decide whether to send us up in adverse conditions. You never want to fly by the seat of your pants. The safe thing would have been for my CO to do it by the book and wait for the weather to clear. But if he'd made that decision, I would have never had the chance to meet the woman who would become my wife. Had we arrived just a few minutes later than we did, she would have been dead. There are times when you can leisurely dot your i's and cross your t's; when you can afford to be deliberate. But sometimes you don't have that luxury. Every day I thank god that my CO decided the right thing to do was to act, not wait. I ask this court to make that same determination."

There was a moment of silence before a nodding Judge Mobley said, "Thank you."

He looked around his chambers and smiled slightly before saying, "Typically, at the conclusion of proceedings such as this one, I announce that I will be taking the matter under advisement before making my decision. Today, however, that won't be the case."

Judge Mobley turned to Michael. "Mr. Carey, I am going to grant your request for expedited discovery."

The lawyer who liked to call himself the Big Bad Wolf began howling. "Your Honor . . ."

"Spare me your outrage, Mr. Wolf. I know your every argument, and I do not deny their potential merits. In the normal course of any judicial ruling, most judges, myself included, err on the side of conservative caution. In this instance, though, I was persuaded by Mr. Carey that being overly deliberate would be the riskier option. I am sure, Mr. Wolf, that you will try and have my decision reversed in an appellate court. That has happened before, and I don't doubt that it will happen again. Still, I am more comfortable with that potential outcome than

I am with denying expedited discovery. Mr. Carey has demonstrated that this is a unique situation, and as such, I believe it calls for a unique ruling."

Wolf tried once more. "But Your Honor . . ."

"Mr. Carey, please prepare an order for me to sign."

"Your Honor," pleaded Wolf.

"As I said, Mr. Wolf, you are free to appeal my decision here today."

The judge looked around his chambers once more and announced, "We are done here. Good day, gentlemen."

XLI

Lily's slight movement caused a sharp intake of breath. For hours she had remained in bed, afraid to move. Last night's violence was the worst yet. Max had kept insisting they "dance." A few times he'd released his grip and sent her flying into the glass. Even when she'd collapsed, it hadn't helped; he'd just pulled her up on her feet and started dancing again.

Shifting her body, Lily clenched her fists at the pain but forced herself to get up. She needed to focus and figure out how to survive another night of her imprisonment.

In the bathroom she used a washcloth to carefully remove the dried blood from the night before. Max's long thumbnails had opened up cuts all over her body. Instead of a mirror on the vanity wall, there was a reflective vinyl that gave her an almost pixelated look, but that was enough for her to see the patchwork of bruises where Mad Max's fingers had dug into her. As ugly as that display was, Lily feared it was only a warm-up for what was coming. Tonight was the full moon. Max had made that abundantly clear.

He had told her, "Tomorrow, on the night of the full moon, we will ascend the Pyramid of the Moon and travel the Avenue of the Dead."

"Are those real places?" she had asked.

"They are."

"So, we'll be going somewhere?"

Had she not asked her question, it would have spared her from hearing his answer.

"There are destinations awaiting both of us, and demands. You have been chosen for your role in the sacrifice, and me for mine."

Demands. Shit. Sacrifice. Shit, shit, shit.

You first, asshole. That's what she should have said. But she'd been too scared.

But not today. "You bastard!" she screamed.

She had to find a way to kill Max. And it had to happen now, before the full moon. Max wasn't a big man, but he was strong and outweighed her by at least sixty pounds. Still, there had to be something she could use against him.

Music suddenly filled the room; some guy began singing about being followed by a moon shadow. Max was responding to what she had yelled. The perv had been watching her, had been listening.

"Asshole," she said.

Lily needed to think. There was something about the song that gave her pause. It wasn't the music or the words, but the way the song had materialized. That wasn't anything new. Max had watched her and reacted to what he'd seen. It was just another one of his games. But for some reason this detail seemed important, even if Lily couldn't figure out why. To the rest of the world, she was a ghost. In the cell of his making, she couldn't be seen. Only he was able to see her, listen to her.

In her jail, the song played on, the singer speaking of lights and shadows.

The answer was out there. It was like a spark in her head; she tried to breathe life into it. The inkling grew, becoming a possibility, a glimmer.

All this time she had run from her nightmare, but Lily realized she could no longer do that. If she was to have any hope of surviving, she had no choice but to embrace her nightmare. Believe in it even. In the nights leading up to this full moon, her lunatic jailer had spent an increasing amount of time standing in front of her bedroom window. It was as if he was drawn to the moonlight. But it was more than that. He had positioned himself at the window so that he could intently listen to what was beyond. A voice or voices talked to him, voices only he could hear. And it wasn't a one-way conversation. Mad Max talked back.

Her jailer spoke to the moonlight, or maybe even to the damn Man in the Moon. And according to what she had overheard, the two of them were conspiring to kill her.

Lily needed to become part of that conversation.

And the singer sang, "Moon shadow, moon shadow."

XLII

Michael turned away from his computer screen to look at the display on his cell phone. Jake was calling. It had only been twenty-four hours since he'd won his motion for expedited discovery, but he was already hard at work preparing for his deposition of Vicky Driscoll. At Michael's request, Jake had driven over to the Pussy Cat Palace to take exterior pictures of the property and make discreet inquiries on his behalf.

"Find any new dirt on Driscoll?" Michael asked.

"Plenty of dirt's being turned up here, but I don't think it's the kind you were hoping for. Were you aware that the Pussy Cat Palace was shut down for remodeling?"

"I was not," Michael said. He didn't like the sound of what he was hearing. "When did this happen?"

"From what I've been able to gather, the club's been closed for almost two weeks."

Michael doubted that was a coincidence. He'd been so absorbed in his work that all he'd been thinking about was getting the chance to put Driscoll on the hot seat.

"What's going on there now?" Michael asked.

"There is a small crew inside the building doing some demolition. I asked to talk to the foreman, but there wasn't one around. The crew working the site are Spanish-speaking day laborers, and they weren't inclined to talk to this gringo."

"Is there signage posted with a construction firm or contact number?"

"Negative. There's only a piece of cardboard with the scrawled message, *Closed for Remodeling*."

Michael got up from his seat and started pacing. "Were you able to get inside to see what's going on?"

"That wasn't a problem. I walked in, and when no one challenged me I took pictures, which I'll be sending to you after our call. They've gutted walls and torn down drywall. The place is full of drop cloths, pails and trays, and industrial-sized containers of paint and paint thinner."

"I need you to do me another favor," Michael said, then made his request.

"I'm on it," Jake said.

Michael started making calls. His first was to the Pussy Cat Palace. After ten rings, he hung up. The strip club's telephone number was still operational, but no message had been left alerting clients to the ongoing remodel.

His next call was to BB Wolf, but Michael was told by the receptionist that the lawyer was out of the office. He left a callback number. Maybe the lawyer had a reasonable explanation for what his client was up to.

As promised, Jake sent him pictures of the construction site. As he studied them, Michael kept wondering about the timing of the remodel. He thought about calling Deke and getting his take on the situation, but decided to wait on how matters developed.

An hour later, Jake called back. "You were right about your suspicions."

Michael had hoped he'd be wrong. He had asked Jake to go on a scouting expedition to the Emerald Hideaway.

"There are no longer any H2B workers at the hotel," Jake said. "I talked to one maid who told me she was a recent hire. She said that starting two weeks ago, lots of temps were brought in to work. Since then, some workers have been offered permanent jobs, including her."

"Which means the old employees aren't returning. Which also means they're probably back in Ukraine."

"That's my take on it."

"Dammit. Driscoll jettisoned all her H2B workers and all our potential witnesses. I never saw this coming."

"It's not like you could have anticipated it."

"And yet I should have."

* * *

Vicky was enjoying being out in her Mercedes CLS coupe. She was feeling like her old self. How did that American saying go? Oh, yes, if life gives you lemons, you make lemonade.

A spa day was just what she needed. It had been too long since she had pampered herself. She would start with a massage, then have a body wrap. After that she'd exfoliate with a salt scrub, followed by a mani-pedi. Her hair appointment wasn't until midafternoon, which would leave plenty of time for tea and cucumber sandwiches.

No, not tea, she thought. I'll have a lemonade instead.

Everything had worked out as planned. Now that her workers were back in Ukraine, a great burden had been lifted from her. Peter Stone had made it easy for her to be rid of them. They had left with plenty of money in their pockets, far more than they would have earned other-wise. There certainly had been no complaints from them.

Or from her. She was doing quite well by this new arrangement. Stone had decided the easiest thing to do was throw money at the prob-lems to have them go away. He had even come up with the idea of remodeling the club. Better yet, he had agreed to pay for the work so as to allow her time to find new employees. The Pussy Cat Palace had always been a dump, but a very profitable dump. When the construction was done, it would look like a high-class club.

Stone could certainly afford the payouts. Vicky had done some research on him. It seemed he had become quite wealthy in the after-math of America's Middle Eastern wars. His profiteering hadn't resulted just from the deploying of his mercenary army. The persistent rumor was that a not insubstantial portion of twelve billion dollars in cash, pal-lets of shrink-wrapped hundred-dollar bills, which the American gov-ernment had sent over to help with Iraq's reconstruction, had fallen into Darkpool hands. Stone had greatly prospered from their spoils of war.

A lack of American governmental oversight had also allowed Vicky to get rich, but not nearly as rich as Stone had grown from his private military contracting. Of course, she hadn't had billions of dollars fall off of some truck right into her lap. But she wasn't complaining. Things had turned out just fine for her in the end.

There was still the lawyer to deal with, but Vicky had been assured there was little to worry about on that end, especially now that her workers had returned to Ukraine. Mr. Wolf had told her that it was likely he would be able to settle the case before she was even questioned by that lawyer who was suing her. The idea of a settlement was fine with her, especially as she wouldn't have to pay—how did the Americans say it?—a thin dime.

Her benefactor Peter Stone would pay.

Karma, she thought, is a beautiful boomerang. It was now rewarding her with lots of his money. And whether Stone knew it or not, there were more debts he would yet pay. Sucking him dry was now something to look forward to.

The sudden jolt to her car threw Vicky forward. She hit her brakes, looked in her rearview mirror, and saw the cause of the collision. An old woman with huge glasses was driving a hulking old Cadillac, a car much too big for her. The crone's head could barely be seen over the dashboard.

"Bitch," Vicky cursed.

Florida was said to have more elderly drivers than anywhere else in the world, and Vicky was of the opinion that most of them should have had their licenses taken away long ago. Why the hell did these antiques still insist upon driving?

Vicky signaled to the right. Luckily for her, it was a quiet stretch of road. The old bitch responded in kind, moving to the side in what appeared to be slow motion, like a turtle. It would take forever for the old lady to get out of her car.

An impatient Vicky muttered, "Shit." Unlike grandma, she didn't have time to waste. And she wasn't going to let this fossil ruin her spa day. Maybe luck was with her and her bumper had gone unscathed.

Vicky got out of her car, slamming her door in fury. Scowling, she walked to the back. Seeing the damage made Vicky throw up her arms.

There was a dent to her rear bumper, as well as a broken taillight. From behind her, Vicky heard a window being lowered. She expected the woman to start profusely apologizing. That's not what she got.

In a raspy voice, the old buzzard said, "You shouldn't have slowed down."

What the hell? The crazy old bitch was trying to blame her for the accident. Vicky stomped toward the Cadillac. If she had her way, the old lady would never drive again. The cops would get an earful. She'd tell them to take her in for reckless driving. Maybe they'd even strip search grandma. That would serve her right.

Vicky opened her mouth to lay into her, but then noticed something odd. The old woman didn't look quite right. She was hunched down in her seat and wasn't nearly as small as she had appeared in the rearview mirror. In fact, she looked positively imposing. That probably had something to do with the gun she was holding in her hand.

Too late, Vicky noticed something else. The old woman wasn't a woman. She was a man in a white wig.

"Don't move," he said, his voice deep and threatening.

Vicky held her hands up as if complying, but then turned and started running toward her car. She didn't get far. The driver wasn't alone. A hidden passenger jumped out of the car and sprinted after Vicky. He tackled her from behind, then began dragging her back to the Cadillac.

No one saw Vicky disappear; no one heard her screams.

XLIII

Lily stepped toward her bedroom window. Normally, she didn't get that close to the glass, but this time she walked into the light of the full moon. Minutes passed. Her eyes were closed and she didn't move, but then she suddenly recoiled and held her hand to her chest.

"Who's there! What do you want?"

She swiveled her head around as if searching for something, her expression bewildered. Clearly there was nothing there. But then she started a second time and took a step back from the window.

"Who are you? Where are you?"

Lily raised her trembling hands up to her mouth; her breaths were rapid and loud.

"What?" she said. "That's crazy."

She said nothing for a few moments, the expression on her face turning from fright to incredulity. Lily began shaking her head in disbelief.

"I don't know what your game is, asshole, but I'm not buying it."

Something seemed to make her reconsider. Whatever it was made her jaw drop. After a few moments of listening, Lily said, "This is some weird shit."

Her face and body showed the conflicting impulses of flight or fight. Curiosity won out. As she inched toward the window, her attention was directed to something outside the glass.

"I'm listening, but this whole thing is crazy."

A minute or two passed, and Lily's body language transformed. The fear and uncertainty on her face and features gradually retreated; she began nodding. Occasionally she blurted out, "Really?" Mostly, though, she listened intently to whatever was being said.

And then there was another voice, this one directly behind her. "What is it? What is *he* saying?"

Lily didn't jump or start, didn't even turn around to acknowledge Max's presence. But she did shush him.

Max wasn't deterred. "What has *he* been telling you?"

"Shh!" she hissed again.

"I need to know."

From the corner of her mouth Lily hissed, "Shut the hell up." Then she turned back to the window. "No, no, not you. Don't go. Stay! Please." Lily did her pleading to something beyond the window. "He won't interrupt us anymore."

She could feel Max's hot breath on her neck, but didn't acknowledge it. All her focus was directed to the moonlight. As the minutes passed, she uttered the occasional "oh wow" and "you're shitting me," laughing a few times and frequently shaking her head in wonderment. Here and there, she voiced cryptic words of agreement, and consternation, and encouragement.

Max decided he'd been patient for long enough. "Tell me," he said.

"When *he's* finished," she hissed.

* * *

He was not finished for some time. At first, Max abided by her directive, but as the hours passed, he began shifting around, with his muttering growing louder.

Lily pretended not to notice him. To appearances, she was transfixed by something else. But inside she was agonizing, torn about what she should do next. Should she try and drive her fingernails into Max's eyeballs? Or should she continue with her pretense?

Stay with the plan, she decided. Every moment that passed brought her closer to dawn. A trickle of sweat dropped from her forehead. She forced herself to take long, regular breaths. Lily believed the only reason she was still alive was that Max had been waiting for the full moon to perform his sacrifice. That hadn't happened, but the night wasn't yet over.

If she could just hang on. Her fervor to live surprised her. There had been too many times over the past year when she had all but welcomed death. She had imagined it would be a relief, an escape from the grunting and thrusting of angry men. But that was no longer the escape she wanted. She wanted to go home and have her mother hold her in her arms.

Mom.

That thought, the need, was so strong that Lily wondered if she'd said the word aloud, and found herself involuntarily drawing her head back. The predator, ever ready to pounce, noticed.

"What is it?" he said.

It was time, she thought. But faced with the moment, the fear almost froze her.

"Thanks a lot," Lily said with the kind of sarcasm perfected by girls her age. "He's gone now, because of all your interrupting. At least he mostly finished with his story."

"Tell me what he said."

"Didn't you hear?"

"You were in the way."

She shrugged. "I don't even know where to start. And I don't have all that music and shit for sound effects."

Max's hand shot out, gripping her by the shoulder, his long thumbnail driving into her flesh. "What music?"

"Get your damn paw off me." She pulled back and rubbed where he'd clawed her. "How in the hell do you expect me to describe music, dude? It wasn't like angels with harps, or any shit like that. It was like nothing I've ever heard. It was like the universe was humming, and I wanted to be part of that chorus. I don't know how you didn't hear it."

"You spent all that time listening to music?" His words were hard, suspicious, just shy of violent.

"Like, no. The music was just part of his story."

"Go on."

"No way."

"What do you mean?"

"The story's crazy. And you're just looking for an excuse to beat the crap out of me, so why should I tell you what I heard?"

Which did he want more, to hear her out, or to kill her? She needed a little more time. Max needed the ritual in his ritual sacrifice. Or so she hoped.

Lily wished she were smarter. But nothing in her life had prepared her for this moment. Or had it? During the past year she had been put into one impossible situation after another, but she was still alive.

"The story," Max demanded.

"All right, but don't blame me if you don't like what *he* said. It's *his* story, not mine."

Lily took a breath and collected her thoughts. Then she said, "Long ago, when even the universe was young, the Moon asked his mother for a special present."

To her ears, that sounded weak and unconvincing. She needed to do better, and fast. Lily didn't dare to look at Max. It was easier to address the moonbeams. That was her audience anyway. The rays of light were spilling into the room. They were her spotlight. Lily wished she had taken a drama class and been one of the theater kids. They'd banded together in their own clique and gone around reciting their own special language.

Screw Romeo. Screw Juliet. They couldn't help her.

Lily steadied herself. Then she reached for the light and pretended to draw it to her breast. "And the Moon said to his mother, 'Please make me a jacket, Mama.'"

Lily moved her hands along the folds of an imaginary jacket, running her fingers along the lapels.

"Jacket?" Max asked.

"Not just a jacket. A very special jacket. He said it had to be perfect, and fit him for every occasion."

"You've kept me waiting all this time to hear some story about a jacket?"

Lily almost fell to her knees, almost decided to pack it in and give up. But she wasn't going to let Max win that easily.

"It's not my story, jackoff. And like I already told you, if you don't want to hear it, fine by me."

"I'm listening."

Lily shrugged her shoulders, feigning indifference. It was a good thing he couldn't hear her heart pounding. "Let's just skip it. It's not like I really believed what he was telling me. But it kept me interested, especially with the music and stuff. Or maybe I've finally gone over the deep end. This place would drive anyone out of their mind."

"Get back to your story," Max said.

"Not my story. *His* story."

Max acknowledged her distinction with a nod.

"Don't expect me to tell it like he did. I don't have his voice, or orchestra."

"Go on."

"So, Mr. Moon told me he was all keen on getting his coat. And not just any jacket. Like I already told you, it had to fit him perfectly and be good for all occasions.

"His mama tried to put the brakes on this idea of his. She said there was no way she could make such a jacket. Mama said, 'There is no coat that is always right for you, young Moon. Yesterday you were the New Moon. And tomorrow you will change again. Every day you're different. Think of the cycle of life. A baby becomes a boy, a boy become man, and a man becomes a grandpa. There is no jacket that can fit a baby, and boy, and man, and grandpa, just as there is no jacket that will fit you for all occasions. You go from being big and bright, to something small and pale. And over time you become little, until you disappear altogether. How do you expect me to make a jacket that would always fit?'"

That was the end of the story, or at least the story Lily remembered having been told as a child. But she needed to buy more time. She looked at Max's hungry expression. He wanted more.

"What happened then?" he asked.

"He nagged her big-time. Kept asking her to make him his coat. But even for the mother of the Moon, it wasn't easy. And when she finally agreed, it took her a long, long time to make, 'cause there were all sorts of things she had to do."

"Such as?"

Was Max leading her on? Playing games with her? Or was he really interested in the story?

"There was a ton of stuff she had to gather. We're talking bizarre shit, like sci-fi kind of crap. She went around the universe, getting some of this, and some of that. It wasn't easy, because she had to take into account the way he changed from day to day."

"His phases."

"Yeah, that's it. His jacket had to work for the *phase* when he was full and bright, and the *phase* when he was tiny and dark, and everything in-between. He said everything had to dance."

Max seemed to get excited at that. "Everything had to dance?"

"Yeah, his coat needed these elements of stardust, and pulsars, and I think even lightning bugs. And that was for his light side. It was the opposite to take care of his dark side. She had to distill the shade from black holes and dark matter."

Lily desperately tried to remember what Mrs. Turner had taught her during ninth-grade earth science. It was a subject she had enjoyed; she had even gotten an A.

Now, Lily wanted another passing grade. If she got one, she might live to see the morning.

"I thought he was bullshitting me when he said lots of secret ingredients went into making his coat. But he had an answer for everything."

Max's eyes didn't leave her. They were his lie detectors. "I would like to hear those answers."

"Fine, but don't blame me for what he said. Like, explain to me how you could use *murky dreams* to make a jacket."

"Murky dreams?"

"That's what he said. They were like a binder that helped the fabric be not totally dark, and not totally light."

"Yin-yang," Max said, not hiding his excitement.

"That's the word he used. I forgot to mention that. He said there had to be this balance."

"Go on."

"He talked a lot about the threading. It sounded all involved, but then I don't know shit about sewing or knitting. Luckily for him, his mom was an expert at those things. She used spiderwebs, and the cocoons of wild silk moths. But it got stranger than that. He said she gathered the mist from moving clouds, and sea-foam from waves coming in and going out. That was necessary for his coat to be able to grow and shrink. It was all very yin-yang."

The word resonated with him. "Yin-yang," he repeated.

Leave him wanting more, Lily told herself. The instinct, the thought, felt right. The light from the moon was retreating. Even a full moon had a limited reign. Dawn wasn't far off.

She raised her hand up to her mouth and yawned. "I'm exhausted. All that music. All his stories. It was like I traveled around the universe."

Lily yawned again. She didn't need to fake her exhaustion; she was spent.

"There's more to tell, lots more, but I'm too tired to go on. Remind me to tell you about the buttons for his coat. Ma Moon took some pieces from orbiting satellites to make those. And for his collar, she got the material from the dust trail of comets."

Another yawn.

Without saying anything, Lily stepped around Max and went to her bed. "We'll talk tomorrow," she mumbled.

She closed her eyes and feigned sleep. Even when she was sure Max was gone from the room, Lily didn't open her eyes for fear of what the cameras would report back to him.

A little later, though, she opened her eyes with just the tiniest slits to see the rays of a rising sun. She had survived. And the next full moon wouldn't arrive for another twenty-nine days.

XLIV

"Sorry I'm late," Deke said, grabbing a chair and sitting down at the conference room table where Gina Romano was waiting for him.

Even though the Welcome Mat trial was still months away, preparing for the contest was an involved juggling act, with the to-do list constantly being checked and revamped. Gina was the point person coordinating with their team of lawyers and staff. Getting ready for any big trial required tending to hundreds of moving parts and delegating areas of responsibility, including motions to be filed, witness outlines to be written up, and exhibits to be finalized. That didn't even take into account the searching of cases, codes, and statutes and the scrutinizing of case summaries from across the country.

"How goes our cases and codes search?" he asked.

Gina pointed to two boxes of paperwork in the corner. "Lots of late-night reading for you. Those are case summaries and published opinions from the Supreme Court, circuit courts, as well as state and appellate courts on any cases that might have a connection with ours. We've highlighted those areas we think might be applicable."

Deke knew that amassing information was the easy part; distilling it was much more challenging. You had to do a lot of mining in the hopes of finding any pay dirt.

"And we're still sifting through potentially pertinent statues and local ordinances," Gina added. "We should get those to you by next week."

Gina pushed a folder Deke's way. "We might have gotten lucky on another front. A few weeks back you suggested we 'follow the brief,' so that's what we did. We studied the amicus brief Nathan Bines filed on lowering the age restrictions on H2B workers. What struck me was that it didn't read like any of the other briefs Bines previously authored. In fact, some of the wording was so atypical we decided to run searches. We wondered if the wording—such as 'American cultural exceptionalism,' and 'age as a fluid concept'—might correspond with any other writings."

Deke started leafing through the folder's paperwork. His face showed his surprise. "GUM?" he said.

Gina nodded. "We found similarities between the wording used in Bines's amicus brief, and in position papers espoused by Global Union Manifest."

"Isn't GUM supposed to be all about human rights, and freedom, and the support of democratic institutions?"

"That's what I thought, but some of their position papers surprised me," Gina said.

"For example, even though GUM claims to support the rights of sex workers, and advocates for the legalization of prostitution, they also suggest that prostitution is a victimless crime."

Deke shrugged. "That's not surprising. Lots of well-intentioned sorts don't know the differences between those who have chosen to be sex workers and those who are sexually trafficked. If it was only a financial transaction between two consenting adults, you could justify GUM's assertion of it being a victimless crime."

"GUM position papers also promote less restrictive borders, including the idea of putting fewer governmental limitations on allowing foreign workers into industrialized nations, including younger workers. GUM's stated position is that they believe workers younger than the age of eighteen should be allowed into the US on apprenticeship programs and be given access to H2B work visas."

"That was Bines's position in his amicus brief."

"It was. And you'll see in a number of highlighted sections that the same wording he used in the brief can also be found in these position papers."

Deke pressed his back against his chair. There was something here, even if he didn't know what it was.

"Isn't there some progressive billionaire behind GUM? Salazar, right?"

"Right name, right billionaire, but our recent findings suggest that the reality of Geofredo Salazar might not be in keeping with his public image."

"So, you're thinking there's a connection between Bines and Salazar?"

"We're finding lots of smoke."

"I'm not usually one for conspiracy theories," Deke said.

"Nor am I, but you're the one who keeps telling me your radar says something is off with Bines working the Welcome Mat case."

Deke found himself nodding. He had thought it an odd pairing.

"You also suspected the mob might have its hooks in Welcome Mat's ownership."

"You're thinking the common denominator between Bines, Salazar, and Welcome Mat is the mob?" Deke said.

"It would explain a lot," Gina said. "Organized crime does control human and sex trafficking. In fact, it's their fastest-growing enterprise, and at one hundred and fifty billion dollars annually, probably their most profitable. Given that, wouldn't it make sense for organized crime to utilize properties with which they have ties or influence for their illegal enterprises?"

Deke thought about the implications. "What do we have that connects Salazar with the mob?"

"When Salazar started his hedge fund a quarter of a century ago, it attracted huge sums of money. The source of those funds has always been a subject for speculation. What if organized crime got its hooks into Salazar early on?"

"That would explain a lot," Deke said.

"Assuming the mob is a silent partner in Welcome Mat Hospitality, it only makes sense that they'd have someone like Salazar working for their interests. As for Bines, Salazar must have some kind of leverage over him, or maybe Bines has been willing to turn a blind eye to what's going on in his case so that the money faucet doesn't get turned off."

Deke nodded. "I've seen that happen time and time again. People don't even know they're on a slippery slope until they're falling off a cliff. Welcome to the contagion that is human trafficking."

"Bines said he had a fifteen-year-old daughter," Gina said derisively. "Maybe we should send him the picture I have on my desk of those billboards in Minnesota." Deke was familiar with Gina's picture. The billboard showed an outline of a girl's head and the caption, WHAT IF THIS WERE YOUR DAUGHTER? accompanied by a damning statistic from the Department of Justice that said the average age of those entering sex slavery in the United States was thirteen years old. Deke knew Gina kept that picture on her desk for a reason.

Sighing, Deke said, "I hope drivers are taking notice of those billboards. These days I'm probably responsible for more billboard advertising in Florida than General Motors. But all of those billboards haven't brought Lily home, or put handcuffs on Rodríguez."

"Carol said they've provided some solid leads."

"Not solid enough, and not soon enough. I need to find another way, a better way, to stir the pot."

XLV

Michael paced the exterior grounds of what had been the Pussy Cat Palace, staying behind the caution tape set around its burned remains. Firefighters were still doing mop-up work on the smoldering ruins, and Jake was documenting the destruction. Overnight, the Pussy Cat Palace had burned to the ground. Michael wondered if his case had gone up in smoke as well.

"I think I've taken enough shots," Jake said. "Are you ready to roll?"

"Unless you've got some marshmallows," Michael said. "This fire was deliberately set."

"That's what I heard you telling the assistant fire chief."

"The chemicals and solvents that were brought in for the supposed remodel were just smoke screens made to explain away the fire."

He hadn't spared the chief that opinion either. The chief had promised that when the conditions were safe for investigators to look around, they would conduct a thorough origin and cause investigation.

Michael added, "That's the same chief who also said that wherever there are hazardous materials and chemicals, the chance of spontaneous combustion always exists."

"We know it was arson, so what difference will the fire department's determination make?"

"Probably none, but it might complicate my Driscoll deposition. Of course, that's assuming she hasn't fled to Ukraine along with her workers."

"Is that a possibility?" asked Jake.

"At this point I'm not ruling out anything. I'll feel more at ease when her whereabouts are confirmed."

* * *

Between her groans and cries, the woman called out, "No more!" Then she began mumbling and muttering in her native tongue.

The man known as the Undertaker checked her vitals. His last interrogation of the woman hadn't gone well for her. She was dying. That was the necessary outcome, of course, but not before he was satisfied that she had told him everything.

The woman had proved far more resilient than most of the men he had questioned during his time being a grand inquisitor. It usually took only five or ten minutes before the toughest of men were spilling their guts. This one had held out far longer. She had eventually broken down, but not without effort on his part. Her reluctance to be forthcoming had only made matters worse for her. During this last session, he had provided a small mercy on his part, sparing her from seeing what he had done to her face. The woman would die with her vanity intact.

The Undertaker began putting away the tools of his trade. He had worked within the privacy of a closed forty-foot shipping container. A small generator provided him with the little power he needed. There was no need to worry about prying ears and eyes; the area was off limits to the ship's small crew. He had been left alone to apply his craft.

The Undertaker was old school. He did not need elaborate implements for his work. The pursuit of truth involved as much psychological torture as it did physical torture. He employed the thought of pain, the anticipation of it, as much as he did the application of it. The waterboarding had started her talking, and the cattle prod had kept her talking. He had brought out other tools, including a blowtorch, a poker, a dull knife, and his vintage dental extractors, items that fit quite neatly in his small leather attaché case.

In the end, she had kept crying, "*Vbyy mene.*" The Undertaker was not a linguist, but then he didn't have to be. He always knew when his victims were begging for the same thing.

Kill me.

It was time for him to see to what she wanted.

In the darkness, the Undertaker brought the body from out of the shipping container. The woman was still clinging to life, but only barely.

He wrapped the chains around her torso and limbs, then secured the weights. Deckhands knew to fear getting caught in the grip of the fishing lines they threw overboard, the weight of which could drag them into the depths. The Undertaker, too, knew to stay clear. It was an apt phrase, he thought. The grip, as in death's grip. The woman was already in that terrible embrace.

*　*　*

Peter Stone had done this to her, Vicky knew. Death was coming. But that thought provided her with an awakening of sorts. The pain was still there, but it no longer dominated her every thought. The devil who had questioned her, who had tortured her, had wanted her soul and more. Over and over again, he'd asked his questions.

Come clean, and the pain will stop. Confess, and you will no longer have to suffer.

More. Tell me more. It was never enough. Along with her screams, he had drawn out her secrets. He had gotten her passwords and her access codes to the security tapes on the cloud. But there was one secret that she had managed to hold on to.

Maybe it would be enough to avenge her death. That thought, and nothing else, had sustained her.

She was no longer aware of her body or her surroundings. Vicky did not know she was now only inches away from death, or that the sea was waiting to take her. Any consciousness she retained was shutting down, or so it seemed.

*　*　*

The Undertaker finally got the body where he wanted it. He moved the deadweight, getting it into position. Another foot, he thought, and he should be good. All was going as planned—until the woman began talking. She was supposed to be dead, but her delirium had her babbling wildly in her native tongue.

When she opened her eyes, she didn't see him but looked beyond him. Whatever she saw terrified her.

Over and over, she began screaming a single word. The Undertaker was glad he did not know what that word meant. The woman should have had the decency to be dead; now she was screaming to wake the dead.

He maneuvered her deadweight over the rail. As she fell to the water, he heard her cry out that word, that terror, that horror: "Rusalki!"

The darkness, and his vantage point, limited his visibility, but the Undertaker was just able to make out the woman's body hitting the water. There was a splash, with the faint moonlight casting a strange reddish hue on the spray. For a long moment, the body remained on the surface, then the sea seemed to boil in swirling ropes of frothing red and white.

The Undertaker stepped back from the railing. He was used to witnessing the throes of pain, and death was a longtime companion of his, but this was like nothing he had ever experienced. His hands, the instruments of his work, were trembling.

XLVI

Michael was used to dealing with unforeseen delays. "Hurry up and wait" was a catchphrase of the military, but it felt even worse in civilian clothes. In the days and weeks that followed the burning down of the strip club, Michael had continued to work the wrongful death suit of Karina Boyko. His efforts felt anticlimactic, though. With Driscoll's disappearance, there was little urgency. Under Florida statute, Driscoll couldn't be declared dead for a minimum of five years. As the legal representative for Karina's family, he was targeting Driscoll's estate, but the process would be long and drawn out. None of this felt like justice was being served.

That was why Michael wasn't surprised when Carol led off her morning call to him with the words, "Bad news."

"What now?"

"Miami Maritime called to say they located a wreck identified as the *Seacreto*."

It had been Michael's hope that the ship would be found with its crew, and that he might get answers out of them. "Where?" he asked.

"A few miles offshore Cape Coral."

"Any sign of the crew?"

"Afraid not."

"Dark Ghoul tied up all the loose ends."

"They're in the process of checking marina videotapes in Cape Coral and should be able to give us a time line on when it was docked and any visitors that might have come and gone. They do seem to share your assessment that the *Seacreto*'s sinking was 'suspicious.'"

"I'm shocked. Gambling in Casablanca."

* * *

Two hours later, Carol called for a second time. "I think you'll want to come over to my office."

"What's up?"

"I've got some news about an elf," she said.

Not more than a minute later, Michael turned the corner into Carol's office. Jake looked impressed by how quickly he'd gotten there. "Did you fly?"

As Michael sat down and regained his breath, Carol handed the two men paperwork she'd printed out.

"It helped having contacts in Las Vegas Metro. It also helped that there's only been one individual in the state of Nevada ever to have an alias of Keebler. Meet Anthony Russo, aka Keebler. It took this long to connect Russo with his alias because during his last stay in the joint he went by the nickname Big Tony."

Michael started going through Anthony Russo's rap sheet, pausing at the copy of his picture. Even though it was grainy, you could see his big cheeks and curly hair. However, Russo was six foot three and weighed three hundred pounds. He'd served time for aggravated assault, battery, pimping and pandering, and carrying a concealed weapon.

"I was told Keebler has the disposition of an angry rattlesnake," Carol said.

"They don't make elves like they used to," Michael said.

"As you can see by his record of arrests and prosecutions, his last conviction was almost a decade ago."

"Don't tell us he turned over a new leaf," Jake said.

"I won't. For the last eight years he's been working as hired muscle for media mogul Max Miller."

All that alliteration prompted Carol to take a breath before adding, "Miller inherited a fortune and built on it. He was a wunderkind in the entertainment business, hitting it big in music and movies in Hollywood. Then he traveled 250 miles to the other entertainment capital of the world after getting a controlling interest in the Double Y, the Yin-Yang Casino and Convention Center."

"Max Miller," Michael said. "I know that name."

"Isn't he the guy who held some poor woman by her ankles from an upper floor balcony?" Jake asked. "I seem to remember there was a video of her screaming in terror."

"That's our Max. Also known by the name of Mad Max because of his penchant for acting crazy. He pulled that high-rise stunt while he was still in Hollywood's favor and bought his way out of any repercussions. Miller took his leave of LA before #MeToo. Since ending up in Vegas, he's gained a reputation as a modern-day Howard Hughes."

"Who?" Jake asked.

"You're making me feel old," Carol said.

"He was that guy DiCaprio played in *The Aviator*," Michael said.

Carol amplified on that. "Hughes was this reclusive larger-than-life billionaire who took up residence in the penthouse at the Desert Inn, and rather than move out, just decided to buy the entire casino so that he could stay put. That's kind of what Max Miller did. He took over the penthouse at the Yin-Yang, and Keebler and the rest of his special security team live on the floor below him."

"Is Miller a recluse like Hughes was?" Michael asked.

She shook her head. "He seems to enjoy playing the big shot; if you google his image, you can see how he's always getting his picture taken with athletes and celebrities. Although for the last few years his penthouse has been off-limits to everyone. That's quite a change from the parties he used to throw up there. Most days Miller just makes the rounds of the Yin-Yang."

"I want to see about getting my picture taken with him," Michael said. "Tomorrow, I'm traveling to Las Vegas."

It wasn't a request, or a question.

"I'd like to go as well," Jake said.

"The two of you going off half-cocked won't help matters," Carol said.

Michael said, "Keebler is my link to Nataliya, as well as the American girl taken from Driscoll's H2B workers' housing compound. And since

Nataliya's family recently retained my services as her lawyer, if there is even a chance my client is in Las Vegas, I'm obligated to try and meet with her."

"Then I would suggest you talk to Deke and get him to agree to your plan."

"What about me?" asked Jake.

"If Michael gets Deke's blessing, you'll get mine."

Michael was already halfway out of his seat when Carol raised her hand and signaled for him to stop. "Hold your horses. We're not done here yet. This morning USCIS finally got back to us. Per my request, they included a picture of Nataliya Nahorny."

Carol handed copies of her photo to Michael and Jake.

"Beautiful green eyes," Jake said. "Sort of reminds me of Lily. All these poor kids who just seem to have disappeared."

"All the more reason for our forming a search party," Michael said.

He hurried out of the office, going in search of Deke to ask about booking a flight to Las Vegas.

XLVII

When Michael arrived home, he inhaled deeply. *Tepsi baytinijan*, a casserole consisting of eggplant, tomatoes, onions, peppers, potatoes, and lamb meatballs served over rice, was a favorite dish of his. Usually Mona reserved making it for special occasions.

"What did I do to deserve such royal treatment?" Michael said.

He and Mona came together just outside the kitchen. The two of them kissed and Michael said, "Better watch out. You're smelling so good I'll want to eat you."

"I was not aware that I was on the menu," she said.

"You are tonight's special."

Michael took another deep breath, but not to take in the aroma of the food. He didn't want to eat his favorite dish under false pretenses. It was better just to come out and tell Mona about his trip, rather than put off the news until after they dined.

"I have to go to Las Vegas tomorrow," he said.

Mona's posture stiffened just a little. "Las Vegas?"

"I'll be going with Jake on business."

She didn't speak for a few seconds, then asked, "For how long?"

Mona never liked it when the two of them were apart.

"I'm not sure. I hope it's just for a few days."

"I see."

"I didn't know about the news until late today," he said.

Instead of answering directly, Mona said, "I need to take our dinner out of the oven, or it will be overdone."

"Can I do anything to help?"

"You can tell me about this business of yours."

"Before I do that, I need to backtrack, and I need to apologize. There are some things I should have told you previously."

"Then I would hear them now."

After Mona turned off the oven, the two of them sat on the sofa in their small living room. Holding his wife's hand, Michael said, "Do you remember that night about two months ago when I told you that Jake and I needed to go to Panama City to meet with my client?"

Mona nodded.

"What I didn't mention is that we went to a strip club where she had been working as a dancer. The reason I didn't tell you is because I know how much you worry, especially when I'm in a potentially dangerous situation."

"And were you in a dangerous situation?"

"The night was not without its risks, but I'd like to think I always had control of the situation. In my defense, I should point out that the US government spent millions of dollars on my training to make sure I'm proficient at handling adverse conditions. I know I should have come clean with you, but as much as I didn't want to let you down, I still felt a responsibility to act as I did for the sake of my client."

"What of your responsibility to us?" Mona asked.

"I always try to be mindful of that."

"In one of the first conversations we ever had, you told me that you wanted to be a lawyer."

"I meant what I said."

"And are you going to Las Vegas as a lawyer?" she asked.

"I'm going there in the hopes of meeting my client."

"Will you be putting yourself in danger by traveling there?"

"I'll try to avoid that." Michael paused before continuing. He didn't want to be evasive to the woman he loved. "But if the situation calls for it, I'm prepared to make this a rescue mission."

Mona surprised him by smiling. "When I thought I was going to die, and you came to my rescue, I wondered if an angel had come to deliver me."

"Sorry to disappoint you."

"You saved my life."

"You can believe that if you want, but the way I see it, from the moment you came into my life, it was you who saved me."

Both of them reached for the other's hands. Mona said, "I do not like the idea of you going into danger, but we will not stand in the way of you and your green feet."

Michael expressed his amusement by saying in a voice of mock alarm, "What is that?"

It was what Mona had said on the first day of their marriage when she spied Michael's backside tattoo. As far as she had known, the only tattoo her husband had was the jade-green $A+$ on his chest. The green feet on his derriere had come as a total surprise.

Since then, whenever either of them wanted the other to laugh, all they had to do was say in a startled tone, "What is that?"

The green feet had been a symbol for pararescuemen since Vietnam. Sikorsky HH-3E helicopters were known for leaving their marks on rice fields and green paddies, massive imprints that looked like huge green feet. Wherever the Sikorsky helicopters went, so did the PJs on their rescue missions, and a catchphrase was born: "green feet mean rescue."

Mona said, "It was a shocking sight to be sure. I did not expect to see lime-colored appendages confronting me as they did."

Michael waggled his backside. "I think you secretly like my green feet."

"I fear you are deluded, husband," she said.

Mona tried to keep from smiling, but was not altogether successful.

XLVIII

Hunkered down together, Michael and Jake strategized during their flight to Las Vegas. For Michael, there was a sense of urgency. Everything he was finding out about Max Miller played to his fears. If Nataliya was with him, he was convinced her life was in jeopardy.

Michael handed Jake a memory card. "I created a file last night with all sorts of stuff about Max Miller. You know how Michael Jackson supposedly got away with crimes in plain sight, and Jeffrey Epstein paraded underage girls for all the world to see? My gut tells me Miller has been doing much of the same for a long time. People say he's an eccentric and don't look beyond that. Michael Jackson had Neverland Ranch, and Epstein had his Pedophile Island; Miller's got the penthouse in the Yin-Yang."

"It's hard to wrap my head around the idea that women might be imprisoned in his penthouse," Jake said.

"That's what Miller and people like him count on. What we know for sure is that a few years ago there was an extensive remodel of his penthouse. After the work was finished, you could no longer see inside. And since completing that remodel, Miller stopped all his entertaining. No one has been in the penthouse since then."

Jake said, "I don't want to throw shade on what you're saying, but it makes no sense to me that Miller would have sent his henchmen halfway across the country to get Nataliya and transport her back to Las Vegas. Why take that risk? Why not target someone local?"

"Maybe he wanted to avoid a spotlight being shined in his backyard.

Or maybe he was quite particular in getting what he wanted, and Vicky was his special procurer, just like Ghislaine Maxwell supposedly recruited girls for Epstein."

"There was something unique about Nataliya?"

"That's my guess. And let's not forget the American girl that Keebler and company traveled to Florida for."

"How is it that wealthy sicko predators always seem to find individuals willing to pimp for them?" Jake said.

"Poor people are crazy; rich people are eccentric. Moon Man buys what he wants. He's also bought his way out of a lot of trouble. It's in that file I just gave you."

"Moon Man?"

"One of Miller's nicknames, along with Mad Max, although neither is said in his presence. Years ago, Miller was known for his full moon parties. He was obsessive about it, people said. You know how the crazies supposedly act up during a full moon? That's Miller all over. But from most accounts, Miller's kind of madness doesn't need a full moon."

"Isn't it about that lunar time of the month?"

"I think we're three or four nights away."

A touch of turbulence shook the plane, and Jake gripped his armrests. "Did I mention that I don't like flying?"

"Not to me."

"The only thing I like about flying is the landing part."

Michael asked, "Ever been to Las Vegas?"

Jake shook his head. "Never. What about you?"

Michael nodded. "For half a year I was with the 58th Rescue Squadron at Nellis Air Force Base, which is around ten miles outside of Las Vegas. The 58th is known as the guardian angel squadron."

"Any friends of yours still at the base?"

Michael nodded. "A few very good friends."

Their conversation tapered off, and both men continued to prep for their mission. Michael used his laptop to review footage taken from some of Miller's full moon parties, before he had chosen to live a cloistered lifestyle. One piece of film, in particular, Michael found himself returning to watch over and over.

In the tape, Miller was heard shouting, "The windows are unbreakable. They are indestructible. The big, bad wolf could huff and puff, but never blow them down. They are impregnable and unassailable!"

His speech was frenetic, and Miller's guests cheered on his pronouncement. The camera zoomed in on his eyes. There was something kaleidoscopic about them.

"They are unbreakable!" he repeated; his declaration was met with applause and shouts.

The partygoers gathered around for a spectacle, and the Moon Man didn't disappoint them. He sprinted toward the window, slamming into it. The loud impact made the spectators recoil, but the window didn't shatter. Instead, Miller bounced off the glass and landed on his feet.

Raising his arms to the loud cheers, Miller once more shouted, "Unbreakable!"

"Again!" yelled a man, and others took up his call. "Again! Again!"

A crowd formed behind Miller. He swayed from side to side, readying for his next assault upon the window. Behind him his guests began to imitate Miller's movements, almost as if they were in a conga line.

"Ready?" shouted Miller.

"Ready for what?" asked a striking-looking woman, an actress Michael recognized. She was one of several celebrities attending the party.

"Ready to dance with the universe!" Miller shouted. His words resonated with the crowd behind him.

And then he ran at the window, throwing himself with his hands and legs spread out as if to embrace the skyline. He struck the glass, the loud crash silencing the crowd, but only for a moment. The revelers began yelling and applauding, then some of them decided to join in on the fun. Men and women ran at the glass, bouncing into it. But Max was not to be outdone.

He parodied a martial arts fighter with screams and posturing, and then ran at the window, striking it with a spinning heel kick.

"Unbreakable!" he screamed.

XLIX

"**A**m I having a conversation with myself?" Gina asked.

Too late, Deke responded to what she was saying. "Sorry," he said, shaking his head in annoyance. "When you started talking about Bines, I got this feeling that I was missing something, but couldn't put my finger on it. That always drives me crazy."

The two lawyers were brainstorming the potential story lines for the Welcome Mat case in the smallest of the firm's conference rooms. Deke believed trials were won or lost through the story that was presented. Complex cases needed to be simplified for the jury. That didn't mean dumbing matters down; it meant making them understandable. Deke had earned a reputation for making things look simple to juries, but as he often said, "Nothing is more difficult than simple."

Gina said, "I was talking about the pushback we can expect from Bines when we personalize the narrative of our Jane Does. By putting them on the stand early, we can humanize them and show the jury that they're victims and flawed humans, not the dregs of society they might imagine. I said the only problem with that is it will allow Bines to tangle us up in the weeds by hammering them on their own complicity and participation in the sex trade."

Deke chewed on his lip. "That's it, but it's not it. One moment I feel like I'm close to the answer, and the next it's gone."

"We could do word association and play a game of hot and cold."

"I don't want to waste our time. It will come to me. Or it won't. Let's get back to the story."

Gina said, "I think we need to introduce Jake's undercover videos early in our presentation. That will demonstrate the complicity of Welcome Mat's truck stop management working in tandem with human traffickers."

"And we should follow that up with the testimonies of our hospitality witnesses, the truck stop attendants and motel desk clerks."

"We know Bines will try to counter that testimony by citing chapter and verse of Welcome Mat's official anti-trafficking corporate policies," Gina said. "The onus will be on us to show that's merely lip service, and that their self-policing has not only been woefully inadequate, but demonstrably disingenuous."

Deke didn't respond. Once more, Gina's bringing up Bines had waylaid his thoughts into trying to identify what was bothering him.

"Warm?" Gina asked.

"I guess my subconscious is insisting upon that game of hot and cold. Keep talking."

"After we finish with the former Welcome Mat employees, that would be a good time to put our expert witness on the stand and let him talk about how he's successfully trained employees on how to observe signs of human trafficking. Of course, that's when Bines will jump on his soapbox and start talking about governmental intrusion, and how businesses shouldn't be required to be their brother's keeper, and that in a free society the onus shouldn't be on the business to interrogate its clients. That's when we redirect his red flags by pointing out that you don't need to be a rocket scientist to identify human trafficking, nor do you need to ask twenty questions of your clientele."

Deke held up his index finger, as if touching something. "Warmer," he said.

The thought was almost there.

Gina tried some word association. "Bines. Soapbox. Free society. Defender of businesses. Guardian of individual freedoms. Creator of smoke screens."

Deke's finger jabbed out. "Hot."

"You got it?"

"We need to turn the heat up on Bines," Deke said. "We need to come at him and make it look as if we're not only gunning for him personally, but for those hiding in the shadows."

"Bines will know it's a fishing expedition. There's no way he'll rise to the bait."

"Normally, I'd agree with you," Deke said. "But in this instance, I believe no one will be happier with our pursuing a new and aggressive agenda than would Nathan Bines."

"What leads you to believe that?"

"An *anonymous source*," Deke said.

He was about to explain further, but was stopped by Carol's appearance at the doorway. "One of your billboards in Jacksonville struck pay dirt! Guess who's on his way to the detention facility at the Leon County Jail in Tallahassee?"

Deke was already on his feet. "What's his ETA?"

"No later than two o'clock."

It was a three-hour drive to Tallahassee, but that would allow enough time for Deke to be there to greet Rodríguez, as well as make arrangements with his welcome committee.

"Sorry," he said to Gina. "Got to run."

And he did just that, racing from the office.

Under her breath, Gina muttered, "Cold. Really cold."

L

Deke paced back and forth at the entrance to the Leon County Jail detention center. Having Rodríguez land here wasn't just happenstance. After Lily's disappearance, Tallahassee State Attorney Bill Fuller had issued a warrant for Rodríguez's arrest. Because of that warrant, and at the behest of Fuller, Tío Leo was now in Tallahassee.

A door opened, and State Prosecutor Gabriella Fuentes interrupted Deke's pacing: "I think you're wearing out the pavement, Mr. Deketomis."

"Deke," he said.

"We're ready for you," she said.

"I appreciate your arranging all this."

"It was my pleasure. The state attorney said that any efforts on my part would be a small price for the admission of seeing you in action."

"I'd like to believe you, but Bill Fuller warned me I shouldn't be taken in by your many charms. I believe his exact quote was, 'State Prosecutor Fuentes can cut off your head, and you won't even know you're bleeding.'"

The prosecutor smiled, her white teeth aglow. "This way."

* * *

Deke entered the interview room, where he was introduced to the sheriff's deputy who had transported Rodríguez, and to Duane Griffin, the court-appointed attorney. No introduction with Tío Leo was necessary. Deke took a seat and was flanked by Fuentes.

Griffin was that rarity of rarities in Florida. Not only didn't he have a tan, but he had somehow also managed to retain his pasty-white complexion. Griffin immediately began voicing his objections. "May I say that all of this is highly unusual? My client hasn't even been arraigned."

Deke leveled a look at the young attorney that gained him the silence he wanted. "The best thing you can do for your client, Mr. Griffin, is to hear me out."

Then he turned his attention to Rodríguez. "I would advise you to inform your mouthpiece that you're interested in what I have to say, and that he should hold off any interruptions until I'm done."

"That's outrageous!" Griffin said. "That's a violation of my client's rights!"

"Your choice," Deke said to Rodríguez. "Just know that I'm not in the mood for games. You can hear me out, or I can walk."

Griffin said, "We don't have to submit to blackmail. All of this is a clear violation of your rights. That's . . ."

"Shut up," Rodríguez said. Even though he was chained, that didn't stop him from leaning back a little. He offered a mocking smile to Deke and said, "Your show, Joe."

"You've got that right," Deke said. "The last time we talked you were holding a gun on me, Mr. Rodríguez. When I informed you that I was an attorney, that seemed to greatly amuse you. If you'll recall, you said to me, 'What are you going to do? Sue me?' I don't think I ever got a chance to adequately answer your question, but will do so now. I don't see the need to sue you, because unless you comply with what we want, you'll be long dead before I even get a chance to file the paperwork."

"That's it!" Griffin said. "We're done here."

Deke ignored the lawyer. He reached into his pocket, pulled out a picture that he had been holding at the ready for months, and tossed it on the table. The photo showed three men arm in arm. One of the men in the picture was a much younger Nick Deketomis.

"They called us the 'three amigos' back in the good old days. I'm the guy on the right. On the left is State Attorney Bill Fuller. As for the man in the middle, that was the chief investigator in the office where Bill and I worked. He is dead now, God rest his soul, but he's not forgotten. Bill was the best man at his wedding, and I was given the honor of being godfather to his only child."

Deke reached out his index finger and slammed it in the center of the picture. "Does this man look familiar, Mr. Rodríguez? Please take a close look. Do you see a resemblance?"

"I never seen that dude."

"I didn't ask whether you'd ever seen him. I asked if you knew anyone who bore a resemblance to him."

Tío Leo looked at the picture and then turned away from it. That was his tell. He'd made the connection.

Deke said, "Art Reyes is the man in that picture. Maybe you should have asked Lily Reyes, the fifteen-year-old girl you sexually trafficked for the better part of a year, about her father."

Rodríguez attempted a look of befuddlement. "Lily who?"

"That's a nonstarter. You ran pictures of Lily on the dark web, saying she was available for good times. We can link you to those. And we have statements from three other underage girls whom you also sexually trafficked that will corroborate what I just said. You're not going to be able to walk away from what you did."

Rodríguez shrugged. "Then why we talking?"

Deke laughed. "That's funny."

"What's funny?"

"You seem to think that you're the one holding the cards. If there's any begging that's going to happen here, you'll be the one doing it."

"You're loco, *pendejo*."

"You want to live? That's the question you have to ask yourself right now. This isn't about our last go-around. Both of us know that should you live long enough to see a trial, you'll be convicted of aggravated battery and attempted murder. That's a given. And in combination with your criminal record, that would result in you getting put away for a long, long time. But I'm not going to go there. You can get a pass on what you did to me. My interest is Lily."

Deke slid his finger over to the picture, settling under the man on the left. "That's the state attorney's interest as well."

Tío Leo looked from the man in the photo back to Deke.

"Sylvia Reyes retained the services of my firm. That means I'll need to periodically ask questions of you in regards to what transpired with her daughter, Lily. State Attorney Fuller tells me his office will need to be asking their own questions of you as well. Because of that, he'll want you somewhere not far away. Since Raiford Prison is in nearby Bradford County, that seems like the ideal venue to serve both our purposes."

Rodríguez slammed his hands on the table. "That's bullshit!"

"Bullshit? I don't understand." Deke's tone made it clear he did understand.

"I go to Raiford, I'm dead."

"Really?"

"Don't pretend you don't know what went down with Cortez, *pendejo cabron*."

Deke pretended to search his memory. "Cortez?"

"MS-13 thinks I had something to do with his death."

"You'll have to excuse me, Mr. Rodríguez, but it's been a long time since I was a prosecutor, and I'm afraid I don't know jack about this gang or that gang."

"Bullshit."

Florida's prisons were arguably the worst in the country. The gang violence was so bad, prison authorities tried to keep feuding gangs from being placed in the same penitentiaries. Rodríguez was a Latin King. Since MS-13 dominated the cells of Raiford, it would not be a good place for a Latin King to go. Especially a Latin King who was believed to have participated in the death of Pablo Cortez, formerly of MS-13.

Griffin said, "This is a blatant abuse of my client's rights!"

Deke said nothing, just let his finger travel once more to the picture of State Attorney Fuller. Rodríguez and Deke locked eyeballs. The stare-down lasted maybe ten seconds, long enough for Tío Leo to get a take on who he was dealing with. Deke welcomed his scrutiny. Rodríguez had survived on the streets by being able to read people. Deke wanted him to see he wasn't bluffing. Either Rodríguez complied, or he'd be dead in a matter of days. And Deke wouldn't lose a minute's sleep over the other man's death.

Finally, Rodríguez said, "You want what I got to say, then I serve time where I choose."

Deke exchanged glances with the prosecutor seated next to him. When she nodded, Deke said, "The state prosecutor believes that can be arranged, provided you give me what I need."

"*Pinche madre.*" Rodríguez said, but his curse sounded more tired than anything else. "What do you want to know?"

"Where's Lily?"

"I couldn't tell you. You'll have to ask that Russian bitch."

"Can you be more specific?"

"She got in touch with me through a members-only message board on the dark web, responding to one of my advertisements. Her interest was in Lily, or at least a part of her. Some clients got specific tastes. Usually they want to see shots of tits, ass, or snatch. But this lady had a different fetish. She wanted close-ups of Lily's eyes. Lady had a thing for green. So do I, but a different kind of green."

"All your communication was through a message board?"

"Not all. She called me on a burner phone. That's when I learned she was female, and when I heard her accent. I figured she might be Russian mob."

"Did you meet her in person?"

Rodríguez shook his head. "She sent the money along with her muscle. The help that took Lily away also sounded Russian."

"You ever learn the woman's name?"

"Her hired help called her Vicky."

LI

Jake entered Michael's hotel room carrying a bag and two large cups of coffee. In the almost three days they'd been in Las Vegas, coffee had been a constant companion of theirs. Michael cleared a space at the table, and Jake set the food down.

"Feels like déjà vu," Michael said, reaching for the coffee.

It was late afternoon, but the two men had stopped being mindful of the time. The hours seemed to blend together, with little difference between night and day. There were no clocks in Las Vegas casinos; management didn't want gamblers to be aware of the passage of time. Michael and Jake had mostly ignored their own sleep needs, but it was possible they were playing for more than high stakes. Lives could be on the line.

"You need to see this," Michael said.

He turned his cell phone in Jake's direction and played a short video. The footage was shaky, with jerky camera angles. There was also the screaming. A young woman was being held by her ankles while being dangled over the side of a building.

"My god," Jake said.

"The woman you hear screaming is Suzanne Cleary. At the time this video was shot, she was an aspiring actress. The man holding her is a young Max Miller. The footage was taken more than a dozen years ago at one of his notorious full moon parties. At the time, Max was a Hollywood producer. That's how Ms. Cleary entered his orbit."

"How high up are they?"

"Seven stories."

The footage neared its end when others came to Cleary's rescue and pulled her up to safety. In the background, party noise could be heard. The camera zoomed into a close-up on a sobbing Suzanne Cleary. Michael hit the pause button, so that he could better see the woman's face.

"Notice her eyes?" he asked.

Jake leaned closer to get a good look. "Green."

"I don't think that's a coincidence. Fewer than two percent of the population has green eyes, so why do women with green eyes keep turning up around Miller? After what he did to her, Cleary sued him. Miller's defense claimed that they were both drunk, and that what they did was consensual."

"Her screams kind of make me doubt that."

"So does her story. Cleary said Miller had a thing for her eyes. It wasn't sexual, she said, but it was bent. Miller told her that the goddess Circe and all great enchantresses had green eyes, but he had the power to resist such spells. She was convinced Miller would have dropped her if the others hadn't been there. He was babbling to her about being a sacrifice to the full moon. She stopped singing, though, when Miller bought her silence and got her to sign an NDA."

"How much was the payoff?"

"Unofficially, five million dollars."

"By the sounds of her screams, she settled cheap."

"I'm sure she wanted to put the whole incident behind her. The problem with that was it allowed Miller to walk. People like him don't change. There's a whole neuroscience around uncontrollable urges."

"You're preaching to the choir," Jake said. "I got to know opioid addiction firsthand, and the urges that came with it, when I became an unwitting junkie."

"So, here's Miller with these overpowering urges. How does he go about satisfying them? No matter how much therapy gets thrown at them, pedophiles can never be trusted around kids. I'm betting Miller's sickness runs just as deep."

"Where's all this taking us that we haven't already been?" Jake asked.

The men had spent their time in Las Vegas learning everything they could about Max Miller and the Yin-Yang Casino and Convention Center. Michael and Jake's initial hope was that they could somehow penetrate or compromise Miller's security team, but they'd made no headway on that front. Miller's inner circle lived on the penultimate floor of the hotel and took their meals there.

"We free our princess from her high tower."

"How?"

The top two floors at the Yin-Yang were surveilled about as well as a maximum security prison. Like all casinos, throughout the property there were eyes in the skies.

"While you were getting our food, I did some printouts."

Michael passed Jake photographic images of the Yin-Yang shot from above. Jake said, "It looks like quite the foreboding castle."

"That's pretty much what it is. And let's not forget there are trolls at every drawbridge we need to cross."

"What's your interest in all this eye in the sky stuff?" Jake asked.

"We've been spending most of our time scoping out the inside of the casino. I wanted a bird's-eye view of the building, especially the penthouse."

"Why?"

"Because that's the best way to meet my client."

"You're not telling me much," Jake said.

"What I've got in mind could go south. Really south. It would be in your best interests if I didn't involve you. This operation could send your career down the toilet, or worse."

"I've already been there, done that. I was disbarred because I wasn't willing to sit by and do nothing while innocent people died. So I'm all in, and I'm all ears."

Michael took a deep breath before finding the words to speak. He had been prepared to go the mission alone—had thought that was the right thing to do—but now he found himself reassured by Jake's steadfastness.

It took him almost an hour to go over everything. When he finished, Jake said, "It's ironic that we're here in Vegas, and you seem to have lifted your plot from the movie *Ocean's Eleven*. Or is that *Ocean's Twelve?*"

"I get all those movies confused, but I think it was in *Ocean's Thirteen* that they tried to make sure the house didn't win. That's kind of what our mission is all about. We need to beat the house."

"Then let's pray that jokers are wild," Jake said.

Michael's cell phone started ringing. "It's Deke," he told Jake, picking up the call.

Without any preamble, Deke said: "I'll be taking a red-eye flight to Vegas tonight."

Michael's response was as immediate as it was firm: "No. That's a bad idea."

The momentary silence on the line told Michael that his reply wasn't what Deke had expected to hear, nor was it a directive an associate typically made to a general partner.

Deke said, "What you don't know is that there were some big developments today. Tío Leo just finished coming clean to us."

"That's welcome news. But you still need to steer clear of Las Vegas."

"You're going to have to give me more than that."

"No."

That word again. But this time Michael amplified on it. "Your presence here would be counterproductive to our mission. We need you for C3—command, control, and communications, especially if matters don't play out as hoped."

"That's all you're going to say?"

"That's all I can say."

"You're missing something here. Based on what Rodríguez told us, I suspect my goddaughter Lily was the mysterious American in Driscoll's compound. And I believe she was taken to Las Vegas."

Michael suddenly realized what should have been obvious to him. Lily had green eyes.

LII

Lily tried to mask the desperation she was feeling. She didn't want Max to see how worried she was. With all the cameras, there was no escape from him. That required her every waking moment to be devoted to her latest role, even though Max didn't seem to be buying it. During the last full moon, she had staved off being Max's sacrificial victim. That had bought her time, but now she was looking at another full moon. Her talking to the moon didn't seem to be cutting it for Max anymore. His skepticism wasn't coming at a good time. Tomorrow, the full moon would arrive.

Still, all she could do was continue with her deception. Maybe she could find a way to win yet another reprieve. As she went to take her place at the window, Lily suddenly found herself feeling light-headed. She took a deep breath and tried to steady herself, but her legs grew increasingly wobbly, and she was forced to take an uncertain step back from the window.

Lily extended a hand toward the moonlight, as if hoping to hold on to its glow, but everything was spinning, and she was forced into a backward retreat. Was her dizziness a result of stress? Lily staggered over to her bed and dropped to it. With each passing moment, she felt more disembodied. She tried lifting her arms, then her legs, but couldn't get them to respond.

With difficulty, Lily opened her mouth. "Help," she cried, or tried to cry, but the word was little more than a whisper.

Her mind was still working, but it would have been easier had she drifted into unconsciousness. Lily's panic was only making her paralysis worse. Max, she thought. He must have drugged her food or drink, or worse, maybe he'd poisoned her. Lily struggled to raise herself from the bed, but could barely shift from side to side. Her breathing felt labored, and she wondered if her lungs were failing her. She tried to scream, but the drugs had taken away her voice.

Her eyes still functioned, though. She saw the face of death coming her way.

The face—the skull—was skeletal, devoid of mercy. It wasn't human. From the depths of its black orbs, a second pair of eyes stared at her through carved slits.

Max's eyes.

"Death is here. Are you prepared for your ascension?"

His voice was distorted, or maybe the distortion was in her head. There was a mosaic pattern to his mask. It was inlaid with turquoise, and shells, and coral. The teeth might have been constructed from bone. Max stepped back, and she could see he was wearing an unusual-looking sleeveless, stained coat. That wasn't like him. Max was always tidy in appearance. But there was a reason for all the rusty droplets and stains.

Lily realized she was looking at old blood splatter.

"I can see how your heart is pounding. Is your blood ready to feed the universe?"

He opened up a fold in his murderer's coat, then withdrew the knife, holding it so that it was all she could see. The black stone blade was aimed at her eye.

"*Ixquauac*," he said. "The ancient ones would tell you this priceless relic has a life of its own."

He changed the angle of his knife, bringing it down to her chest. Lily had no idea if the knife was cutting into her. Tears ran down her face.

The man in the mask slashed his blade, and the torn nightgown fell away from her.

"It is time you were purified for your consecration," he said.

He reached into his butcher's coat again, exchanging the knife for a porous, chalklike stone. Max rubbed the chalky substance up and down her body. Lily was glad there was no sensation to his touch, but just the thought of what he was doing made her retch; she fought off her nausea so as to not choke on her own vomit.

"You are almost cleansed of your sins. Almost."

Max stared at her from the slits that had been cut in the black mask. He retrieved his hard, black blade, then ran it along her flesh. Judging from the fast breaths coming from behind the mask, he could barely hold his excitement in check.

Then he lifted the blade with both hands, raising it up to his forehead.

Holding it high so as to plunge into her.

LIII

D eke resisted the urge to call Jake and Michael for an update. Somehow the young lawyer had gotten Deke to promise he would stay put in Florida. How the hell he'd managed that, Deke wasn't sure. But maybe it was for the best. Things were heating up on his end as well.

As if on cue, Diana appeared at the doorway to his office. "That call you've been expecting has been on hold for around two minutes now."

"Two minutes?"

"He demanded to be put through to you 'at once.'"

"In that case, keep him waiting another two minutes."

Two minutes later, the call was put through. "Good morning, Mr. Bines."

"I just got the paperwork for your bullshit class-action suit. Is it a desperate plea to be noticed, or a publicity stunt?"

"I'm good with either one of those outcomes," Deke said.

"Your suit is so transparent it can't even be called a ploy," Bines said.

"I'm sorry you feel that way."

"Today I'll be filing a motion to dismiss," Bines said. "After it's upheld, your class-action suit will go away."

"If it happens that way, then you won't have to wait long for me to amend the original motion, and then refile."

"And I'll see to its dismissal once more."

"Oh dear. By the sounds of it, this will be a protracted affair. But I'm okay with that. The longer it takes for things to play out, the better it will be for our side."

"What leads you to that conclusion?"

"Because the more we cross swords, the more likely it is that the media will take an even greater interest in not only the class-action suit we just filed, but in the ongoing Welcome Mat Hospitality lawsuit. In fact, our office contacted Storm, and she seems quite willing to offer her thoughts on the case. She might even release a single from her album *Chains* around the time she makes her statement. That sounds good to me. What about you?"

The class-action suit had been filed in the state of Florida and framed the argument of economic losses being suffered by H2B workers who were sexually trafficked at Welcome Mat properties. Because federal law in the US didn't allow for class-action suits asserting individual injury, Deke was basing his case on alleging economic loss. By attempting to put a price tag on prostitution, Deke was hoping to turn the usual equation—and law—around. Since those being trafficked weren't receiving any money for their services, Deke was asserting that compensation was due to them. As precedent for the class-action suit, Deke cited several Fortune 500 companies that had been deemed to be liable for essentially forcing their employees to work off the clock. Deke had more than a passing familiarity with a number of the cases he had cited, as he had successfully litigated them. Among those named in the class-action suit were Nathan Bines, Geofredo Salazar, and the Global Union Manifest foundation.

"It sounds like a complete waste of time. If you'll excuse me, I need to go file our motion to dismiss."

"That won't stop me from putting the dots out there."

"Dots?"

"Dots that I'm counting on enterprising reporters helping me to connect. There are lots of questions pertaining to the ownership and operation of Welcome Mat that need answering. We know Welcome Mat is dirty. Given time, we plan to show how dirty."

"Good luck. You'll need it."

"I don't think so. It's strange how my team keeps digging up things and finding Mr. Salazar's fingerprints. Maybe you can explain to me why the amicus brief you filed contains much of the same language found in a Global Union Manifest position paper that advocates lowering the age for H2B workers."

"I'd call that a coincidence."

"Coincidence? That's one explanation. Another might be the ugly story going around that Salazar fronts the interests of the mob, and uses GUM to promote those interests."

"I'm glad, then, that the rule of law is based on facts, and not ugly stories and supposition," Bines said.

"Facts can be very ugly things, Mr. Bines, when they are not on your side. And I intend to reveal those facts. But if we're to continue this conversation, I suggest you call me from a different phone and location."

"And why is that?"

"My firm is not on the best of terms with certain multinational corporations, and because of that, all workplace conversations are conducted over secure telephone lines. As part of that security system, we are able to tell if there is any monitoring going on by a third party."

"So, what are you saying?"

"Your line is bugged," Deke said.

* * *

Half an hour later Bines called back on a cell phone he'd apparently borrowed from someone outside of his workplace. If Bines was expecting to resume the conversation where he and Deke had left off, that didn't happen.

"Satisfied?" Deke asked.

"About what?" Bines sounded mystified.

"Didn't I play the role you scripted for me to perfection?"

"I must be missing something."

"You can stop your games," Deke said. "I know you leaked what went on in Irwin's courtroom to the *Times*. You were the anonymous source, or at least you had someone close to you funnel that information to the reporter."

"Why would I have done that? I came out looking worse than anyone in that proceeding."

"That's why."

"You're suggesting I wanted to look bad?"

"Not suggesting. Stating it as a fact."

"Based on what?"

Deke didn't directly answer. "When I was a wet-behind-the-ears lawyer, I was handed a child custody case over a six-year-old girl. The mother and her new husband were trying to freeze out the biological father's visitation rights. It was a David-versus-Goliath fight. The father was a working-class stiff; the new husband was Mr. Moneybags. When the biological father got on the stand, I started asking him about his daughter, and he told the court, 'If a tiger was coming at my little girl, I wouldn't hesitate for a moment to put myself between it and her.'

"Everyone in the courtroom heard the truth in his words, and I heard the same thing from you the other day. My guess is that you would throw yourself into the jaws of a tiger in order to protect your daughter. And having your own personal connection made you think about other daughters, and how many of those girls had no one looking out for them. You knew that what Salazar and his cohorts wanted was to make these young women even more vulnerable."

There was silence for a few long moments. When Bines finally spoke, he sounded relieved. "It was damned if I do, damned if I don't. My professional obligations were personally repugnant. There didn't seem to be a good way out."

"There is now."

"I think I can convince . . . a certain individual that it is in his or her best interests to settle the Welcome Mat case, provided you drop the class-action suit."

"What kind of terms are you talking about?"

"I will make sure the sixty Jane Does you represent are adequately compensated."

"There is no adequate compensation."

"We will follow the metric settlement that you proposed," Bines said.

Deke had asked his clients be paid $1.5 million dollars per year for every year they'd been sexually trafficked. As pricey as that might have seemed to outsiders, Deke knew it wouldn't even come close to compensating for their pain and suffering.

"That's a start," Deke said. "But we're also going to need to have Welcome Mat Hospitality put anti-trafficking safeguards in place that will assure all their properties are free from sex trafficking now and in the future. Lip service isn't going to work. We'll need complete transparency, and outside oversight."

"I will make that happen," Bines said.

"In addition, the ownership of Welcome Mat needs to pay for a national informational campaign combating human trafficking."

"You're asking for a lot," Bines said.

"The way I see it, I'm asking for the bare minimum."

Bines sighed. "I'll advocate for it."

"You'll need to do more than advocate. It's nonnegotiable."

"Done," Bines said. "And if our official business is concluded, I'd like to thank you for your *understanding*."

Deke didn't need to read between the lines. As a lawyer, Bines had a duty to his client. As a father, Bines had a duty to his daughter, and girls like her.

Like Lily.

"Anything you can tell me about my being set up for the *Enquirer* and their hit piece?" Deke asked.

"What I can tell you is that I would never be a party to such an action. And had I been privy to anyone voicing threats your way, I would have strongly advised against that course, although I doubt my objections would have been listened to."

"I understand."

"Beware the tigers out there, Mr. Deketomis."

"I think they better beware of me," Deke said.

LIV

The sound of her own groaning roused Lily. For a few minutes she drifted in and out of consciousness, but finally awoke and staggered over to the toilet. After taking care of the needs of her bladder, she returned to bed.

That Max had drugged her wasn't surprising. Her still being alive was what was unexpected.

She remembered how the masked Max, wearing his butcher's outfit, had come at her with his black stone knife. But instead of cutting her open, he had used his ancient blade to hack away her hair. She ran her hand along her head and felt the stubbled remains. A single tear ran down her cheek.

The afternoon shadows were already giving way to night; Lily had slept away most of the day. Max had probably wanted her to slumber until the full moon showed itself, and he along with it.

Her gaze ran down her naked body. The chalky substance he had rubbed on her skin still covered her flesh. It was for purification, Max had said. He had applied it in preparation for the full moon and what would come with it. She looked like a ghost. And soon, Lily feared, she would be one.

* * *

In the last twenty-four hours, thought Michael, it had felt as if he and Jake had moved heaven and earth. Now there was time enough for him to make one last call. When he'd been a PJ, many of those he had served with had written "just in case" letters, notes to be delivered to loved ones in the event of death. Because of his own circumstances, and having no family, Michael had never felt the need to write a just in case letter. Only now did he wish he'd inked one.

"Husband?" Mona said. He could hear the concern in her voice. Michael had told her not to expect a call from him until the following morning.

"No cause for alarm. I just wanted to hear your voice."

"Are you sure everything is all right?"

"Can't your husband call to say he loves you without you getting worried?"

"Hearing those words makes me glad, but I would rather they were said in person."

"Next time I'll just text," he said.

Mona's playful tone matched his. "If you do so, remember to include one hundred heart emojis, as well as a dozen emojis of roses."

Although Mona still didn't sound completely reassured, Michael was glad to hear her playing along with him.

"You drive a hard bargain," he said.

The door to his hotel room opened. "It's time," Jake called. When he saw Michael talking on the phone, he signaled his apology.

"Jake's telling me we have to go."

"Husband?" Mona asked.

Her intake of her breath made it sound as if she was about to say something else before reconsidering.

Michael said, "My turn to ask. Are you okay?"

"Of course. I just did not want our conversation to end without my saying, 'We love you.'"

* * *

Three hours later, Michael thought about his wife's parting words. Even now they sustained him, providing an irreplaceable warmth. Thinking of her made his mission easier. No, it wasn't so much a mission, he thought, as a wing and a prayer.

Or maybe a leap of faith.

He wasn't making that leap alone. There were plenty of people who had put their necks on the line for him. If he failed, it could mean the end of their careers. Michael would have understood had they refused his request for help, but no one had even hesitated. His band of brothers had made this mission possible.

The airspace around Las Vegas, like all metropolitan cities, was carefully regulated. Michael was fortunate that air traffic control at McCarran International Airport had a longstanding relationship with Nellis Air Force Base. Because of their proximity to one another, the civilian and military air traffic controllers were used to working closely together. McCarran was also used to accommodating a wide variety of military training missions involving aircraft.

Tonight was supposedly one of those missions. The Cessna 182 that was transporting Michael was flying at a low altitude toward the restricted airspace of Las Vegas. That wasn't a problem, though; their unusual flight plan had secured approval through McCarran.

From his pilot's seat, Captain "Corky" Corcoran called out, "Five minutes to DZ."

DZ was drop zone. The plan was for Michael to leave the plane from five thousand feet, an altitude much lower than he usually jumped from. Still, in hot zones it was often necessary to come in low. Both he and Corky were used to nighttime missions. In the darkness you weren't as much of a target. Michael suspected the Cessna felt more like a toy to Corky than a real plane. He was used to flying much bigger birds, mostly military transport planes like the HC-130 Hercules. Still, the old Cessna jump plane suited their purposes.

Corky yelled to be heard. "Mid-level winds are light. Under ten miles per hour."

The wind gods were always fickle, especially in deserts. Michael had been monitoring the wind levels all day. Desert winds are notorious for being blustery and wild. Tonight, there was only a gentle zephyr. Had it been too windy, their mission would have had to be scrubbed.

There was no jumpmaster for this flight. They had taken off with the cabin door open. For Corky, it would be a short flight: fifteen minutes to altitude to destination, and about the same amount of time to land. Corky had departed with one passenger, and would return with none.

Michael checked his rig for the umpteenth time. His harness was snug and secure. He would deploy an MC-6 steerable parachute, a canopy used for accuracy jumps. Its hollow steering toggles would allow for better maneuverability and easier braking. For this mission, that would be absolutely necessary.

It was a cloudless night. The full moon would provide more than ample illumination. As he had been doing for much of the day, Michael visualized his jump. To prepare for the mission, he had pored over the DZ map, familiarizing himself with all the cardinal headings of north, south, east, and west, and the landmarks associated with them. He had prepared as if his life depended on knowing that information cold. It wasn't an overstatement to say that it did.

Worldwide skydiving accuracy competitions—landing at a dead center target—were often determined by as little as a centimeter. The best skydivers were able to land on a dime. Michael wouldn't have to be quite that precise, but close to it.

PJs constantly worked on accuracy in their landings, but setting down atop a building's roof wasn't something he had ever trained for. Michael wasn't even sure if that was something you could train for. The jump, and especially the landing, posed significant dangers.

Looking out the open cabin door, he could see the skyline of Las Vegas and its kaleidoscope of colors below him. Among all the flashing, in the midst of the city's sparkler show, he identified his target. It wouldn't be as easy to do so while spinning around in the air.

"One minute," Corky said.

Those who skydived were wont to use the expression "Blue skies." It was a phrase often heard before jumping, or after landing. Michael said those words now: "Blue skies."

Then he stood up and made his way toward the opening. The wind grabbed at him with its unseen fingers. In his head, Michael recited Psalm 56, verse 3. It was short and to the point: *When I am afraid, I put my trust in you.*

No question about it, he thought. I am afraid. But that didn't stop him from positioning first one foot atop the small ledge above the right wheel, then the other. It was time for his leap of faith.

He jumped.

* * *

Freefall. PJs liked to call low-altitude jumps "hop and pop," as there is little time to do anything but deploy your canopy.

Still, there was time enough to spread his wings to the wind around him and take in the earth below. All of Michael's senses were instantly engaged, supercharged with the hyperawareness that comes with freefalling from the heavens.

He could hear Tom Petty singing the chorus to "Free Fallin'" in his head. Michael felt as if he was part of the song.

The bliss that came with his fall was its own drug. Beneath him was the biggest amusement park in the world, with all of its vying light shows. The wind was singing in his ears, and another song came with it, "Purple Haze" by Jimi Hendrix. The universe opened up to him; Michael was kissing the sky.

Two selves on the same skydive. Altimeter check, mental countdown to terminal velocity of 120 miles per hour. Ten seconds of freefall to one mind, eternity to the other. His rapture told him to follow the wind, his mission mind noted the speed and direction of that same wind.

Too soon, time for the big brake. Too soon the release and the canopy above him.

Michael took in the window in the sky. He descended on the experience of more than a thousand prior jumps, but asked for the wings of angels on this one. His eyes took in the Yin-Yang, a visual more reliable than GPS, and he traveled along the glide path he had been studying and visualizing for. Like a pilot preparing to land, Michael worked his own controls, using brakes, wind-checks, and crabbing to slow his descent, but not stall his canopy. He employed S-turns to get the best approach to the roof, aiming for dead center.

The Yin-Yang's low-slope rooftop drew closer. Michael knew it through aerial photographs; now he would see it up close. He needed to avoid the ductwork and piping. The building rose up at him.

Stick the landing, he thought.

There was no alternative, or none he wanted to imagine.

* * *

Lily's heart was pounding as she awoke from her drugged sleep. She had heard loud knocking and feared Max was coming for her. Lily looked around, alert to the sounds of more banging. She turned her head from side to side, trying to identify where the noise was coming from, but then it stopped.

Max, she thought. Bile rose up in her throat. Max had to be behind the sounds, even though he was nowhere to be seen.

Seconds passed. She was on the alert for anything. But what she didn't expect was someone calling her name.

"Lily!"

Or at least she hadn't expected a voice calling from outside her bedroom window.

"Are you there, Lily?"

The voice was faint, not much more than a whisper. But the best thing about it was that it didn't sound like Max. Another man was calling her name. But that was impossible. She looked toward the window. Even though it was dark, Lily could just make out a figure.

No. It couldn't be. Max had to be playing a final trick on her. He was getting back at her, pretending the moon was talking to her.

"Nataliya? Lily?"

The voice sounded more desperate now. Lily wondered if she was going mad. Perhaps, on this night of the full moon, it would be a mercy to not be in her right mind.

She rose from the bed, driven to go see. Once at the window, she put her face up against the darkened glass. Something was out there. That wasn't possible. The figure was awash in the moonlight. He looked to be hovering in the air.

She stepped back, afraid. That was madness, she thought, unless . . .

"Are you an angel?" she said, shouting the words so that they might be heard.

"No," the voice said. "My name is Michael Carey. I'm your lawyer."

LV

"**A**re there any other captives in there?" Michael shouted.

"Only me," Lily said.

That would make the rescue mission easier, Michael thought, but he was disappointed Nataliya wasn't there as well.

Michael tried to speak with a calmness he didn't feel, and with an assuredness he didn't have. From atop the roof he'd anchored a line to the dampening system, and for added insurance had hammered pitons into the building. That had made it a little easier for him to step off the roof. He was now suspended from above, his harness secured with ropes and carabiners. The platform he was standing on was a rigid hammock, the kind used by rock climbers.

"The setup out here is very safe," he shouted.

That's what rock climbers liked to say; to Michael's thinking the platform felt shaky.

"I hate heights. I'm scared shitless."

"If you do what I tell you, everything will turn out just fine. Before you squeeze your way outside, I'll make sure you're secured into a harness. Even if you weighed ten times what you do, the arrest line would still hold you safe and sound."

As loudly as Michael was speaking, he knew Lily was still having trouble hearing what he was saying. Projecting confidence was the important thing. She needed to believe in him. Besides, this wasn't a time to say too much, especially with her fear of heights. He needed her to take one step at a time.

"I can't do it," she said. "I just can't."

"We'll get through this together. Before becoming a lawyer, I served in the military where my job was to rescue people from very difficult situations. You will need to trust me."

"But how in the hell can I even get outside? The glass is . . ."

Michael spoke for her. "Unbreakable. I know."

* * *

For most of the day, Max had felt as if he were a stranger inside of his own skin. It was the full moon, of course. And the anticipation.

Unfortunately, business had delayed his pleasure. Heavy was the head that wore the crown; there had been no avoiding today's meetings. But now the day's duties were finally behind him. It was time for Max to unwind. He had been looking forward to this evening from the moment his latest enchantress had come into his life.

Usually Max enjoyed spending time monitoring his special guest, but today he'd had little time to pursue that pleasure. An hour earlier he'd spent a few minutes on his phone looking at the live surveillance cameras monitoring her. Max had been somewhat surprised to see the woman up and about. With all the drugs he'd given her the night before, Max had thought she would surely be asleep. Instead, she'd been standing at the window, doing a lot of talking.

And a lot of pretending. Max had learned his lesson. Now he knew the voices she heard were not there. He knew this because the voices she heard were not the voices he heard.

Those voices that were telling him it was time for her to die.

As Max opened the security door to her special area of the penthouse, he came to an abrupt stop. In the distance he heard what sounded like a woman's scream. The cry was not repeated, though, and Max wondered at the source of the sound.

He moved silently through the penthouse, wanting to come upon the woman unawares. For the second straight night he wore his *xicolli*, the kind of garments worn by Toltec and Aztec priests. In his hand, held at the ready, was his special *tecpatl*. The priceless *ixquauac* showed a glyph of the moon that had been chiseled into its obsidian blade long ago. Max could feel the knife's hunger. By his hand, it had been fed on three occasions before, and it was hungry again.

It was time to perform the sacred duty.

He took one stealthy step after another. The anticipation was delightful. It coursed through his veins. Like the priests before him, Max would cut out the woman's still-beating heart, place it in a vessel, and make a sacred offering of it to the light of the moon.

Max turned the corner, expecting to see the woman in all her terror. Her frightened green eyes would speak volumes. But his expected gratification didn't materialize. The woman was nowhere to be seen.

He whirled around, anticipating some sneak attack, but she wasn't there.

So be it, he thought. She wanted a last game. "Are we playing hide and go seek?" he called. "Am I 'it'?"

Max began moving through the penthouse. "How about a hint? Am I getting warm?"

He lifted up his death mask so as to better see around him. Before paying a fortune for the mask, Max had verified its authenticity. It was believed to be eight hundred years old and had been made before Cortes arrived in Mexico. The mask was meant to adorn the face of the dead, which was why its eye sockets were sealed closed. To see out from it, Max had cut pinhole openings. Now, even with the mask removed, the woman was not immediately visible.

"Are you in the tub?" he said. "Should you be calling out, 'Marco'?"

He moved toward the bathroom, but the woman was not there. Strange, thought Max. His special penthouse guest quarters had been designed to be open, with very few potential hiding places. It didn't take him long to check those spots, but the woman was still not to be found. It was almost as if she had disappeared.

Max went back to the bedroom. There was no platform for the bed, and no baseboard or headboard. There was no place for someone to hide underneath or behind it. But what if his guest had managed to hollow out a space between the box spring and the mattress? What if she was hiding there right now?

When he'd been a boy, hide-and-go-seek had been a favorite game of Max's. What was the cry used to end the game? Max remembered the words.

"Olly, olly, oxen free!" he yelled.

He put the death mask back on his face, grabbed the mattress, and pushed it to the side.

She wasn't there. He stared at the intact box spring. Then, just to be sure, he turned that over as well.

Nothing.

"Impossible," he said.

Or was it? Max had seen the woman talking to the Moon and been sure it was another one of her ploys. What if it hadn't been?

He would review the surveillance tapes, of course. Maybe they would explain her disappearance. But at the moment, Max did not know quite how to react. There was nothing to suggest that the girl had found a way to escape, and there was no visible handiwork of her having done so. In prison escape films, tunneling was always revealed, or some broken-down door. None of that could be seen here. The penthouse prison had been designed to be impregnable. There was nothing that suggested otherwise.

Nothing except the missing girl.

Max wasn't sure whether to feel deflated or exultant. He had been denied the transcendent evening that he had been so looking forward to, but the possibility that something else had happened, something greater, excited him.

The light from the Moon shone into the room. What was its illumination telling him? His *xicolli*, he noticed, was alit. All the old spilled blood was showing itself.

"I'm all dressed up, and nowhere to go."

He had worn his bloodstained xicolli for the ultimate party, but the festivities had been put on hold. There would be no last dance.

And yet . . . the Moon called to him.

It did seem like a marvelous night for a moon dance. Why not?

Max ran at the window and threw himself at it.

He was falling for a full second before his voice caught up with the realization that he was plummeting toward the ground. It was then that he started screaming.

And screaming.

And screaming.

All the way down.

In the time it took for him to fall, Max remembered a little-known fact. When he'd taken over ownership of the Yin-Yang, Max had been told the penthouse was actually located on the forty-fourth floor. It was something that had never been advertised. From its inception, the property had banished the number four. It was as if it didn't exist. Max had always thought it silly that so many of his Asian clientele suffered from tetraphobia.

Until now.

The window hit the ground just before he did. It survived the fall. It was unbreakable.

The same could not be said of Max.

LVI

The scream was something that could never be unheard. It was like a shard of ice being repeatedly hammered into the ear canal. The terrified cry went on and on, until it didn't. In the shocked stillness that followed, Jake said, "What the hell just happened?"

Michael and Lily's heart-stopping jump had landed them several blocks from the Yin-Yang. They were too far away to see Max Miller's fall, but not too far to hear his end.

"Someone danced with the devil," Michael said.

Lily turned toward Michael. She was wrapped up in a sweatshirt that Jake had provided her, but it hadn't stopped her violent shivering. Now, it looked like she had found her peace. All of her trembling had stopped.

"Thank you," she said to Michael.

Freeing Lily from her prison had been the easy part for Michael. You could thank Max Miller's remodel. He'd insisted upon a decorative Yin-Yang pane that was about the size of a doggie door, located beneath the huge high-rise glass window. Miller had said in an interview that the window was his "portal to the universe."

Removing the pane hadn't been easy. Though it was small, it was still exceptionally heavy. Once it was out, Michael had secured Lily into a safety harness, and she had squeezed through the tiny space. It was a good thing she was so slight. That's when Michael had secured the window and continued with his work.

Lily hadn't watched his progress. Her eyes were shut tight the whole time she was suspended forty-four stories above the ground. She had been rigid, terrified, too scared to move a muscle.

"Breathe," Michael had kept telling her. "Breathe."

Michael hadn't explained what he was doing with his tools.

The installation of high-rise windows requires cranes, suction tools, pulleys, and ropes. The windows were heavier and thicker than residential windows, with an insulated spacer between the glass. Removing such glass required specialized equipment, including hoists. It had never been Michael's plan to remove the big window, though. The tools he'd purchased at a high-rise window replacement company had served a different purpose.

Michael had used them to loosen the frame surrounding the window.

For ten minutes, he had worked on the frame. Only when he was finished did Michael tell Lily that it was time for them to be leaving. Then he explained that in order to get down to the ground, they would first have to climb up to the roof. That had almost scared Lily senseless, even with a safety harness.

When they reached the roof, Lily thought she was finally safe until Michael explained what came next.

Doing a solo BASE jump from a skyscraper was risky enough; doing a tandem jump was insanity. In the end, Lily put her life in his hands and skills, and they vaulted from the roof. Lily's scream as they plummeted was so loud, Michael feared it might displace the window he'd been working on.

It hadn't. That had been left to Max.

"What am I missing here?" Jake asked.

He looked from Michael to Lily, his eyes demanding an explanation.

"Those screams we heard were Max Miller falling to his death," Michael said.

"And how is it you know that?"

"Educated guess," Michael said.

"Based on what?"

"While seeing to Lily's escape, I might have inadvertently not fully secured the window."

It almost sounded like a reasonable explanation, or perhaps it would have if Jake hadn't also seen the footage from Max's full moon parties where he kept throwing himself at the bedroom window over and over again. Even though he was a lawyer, Michael knew to be distrustful of the legal system. Sometimes justice needed a helping hand.

"I want to go home to my mom," Lily said.

The sounds of sirens began filling the air.

"Let's go then," Michael said.

LVII

Mona was there to meet Michael at the entrance of their apartment. As the two of them came together for a long embrace, she said, "Oh, husband, it has been far too long."

"Yes," Michael said. His throat was so constricted it was all he could do to get that one word out.

The two of them clung to one another until Mona stepped back from their embrace. "I do not want to leave your arms, husband, but neither do I want to overcook our dinner."

"We can't have that, can we? What can I do to help?"

"You can find a vase for those beautiful roses you are holding."

"This feels like déjà vu," Michael said. "You were making my favorite meal the night before I left for Las Vegas, and that's what I'm smelling now, isn't it? I thought *tepsi baytinijan* was only for special occasions."

"It is," she said.

There was something in his wife's voice that made Michael take a read of her face. "Am I missing something?"

"Something, and someone," she said. "Since even before you left on your trip, I have been offering you hints, but you never took notice."

"What are you saying?"

"Do you remember when you told me of your plans to go to Las Vegas, and I said to you, '*We* will not stand in the way.'"

Michael tried to make sense of what Mona was saying.

"And for the last five days, there hasn't been a phone conversation where I didn't tell you, '*We* miss you.' And '*we* love you.'"

"*We?*" Michael said.

"We. I made your favorite dinner to celebrate, but when you told me about your trip, I decided the news should wait. Still, I could not resist passing on hints. I half hoped you would pick up on them."

"We," Michael said, realizing the import of that word.

The two of them—no, the three of them—embraced.

Once again, dinner had to wait.

LVIII

When Michael's mother had died, the Air Force had provided him with an extended family and given him a good life, a fulfilling life, but he had always dreamed for more even if he hadn't been sure what that was. Love stories didn't usually involve someone recovering from gunshot wounds and the other person having to do his courting with a broken back, but that was his life, and his love story. Somehow, he had come out on the other end of the rainbow.

Mona was showing now. The two of them were planning for their family. Their fairy tale was ready to end with the words, "And they all lived happily ever after." But Michael was having trouble with the words, "The end."

Peter Stone, or someone in his employ, had gotten away with murder.

Some days Michael could almost forget that, but it still ate at him. Deke had tried to help him see the big picture, how their actions had improved the lives of so many. Michael tried to see it that way.

Miami Maritime Investigations had just sent over their final report. The firm had tracked down all the movements of the *Seacreto* until its sinking off of Cape Coral. Their forensics investigation of the wreck had determined that at least five limpet mines had been attached under the hull of the yacht. As their report noted, it wasn't easy to legally obtain limpet mines, especially as they were a preferred weapon of terrorists. Limpet mines—named for the mollusks that clung to rocks—had been used against US Navy ships and oil tankers.

A last dead end, thought Michael. Dark Ghoul had been cautious from the first. There was nothing to link Darkpool with any of the deaths or destruction. A frustrated Michael had looked at the marina tapes dozens of times. The beginning and ending never changed. There was no footage of any Darkpool employees going onboard the *Seacreto*. And Karina Boyko had never come back.

The universe is telling me it's time to move on, thought Michael. Like Deke had told him, he needed to take solace from all the good outcomes their work had yielded. He reached for the report, prepared to put it away in a drawer. It would follow the path of good intentions, he knew, and bit by bit find its way deeper into the drawer. If he was lucky, with each passing day its hold upon him would ease, but to his thinking, what passed for wisdom felt more like capitulation. Michael still wanted to nail the bastards.

Michael took a last look at the pages, then noticed there was a new link to marina footage. According to the time line, on the day after the booze cruise, Vicky Driscoll had visited the marina and had boarded the yacht. Her visit had been a short one.

Curious, Michael decided to look at the footage.

From his computer, he called up the file. In fierce wind and rain, he watched Driscoll moving around a deserted marina where hazardous sea warnings had kept everyone and everything hunkered down in port.

Everyone but Vicky.

In pouring rain and buffeting winds, she made her way to the *Seacreto*. Although she was wearing a trench coat with a hood, it wasn't a match for the storm. For extra protection, she'd wrapped a tote bag over her head. To get to the *Seacreto*, she passed through two locked security gates. The surveillance cameras showed her walking along the dock, but they didn't offer a vantage point to her movements on the *Seacreto*. Whatever had brought her out that day didn't keep Vicky long. She only stayed aboard for five minutes before making her way out of the marina. There appeared to be a slight detour in her route out to the parking lot, but the pouring rain from the fall squall obscured the surveillance footage and blurred her movements.

Still, from what Michael could observe, she paused along the walkway. With her back to the camera, and the image grainy, it was all but impossible to see what she was doing, but whatever it was didn't take more than a minute. Michael tried manipulating the screen to get a better picture, but his efforts didn't yield much in the way of additional clarity.

He could just make out a white rectangular object next to where she was standing. It had to be a dock box, he decided. Most berths had their own dock boxes, but this box wasn't located in proximity to the *Seacreto*. Michael remembered having read something about dock boxes in Miami Maritime's report and began flipping through the pages. Yes, there it was. Several dock boxes at the marina had been broken into, including the box in front of where the *Seacreto* was berthed. The break-ins had occurred not long after the fall squall.

Was that just a coincidence? Michael wondered. Or was it something more along the lines of how the Pussy Cat Palace had been burned down and the *Seacreto* sunk?

Michael reviewed the tape once more. His heart was pounding, even though he didn't want to get his hopes up. Maybe Vicky had visited the marina for some innocent purpose, but most people don't go out into pelting rain and forty-mile-per-hour winds without good reason.

He still couldn't see what Vicky was doing at the dock box. She could have been reading some notice, or adjusting her clothing, before hurrying to get to the safety of her car.

That's when Michael saw it. Vicky was no longer carrying her tote bag.

For a third time, he followed her route. The bag was covering her head when she went to board the *Seacreto*, and it was still in her possession when she got off the boat. Now, though, Vicky wasn't using it as a head wrap. She carried it at her side. To Michael's eye, it looked as if there was something in the bag.

There was another thing he noticed. Vicky had bypassed the *Seacreto*'s dock box in favor of using another one. It was likely that no one had known about her second dock box.

Michael ran out of his office.

LIX

"**Y**ou're going to want to see this."

The serious tone of Michael's voice was enough for Deke to reply in a single word: "Where?"

"Conference room C," Michael said.

"Five minutes."

One of the AV specialists had helped Michael set up the DVR in the conference room. Michael now knew the reason for Vicky's going to the marina on such an inclement day. Unbeknownst to anyone else, there was a secret compartment on the *Seacreto* that housed surveillance equipment. When she'd ventured out on that blustery, rainy day, she had gone to gather insurance.

I should have known, Michael thought. In all her businesses, Vicky had kept tabs on her employees. He wondered if the *Seacreto*'s crew had known about the existence of her spy room. I doubt it, he thought. The two crew members hadn't been seen since the *Seacreto* had been scuttled. Michael believed it was highly unlikely that they were still alive.

There was no sound with the tape, but that didn't diminish the brutality of what was on it. Michael was glad he was spared seeing Karina's struggles in the sea. There was only the wide-angle view that did not encompass the water, but seeing the laughter of Stone and his men was sickening enough. Even some of the women aboard had seemed to take pleasure in Karina's drowning. Or perhaps they had been too afraid to not go along. Maybe the alcohol and drugs, combined with the shock of what they had witnessed, had caused them to react as they did.

"I've seen enough," Deke said.

Michael stopped the recording. Both men sat for a minute in stunned silence. Finally, Michael got to his feet.

"I've got business to attend to. I'll trust you to put the DVR in lockup when you're finished with it."

"Wait a second," Deke said.

"What?"

"This isn't a time for another special forces rogue operation."

Michael seemed at a loss as to how to respond, prompting Deke to speak with that much more forcefulness.

"You're lucky that what happened in Vegas hasn't come back to bite you in the ass. You can't count on that luck a second time. We need to do this the right way. We need to involve law enforcement."

Michael opened his mouth, but Deke still didn't let him speak. "No vigilante crap. No frontier-style justice. You hear me? This isn't some PJ mission."

"I know that," Michael said, finally getting an opportunity to talk.

"Then why are you running off? And what are you up to?"

"I'm going to my office, where I'm planning on doing my job."

"And what job is that?"

"The one you hired me for. I'm a lawyer."

The words were said with pride. Michael was still a rescue ranger and always would be, even though he now wore a very different uniform.

"And as a lawyer, I need to prepare for what I imagine will be the biggest wrongful death suit this firm has ever filed," he continued.

Deke had the reputation of being unflappable; Michael's announcement revealed Deke was flappable.

Stumbling to find the words, Deke managed to say, "That's—that's—really good thinking."

"One thing. I need to be there when Stone's arrested. I'm going to be the one serving him papers right before he's handcuffed. I'll want him to have some good reading material for his send-off to prison."

"In that case, don't let me detain you," Deke said.

* * *

When Michael reached his office, he decided to make a call before beginning his work.

"I'm afraid I won't be home until late tonight."

"Are you once again saving the world, husband?"

"Something like that," he said.

"Then do as you must, and when you get home, we will greet you with open arms."

"That's what I wanted to hear," Michael said.

Epilogue

The yacht *Jurisprudence* was following the course laid out by a sun making its slow descent into the Gulf of Mexico. With his hands on the wheel, Deke aimed for the trail of light that was setting the emerald water aglow. Miss Prudence, as Deke liked to call her, was nearing her destination.

They had timed their journey to arrive a little before sunset. The day was balmy, with just enough breeze to keep the heat at bay. The dozen passengers aboard Miss Prudence were congregated on the main deck.

Deke caught the eye of the organizer. This was her show.

"Permission to drop anchor, Captain," he yelled.

Lily smiled. This outing was her idea. She looked around and seemed to test the area with all of her senses, making sure it was just the right spot. After a few moments of surveying, she offered a satisfied nod to Deke and called, "Drop the anchor!"

"Aye, aye," Deke said.

Almost half a year had passed since Lily's rescue. She was seeing a therapist three days a week, and her godfather checked in with her once or twice a week, which was probably as much as any teenager could stomach, but she humored him.

The healing process for what Lily had been forced to endure was slow. You don't walk out of hell unscathed. But his goddaughter was coping, and her support system was doing its best to make sure she had more good days than bad days. During their voyage, Deke had been heartened to hear her laugh a few times. In coming to this place, she was looking for some closure. And Lily wasn't the only one needing that.

For once, the bad guys hadn't come out on top and had ended up either dead or in prison. It was rare for the universe to get it right. Peter Stone's own soldiers had flipped on him and were testifying against him in Karina Boyko's homicide. It was looking more and more like Stone would spend the rest of his days in prison. And even Geofredo Salazar and all his money hadn't proved to be immune from retribution. A month earlier, he'd been shot and killed. There had been no witnesses to the shooting.

Karma, Deke wanted to believe.

Lily and Sylvia made their way to the center of the main deck where everyone had gathered. Conversations stopped, and the mood suddenly turned somber.

From his vantage point in the wheelhouse, Deke watched Sylvia give her daughter an encouraging shoulder rub. Even though she was among friends, Lily looked nervous. Or maybe she only looked like the uncertain sixteen-year-old kid that she was. For her to just be able to act her age again, Deke thought, was a good thing.

After getting a reassuring nod and smile from her mother, Lily found her voice. "I'm glad you guys are here," she said.

She looked down at her feet and took a moment to gather her thoughts. When she raised her head, Lily's eyes were wet.

"Today, I wanted us to come to this place to remember a friend. I never got a chance to know Karina Boyko like I would have wanted to, but because of her, I'm alive. I was a stranger who asked Karina to help me. And just before she died, Karina made a call on my behalf, and someone listened."

Silent tears coursed down Diana's cheeks, but she managed a smile for Lily.

"I know it's kind of a miracle I'm alive, but that's because of you guys. And because of Karina."

Lily held up a picture of a red-haired young woman for all to see.

"I was the only one here who had the chance to meet Karina while she was still alive, so her mom sent me this picture to show everyone today. Even though Mrs. Boyko couldn't be here, Michael and I have been talking with her through a translator, and she wanted everyone to know how glad she is that we are remembering Karina like this.

"Anyway, you can see Karina had really red hair. Because of that, she had this nickname. The other girls called her rusalka, which is like a mermaid with red hair. What sucks, though, is that you only become a rusalka after you've violently drowned. That's the story, at least. But what really, really sucks is that's how Karina ended up dying. If you believe the tales, most rusalki are pissed off at the world because of how their lives ended, but it's not only that. The stories say the drowned woman's soul will forever haunt the waters where she died unless her death is avenged.

"I'm not saying I believe any of that, because I know it sounds bat-shit crazy, but I've been through enough of my own crazy stuff to not want to take any chances for my friend Karina. I want her to be at peace, and hear from all of us that she doesn't need to haunt these waters, because there are people here who have avenged her death, and who continue to avenge it."

Lily stopped talking and took a few moments to look out to the sea. "You can rest in peace, Karina."

There was a chorus of people saying, "Amen."

Lily said, "My mom told me in ocean memorials like this, flowers are traditional, so we brought lots of red and white roses for everyone to remember Karina."

Lily reached into a five-gallon bucket, removed a handful of roses, and made her way to the railing. After whispering some private words, she tossed the colorful blossoms into the air. More roses soon followed. Deke left the wheelhouse and joined the others in the floral ceremony. Everyone said their goodbyes in their own way. In the aftermath of Karina's send-off, roses bobbed on the water's surface, seeming to catch the last throes of light cast by a spectacular sunset. The end of the day was marked by a glowing red sky.

"Red sky at night," Deke said, "sailor's delight."

And not only sailors. The gathering suddenly became convivial. Deke went around sharing conversation and laughs, but he didn't linger for long. Even on calm seas, and with the ship anchored, he felt his place was in the wheelhouse.

Lily took her hosting duties seriously, going from person to person and spending time with everyone. She saved Deke for last, finally joining him at the helm.

"You're missing all the good food."

"No chance of that. Teri made sure there was enough for an army."

"In that case, you're missing the company."

"I'm talking to you now, aren't I? Besides, it's the job of the captain to see to the needs of the passengers."

"I had no idea how big this thing was. It's like the size of a battleship."

"I'm glad it's big enough that you had a nice stage. Your father would have been very proud of his daughter."

"Do you think so?"

"Without a doubt."

"I don't remember him very well," Lily confessed.

"The only thing you need to remember is how much he loved you. In his own way, your father was a romantic. When I first got to know him, we were both single, but even then, Art knew what he wanted. He was thinking about you even before he met your mom."

"Come on."

"I kid you not. One night the two of us were out having drinks, and I can't remember how the conversation came up, but Art asked if I would be godfather to his first child. That sounds crazy, right? Here was a guy who didn't even have a steady girlfriend, and he was asking me to be godfather to some imaginary child in the distant future."

"What'd you say?"

"I told him, 'I'd be honored.' And I was. Even though it wasn't until about ten years later that you came along."

Lily tried not to show it, but Deke could see how pleased she was.

"You've probably seen some of the pictures from your baptism," Deke said. "If you can't tell from the photos, your father was absolutely beaming. I don't think he wanted to share you with anyone. At the party, I'm not sure if he ever let go of you."

"Did you see him much after that?"

Deke shook his head. "By then I had entered private practice, and

Spanish Trace is the better part of seven hundred miles from Fort Lauderdale. I wish I'd made an effort to bridge the distance, but I didn't."

"I'm kind of glad he didn't live to see what happened to me."

"Why?"

"Because of all the bad shit I went through."

"Nothing that occurred would have tarnished your father's opinion of you."

"Yeah, right. Every dad wants his daughter to be a sex slave."

"Art would have been proud of your grit, and your smarts, and your finding a way to hold on long enough to survive."

Lily blew out some air, not hiding her skepticism.

"It's true," Deke said. "A German philosopher named Nietzsche once said, 'What doesn't destroy me makes me stronger.' If Nietzsche's right, that makes you one of the strongest people on this planet."

"I don't feel strong."

"I'm not about to tell you that you haven't had more than your share of adversity, but bad things have happened to everyone here, and they've still managed to come out on the other side of that."

"Really?" The word came out as a challenge. Lily turned her attention to the passengers and settled on a laughing Gina. "What about Gina? She's got it going."

"Yes, she does. But Gina's father was a piece of work. He was abusive. Gina can tell you just how abusive. For a long time, her personal life was a train wreck because of him."

A begrudging Lily said, "You'd never know."

"No, you wouldn't."

Lily still wasn't convinced. She looked to the deck again, in search of another happy face. "What about Jake?"

"A week before graduating from law school, Jake lost his twin brother, Blake, to an opioid overdose. That same addiction almost killed Jake. It's been a long road back for him."

"I never would have guessed," Lily said.

"No one would."

Curious now, Lily pointed to the very pregnant and glowing Mona. "Mom-to-be looks like she's won the lottery."

"Looks that way, right? And yet Mona's entire family was slaughtered in war, and she barely survived. The severity of her wounds made it difficult for Mona to conceive."

"And I suppose Michael's got a sob story as well?"

"Did you notice that tattoo on his chest?"

"When he was sunbathing earlier, it was hard to miss. I thought about giving him shit for advertising he was an A-plus student."

"You'll have to hassle him about something else. The tattoo is his blood type. Michael is A positive. He and the other rescue rangers in his unit had their blood types inked into their skin so that in the event of a severe injury, the medics would know how to treat them."

"Wow."

"Michael was only a year older than you are when he became an emancipated minor. He and his mother had to do some serious planning when she was diagnosed with terminal cancer. At the age of seventeen Michael got his GED, which allowed him to skip his senior year and join the Air Force early when his mother died. That couldn't have been a cakewalk for him. I know his service wasn't. He came home with a broken back and traumatic brain injury."

Lily wasn't making any more skeptical sounds.

Deke said, "That's how it's going to be with you one day. People won't know what happened to you unless you tell them."

"What about you?"

"Too much baggage to mention."

"Bullshit. You're this hotshot lawyer who's got everything going for him. I mean, who could afford this boat? And you've got the perfect wife and family. It must be nice."

"It is nice. But when I was your age, there wasn't a person in the world who believed in me. If you'd asked anyone, they would have told you there was no way I would ever succeed in life. I would have told you the same thing myself."

"Come on."

"My parents gave me up to foster care when I was just a kid. I lived in four separate foster homes until I aged out of the system at eighteen."

"For real?"

"Cross my heart. I know there's a part of me that will always feel like an abandoned kid, but I've refused to let it define me. In some ways it's even been a strength. It's made me want to take on cases representing the dispossessed and the voiceless."

Neither spoke for a minute. Deke could see Lily was thinking about what he'd told her. Her eyes kept looking at those out on the deck. She seemed to be seeing them differently now.

"So, we're all misfits?"

"Every single one of us," Deke said.

"That's kind of cool."

"Yeah, I guess it is."

"You don't always have to be the one steering the ship, you know."

"It's an old habit."

"The anchor's in the water. I'm thinking we should join the others."

"I'm thinking you're right," Deke said.

THE END